THE PRINCE & THE PLAYER

By Tia Louise

Cover design by Steven Novak.

For Mr. TL, my favorite movie buddy, who introduced me to Dirty Rotten Scoundrels.

CONTENTS

PROLOGUE

Zelda Wilder

My legs are wet. Thunder rolls low in a steel-grey sky, and the hiss of warm rain grows louder. I lean further sideways into the culvert, closer against my little sister Ava's body, and grit my teeth against the hunger pain twisting my stomach. There's no way in hell I'm sleeping tonight.

Reaching up, I rub my palm against the back of my neck, under the thick curtain of my blonde hair. A shudder moves at my side, and I realize Ava's crying. We're packed tight in this concrete ditch, but I twist my body around to face her.

Clearing my throat, I force my brows to unclench. I force my voice to be soothing instead of angry. "Hey," I whisper softly. "What's the matter, Ava-bug?"

Silence greets me. She's small enough to be somewhat comfortable in our hideout. Her knees are bent, but unlike me, they're not shoved up into her nose. Still, she leans forward to press her eyes against the backs of her hands. Her glossy brown hair is short around her ears and falls onto her cheeks.

Our parents were classic movie buffs, naming her after Ava Gardner and me after Scott Fitzgerald's crazy wife Zelda. We pretty much lived up to our monikers, since my little sister wound up having emerald green cat eyes and wavy dark hair. She's a showstopper whereas I'm pretty average—flat blue eyes and dishwater blonde. So far no signs of schizophrenia (*har-har*), but you can bet your ass I can keep up with the boys in everything, which brings us to this lowly state.

"Come on, now," I urge. "It can't be as bad as all that."

Her dark head moves back and forth. "I'm sorry." Her soft whisper finally answers my question. "This is all my fault."

"What?" Reaching for her skinny shoulder, I pull her up. She's the only person I've ever known who looks pretty even when she's crying. "Why would you say something like that?"

"I tried cutting my hair off. I tried not brushing my teeth—"

"Don't be doing shit like that!" I snap, turning to face front. The rain keeps splashing on my side getting me even wetter. "We can't afford a dentist."

"I don't know what to do, Zee."

Pressing my lips together, I clench my fists on top of my knees. "We ain't going back into no foster home. I'll take care of us."

"But how?" Her voice breaks as it goes high in a whisper.

"Hell, I don't know, but I got all night to figure it out." I press my front teeth together and think. We're not that far from being legal. I'm seventeen, but Ava's only fifteen. Looking at the sand on my shoes, I get an idea. "We got one thing going for us."

"What's that?" My little sister sniffs, and I hear the tiniest flicker of hope in her voice. She'll trust whatever I tell her, and I take that responsibility very seriously.

"We live in the greatest state to be homeless. Sunny Florida."

"Okay?" Her slim brows wrinkle, and the tears in her eyes make them look like the ocean.

"We don't have to worry about getting cold or anything. We don't have to worry about snow..." I'm thinking hard, assembling a plan in my mind. "During the day, we fly under the radar—keep your head down, don't attract attention. I'll see what I can find us to eat. At night we can sleep on the beach. Or here, or hell, maybe one of these rich assholes forgets to lock his boathouse. Have you seen how nice some of these boathouses are? They're like regular houses!"

Her eyes go round with surprise. "Why are they like that?"

"Hell, I don't know. Rich people are crazy. Some rich men even get their nails polished, and they aren't even gay!"

Air bursts through her lips, and she starts to laugh. I smile and pull her arm so she can lie down with her face on my bony, empty stomach. "Now get some sleep."

The rain is tapering off, and my little sister is laughing instead of crying. I don't have any idea if anything I just said is possible, but I'm going to find out. I'll be damned if I let another foster asshole touch her. It's what Mom would expect me to do. I'm the biggest. I have to take care of us, and I intend to do it.

* * *

The navy fabric of my father's uniform coat stretches taut across his shoulders. It's the tangible warning sign his anger is rising, and the person addressing him would do well to *shut up*.

"Monagasco has been an independent nation for eight hundred years." His voice is a rolling growl pricking the tension in my chest.

The last time my father started on our nation's history, the offending party was thrown out of the meeting room by the neck. He's getting too old for such violent outbursts. I worry about his heart... and my future. My *freedom*, more specifically.

"I think what Hubert was trying to say —" The Grand Duke, my mother's brother Reginald Winchester, tries to intervene.

"I KNOW what Hubert is trying to say!" My father (a.k.a., The King) cuts him off. "He thinks we should cede our southwestern territory to Totrington! Even though their raiders and bandits have pillaged our farms along the border for *generations!*"

Leaning back in my heavy oak chair, I steeple my fingers before my lips and don't say what I want. As crown prince, I've attended these meetings for three years, since I turned nineteen. I've learned when to speak and when to discuss things in private with my father.

I could say I agree with Reggie, we should consider a trade agreement with our neighboring nation-state, but I'm more concerned about the King's health. I've never seen him so worked up before.

"Independence at all costs," he continues, his naturally pink cheeks even pinker. "We will not give those savages an open door to the control of Monagasco."

"No one's suggesting—"

"Shut UP, Hubert!" My father shouts, and I glance down to avoid meeting the earl's offended eyes.

Hubert's sniveling voice is like nails on a chalkboard, and I privately enjoy my father chastising him. I've always suspected him of conspiring with Wade Paxton, Totrington's newly elected Prime Minister, from the time when Wade was only a member of their parliament.

"I've had enough of this." My father walks to the window and looks out. "I'd like to speak to Rowan in private. You can all go."

"Of course." Reginald stands at once, smoothing his long hands down the front of his dark coat.

Tall and slender, with greying black hair and a trim mustache, my uncle embodies the Charmant line of our family. I inherited their height and Norman complexion. My father, by contrast, is a Tate through and through. Short, pink, and round.

As soon as the room is cleared, he stalks back to the table, still brooding like a thunderstorm. "Reggie's in league with them as well," he growls.

"Not necessarily." My voice is low and level, and I hope appeasing. "My uncle does have an idea, and of the two, it's the least offensive. Hubert would combine our countries and walk away—"

"Exactly!" Father snaps, turning to face me, blue eyes blazing. "My own cousin, born and reared in our beautiful land. He's been promised a place in the new government, I'll bet you. They'll throw the lot of us out—behead us if they can."

"I'm pretty sure beheading is no longer tolerated in western civilization."

"Harumph." He's still angry, but at least he's calmer. "It would break your mother's heart. The Charmants founded Monagasco. We can't let those Twatringtons in."

His use of the unofficial nickname for our southwest neighbor makes me grin. Rising from my chair, I brace his shoulder in a firm grasp.

"We won't let that happen." Our blue eyes meet. It's the only feature we share. He's a few inches shorter than me, but he makes up for it in stubbornness. "We're flush with reserves, and the economy can change at any time."

His thick hand covers mine. "I'm doing my best to leave you a strong country to rule. The country I inherited."

"We would do well to reduce our dependence on foreign oil reserves." He starts to argue, but I hold up a hand as I head for the door. He's finally calm, and I'm not interested in riling him up again. "In any event, you'll be around long enough to see the tides turn. Now get some rest." I'm at the enormous wooden door of the war room. "We can't solve all our problems in one day."

"Goodnight, son."

The tone in his voice causes me to look back. He's at the window, and a troubled expression mars his profile. A shimmer of concern passes through my stomach, but I dismiss it, quietly stepping into the dim hallway. It's enormous and shrouded with heavy velvet curtains and tapestries.

I grew up playing in these halls, hiding from my mother and chasing my younger brother. I'm tired and ready for bed when the sound of hushed voices stops me in my tracks.

"Pompous ass. He's going to kill himself with these outbursts. We need to be ready to move when that happens." The glee in Hubert's sniveling voice revives the anger in my chest. I step into the shadows to listen.

"By climbing into bed with Wade Paxton?"

I recognize my uncle's voice, and my jaw clenches. *Is Father right? Is Reginald conspiring with that worm against the crown?*

"Wade Paxton would unite the kingdoms and make us both leaders in the new government."

"Wade Paxton is a thug."

"Not very respectful verbiage for the Prime Minister of Totrington, also known as our future partner."

"He's no better than one of those mob bosses on American television. Savage." Reggie's voice is laced with snobbery. "He'd tax the people and change the very nature of Monagasco."

Hubert's tone is undeterred. "Some things might change, but as leaders, you and I can help maintain the best parts, the heart of the nation. Once Philip is out of the way, of course, which could be sooner than we think."

My fists tighten at my sides. I'm ready to step out of the shadows and shake Hubert's traitorous neck until his teeth rattle. The only thing stopping me is my desire to hear the extent of this treachery.

"You're right about one thing," Reggie says. "Philip's health is tenuous. We need to be prepared to act should a crisis arise."

"What about Rowan? If he's not on our side, we could end up in the same position — and with a much younger king to wait out."

"Possibly." My uncle pauses, and I feel the heat rising around my collar.

"Wade has a plan for managing such a contingency. Should Rowan prove… difficult."

"I'm sure he does," Reggie scoffs. "And Cal? Shall we wipe out the entire Tate line?"

Hubert's voice is low and wicked. "Perhaps being in league with a 'thug' as you put it has its advantages."

How dare these bastards! What they're saying is high treason! My body is poised to move when Reggie's words freeze me in place.

"I'm sure Wade's tactics won't prove necessary. When the time comes to do the right thing, we can count on Rowan."

Count on Rowan? Is it possible he thinks I would even consider a merger with Twatrington? Their voices recede down the corridor as my level of disgust and loyalty to my father rises. The king has had a difficult evening. I'll let him rest tonight, but I will present him with this conspiracy first thing tomorrow. Reggie is right. When the time comes, I will do the right thing.

Looking back, I had no idea the time would come in less than twenty-four hours…

CHAPTER 1: SURVIVAL SKILLS

Zelda - Six years later...

Lifting my chin, I shove my pale-blonde hair behind my ear and straighten my shoulders as I enter the Hard Rock casino in Hollywood, Florida, five miles north of Miami.

The carpet is a dizzying pattern of swirls and diamonds, driving my eyes up and through the large, open gambling space. Neon lights chase their tails around the metal slot machines, and the musical tones battle like dueling carousels.

Since smoking is banned in bars and public spaces, the air is clear. I've only been to one casino where it wasn't, and I went home reeking of cigarette smoke. Now all I catch is the faint scent of the citrus used to invigorate gamblers and make them stay longer. No clocks are anywhere to be seen, of course, but I know it's nine, the precise hour I'm scheduled to enter this establishment and make my way to the roulette wheel.

My flesh-toned, halter-top pantsuit is covered in tiny silver beads that shimmer in the flashing lights, and I carry a white alligator-embossed clutch. My hair is arranged in long, sixties-inspired curls, and my makeup is smoky cat-eye. A gold cuff and large yellow-topaz earrings complete the look. I'm somewhere between a Bond girl and Charlie's Angels, and as I walk, I mentally note the positioning of the security guards.

South Florida isn't known for its gambling scene, and the Hard Rock is a small casino. It's perfect for the scam we have in mind. I count only four men in suits with curly earpieces dotted around the space. They're casual and easily distracted by a flirtatious wink or a nod.

Seth is five minutes behind me. He's the mastermind of this gig. We're running a short con, but if things go as planned, it'll yield enough payoff to keep the three of us in hundies for the next few months. Long enough for him to come up with another scheme far away from the crystal shores of Miami.

This job only works once, so we have to get it right the first time or we're done.

An enthusiastic round of applause breaks from one of the card tables in the back corner, where I can only assume a patron won a minor victory over the House. It will soon be gobbled back up in his or her losses. Just as I pass the bar in the center of the room, I see Ava. She's in a short black strapless dress that has a sheer panel over her slim, elegant shoulders.

Her long dark hair is styled in a low ponytail that hangs in a dramatic curl over one shoulder, and a grey-haired man in a tux is leaning toward her grinning like a wolf. I spot his telltale earpiece, and a smile lifts the corner of my mouth. *Good work, Little Sister.*

She blinks those emerald eyes at him, and I watch as her slim hand gingerly touches his forearm. She'll keep him distracted for the next several minutes, and if she's feeling brave, he just might discover his watch or gold cufflinks are gone an hour after she leaves him. He'll never suspect her. Who would suspect her angelic sweetness hides devilishly light fingers?

Only two other patrons are at the roulette table when I arrive. One is an elderly woman with silver-blue hair and a navy sweatshirt with "May contain alcohol" plastered across the front in white.

She's throwing chips around, vaguely distracting the dealer. Across from her is a guy who looks barely twenty-one. He's wearing jeans and a long-sleeved grey shirt with a bit of shimmer in the fabric. As I open my clutch, he gives me a sly grin, but I turn to the stocky casino worker. His hairline is receding, and he wears an ill-fitting cummerbund.

"Fifty in dollar chips." I pass him a crisp bill.

He slides me fifty round blue plaques the size of my palm, and I glance at the sign telling me it's a dollar table. I'll have enough time to lose a few rounds before Seth appears and the con begins.

My heart beats faster. The rush of what we're doing is more powerful than any drug, and the fine hairs on my shoulders tweak when I spot Seth's auburn head across the room at the entrance. He's dressed in a beige linen suit and black slacks, and to complete the look, he's added a pair of fake horn-rimmed glasses—very hipster.

Reaching forward, the beleaguered dealer starts the wheel, and everyone places his or her bets. It's a double-zero table, which is the least favorable to gamblers, so I place two corner bets and five chips on the black. The little ball clangs into play, spinning faster than the eye can track it around the wheel.

"No more bets!" The dealer calls, passing his hand over the table.

With a clatter, the silver ball shoots toward the center of the wheel, bouncing up once again to the rim before landing solidly on seventeen black.

"I WON ONE!" The old lady screams, pushing both arms in the air. She does a little shimmy as the chips are quickly slid away and the winners paid. "I WON ONE! Did you see that???"

I smile, not bothering to point out I doubled my stack of five. My job is not to attract attention, although with the way this crowd is dressed, it's practically impossible. Mental note: Hollywood, Florida, is not Reno, Nevada. *Dress down.*

"I'm feeling lucky tonight!" Granny doubles her stack of chips on a corner bet, and I leave my ten on black.

Seth is at the table now, and he nods all around. "Mind if I join y'all?" His voice is loud, and his accent is exaggerated.

I don't engage. My role is that of cool disinterest, and I reach down to adjust my gold cuff bracelet. If all goes as planned, he's about to hit a winning streak.

"Y'all from around here?" He grins big at the old woman and the boy. "I'm from a little ole town in Kentucky."

"I'm from Dallas!" The lady answers equally loudly. "My church group took a bus all the way here!"

Well, hallelujah. I look over my shoulder as Seth monopolizes the table. I don't like leaving Ava alone in skeezy joints like this. A server appears, mistaking me for wanting a drink.

"Gin and tonic," I say, doing my best to keep my voice low.

"It's my birthday!" The young guy loudly announces. I'm beginning to think he may contain alcohol as well.

"Well, I declare, let me guess!" Seth is really laying it on thick. "Twenty one?"

"That's right!" Baby's ears pink, and he glances at me again.

My eyebrows rise when he gives me another grin coupled with a wink this time. *Dream on, little man.*

"Dealer, here's a hyundai!" Seth announces, passing him a hundred dollar bill, and I almost *do* laugh at that intentional screw-up. "Mr. Bourie says to get in and get out fast. That's the way to play roulette, right? Win quick and walk away?"

"Who's Mr. Bourie?" Grandma asks.

"Oh, he wrote the book on how to play roulette and win. Steve Bourie. You have to look him up."

The dealer's stoic face doesn't change as he pushes Seth's hundred into the drop box with a clear plastic paddle. A hundred plastic chips are shoved across to my covert partner in crime.

"He actually says not to play roulette at all..." Seth continues getting cozy with the old lady.

I reach down to adjust my gold cuff when a deep command from over my shoulder startles me.

"Fifty," the accented voice says, and a tall, elegant-looking gentleman in an expensive blazer leans beside me. I glance up as he straightens. He slides a long black wallet into his coat pocket, and a gold pinky ring catches my eye.

He smiles, and I blink away, trying not to move my panicked gaze to Seth. He hasn't broken character yet, but with this intruder right behind me, it's going to be impossible to activate the switch without being seen.

A tremor of fear moves through my chest, and a tiny bead of sweat tickles down the line in the center of my back. I'm breathing faster, and I reach up to push another strand of hair behind my ear.

"I hope I'm not making you uncomfortable, mademoiselle." The older gentleman's voice is right beside me, over my shoulder.

"Not at all." I'm irritated by his proximity, and I shift to the right to get away from him. The only problem is I'm now closer to Birthday Boy.

Shit. Our plan is coming apart.

"Why you sound like a foreign gentleman," Seth says, attracting my unwanted tablemate's attention. "Where does one get an accent like that?"

"My accent is Monagascan, monsieur."

"I'll be damned. I didn't know they spoke French in Madagascar!"

"No, monsieur, it's *Monagasco*."

Seth has the man's complete attention as I slide all my winnings onto the black space. The dealer passes his hand over the table.

"No more bets!" he calls.

I dip my finger inside my gold cuff and press the tiny button hidden inside. The silver ball immediately drops, bounces, and then swerves into the tray labeled fifteen black.

"Holy shit! Ho-lee *shit!*" Seth hops off his stool and does a little jig. "I WON!"

"SO DID I!!!" Granny looks like she might have a heart attack. She's holding her chest heaving hard, and I notice a security agent drifting to where we're sitting.

We only have one more spin before we have to get the hell out of here. Odds against roulette players add up faster than any other game in the casino. Our winning streak can't last long, or we'll be detained and questioned.

"I feel as if I'm playing the wrong end of the table," Frenchie says, sliding closer to me.

I'm trapped with nowhere to go. Another scoot to my right, and I'll be in Mr. Twenty-One's lap. Leaving my two hundred chips on black, I attempt to angle my body so it's away from Frenchie's line of sight.

Movement behind the dealer causes me to glance up. Security has his eyes on me. Now I'm really freaking.

Seth happily moves all his chips to the other end of the table. "Mr. Bourie says the odds build up fast on roulette." I watch as he places two huge corner bets.

In a subtle movement, I pass all my chips over to red before quickly returning to my contorted state. I turn my body so I can get my finger inside my gold cuff without being seen.

"No more bets!" The dealer says.

Security's eyes are fixed on me, and they narrow. They follow a burning line down my bare shoulder, along my arm, to my wrist, when all of a sudden a slim, olive hand appears on his lapel. His eyes leave me fast and then widen as Ava steps between us, her beautiful face lined with worry.

"Excuse me!" I can just hear her dewy purr. My little sister has perfected the art of innocent tease. "I'm so worried. I seem to have lost my handbag, and it has all my chips in it... my phone..."

Seth's eyes are on me, his hillbilly pretense gone. Ava's handled security, now I have to finish this job. The ball is slowing on the track, and I pray I haven't missed my chance. My breath stills as I activate the device hidden in my bracelet. At once the ball drops, bounces up again, and hovers in air. It seems to wobble uncertainly. Sickness fills the pit of my stomach. A roaring noise is in my ears.

All this work, and we're going to lose every last…

Thirty-two red.

"WE DID IT!" The old lady shrieks. "We WON! WE WON!!!!"

She's jumping up and down, hugging Seth so hard his glasses bounce on his nose. He's grinning, eyes sparkling.

"God Damn!" Seth slaps the table. "I'm hotter than a Billy goat's ass in a pepper patch!"

I do my best not to burst out laughing as the silver ball rides around in a circle sitting on that red thirty-two. I'm just about to stand when something icy-cold and hard slips between my breasts.

"Oh!" I jump up, clutching my chest.

"*Mon dieu!* I'm so sorry!" The Frenchman steps back, facing me.

My eyes widen, and I hold my arms tight at the top of my ribcage. "What the HELL did you do?"

His dark brows furrow. "I seem to have lost my grip… The excitement." He seems to be trying not to laugh.

My arms are tight around my torso when I turn to the dealer. "Cash me out." I snap.

The man quickly slides my chips away and passes me a five hundred dollar bill. With one hand, I slip it into my white clutch and start to leave, but the Frenchman's fingers close like a steel trap around my forearm.

"I'm so sorry, mademoiselle, but that was a thousand-dollar plaque I dropped!"

I can feel the hard piece of plastic wedged between my skin and the side of my bra, and

I'm holding it tight with my arms so it doesn't fall out.

"Then you should've held onto it better." I yank my arm from his grip and walk quickly away from the table.

In the background I notice Seth and the old lady shaking hands and cashing out. Seth says something about Mr. Bourie advising when to walk away, and the old woman nods, taking his arm. The dealer's face is confusion mixed with embarrassment, but I don't have time to waste. I'm across the gambling area nearing the exit with the foreigner hot on my heels.

"Mademoiselle... Miss! Wait!" He's after me, and I see security closing in around him.

"Take it easy, pal." A hearty growl cuts through the din, and I'm feeling more confident than ever I'm getting out of here with a thousand-dollar bonus.

"You don't understand," he continues. "That lady. She has my money!"

Ava is at the door waiting for me, her eyes round. I'm doing my best not to run when I hear the same meaty voice calling after me.

"Lady! Stop!" My shoulders tense. "Stop her," the guard says, and at once, another man in a suit steps into my path, blocking my way.

I deflect, taking a step to the side. "Oh!" I cry softly.

"Hang on a second, sister." The beefy security guard holds both hands up to the sides. "We just need to ask you a question."

My sister gives me a subtle nod and immediately disappears into the coatroom. The other guard and the Frenchman join us.

"Forgive me," the man says. "I... er... how do you say? I dropped my chip in her... er... *décolletage*?"

"Miss," the guard behind me says, "do you have the man's money?"

I turn to face them, but I'm not backing down. "I don't know what he dropped *down my top*." I infuse my voice with venom, narrowing my eyes. "But I can assure you, I'm not allowing him to retrieve it!"

"Er... no. Of course not." The older gentleman glances to the guards. "However, if you could perhaps step into the powder room?"

He gestures toward the coatroom, and I make a show of exhaling deeply. "If you insist." Squaring my shoulders, I step toward the narrow space where Ava waits.

"But... no. Excuse me?" He calls. I pause, but don't turn. "Would you mind leaving your bag with the guard?"

My head snaps, and I look over my shoulder at him. "What do you think I'm going to do? Hide it? I've already said you dropped something in my top."

"It was a thousand dollar plaque, Mademoiselle."

"So you say. I don't know what it was," I snap.

"I can assure you it was."

Flashing my eyes at the guards, they both shrug. "If you don't mind handing me your purse. I won't open it."

Pushing my white clutch against the guard's chest, I storm into the coatroom as if I'm highly offended. Actually, I'm pretty impressed at this Frenchman's audacity. I'm not sure what he's after, but he's barking up the wrong tree with Zelda Wilder.

Once inside, I hastily unfasten the beaded collar of my dress. Ava is right behind me, holding the top so my breasts are covered.

"He must've been working hard to get that thing down your top," she whispers. "It's a halter!"

I reach down to lift out... sure enough, a powder blue thousand-dollar rectangular chip. "Well what do you know," I sigh.

We both stare at it in wonder for a moment. All of our cons are small, petty-cash jobs that build to real money. It's the first time we've held the real deal in our hands all at once.

"Here, quick!" My sister snaps opens her clutch and whips out a red and black fifty-dollar chip, exchanging it for the plaque, which she drops into her bag. "This is what was in your top."

Our eyes meet, and hers flash with determination. "You think I can get away with it?" My voice is hushed.

"Who's going to prove what he dropped? You already said you didn't see what it was. *He* made the mistake. And who the hell is he anyway, to go around dropping shit down your top? He deserves it. Pervert. Now fasten up. Hurry!"

My heart beats faster as I do the buttons behind my neck. "If we get away with this, we're driving to Fort Lauderdale tomorrow and chartering a sailboat. We're going to spend the whole day on the water."

"Good thing I bought a new bathing suit!" She steps to a small room and shuts the door. "I'll meet you back at our hotel in an hour."

"I'll settle this then I have to meet up with Seth," I pause before going to the door.

"You did good tonight, Sis!" I say.

"I got my bonus. Be careful."

Three men glare at me expectantly when I step from the small room. I square my shoulders and push my hair back. Striding across the space to the men, I resume my offended act.

"I don't know what kind of con you're running, Mister, but that wasn't a thousand dollar chip in my top." Shoving the red and black plastic in his hand, I reach out for my clutch from the guard. "Nice try."

"*No!*" Frenchie shouts. "This is not right! I did not drop fifty dollars down your shirt! Give me my money!"

"I will not stand here and be harassed any longer!" Flashing my eyes at the guards, I zero in on the weaker of the two. "I am not accustomed to such treatment, and I know this is not how the Hard Rock HQ expects their female guests to be treated. This is sexual harassment!"

Both guards look constipated and confused, and I don't give them a chance to collect their thoughts. I'm making my way out the door while the Frenchman is still arguing, lapsing into his native tongue at times as they hold him from chasing after me.

Running out into the night, I wave at a yellow cab waiting on the corner. He lurches forward, and I jump in, slamming the door. "Ramada Hollywood Downtown!"

The cab heads south, leaving the Hollywood reservation and driving toward the coast. The radio plays softly, and the guy isn't chatty. Looking in my clutch, the five hundred is still intact along with a few hundreds I picked up playing blackjack. We'll pool it all once I get to Seth's place.

In minutes we're turning into the cheap hotel parking lot. I pass a ten to the driver. "Keep the change," and I'm out the door, slamming it behind me.

The air is heavy and thick with heat. It smells like rain and cooling asphalt, and I give the parking lot a quick scan. I'm alone, but I see Seth's green Civic in the lot.

I pop open my clutch and pull out the door card he gave me, swiping it so I can enter the courtyard. Tall palm trees outline the perimeter, but I can tell it's empty. A kidney-shaped swimming pool is in the center, also empty, but as I'm making my way to the balcony stairs, I hear a woman's gravelly voice.

"Zee," she calls. "Over here."

Squinting in the dim light I see two figures sitting at a table in shadows. Hustling toward them, I recognize Seth. His coat is off, and the fake glasses are shoved up on his head. He's counting out our winnings.

"Think it's safe to do that here?" I pull out a heavy iron chair and drop into it with a sigh.

"What happened to you?" Helen takes a long pack of brown cigarettes from her bag and flicks her Bic. The small yellow light briefly illuminates her "May Contain Alcohol" sweatshirt, and I can't help a laugh now that we're safely away.

"Where the hell did you get that shirt?"

She looks down and coughs a congested laugh. "On the strip in Fort Lauderdale. This shop has every kind of shirt you can imagine."

"I bet," I exhale, but Seth leans forward.

"Okay, what you got Zee?" All trace of accent is gone, and he's back to flat Kansas, as nondescript as you can get.

Opening my clutch, I scrape out all the contents. "The five hundred." He takes it and adds it to the pile. "And a few *hyundais* I picked up at blackjack before you arrived."

He grins and waves it away. "Keep 'em. Your winnings outside the con are yours."

"Thanks," I say, leaning back. I can't help wondering if he caught what happened after his big win — my encounter with our foreign tablemate.

He's back to counting our pot and then dividing it into thirds. "That guy was crowding you tonight," he says, and my heart stops.

It's quiet a moment, and Helen takes a pull on her cigarette. The orange cherry glows in the darkness.

"Yeah," I say, keeping my voice calm. "I was worried for a second he might see me."

"That's why this is a three-person job." He leans back and looks at me. Three even stacks are before him on the table.

"Ava played an important role, in case you didn't notice." My chest is tight, and if we hadn't run our own, separate con, I'd be pissed. Seth never acknowledges Ava's role in keeping security distracted. "You guys made as much noise as possible. I'm surprised we didn't have the entire police force standing around watching us play."

That makes him laugh, and he leans forward. "Take it easy, Fireball. I know little sister is an asset."

"You never include her in the winnings."

Lifting his eyebrows, he does a little shrug. "If she brings in cash, she can have a share of the winnings."

I'm still not sure if he's waiting for me to confess what happened with the thousand-dollar chip. The old saying "no honor among thieves" drifts through my mind, and he can wait all night if he thinks I'll cave. Whatever he knows, if anything, he'll have to say it.

"It was so much easier when they let us smoke in the casinos," Helen sighs a long cloud of blue smoke. "Hiding that transmitter in your cuff is not ideal."

"Either way, we've burned up our chances of winning any more here." My eyes ache. My spine is tired from absorbing all the stress of the evening, and exhaustion is rolling over me like the warm surf.

"We'll lay low for a month or so. I'll call with our next rendezvous point." Seth shoves a pile of money toward me, and I stand. "You should have enough there to keep you both comfortable until I call."

Picking up my clutch, I tuck the stack inside without bothering to count it. "I'll be waiting to hear from you."

He's on his feet equally fast. "Hey, Zee..." Hazel eyes twinkle in the tall lights, and he reaches up to slide the black glasses off his head. "That's it? No hug before you go?"

I pause, evaluating his request. I've known Seth Hines since I was twenty-one, hustling pool players in panhandle bars while Ava lifted food and petty cash off vendors in the farmer's markets.

Seth is two years older than me, and when we met, he was selling human growth hormone in South Beach. He cleaned us up, taught us to how to talk right, made me stop saying *fuck* all the time. That swear jar almost broke me on the F-bomb alone. I'd never realized how useful (and versatile) that term was.

Basically he turned us into knock-off Bar Harbor society girls as opposed to the panhandle hicks we truly are. He also taught me how to gamble in nice casinos, which is different from gambling in shit-hole dive bars.

He taught me how to stay cool when it looks like I'm about to get busted. He taught me to be a pro. But not Ava. Back then she was too young. Then when she was old enough, he said she was too pretty.

"Targets will want to sleep with her or at the very least hit on her," he'd said. "Having a memorable face is a liability in this game."

By saying that, he had essentially called me plain and forgettable, but I shook that shit off. He was right. Ava's beauty was the reason we were forced into a life of petty crime in the first place. It wasn't what I promised her when I said I'd take care of us, but we were making it. I didn't want her taking chances like me.

Two years later, and we've graduated from small-time card tricks to more complex schemes with bigger payoffs. We're only loosely associated with Seth, and I like to keep it that way. He has a mean side. He's never hurt me, but I don't get too close. I don't trust him.

Seth's a grifter like me, and a grifter like me will do anything to get what he wants. In my case it's security, a safe place for Ava and me. In Seth's case, it's the big score, the ultimate win.

I step forward into his outstretched arms, but I only hug him briefly before pulling back.

"What? That's it?" he laughs.

"Ava's back at the hotel alone, and I'm ready to crash."

He waves and drops in his chair. "Suit yourself."

"Night, Helen." I wave at the part-Seminole granny, who always adds color to our jobs. "Can't wait to see what you show up wearing next."

She takes another pull off her cigarette and exhales a chuckle. "Night, Zee. Take care of you two."

"It's what I do," I say as I go.

It's what I've been doing for the past six years, and I don't intend to stop. Survival skills have gotten us this far.

I think about earlier this evening and how Ava knew instinctively to sneak into the coatroom and wait. My sister and I have become a well-oiled machine. I can't take credit for being the brains anymore because my little sister is right there spotting every angle and preparing to maximize any situation.

One day we won't need Seth to come up with cons. One day we'll have enough money to take care of ourselves for a long, long time.

One day we'll be free.

CHAPTER 2: PLAYBOY PRINCE

Rowan

Shoving the clutch into fifth, I steer into the straight and punch the accelerator all the way to the floor. The noise of the engine rips through the air, and the speed of the Mercedes CLR vibrates up my legs as the needle moves past a hundred.

The track is slick and the tires of my Formula One car are slicker. A single wrong move could send me into a potentially deadly spin. Every muscle in my body strains as I ride the lightning, as a bead of sweat glides down my neck. A curve is ahead. I'll cut the first one to nail the second exiting into another straight to pick up more speed.

Pushing the breaks hard, the wheel fights me as I turn it. I cross my arms like a pretzel, never letting go as I guide the car through the first turn, only to whip it around again coming out and hitting the gas hard, flying into the straight.

The black and white checkered bar of the finish line is in view, and I let her rip, giving everything to beat my previous time. Scenery blurs into a wash of color. My eyes are fixed on the top third of the windshield. I blaze past the flagman faster than a blink, his frantic waving barely registering in my vision.

Foot off the gas, I exhale, my muscles vibrating with adrenaline. Coasting through the downshifts, I bring it into the pit.

"Fuck me, you did it! Seven seconds!" Cal is laughing and shouting at the side of the car, grasping my underarm and pulling me up. "You're one away from the record."

Pulling off my helmet, I scrub a hand back and forth through my dark hair. "It's not enough," I say, pulling the zipper down on my red and white fireproof suit.

It's a gorgeous day on the track. The sky is brilliant blue, and the air is dry. Zero humidity, and not a cloud obstructs the sun from beating down on us. Standing on the black asphalt, my entire body is covered in sweat from both the exertion of the trial run and the heat. If we were closer to the coast, at least we'd have the constant breeze.

"You're the best racer in the country," my brother continues. "It's a shame you'll never compete again."

Regret twists my stomach. "You always know just what to say, don't you, Cal?"

"Come now, we can't have our future king going out in a blaze of glory." He slaps my back as he braces me. "You've got enough shit to deal with at the palace."

Even after all this time, it's tough for me to let it go so easily. "Did you see Gutierrez's crash last week? He climbed out and walked over to do an interview right after."

"What are you saying?" My brother's eyes flash.

"Nothing." One of the pit crew shoves a Gatorade in my hand, and I rip the top off and take a drink before dismissing my fantasies of freedom. "Only that it's impressive how far safety has come. Racing sets the standard for the entire automobile industry."

"You want to say *fuck it*? Grand Prix qualifications are only a few weeks away!"

"No." I push off the side of the car and slowly make my way to the track exit. Cal would never talk me out of doing something completely insane and irresponsible. He's perfected such behavior. "*Fuck it* is not in the royal vernacular."

"Ah, shit." He walks beside me, pulling out his phone. "I thought for once we might have a little fun around here."

As I'm passing into the covered area under the stands, I nod to the guards standing watch.

"I need a shower," I mutter.

"Hello hello! What's this? It appears someone is having fun on his own." My brother grabs my shoulder, stopping me. "Is *hummer* in the royal vernacular? Ha! And it's all over the blogs..."

The last thing I care about is tabloid news. "I really couldn't give a rat's ass—" The words die in my throat as my brother shoves his smartphone in my face, and I immediately recognize the billiard room at our estate in Occitan. "What the hell?"

On the screen is a blurry image of me leaning against the wall. My head is back and my eyes are closed. On her knees in front of me is a blonde I know too well, her head level at my crotch.

"Shit!" I snatch the phone, adrenaline spiking in my veins.

"Now who was this young lady?" Cal teases, elbowing my side. "Is she practicing her genuflection?"

"Who took this?"

"More importantly, who is she and was it any good?"

My jaw grinds in anger as I remember that night a few weeks ago, the daughter of a duke was visiting with her father. She and I have known each other since we were kids. I was tired, she was charming, a few drinks later...

We haven't spoken since, and there's no way in hell I'll reveal her identity.

"How dare they... Find whoever did this and have these images destroyed!"

Taking his phone back, Cal laughs louder, increasing my fury. "What century do you live in? These photos are out there for the duration. I'm just glad to see you're finally getting some action." He slaps my shoulder. "I was worried about you, old chap."

Stopping at the exit wall, I lean against it thinking of all the eyes that will see that photo — the queen mother, the lady's father, the god damned assholes in the cabinet who treat me like I'm not old enough to rule. It's yet another reason for them to delay the referendum naming me King of Monagasco. As if we can afford another delay...

"I hate the Internet," I growl.

"Welcome to the club." Cal turns his phone. "It's an incredibly clear shot. You must've been drunk to be so careless."

"I was very tired. I didn't ask for that." I honestly never expected it either.

"What I wouldn't give for that whole *future king* moniker you continually waste. Do you know how much tail you could be getting on a regular basis?"

"You're the heir presumptive. If *future king* is all it takes, you can cash in on the lineup at any time."

He shakes his head. "Nobody wants the bitter younger brother of the future king. The one silently calculating the day his elder sibling dies and he seizes all the power."

"Is that what you're up to?"

"I'm just saying. Don't you watch any movies?"

Narrowing my eyes on my younger brother, I joke, "I seem to recall that Loki fellow has quite a following. Isn't he always trying to find creative ways to kill Thor?"

"Part of the problem is I actually like you, old bean." Cal throws an arm over my shoulder. We're the same six-foot-two height, so it works. "I wouldn't trade the shit you deal with every day for all the pussy in the world."

"Look out—" Shrugging his arm off, we both launch into a full-out sprint toward our waiting town car.

We're only steps ahead of a mob of paparazzi flying in our direction, camera flashes popping. I fling open the door and dive in. Cal's right behind me, pulling in his feet just before the door slams with a solid *thunk*.

Our most trusted driver Hajib hits the gas, and we're pushing away from the crowd as the strobe of flashbulbs blinds us.

"Next time you're feeling hard up, let me know." Cal pants. "I'll find you someone more discreet."

"I can't fucking believe this." Leaning forward, I pinch my fingers over my closed eyes, calming my breath. "It had to have been someone on staff."

"You're not going to tell me her name?"

Hesitating, I consider his request, but waiting for my answer is forgotten as he checks his phone again.

"No!" he cries. "They can't do this!"

My blood freezes. "What?" I lean toward him, stomach tight. *Could it possibly get any worse?*

"*I'm* the Playboy Prince. *Me!*" He jams a thumb in his chest. "Leave me something, man!"

"Jesus," I hiss leaning back in the seat and looking out the window at the passing scenery. Every few seconds I catch a glimpse of the turquoise water of the Mediterranean. "We're supposed to be in Occitan to relax."

"You're one step ahead of us on that front."

I'm about to lose it when my phone buzzes. "Shit," I mutter when I see the screen. "Mother."

"Here we go." Cal turns my phone to read her text aloud. "We need to talk."

I lean forward again, putting my hand over my mouth as I try to sort this out. Of all things, my mother had to see me getting a blowjob from an unnamed female. She won't be angry at the act necessarily — just that I got caught.

"Chin up. It could be worse." My brother stretches his legs. "It's not like your royal ass was in the air or you were caught in a *ménage*."

"Both of which *you've* already done."

He exhales dramatically, "It's been a while, my brother."

"Two days?"

That only makes him smile, and he slaps my shoulder. "Think of it this way, getting a hummer from an attractive young courtier is the royal way. You're just keeping with tradition. Shows you're a man."

"More like a careless frat boy. Not the future leader of our country."

"It didn't hurt the President of the United States, and they're supposedly the world leaders."

"I'd hardly model my personal life after a U.S. President. They're all commoners."

The car stops in front of our seaside estate, and I glance down at my racing suit and dirty hands. At least the sweat is dry from our air-conditioned ride. "I suppose I should get this over with now."

Hajib opens the door, and I step out, not missing his attempt to hold back a smirk. *I can't believe I'm plastered all over the fucking tabloids...*

"You could've been experimenting with coke," Cal continues as we jog up the white front steps to the grand entrance.

"Again, something you've already done," I retort.

"It was only once. The sex was insane, let me tell you."

My mother is standing in the foyer waiting for us. She's dressed in an olive green suit, and her silver hair is smoothed back in a controlled helmet. A three-stranded pearl necklace is precisely positioned at her throat. Everything about her is planned, controlled, and exactly as it should be.

"Your royal highness," she says to me, a definite tone in her voice. "Would you step with me into the parlor?"

"Of course," I say.

She leads the way, and my brother is right on my heels, never one to miss a royal scolding.

"Close the door please, Cal," she says, turning to sit on the edge of a chaise upholstered in yellow satin.

"If you don't mind, I'll stand." I say, doing a slight nod. "I've been at the track."

"Certainly," Mother's voice is sharp. "This won't take long. I suppose you've seen the news."

"Just now. Cal noticed—"

"Your great aunt Daphne brought it to my attention. You know how I despise that woman." Straightening, she runs her palms down the front of her light blazer. "You know, Rowan, when you first took over after your father's death, you made several bold moves. Exiling Hubert and Reggie, although I don't know I agree with the latter, you demonstrated strength, that you were not afraid to crush insubordination. I was proud of you."

"Thank you," I say, knowing exactly where this is headed.

"You also have powerful critics, who think you're young, inexperienced, and reckless. Your racing hobby, for instance, and now this."

"I can assure you, Mother—"

"I'm not angry, Rowan. You're a man, after all." Her lips are tight, and her ice blue eyes fix on mine. "You're very handsome, you're twenty seven, you have needs."

Actually, I've changed my mind. I have no idea where this is headed. "What are you saying?"

She inhales and looks around the well-appointed room. "We can't afford to have you engaging in frivolity while the people suffer and unemployment is high."

"I couldn't agree more. I spend most of my time looking for ways to improve the economy—"

"Looking for ways is not enough, Rowan." Her eyes return to mine. "I'm ready to retire. I need you to do something bold. Take action. Force their hand on the succession referendum."

Frustration twists in my chest. My succession to the throne has to be put forth to the people by the very cabinet members intent on criticizing me.

"I have several projects in the works. I'm moving us away from oil dependence. I've drafted an agreement with an American tech billionaire —"

"Which I'm sure will pay off eventually," she sighs.

For a moment, she's quiet, thinking. I don't know what to say to ease her concerns, partly because I know she's right. I've got to do something to control the narrative.

"Many things about our way of life never change, no matter how many centuries pass," she says. "If your only press is of you acting the playboy while the people suffer, you might as well tell them to eat cake as they starve."

"That's hardly fair, Mum," Cal jumps in. "Everyone knows what a stiff Ro is. So he had one slip up. Now all the old biddies can stop saying he's gay."

"What the *hell*?" If I wasn't angry before...

"MacCallum Lockwood Tate! Don't make me send you from this room."

My brother only laughs, but I ignore his jokes and address my mother's concerns.

"I understand what you're saying, Mother. I'll double-down on appearances. Perhaps I can do something with the regiment..."

"It's not enough."

Our eyes lock. We're wealthy beyond belief. We're sitting in a plush room with arched windows covered in gold-velvet curtains. Two couches are arranged back to back on a red-Persian rug, which protects gleaming wood floors. A gilded lamp sits on a small, round mahogany table. I'm trying to figure out how I can change what we are.

"What more I can do?"

41

"You have to show your focus. Engage in an act of maturity." Her eyes harden. "It's time the king took a wife."

The noise of Cal dropping the brass paperweight echoes from the desk behind me. My throat closes. "I don't think *that's* necessary."

"You need to appear rooted and settled down, Rowan. Or at the very least focused on the future. France tolerates us, but if it appears Totringham is poised to invade, they will move. We're not in a position to fight with this recession dragging on."

Everything she says is true. The country is in a precarious position and any indication of weakness in power makes us vulnerable. Still, I can't tolerate the meaning of her words. I'm out of my seat and pacing. It's my absolute last shred of freedom stripped away.

"So I marry some cousin or daughter of an earl to save our independence? It's ridiculous."

"Or you become a celibate, which is even more ridiculous." She stands and does a little wave. "It's time you settle down with someone royal and start producing royal heirs. Now get cleaned up."

She exits the parlor, and Cal rocks back in the chair, watching me with a smirk. "I sure hope that was one superior hummer."

A five thousand kilo brick is in my stomach, and I can't think about this right now. "I need a shower."

CHAPTER 3: A PROPOSITION

Zelda

The water of the Atlantic gleams turquoise under a cloudless sky. I lie back on the catamaran and let the blazing sun beat down on my golden skin. The warmth and salt air combined with the lapping of the waves is delicious.

"A perfect day after a perfect crime," Ava says with a laugh, joining me on the bow of the sailboat. "Check it out."

Propping on my elbows, I look over at her latest acquisition. She holds up a thick gold herringbone men's bracelet. I sit up all the way and reach for it.

"Let me see!"

She sits in front of me, and I turn the half-inch-wide gold strand over in my hands. "It's very expensive."

"Yes, but what man wears a gold bracelet anymore?"

"I can think of a few."

"Rap stars."

"So hook up with a rap star." I blink up at her and grin. "Your pretty head would probably explode with all the jewelry you could steal."

That makes her laugh. "I wonder if I could get a diamond stud out of someone's ear without him noticing."

"I wouldn't put it past you."

"Maybe if I used my mouth..."

"Gross!" I throw my hands up. "Don't tell me. Show me when you've done it."

My sister started her game of "trade" when she was only eighteen and helping me distract security guards in the Indian casinos in north Florida. She'd talk to them, flirt and giggle. She'd hang on their arms and ask them all about their jobs in breathless rapture. They wouldn't even notice me counting cards and palming the decks.

At some point in the night, she'd grow sad and wistful and tell the unsuspecting male how much like her late father he was. Then she'd give him a gift—either a gold cigarette case or a pair of onyx cufflinks. Or maybe a shiny brass Zippo. The men would be so flattered, they wouldn't even notice her stealing their watch or money clip or whatever expensive item they happened to be wearing. In Ava's mind, the gift made up for the theft of something new. It was her own private jewelry exchange.

I watch as she wraps the thick piece of gold around her slim wrist. "Maybe I'll have a few links removed and keep it for myself."

"But then what would you give your next victim?" I lie back, closing my eyes against the blazing sunlight.

"I don't know." She's quiet, and I glance over at her stretched out, long and lean, brown skin in a white string bikini.

Suddenly her chin jerks in my direction. "Don't you ever wish we could do something really exciting? Like rob an art gallery that has laser tracking? We could sprinkle powder everywhere and climb through it like Catherine Zeta-Jones in *Entrapment*."

"No." I frown at her, and she laughs, turning away again.

"*C'est la vie.*"

"What we do isn't for kicks, Ava. We only steal so we can eat. And live."

"And take charters off the coast of Miami."

"This is a bonus, and you know it." Sniffing, I take a sip of my rum punch. The sweet, fruity flavor fills my mouth. "That jerk was an asshole dropping his chip down my dress. He got what he deserved."

"Did you tell Seth?"

I don't answer, and the sound of the waves licking against the side of the boat fills the empty air while she waits. A seagull cries as it passes over, and I look up at it.

With a little sigh, she relaxes on her towel, letting my non-answer pass. "How come you and Seth never hook up?" she asks instead. "He's been with us since Tampa. You claim he taught you everything you know about scamming casinos. What's the problem?"

"He's not my type." Seth is about control, and I'll be damned if I let any man control me.

"Tell me," she flips onto her stomach. "What is your type, Zelda Wilder? Some tall, dashing pirate with doubloons galore? Or a cowboy?"

All these questions are harshing my buzz. "I thought we came out here to relax."

"I'm relaxed. I'm ecstatic!" She laughs and kicks both her feet up. "We've got four thousand dollars! Can you believe it? We can live on four thousand dollars for—"

"About a month." I take another sip of rum.

"Not true! The hotel room is only three hundred. We can scrimp on meals."

"It's still going to run out, and then what?" I'm not sure why my mood has taken a turn, but I'm less breezy and more reality all of a sudden.

"Then we do it again!" Ava cries, and I hear the impatience in her tone.

For a moment I'm quiet, looking at her stretched out in the sun smiling. My sister is smart and attractive. I might have saved her from abuse in the foster system, but what have I done for her?

"I'm going to burn," I mutter, pushing up and walking low to the back of the boat, my empty silicone glass in hand.

Miguel, our captain, is stretched out smoking a joint. "Sexy Zee," he says smiling. "Have a hit?"

"No thanks." I shake my head and give him a wave. "I'm not in the mood for grass."

"Drinks in the cabin."

Nodding, I start down the ladder, but I pause midway. "Thanks for taking us out today."

He shrugs. "I didn't have anything else to do. Beautiful day, beautiful view." He winks and nods toward the bow.

"Yeah."

Miguel is harmless, and he's always been nice to us since we arrived in south Florida. Our first few days, I snooped around the docks looking for scraps and easy work. He hired me to be first mate on a few of his snorkeling charters, and in return, I've sent him business pretty regularly. Him being at the dock today looking for tourists was a stroke of luck, and now three lucky breaks in a row has me looking over my shoulder.

I spray sunscreen on my chest and arms then lean down and coat my knees again. A little more lotion on my face, a refill of rum punch, and I'm headed back up front to where my sister is sitting cross-legged, looking into the breeze.

"I didn't ask if you wanted anything, sorry," I say, sitting on my towel again.

"It's okay. I'll get something in a minute." She's looking up and down the shoreline. "One goes down, and another, bigger one springs up in its place."

Looking at the shore, I think about where we are and where we're headed. "We should try to get a job at one of those places."

"A nine to five?" She looks at me like I just sprouted an additional head.

I trace a path along the frosted edge of my glass with my finger. The pink beverage inside is thick and sweet. "We gotta do better than this, Ava-bug. This is no kind of long-term plan."

She growls softly and stretches her legs in the sun. "You always get like this after a big job. You're small-time, Zelda Wilder."

Her carnival barker voice makes me grin. "What are you talking about?"

"The more zeros you bring home, the more you fret about changing the way we live. How *we gotta do better than this*." She's imitating me now.

I think about how I'm feeling. "We *are* better than this. At least you are."

"Better than the cheating husbands who grab my ass? Okay, sure." Scooting closer, her voice gets a little harder. "Better than the casino owners who rig the games to dribble out a little money at a time so the addicts keep coming back for more? I guess I'm better than them."

Lifting my glass, I smile as I take a drink.

"See how smart you are? You should be in school somewhere learning how to run a business."

Ava eases back onto her towel, tilting her head to the side. "I'm no smarter than you are. I've learned everything I know from watching you."

I groan a laugh. "That's not encouraging."

We're still again, listening to the sounds of the ocean, the waves splashing gently as the catamaran cuts through the water, the birds overhead, the occasional tug of a cruise ship passing in the distance, taking off for some Caribbean voyage.

In my mind I replay last night, my time at the table, the old man who slipped up behind me and tried to pull a fast one. My little sister at the bar touching security guards, leaning forward to give them a teasing glimpse of her cleavage as she steals their gold bracelets.

"It never ends," I answer. "Or it ends badly."

"Which is why you love it." Her forceful reply snaps me from my melancholy thoughts. "You would be miserable doing anything else. You live for the adrenaline rush of going in there, taking chances, not knowing what might happen from one moment to the next."

"Maybe." I can't deny what she's saying, but I can't let her win that easily. "Still... Momma would've expected me to do better by you."

"Don't you do that." She grabs my arm in a surprisingly strong grip. Our eyes meet, blue on green, and I see the fierce protectiveness burning in hers. "You saved me. You got us away from those abusive assholes. Don't you ever think Momma would doubt you. I never will."

We stare at each other, and as much as I don't want it, my mind goes tripping back to that last night in foster care. To the sweaty, meaty hands running up my little sister's smooth legs, higher… to the hem of her gown as she lay still as a statue shivering and praying. I saw the fear in her eyes, and I snapped.

Bile rises in my throat, and I remember taking the lamp and smashing it over his head moments before we ran. "I didn't have a plan," I confess. "I just couldn't let him touch you like that."

"You kept me from being hurt. I'll never be able to repay you for that."

I exhale, straightening my legs and looking down at my drink. "I'm your sister. You don't have to repay me."

I'm back in that concrete culvert holding her small body as she cries. I'm vowing to do whatever it takes to keep us on the road, free, even though I have no idea how the hell I'll do it.

I'm lost in thought as a blast of noise cuts through our tranquility. The loud buzz of a speedboat races toward our vessel.

"What the—" Ava's voice trails off as she reaches for her cover-up, and I turn in time to see a gleaming wood, clearly expensive cruiser glide up beside us.

The captain reaches for the side of the catamaran and throws a rope across just as my eyes register his passenger. *It's the Frenchman from last night! Mr. Thousand-dollar Chip!*

"Miguel," I scream. I scream until my voice cracks, but it's no good. He's asleep in the back, and the noise of the boat drowns me out.

The speedboat captain puts one foot across to our boat, and before I can protest, he grips my arm roughly, jerking me off the catamaran and into the bed of his cruiser.

"You too, Miss!" he yells at Ava, whose eyes are round saucers.

Uncertainty ripples through her limbs, and I see her trying to decide whether to follow me, or run and try to wake Miguel.

"Stay where you are, Ava!" I shout. "I'll be okay."

"Zee?" That tremor of fear I haven't heard since the night we ran is in her voice.

The Frenchman steps up on the side of the cruiser and holds out his hand. "Please come with us, Mademoiselle." His voice is low and smooth. "I won't hurt you. We have business to discuss."

Her brow lines, and her eyes flicker to mine. She's like a sparrow caught in a trap. I turn my attention to the well-dressed man speaking to my sister. Living on the street has taught me to read people, and one thing I've learned is when someone intends to hurt you, they don't typically mention business. They don't make requests. They push you down or pull out a weapon.

Ava doesn't move, waiting for my direction. With a fortifying breath, I nod. Her posture is defensive, but she scoops up my bathing suit cover before placing her small hand in his and climbing slowly across to the speedboat.

Once she's in, the man turns to me. "Sir Reginald Winston." He extends a hand, but I'm trying to figure him out.

Today he's dapper in khaki slacks and a white polo shirt with a navy blazer on top. His dark hair is streaked with grey, and that moniker sounds like royalty.

"Zelda Wilder," I say, not shaking his hand. "How did you find us out here?"

"There's very little money won't buy, Miss Wilder, including the whereabouts of an attractive, street-smart blonde with a brunette who could pass for a model."

Chewing my lips, I silently acknowledge what Seth has been saying all along. It's hard to fly under the radar with Ava.

"Zee! Zee!" I look over my shoulder to see Miguel is up and waving frantically at us from the catamaran. "What's going on? What's happening?"

"Tell him you're fine," Sir Reginald Winston says to me in a low voice.

I survey the plush speedboat we're in and the relaxed captain waiting for further instruction.

"Will it be a lie?" I ask, arching an eyebrow.

"Of course not. As I told your sister, I have no intention of hurting you."

A few moments pass, and I study his steel grey eyes. I see something in them, something I recognize—and it's not deception.

Stepping to the side, I call back to our friend. "If we're not back in an hour, call the police."

He hesitates, looking from me to the captain of the speedboat to the tall man standing beside me.

"One hour," he shouts, and I nod, giving him a wave.

"Let's go," the man to my right says, and the speedboat roars to life. "Please, take your seats."

Ava is already sitting with her arms hugging her stomach. I take the seat beside my sister, putting a protective hand on her. Miguel doesn't move as we turn and shoot away from where he's anchored.

"A thousand dollars for an hour." The man's accent is thick, and it makes his words sound slurry. "Your time is quite valuable."

"Then you'd better get on with it," I snap.

Unlike Ava, I'm sitting straight, unafraid on the outside, shaking like a leaf on the inside. This could be one of the dumbest decisions my curiosity has made.

The man laughs as he reclines in the leather seat beside me. "I like your spirit, Miss Wilder. I was quite captivated by it last night at the tables."

"Is that why you pulled that stunt with the chip? You must think I don't watch movies."

His eyebrow quirks, and his blue eyes twinkle. "Hats off to you. Few people would catch the Hitchcock reference."

"Our parents loved classic movies," Ava's voice is quiet.

"No, I used the 'stunt with the chip' as you put it hoping I might secure a meeting with you."

"Perhaps you should look up the term *backfire* in your French-to-English dictionary."

His expression hardens, and he straightens his coat. "I'm an official in the Monagasco government, and the con you pulled at the roulette wheel last night was first executed in one of our most luxurious casinos. Only that time, they used a pack of cigarettes to activate the transmitter."

My stomach drops. He's with the gambling commission! Ice filters through my veins, and my mouth goes dry. "I-I don't know what you're talking about."

"Of course you do." He's smiling, but it's like the cat that has the mouse cornered and is ready to pounce. "The trick you and Mr. Kentucky pulled involved your gold bracelet emitting a radio transmission that guided the ball into one of three possible trays."

Ava stiffens at my back, and I'm glad she's wearing her dark sunglasses. My sister does not have a poker face—one of the many reasons I don't let her gamble.

"You must have watched one too many movies yourself, Mr. Winston. I'd never laid eyes on that man from Kentucky before last night."

He's quiet, smiling as we continue to bounce along the waves. A little spray of water shoots over the side, and he pulls out a cloth handkerchief to wipe it away.

"That's good," he nods. "Very good. You lie in broad daylight as well as you lie in the evening. I suspected as much."

I'm sick of this shit. "You'd better get to your business before you run out of time."

"My business won't take long to explain. We've time for a little polite conversation."

"I'm not known for being polite."

"Or for being honest," he grins, "but I won't hold it against you."

"You took a chance. Too bad it didn't pay off for you."

"I wouldn't say that." His eyes move to my sister, and then back to me. "I've got other things in mind."

Scooting closer to her, I lower my brow. "You and every other straight man on the planet. Take a hike, Frenchie. She's not interested."

He leans his head back and laughs loudly. "What did you call me?"

"I'll call you worse than that if you try to put your pampered hands on my sister."

The cloth handkerchief is back out, and he's dabbing his eyes as he shakes his head. "You're mistaken, Miss Wilder, it's you I want."

My heart lurches, and I speak before I realize. "Me?"

"We got off on the wrong foot." He holds both hands up. "I only meant to say I admire your work. I have a proposition for you that will make that thousand-dollar chip look like... how do you say? Chicken feed?"

We've slowed to a crawl, and the waves rock the small boat roughly. I study his expression. All the humor is gone. He's serious.

I frown, but he rises from his seat with a flourish. "I have a job for you that would eclipse all others. If you're successful, you'll never work again for the rest of your life." His eyebrow cocks. "Unless you get bored and simply want to."

So many questions jam together in my brain, I don't know which to ask first.

Ava's hand tightens on my arm. "What is your proposition?" she says.

The man winks and does a little point at her. "I see you have a head for business, Miss..."

"You can call me Ava."

"He's not calling you anything." I grab the reins on the conversation. "I don't like your looks."

"Not a problem," he says, waving a hand. "I'm not the one you'll be interacting with. Does the name Rowan Westringham Tate mean anything to you?"

Ava and I shake our heads no. "Who is he?" she asks.

"He's the crown prince of Monagasco, and believe me, women *do* like his looks, *very* much. Some men as well, from what I understand—"

"What about him?" I'm impatient.

For the first time, I see anger fire in our host's eyes. "I have a score to settle with his royal highness." Reginald's jaw clenches, and he levels his gaze on me in a way that makes my insides squirm. "I confess I never saw you coming, but you are perfect. You're the answer to my prayers."

"Your twisted prayers, I'll bet."

"Hear me out." He returns to his seat facing me. "Last night you demonstrated your skill with playing a part all the way to the end. You showed you don't crack under pressure, and you're quick on your feet."

"What's your point?" Flattery has never distracted me from the bottom line.

"The way royal succession works in our country, when the parliament decides the heir is ready to take the throne, they propose a formal referendum upon which the people vote." He leans back, and I don't like the darkness in his eyes. "I have a plan to expose the crown prince of Monagasco for the immature, selfish... *careless* leader he is. A leader who jeopardizes the future of our country."

"Is that so?" I say, shifting uncomfortably.

"He won't listen to his advisors. He threw out the cabinet. The only way to break him is to show him he's a fool—to demonstrate it for the entire country to see."

I don't like the sound of this. "I don't have a dog in your fight. Why do you need me?"

"It's very simple, actually." He straightens, the menacing expression gone. "You will pose as the heir of Lux Benedict, a colleague of mine who I've recently established as a Texas oil baron."

"Hang on..." I'm following his words closely. "Is your friend really a Texas oil baron?"

"Of course not."

"And you think that's going to work?"

"Again, you'd be surprised what money can do. As Benedict's daughter, I'll escort you to Monagasco on a holiday—Ava can be your sister or your friend, whatever makes you comfortable. While there, you just happen to cross paths with the dashing future king. You fall in love, he proposes, makes a grand public engagement, and *Voilà!* You're free to leave. I'll take care of the rest."

My mouth has dropped open. Ava's hand is still on my arm, but she's not talking either.

Reginald grins. "Did you never dream of being a princess when you were a little girl?"

"No." I glance over my shoulder, and my eyes meet Ava's. "I dreamed of finding us a safe place to sleep, of no one catching us stealing food or breaking into boathouses when it rained. I dreamed of a place where we didn't have to be afraid..."

"Of course, your experience was different."

"We learned to cope in ways most people never do."

My words seem to invigorate him. "Which is why you must say yes to me now." He scoots forward slightly and takes my hand. "You'll be pampered, treated to the finest clothes, food, wine... You'll stay in the most luxurious suites, and visit the most beautiful beaches in Europe."

Sliding my hand out of his, I scoot back. "And in the meantime I help you humiliate some guy I don't even know in front of his entire country?"

"It's to *save* the country."

My eyes flicker up, over his shoulder, and I see Miguel in the distance. *Perfect timing.* "I'm sorry, Mr. Winchester—"

"Call me Reggie."

"I'm sorry, Reggie, but that's not who I am. You've got the wrong girl." Ava makes a noise like a puppy behind me. "Find someone else to play your game. We're not interested."

He leans back, pressing his lips into a thin line. "I had hoped it wouldn't come to this."

I pause and study his disappointed expression. "Come to what?"

"You owe me money, Miss Wilder. I was hoping you'd agree to help me without the need for coercion. However, if you choose to be difficult, I'm afraid you'll force my hand."

My fists tighten, and I'm ready for a fight. "What is that supposed to mean?"

He rises, and to my dismay, without my heels on, my face only reaches the middle of his chest. I'm like a petulant child.

"Last night at the roulette table, I took pictures of you activating your bracelet. I'd hate to turn them over to the gambling commission. I also requested the security footage from the coatroom, which shows your sister trading out my thousand-dollar plaque for the fifty-dollar chip, which makes her your accomplice."

He reaches down to straighten first his left cuff then his right. "Third-degree Grand Theft is a felony in Florida with the penalty of five years in prison, not to mention your unforgettable faces blasted to every casino security team across the U.S."

As he speaks, I slowly sink back into the seat beside my sister. My stomach sinks further, through the bottom of the boat all the way to the ocean floor. We're trapped like rats.

"But there now," he smiles. "Let's not fight. I don't want anything bad to happen to you. I want you to help me, and in return, I help you. It's a win-win, yes? What do you say?"

Swallowing the lump in my throat, I can't shake the bad feeling twisting my guts. "You said we'd be set for life. How can I trust you'll keep your word?"

"Of course, I almost forgot." He hastily reaches inside his coat and pulls out a slim wallet. Opening it, he retrieves a black card. "Ten thousand dollars is on this card, prepaid. All you have to do is register it to your name and set up a password. It is yours free and clear."

Now I really can't breathe. "What is that?"

"Your first payment." He smiles, and I see in his eyes he knows he's got me. "You'll get another ten as soon as you reach Monagasco, and I'll reload the card as needed. You only need to text me."

Ava's nails bite into my arm. I can feel her breathing quickly behind me, and I know her eyes are fixed on that piece of black plastic just like mine. One word rattles around in my head: *Freedom*.

"We don't have passports... visas..." It's my last ditch attempt at saying no.

"I'll have ambassador's visas made up for the both of you. You're my personal guests."

The smallest nudge comes from behind, and I know I'm making a deal with the devil, a deal I'm going to regret. Still, like an out-of-body experience, my arm rises, and I take the card from Sir Reginald's fingers.

We're in.

"Very good," Reggie nods, lifting his chin to signal the captain. "Let's get to Bal Harbour. We have quite a bit of shopping to do."

Chapter 4: Unwelcome Guest

Rowan

Reaching down, I take my mother's hand to assist her out of the shiny black Mercedes town car. A strobe of camera flashes explodes around us making it difficult to see her foot wrapped in a strappy silver heel as it clears the curb. My mother is as accustomed to such events as I am, and she exits the vehicle with practiced grace.

It's been two weeks since my royal indiscretion was plastered across the front page of every blog and cheap tabloid on the continent, and in that time I've performed nonstop penance.

I've been photographed at two charity auctions — the first for a children's home in Romania, shaking hands with the chief architect. The second was at a benefit for the rail workers' union. I donned a hard hat and stood beside men I equaled in height but didn't match in sheer brawn.

Behind closed doors, I've met with two entrepreneurial startups. I've chatted with an American tech billionaire on possibly locating one of his clean-energy electric storage facilities in the northern hills of Monagasco. It's so risky and new I've only discussed it with Cal, but it's the closest I've gotten to revolutionizing our economic basis and moving us away from oil dependence.

Tonight I'm at the royal gala benefitting the Monagasco Red Cross. The annual event draws celebrities and dignitaries from all over the world, and once it's over, they filter into the streets and the casinos to flood the town's coffers with high-end tourist dollars. As we walk slowly toward the Royal Sporting Club, my mother leans on my arm.

"Make the most of this night," she says through her smile. "Look at all the eligible young ladies in attendance. Many are daughters of our allies."

Her words cause the muscles in my neck to tighten. Glancing up, I notice the Earl of Bishopsworth standing near the entrance with his daughter Graceland at his side. Speaking to him is the Duke of Westingroot. My throat goes dry when I see his eldest daughter Lara on his arm. *Lara...* The reason I'm in this fucking mess.

I don't have time to dwell on it. Beside them is another earl or baron whose name I don't recall... along with what appears to be his daughter, and the pairs continue into the Club.

I lean into my mother's ear and speak through clenched teeth. "What have you done?"

She smiles and nods to an old crone who arches an eyebrow at me. My smile clenches harder. As if what I did was so blasted unheard of. So I allowed an overzealous courtier to suck my dick. So sue me. It isn't the first time something like that has happened.

Straightening, my mother speaks softly through her smile. "I simply put out the word the crown prince is ready to marry."

It takes all my strength not to explode. We've made it to the entrance, and the duke is waiting.

"Rowan," he says heartily, gripping my shoulder in one hand as he shakes my hand with the other. "It's good to see you keeping with tradition. You remember my daughter Lara?"

All too well... "Yes, of course," I say, nodding my head while focusing on her mouth. Indeed, that was a superior hummer.

Lara lifts the side of her blue dress and bows her blonde head as she curtseys. "His royal highness and I took riding classes together in Nice," she says, glancing up at me with a knowing grin.

"You were a far better rider than I was," I say, giving her a brief smile in response.

I'm not a dick, even if these ancient assholes are royally pissing me off. I really liked Lara that summer. Our memories of being fifteen, riding along the shore, and passing the time together in the twilight hours of Nice are what preceded her dropping to her knees. We'd both had a little too much alcohol that night.

"Perhaps you'd like to dance," her father says in an encouraging tone.

"Ah, yes... Right after I see Mother in." I use my mother's arm to push us through the entrance.

It's a shitty thing to do. Lara's a pretty girl, we've had some fun times, but nothing puts me off wanting a woman like having her shoved down my throat.

"Oh!" Mother squawks like a hen, but I guide her around the corner into a narrow hall.

"What is this? Some kind of reverse Cinderella scheme?"

She straightens her dress as if I've offended her. "Actually, it's a very straightforward Cinderella scheme."

"Jesus!" I couldn't be more humiliated. My fists tighten at my sides as I pace the small space. I wonder how far back it would set me in my PR efforts if I walk out on this charity gala. "So what did you do? Put a link on the royal website? Send out a royal text alert?"

"Of course not," she sniffs. "I wouldn't even know how to do such a thing. I simply called a few of my friends, your great aunts…"

Striding back to where she stands, I pause to control the volume of my voice. "I would appreciate being allowed to control my personal life."

"I'd be happy to allow that, darling, if you hadn't already lost control of your personal life."

"I have not lost control of anything."

"Hello? What's happening back here?" Cal enters the narrow space all smiles and decked out in his navy Carabiniers jacket.

"MacCallum, would you please escort me to the ballroom. Your brother needs to collect himself, and I have guests to welcome."

"I'd be honored, Madame." He gives me a wink and extends an elbow to our mother, who takes his arm and slowly follows him out to the evening's festivities.

I almost laugh at the irony. The Carabiniers are a small division of soldiers charged with defending my person against attack. How appropriate he should lead my chief attacker away.

For a moment, I consider my fate. I've lost my father, I've lost one of my most trusted senior advisors in Reggie, I've lost my racing, and now it appears these old women are attempting to force me to marry.

My mind travels to when the king was still alive. What would he tell me to do in a situation like this?

How can I best serve my country? It only takes a moment for me to know the answer. *Be the king.*

Straightening my shoulders, I tamp down my anger and find the control switch. Stepping out into the dark hallway I walk to the ballroom. The entire place is filled with ladies and gentleman in formal attire.

Blue and red lights alternate in the tall windows around the room, illuminating crystal chandeliers. A DJ is in the far left corner, and white-clothed tables of hors d'oeuvres line the walls. I'm surrounded by the glittering eyes of scores of young ladies breathless at the thought of being the future Queen of Monagasco.

My eyes roam the various couples when a young lady in an olive-green silk dress approaches. "Hello, there," she says with a smile.

I smile in return. "How do you do."

"My name's Felicity," she says bluntly. "I'm the Baron of Rothingham's daughter."

"How do you do, Miss Rothingham?"

"You can call me Felicity, and I'm all right, I guess. Mum says we're supposed to be here putting on a show for you or something. It seems rather stupid to me."

"Seems rather stupid to me as well," I agree in a low voice.

Felicity doesn't miss a beat. "When I was sixteen, my parents didn't think I was showing enough interest in boys, so they threw me a grand ball." She leans back and gives me a squint. "When I walked in, I expect my face looked exactly like yours does now."

Her manner causes my insides to relax slightly. "How is that?"

"Irritated…" she pauses to think. "And quite a bit embarrassed."

"I'm not embarrassed. I'm the crown prince." I sound more defensive than I feel, and we're quiet a moment.

"I'm also Lara Westingroot's cousin," she continues, "and possibly one of three people who know whose mouth your royal wank was in in all those Internet pics."

Explaining myself to a near stranger is not something I intend to do. We're standing at the edge of the dance floor, and all eyes are fixed upon us.

"Shall we dance?" I say, motioning to the floor.

"I suppose we have to now."

The music starts, and we turn to face each other. My hand is on her waist and hers is on my shoulder. Our other hands clasp at the side, and I study Felicity's light brown hair styled down to the side in a ponytail. Her makeup is simple powder on her nose as far as I can tell and her lips are glossy nude. Still, her appearance is pleasant. Her eyes are the same olive drab as her dress, but I feel oddly at ease with her.

"What's your game, Felicity?"

"I suppose I'm trying to figure out yours. You didn't tell who the girl in the photo was, which makes me want to like you."

"You're one of the few," I say, looking around at the scowling old bitties watching us.

"At the same time, you haven't spoken to her since, which makes me think you're a dick."

My jaw tightens, and I don't smile. Lara and I had been having a pleasant time that night. However I felt for her at fifteen, my feelings didn't stand the test of time, and I found our connection dwindled no matter how much we drank. Dropping to her knees felt more like a last-ditch effort to forge some kind of bond.

"Why'd you do it?" Felicity's eyes move around my face. "I've watched you since you nearly won the Grand Prix seven years ago. You're very handsome, and you're the most controlled royal I know. I admired you."

The dance ends, and her hand is in the crook of my arm. We walk a few paces from the floor as I think about her question. No one's asked it that way, and I consider it would be more accurate to ask why I *let* it happen. I didn't do much of anything besides lean back and enjoy the release.

"I was tired," I confess. "It's been a long six years, and I wanted..." I can't say I *wanted to feel free*. That sounds pathetic. "I needed a break. It felt good to let go."

"It felt good to get your nut off more like," she quips. I can't argue, and she exhales a laugh. "It's all right. I understand. I don't think *they* understand, but I do. I forgive you."

"Thanks, I guess. I'm paying for it now if that gives you any satisfaction."

"It doesn't, but thanks for the dance. Don't feel pressure to pick me. I don't care for men." She does a little sigh. "I'm only here out of curiosity. I find you very interesting."

That almost makes me laugh, and I give her a wink. "Are you telling me you're a lesbian, Felicity?"

"Must we label each other, Playboy Prince?"

"Hmm," I pull back with a frown. "I see what you mean. Let's not."

"Lara *is* very interested in you, or at least the chance at being queen." She glances around the room. "From the looks of death I'm getting right now, I'd say she's not alone. I wouldn't be in your shoes for anything."

"I owe you a debt of gratitude."

Her slim brows pull together. "How so?"

"You distracted me from what was shaping up to be a horrid night."

"Oh, it's only just started." She does a little bow. "Good luck, your majesty."

I bid my strange new friend *adieu*, and Mother appears to make sure I dance with Graceland next. After her follow a string of noble females, who all look alike to me. I manage to avoid being paired with Lara, who I happen to remember is as fine a dancer as she is a horsewoman.

Still, after talking to Felicity I'm convinced dealing with her would be more than I can tolerate this particular evening. My patience has reached its limit. As a matter of fact, I'm counting down the minutes until I can leave. None of these fine ladies interests me, and they shouldn't be the targets of my irritation. They only answered the call.

I manage to escape to the broad patio leading off the back of the ballroom, and by some miracle, I'm alone. I spot Felicity on my way out sitting on the sidelines chatting with a woman who looks older than my grandmother. She does a little wave, and I nod as I discreetly back out through the French doors.

Outside, in the fresh air, I take a deep breath and exhale a groan. I walk slowly across the flagstone pavement wanting to rip the bow tie off my neck and throw it over the balcony.

The moon is high and bright and far off in the distance. The noise of the ocean whispers like a taunt, and I wonder how difficult it would be for me to climb over the rail and escape, dash down the hill to the shore below. What I wouldn't give to be my former self before my father died, free and easy for just one day.

Several moments pass, I stand looking out at the waves now black and tipped in silver by the moonlight. In spite of the annoyance of the evening, the night feels almost magical, like the universe shifts.

A soft voice catches my ear, and I realize I was wrong—I'm not alone. Through my exhaustion, I recognize the words softly spoken from the other side of the small rose bush planted in the center of the patio. A female voice recites a poem I learned in school.

And yet with all this help of head and brain,
How happily instinctive we remain.
Our best guide upward farther to the light:
Passionate preference, such as love at first sight.

I step around the roses, and I'm frozen on the spot. A young woman sits, leaning back on her hand, and she seems to glow in the moonlight. Her dark hair is down her back in long waves that curl gently at the ends. I want to thread my fingers through it and see if it's as silky as it appears. Her lips are full and pink, and her skin is the color of caramel.

Her strapless gown leaves her slim shoulders bare, and her chin is tilted up, eyes closed. All my tension falls away, and I burn with desire to take her in my arms and kiss her.

I want to run my mouth all over her body and taste her. I want her in my enormous bed in my chamber where I can inhale her scent and have her all around me all night. It's an insanely primitive response unlike anything I've ever felt, yet I have to know who she is. I have to know her better.

"*Bonsoir,*" I say as gently as possible, despite my growing hunger.

Her eyes flash open, and I'm hit with a blaze of deep emerald green. It's like a sucker-punch to the chest.

"I'm sorry!" She leans forward and moves her long dress aside before standing. She's American.... And she's trying to leave! My insides revolt. I can't let that happen.

"Wait!" Dashing forward, I catch her hand. It's slim and cool in my noticeably larger one. "I was just..." I motion back toward the ballroom. "Taking a break, and I heard you. Were you reciting poetry?"

"I love your accent." Her chin drops, and I'm pretty sure she's blushing. I almost can't control the urges burning under my skin.

"It's so beautiful here..." She slowly pulls her hand out of mine and points over the hill. "The ocean is just there, and the roses smell so nice."

In that moment, I remember. "Were you reciting 'In the Clearing'?"

"You like Robert Frost?" Her eyes sparkle, and I only want to see that light in them forever.

I look around, thinking. "He's American, but his poems were easy for me to remember. They rhyme, and they feel logical. Intuitive."

"Yes," She smiles and nods, as if I've read her mind. "That's how I feel!"

Again, I reach for her hand. Looking down, I notice our skin seems to match, although I can tell she's been in the sun. Her hands are soft and elegant, and I want them on my body. I want her on my body. I want our bodies entwined, our sweat mingling in the throes of passion…

When she pulls away, it physically hurts. "I'd better get back. I only stepped out for some air. They'll wonder where I am."

I capture her hand again. "Who are they? Who are you here with?"

Her chin drops, and she looks worried. "Oh, well, umm…" I watch as her eyes trace the flagstones searching for an answer.

I'm hypnotized by those eyes, by her full lips. Reaching out, I touch her cheek. Moving closer, I'm ready to taste her. Her chin lifts, and her pink tongue slips out to touch her bottom lip. It's like a match to gasoline, and I know the moment we meet, we won't be going back.

"There you are!" A clear voice cuts across the patio, breaking the spell. "I've been looking everywhere for you!"

I look over my shoulder to see a pretty blonde, who only appears to be a little older than the angel I've found. Her hair is tied back, and she's wearing a dark silk gown. When she sees me, she stops moving, and her eyes widen.

"Are you…?" Her voice trails off as she stares at me.

My attention is pulled away when the one I want struggles out of my arms and rushes to her side.

She takes the blonde woman's hand and whispers. "I'm so sorry, Zee. I didn't mean to…"

I've had enough of all this. I'm the king, dammit. "Who are you?" I demand. "Who did you come here with?"

"Good evening, your majesty." The one called Zee does a little curtsey, but before I can respond, I see a face that changes my burning need to raw fury.

The beautiful woman is momentarily forgotten along with her friend. I cross the space as the heat rises to my eyes.

"How dare you step foot in this place," I say through clenched teeth. "How dare you step foot in this country!"

Reginald Winchester stands in front of me, his cold blue eyes narrow as he evaluates my response. "Your majesty," he says in a voice dripping with insolence.

My late father's suggestion of the guillotine floats through my mind. "You've got ten seconds to leave here before I order the guard to throw you out."

Reginald only sneers down his nose. We're the same six-foot-two height, and I am not intimidated by his scowl. "You might want to hold the threats until you hear what I have to say."

I can barely control my anger. One of my first acts was to banish him from Monagasco along with his scheming cousin Hubert and the rest of their traitorous ring. He conspired against my father, and I hold him indirectly responsible for my father's death. If it weren't for this disloyal asshole, I'd still have a life. I wouldn't be forced into the life of a retired monarch at twenty-seven.

I'd still have my father.

My jaw is clenched so hard, I can barely speak. "There's not a word you can say that will change my mind—"

"Your mother invited me here."

My mother?! I can't decide if I want to shout or throw something. *My own mother went behind my back?* It doesn't make any sense. Only last week she was saying how proud she was of me for cleaning house.

"You're lying."

"Ask her yourself." He walks fluidly to where the two young women stand.

The blonde has positioned herself in front of my angel, and while she's strong, I can tell they're both afraid of what's happening here. I can't help wondering who they are and how they're related to this traitor. I have to believe an explanation exists I can accept.

My uncle fills in the blanks. "Your majesty, Rowan Westringham Tate, I'd like to introduce you to Miss Zelda Benedict and Miss Ava Wilder." He leans closer to me, and I flinch away. "Miss Benedict is the heir to Lux Benedict of San Angelo." He pauses as if waiting for me to understand. "Texas."

"How do you do," I give them a little bow, but my anger is barely controlled below the surface. "I don't see how this changes my direct order."

"If you please." He gestures for me to walk ahead with him. I only comply out of simple curiosity.

"Miss Benedict recently inherited a quarter of a billion in oil from her late uncle. Your mother thought it would be a nice idea if the two of you spent some time together." He glances back over his shoulder and smiles. "In case anything happens."

As angry as I am with Reginald, when I glance back and see Ava, the fist of anger in my chest loosens slightly. I know Reggie's schemes. I kicked him out for conspiring with Hubert against my father, but unlike Hubert, I know my uncle still desires independence for Monagasco. It's in his blood. Also, lurking in the back of my mind is the notion that time spent in Miss Benedict's presence equals time spent with Miss Wilder.

"Where are they staying?"

"They currently have rooms at the Fairmont."

Nodding, I look down and clear my throat. My mind wanders from the sea of females in the ballroom to the one I found lingering in the moonlight, drinking in the sound of the waves, just like me.

"I'm willing to overlook your audacity this time." When my sharp gaze meets Reginald's gloating expression, I have to fight the urge to pop him in the mouth. "Only because I know you're loyal to Monagasco."

"I live to serve my country." He does a little bow.

I push past him, returning back to where the blonde Miss Benedict stands with her friend Miss Wilder. Our close proximity stirs the desire only momentarily cooled in my chest, and I have to force my eyes away from the lovely brunette.

"Miss Benedict, forgive my rudeness. I'm delighted to welcome you."

Ava steps away, taking my insides with her, but her friend smiles and nods her head as she bows. "It's an honor, your royal highness."

My eyes have followed Ava when I realize what Zelda just said. "Call me Rowan, please."

She straightens, and her blue eyes meet mine. "Then you must call me Zee."

Her voice commands my attention. She's smart. I like that. Although her friend has stolen my fascination, getting to know Zee Wilder might be interesting. I'll see what Reggie has in mind for this partnership and if there's any way I can help the country while pursuing what I really want.

CHAPTER 5: TWO PRINCES

Zelda

Sometimes I wonder if Ava and I are truly related. Stepping out of the sleek black Mercedes into the blinding strobe of camera flashes at the entrance to the Royal Sports Club, I feel like a fish who just leaped out of her bowl.

I can barely breathe. I can't see a thing, thanks to the paparazzi. The bustier bodice on my black tulle and satin formal gown is pinching me in half. I know I'll walk like I'm in a body brace through the crowd of nobility—that is, if I can stay upright on my too-tall stilettoes.

My sister, by contrast, sweeps out of the Town Car in her flowing dusty-rose gown as if she were born in this scene. I swear, she seems to move in sparkling slow motion, and as she turns to smile at me over her shoulder, her dark hair swirls around her arms in a shiny curtain. A ripple of whispers passes through the crowd as everyone tries to figure out who we are.

Reggie is right behind us, nearly bumping into me as I lean down to adjust my heel.

"Watch it!" I have to grab his arm to keep from falling.

His smile is plastered, and he looks straight ahead. "Hold steady. Every single one of those flashes is a photograph. You don't want to look like a shrew on tomorrow's gossip sites—or constipated."

Freezing a smile on my face, I lower my leg, push back my shoulders and make my way as quickly as possible to the entrance. The sooner we're off this freakin red carpet, the better.

"What happened to Miami?" Reginald huffs once we're safely in the building and out of the strobe lights. "You waltzed through that casino like a supermodel on a catwalk."

"I was wearing a romper and platforms. You've got me in a corset and stripper heels." I gasp, straightening a pinch of skin near my ribcage. "I'm starving, and this damned dress is too tight."

"You're wearing Gauthier and Louboutin. The finest designers in France."

"I look like a demented ballerina... or a dominatrix who got off at the wrong stop."

"Look at me." His tone is stern, and he stops short.

I look up at his face, and over his shoulder, I notice Ava is ahead of us peeking into the ballroom where a rainbow of lights flashes and music plays loudly.

"Eyes," he orders, and mine snap to his. "You actually look quite lovely tonight. You're every bit Miss Zelda Benedict, the richest woman in Texas." His expression softens, and the unexpected warmth makes my insides squirm. I start to move away but large hands grasp the tops of my bare shoulders. "You've got this."

My lips twist, and for a moment I feel obstinate. "I want to be at the beach."

He laughs gently. "Tomorrow you can spend the day at the beach. You only have to be noticed tonight. In a *positive* way."

Nodding, I slide my hand into the crook of his arm, and we start for the ballroom. Holding his arm helps me balance as I walk, and once we reach the large space filled with men and women in formal attire, I start to relax. The venue is very crowded, and it's more like a nightclub than something out of the eighteenth century, which is what I expected when he said *royal ball.*

Purple and red lights shine from the ceiling to the floor in large spots, and a DJ is in the back corner spinning smooth techno. Looking around, I can't spot Ava, which makes me nervous. I'm not sure how proficient she is with our story.

We opted with her being my friend instead of my sister. It was my idea, as I figured it would be easier for her to make a quick escape if we were caught.

Reggie and I take a slow pace around the perimeter, and my mind drifts over the last week and getting ready for this show. The moment I took the black card from his hand on that cruiser in Miami, everything shifted into fast gear...

One Week Earlier

The black card is barely in my grasp when Reggie turns to the captain of the speedboat. "Take us into port. We have work to do."

"Hang on!" I hold the top of the white-leather seat still looking at the black American Express in my hands. "I want to verify this before we go anywhere."

"Of course," Reggie sniffs. "Check it while we go."

A sleek, rose-gold iPad is shoved into my hands, and I do my best to type in the card number and register a new account while bouncing over waves in the speeding boat. Sure enough, ten thousand dollars is in the account, now owned by me.

"It appears we're all in," I mutter through the tightness in my throat. I can't shake my nerves about this job.

Ava seems to know instinctively what's happening inside my chest. She scoots closer to me on the seat and rests her chin on my shoulder.

"It's just another zero, Zee," she whispers, holding my arms. "We can do this."

The captain pulls us up to the pier and hops out onto the wooden platform to tie up the boat. Reggie gathers his belongings and steps out, extending a hand back to me.

"We're not going to Bal Harbor in bathing suits?" I look down at my flimsy cotton cover-up. The material is practically transparent, and the plunging V-neck does little to cover up my bikini.

At least Ava's strapless dress has a ruched top and hangs to her mid-thigh. It could pass for dinner attire in South Beach. I am clearly straight off a boat.

"When we start throwing around the money we're about to spend, they won't care if you walk in naked." Reggie leans forward and grasps my arm, half-helping, half-pulling me onto the pier.

Ava exits the boat without assistance, and I don't miss the definite bounce in her step. While I'm churning with second thoughts, she's invigorated. Maybe she's right about me and the additional zeros. Maybe I can't handle the long cons or big payouts.

"Are we going to Bal Harbor Shops?" Her voice is breathless as she practically skips beside us. "I've always dreamed of strolling the promenade, stopping at the fountains, eating at a little café..."

"You have?" I stare at her in wonder. "I didn't even know you knew about the place."

"I don't live under a rock!"

Reggie observes all of this in quiet amusement. We've followed him to a shiny black Mercedes. A driver steps out and holds the door open, but our host steps back to let us get in first.

"I'd give anything for at least a sundress," I grumble pulling the hem of my tunic top to the middle of my thighs.

"Don't be a grump," my sister says. "You have lovely legs."

It takes less than ten minutes for us to be at the two-story outdoor mall. We're let out under an awning near the Ralph Lauren store, and we pass through the breezeway, entering a wide passageway between the lines of stores. The pavement is speckled beige granite, and in the center is a long, rectangular fountain with neon orange, yellow, and white Koi fish swimming among reeds and palms.

"This is really beautiful," I whisper, inhaling the fresh scent of plants and outdoor air conditioning.

"Isn't it?" Ava looks up and around the plants and flowers spilling over around us. "Those fish are as long as footballs!"

It's like shopping in a tropical paradise. Bright coral blooms spring out of the center of fleshy hosta plants and tall, slender palm trees tower over shorter fringy plants in dense clusters. In the center of the walkway every so often, the fountain area joins, and a little coffee shop or café is stationed with chairs and tables under huge canvas umbrellas.

The only thing more vibrant than the foliage, fountains, and fish are the women going from shop to shop. Some have multiple bags with the names of stores printed on them. One woman wears a 1950s-style tea-length floral dress with a bright green cardigan over it. Another is in a striped shorts-romper with a huge straw hat. Occasionally a man in a suit walks past.

"Here," Reggie says, catching Ava's arm. "We'll start here."

I look up to see he's leading us into Balenciaga, and my knee-jerk response is to protest, saying we can't afford it. Yeah, it's going to take me a little time to get used to our new situation.

A woman crosses the floor to us, and Reggie holds out a hand. "Size two for Mademoiselle Ava, and…" He sweeps his eyes over my slightly shorter, more athletic build. "Four for Mademoiselle Zelda."

"Of course, this way to your rooms." The young woman motions for us to follow her.

Ava takes off as if nothing strange just happened. I chase to catch up with her, catching her arm and whispering in her ear. "Aren't we supposed to pick out some things we like first?"

My sister shrugs. "I'm just playing along."

Moments later we're in separate dressing rooms, each the size of the hotel room we've been living in. They're all white with black doors and long white upholstered benches in the center. A soft tap, and the sales clerk enters with a short rack holding several different outfits all on hangers.

"These are the editor's picks from the Spring-Summer collection," she says. "Please take your time. Can I bring you something to drink?"

My head is spinning, and I could probably use a bottle of water, but I decline. I'm walking slowly toward the rack of monochromatic beige outfits. Most are dresses, but a few are short sets with filmy coats on top.

I'm just slipping on the first completely sheer lace dress when my door slings open. "Check this out!" Ava cries.

Her long, tanned body is clad in wide-legged beige-satin pajama pants with navy pinstripes running down them. Her top is a wide bandeau, and over that is an oversized, triangular-shaped beige coat. She's holding a white leather clutch that's round like a cylinder with fringe hanging off it on every side.

"That's... interesting?" She paces around the room swaying her hips like a model. "Would you wear that out on the street? With your stomach showing and all?"

"I don't know!" she laughs, "but I love it!"

My sheer dress is on the floor, and I'm pulling on wide-legged shorts in the same material as her pants. The top for me is a V-neck halter contraption with a wide band around my ribs. A long, sheer-chiffon coat is on the hanger with it, which leads me to believe I'm supposed to put it on top.

"Halter and shorts with a chiffon... coat?"

"Oh!" Ava spins around and catches my hands. "You look amazing!"

I pick up a large fanny pack made of pleated and gathered silk. It has a wide zipper across the top and long wide satin strips. "Am I supposed to tie this around my waist?

"Who knew fanny packs were making a comeback?"

"This is a lot bigger than the fanny pack our mom used to wear."

We finally decide on two outfits each from the lot and head out to meet Reggie, who's sitting in an elegant leather armchair sipping champagne.

When he sees us with our selections, his nose curls. "That's hardly enough!"

He stands and stops the clerk, who is heading back out with the two racks from our dressing rooms. He pulls two more items off the racks. One is the full-length halter dress with a midriff Ava had put back. I thought it looked stunning on her. The other is the silly shorts ensemble I rejected. I don't even try to argue.

We head to the checkout, and I almost have a heart attack when I hear the total. Ava cuts her eyes at me, and I hand over the black card sadly.

"At this rate, we'll be broke by noon," I say, but Reggie catches my wrist.

"No, no." He pulls my hand back and hands the clerk his card. "I'll get this."

Relief washes over me, I won't lie. Even though we're pretty much committed at this point, I like the idea that I still have Ten-K should we decide to bolt.

From that store, we head to Alexander McQueen, where we pick up several unusual evening gowns in mostly black with turquoise butterflies all over them. Ava chooses a neon-pink chiffon mini-dress with a black leather bustier-style vest, and while I can't imagine where she'll wear it, I also have no idea what our future holds.

Finally, Reggie decides we've bought enough, and we make our way through the jungle walkway back to the entrance where I expect the black Mercedes to be waiting.

Ava hums softly as we walk, and I notice she's holding a round piece of dark chocolate near her mouth. It looks very fine and decadent, and she takes her time consuming it.

"Where did you get that?" I whisper, my stomach pinching.

"What?" She snaps out of her spell and realizes I'm watching her eat. "Oh! Here—" The large fanny pack I rejected is now tied around her waist with a satin bow. She unzips it and holds it open so I can see a pile of identical chocolates to the one she's holding inside.

"Where did you get all these?"

She shrugs. "They were on a tray inside the last store."

"Ava!" I start to laugh. Reaching in, I take one of the smooth chocolates from her bag and eat it.

I have to stop walking when the rich flavor fills my mouth. "Oh my god. That is so good."

"I know, right? Have another one."

I'm holding the second stolen treat to my lips as we walk. Reggie's up ahead of us, and my eyes travel to the second floor and around the treetops. Birds sing, and the air smells like rain. My anxiety about our future has diminished with our new wardrobe packed up and headed to our hotel. I suppose that's what they call "retail therapy."

"I've cancelled your room at the New Yorker," Reggie says once we exit the courtyard full of designer boutiques. "Your few belongings have been sent to the St. Regis where I'm staying."

I freeze in the crosswalk, but Ava pulls my arm. "Come on," she says. "You're going to get run over."

"Wait—you cancelled our room? You moved our stuff? How—"

"Your questions all have the same answer, my dear." Reggie grumbles as he holds open the heavy glass door of the high-rise luxury hotel just across the street from the lavish mall. "Instead of *how*, you should be asking *why*, which I'll save you the trouble. We need to be close so we can spend our remaining time going over everything you need to know about your new identity."

"I didn't think I'd need to learn much if it's going to be an *accidental* meeting," I follow him into the shimmering elevator. Ava leans her forehead against the glass wall and looks down as we shoot up to the fourteenth floor.

"You won't have to learn much about him, but you do need to decide where you went to college, your major of study, your favorite designer, place to eat, resort destination—"

"So I have to tell lies." That gross feeling trickles through my stomach, carrying all my hesitations about this job right back with it.

He lets out an exaggerated sigh. "Perhaps it won't come up, but in case it does, yes. You might have to tell a few... *half-truths*. An heiress of your caliber has more experience than an afternoon shopping at Bal Harbor."

My lips press together, and as much as I hate it, he's right. "I see what you mean."

"But you'll have done quite a bit of traveling when we arrive. Perhaps some of your answers will be true by the time you give them." He uses a slim white card to unlock our door then hands it to me. "We'll meet for breakfast tomorrow and get started. I'm right across the hall if you need anything. Your new wardrobe should be delivered within the hour. I want us on the plane for Monagasco in two days, so get some rest."

It's all moving so fast. My shoulders are tight as we enter the expansive suite. Ava squeals as she runs across to the wide balcony. We have a clear view of the ocean from fourteen floors up, and I peek into the marble-lined bathroom. My jaw drops. It's as big as the room, and has a shower *and* a tub!

"We have to celebrate!" Ava's back, opening the well-stocked mini-fridge and pulling out a pink bottle of Veuve Clicquot Rose. "It's like we're living in a dream!"

All the clothes and pampering and tropical gardens distracted my insides, but now I'm back to straight-up worrying. "I don't know, Aves. What if this is a mistake?"

The cork pops, and she wrinkles her nose at me. "Don't start that again. We're helping Reggie take back his country!"

"From some crown prince we know nothing about!" I watch as she pours two tall glasses with pink sparkling wine. "What if he's really the good guy?"

A clink and she takes a sip. "Mmm," she smiles, eyes closed. "I'm willing to take that chance."

I try mine. *Not bad.* Only very slightly sweet, but mostly crisp and refreshing.

Her eyes pop open again, and she holds my arm. "Listen to me, Zee. We only said we'd go with him. We haven't made any promises. If we get over there, and it turns out he's really the bad guy, we'll leave!" Pressing my lips together, I watch as she lays back on the bed. "In the meantime, we get to go to Europe! And all those clothes…"

"I'm going to talk to Reggie again." Ava calls after me, but I'm out the door and across the hall banging on Reggie's door before she can stop me.

A few moments pass, and he opens the door. His navy blazer is gone, and now he's only in khaki pants and the white shirt with the sleeves rolled up. If not for his posture and the way he carried himself, I would've mistaken him for a regular person he's so casual.

"I didn't expect to see you until tomorrow," he says, stepping back and allowing me to enter. "Aren't you tired from all that shopping?"

I'm exhausted, but I'm not letting him deter me from my reason for being here. "We need to talk."

"Yes, we do. I intend for us to do quite a lot of talking. Tomorrow." He crosses his room and lifts his own slim glass of pink champagne. "Tonight, order room service, take a hot bath, relax."

My brow lines, and my fists go to my hips. It's a defensive stance, but I have to know. "Are you being honest with us, Reggie?"

He sits in the beige chair that matches the one in our room across the hall. "About what?"

The question exasperates me. "All of it. The crown prince, the money — "

"Look." The cool tone in his voice cuts the heat in the room like ice. "I know you're used to small-time cons, selfish games, working only for yourself and for the score. Get that out of your head. You've gone beyond counting cards and manipulating roulette wheels. This is politics. Government. Lives are at stake. You're helping to save a country."

A faint echo follows his last words, then for a moment the only noise is the hum of the window unit. I take a few moments to consider what he said.

I think about what little I know of politics and the deals made to run governments. We don't want to see how it works just as much as we don't want to see the sausage being made—at least that's what I've heard. Now I'm a part of it.

"But how do I know which is the right side?" I'm not angry. It's an honest question.

His steel-blue eyes meet mine, all seriousness. "How does anyone ever know that? History will tell us. In the meantime, we simply fight for the right."

"You make me sound like a hero."

"You never know."

Fast-forward to the Ball

An elegant older woman snaps at my escort. "How dare you show your face here tonight?" I have no idea who she is, but she's someone powerful enough to chastise Reggie.

"Forgive me, your grace." Reggie bows, and for the first time, I see him genuinely meek.

"Rowan will be furious! You'll ruin all my plans." Her eyes flash, and I take a subtle half step behind him, hoping in my black dress I blend into the rave atmosphere.

"Not if I come bearing gifts," he says, motioning to me. "Would introducing him to the heiress to the Benedict oil fortune appease my nephew's wrath?"

I actually feel the moment her ice blue eyes spot me. "Come here, girl," she barks the order, and I dutifully step forward on my needle-thin heels.

"Zelda, may I present the Queen of Monagasco," Reggie says.

The words make my pulse jump. Holding the side of my dress, I do a careful curtsey, bowing my head. "Your majesty."

"You're Zelda Benedict? Daughter of the Texas oil tycoon?"

"Niece, actually, ma'am." My head is still bowed, both because I don't want to risk her reading my expression and because I'm not sure when it's okay to rise.

"That's enough, you may rise."

Straightening, I see she's stepped closer to me. Our eyes are about the same height, which means she's taller than me. She also bears a striking resemblance to Reggie...

"You're here to meet my son, is that so?"

"I'm sorry, your majesty, I'm here as a guest of Sir Winston. My... *friend* and I met him in Texas, and he has been gracious enough to escort us to your beautiful country on a holiday visit—"

"Yes, yes," she waves a hand between us as if she's heard enough. "That will do. You might as well get in line with the rest of them. The crown prince has danced with almost every girl here tonight, and I haven't seen a spark of interest in any of them." She shakes her head and turns. "Unless you count that first dance with Fredrick's niece. Of course, he chooses a *lesbian* to have chemistry with."

Her statement catches me off-guard, and I almost laugh. "Thank you, ma'am," I say and do another careful curtsey-bow.

"Come with me, Reggie. I'll allow you to tell me your plan, and perhaps I can soften my son's anger." The woman takes his arm and pulls him away. He looks back and gives me an arched eyebrow and a slight nod.

I flick an eyebrow in response. I know what to do. I have two purposes tonight: to be seen and to make a *positive* impression. I do my best not to be annoyed every time Reggie emphasizes the word *positive*, as if I might do otherwise.

With him gone and everyone focused elsewhere, I take a moment to exhale slowly. *We're here, we're doing this.* The song changes to a dance tune I know from home, and I close my eyes as the beats wash over me like soothing water. If things were different, I'd go out on the floor and give in to the rhythm. As it is...

"Oh!" I yip, nearly jumping out of my skin when a strong hand closes over mine.

"Sorry." A low, accented voice vibrates near my ear, causing the little hairs to rise on my skin. "I didn't mean to startle you, *Mademoiselle.*"

"No, it's okay," I say quickly.

He scared the shit out of me, but that luscious accent is *to die* for. My poker face is firmly intact—until our eyes meet, and I almost forget everything. His are warm hazel with the most irresistible, devilish twinkle in them. He has wavy, light-brown hair that my fingers itch to caress, and he's wearing a navy military jacket, which surprisingly turns me on. I've never been into military men before... most likely because of my checkered past. I run away from men in uniform.

Actually, in the past I've done my best to avoid *all* male entanglements entirely. If I'm going to take care of us, I can't afford such distractions. Whoever this sexy soldier is, I can tell one thing right away. He's a player, from the dimple at the corner of his mouth to the scruff dusting his square jaw. He smiles, and my stomach flips.

"I don't think we've met." That naughty grin grows a little wider. "You're American?"

I take a step back. *Focus on the job, Zelda Wilder. Focus on that ten thousand dollars.*

"No," I say, clearing my throat. "I mean yes! I'm visiting. I'm here with my... *friend*!"

Jesus! That's twice I've almost said *my sister!* And I was worried about Ava being confident in her role.

"Visiting?" He slides a warm hand around my waist and pulls me flush against his torso. A brief kiss to my cheek steals my breath. "Is that so? Tell me more."

A sultry dance song begins, and we sway together. I have to hand it to this guy. He's good. Still, I'm no rookie, and I force my control back in place. I haven't worked the angles as long as I have to be thrown off by the first charmer I meet.

"My friend and I are from Texas. I've always wanted to see Monagasco, so she came over with me."

"It is your first time in our country?" His smile grows and that dimple deepens. "I'll show you everything. Where are you staying? We can meet in the morning—"

"No! I mean... I'm sorry. I can't do that."

"What? Why the hell not?"

"Because I'm... well..."

"You're...?" His eyes narrow playfully, and I'm racking my brain for an acceptable excuse. I can't say I'm here to *accidentally* meet someone in particular.

"Oh! I already have a guide!" *Real smooth, Zee.*

"Is that so?" He's not buying it. "Who?"

Luckily we're interrupted by the sudden appearance of Reggie. "Cal, what a pleasant surprise." The tone of his voice implies just the opposite, and he grips the shoulder of my dance partner firmly, forcing us apart.

"Holy... What the *fuck* are you doing here?" Sir Sexy Cal snaps. "You know what will happen when he sees you. It will ruin HRH's ball."

Reggie ignores his words. "I see you've met my friend Zelda Benedict." Yanking me to his side, Reggie motions between us. "Zelda, this is MacCallum Lockwood Tate, younger brother of the crown prince, heir presumptive, captain of the Carabiniers, and Duke of Dumaldi."

Something about all those titles makes my head spin. How is it possible I find this guy even more attractive once I know I'm supposed to be seducing his brother?

Taking a half step back, I start my bow, but Cal's warm hand covers mine. "My friends call me Cal, and absolutely none of them bow to me... Unless they get off on that sort of thing. Do you?"

My cheeks heat, and dammit if I don't want to kiss those royal lips. "It's an honor to meet you, Sir. I had no idea I'd be surrounded by so much nobility my first night in town."

Cal moves around to my other side, avoiding Reggie's cock blocking, and pulls my hand into the crook of his arm. "Now about that tour guide. You can't tell me Sir Reginald is showing you around. *Mon Dieu*, he'll probably take you to the aquarium."

I want to laugh. His manner is irresistible, but I feel Reggie's gaze burning a hole in my back. "I'm sorry, your majesty —"

"Cal — *please*."

"Cal." I pull my hand back. "I'm sorry, but I already promised the duke."

"I'm a duke! Didn't you hear all that shit he said after my name? I'd make a far better tour guide."

I can't suppress a smile, and Cal's eyes light. "Yes, that's *much* better. Why don't we start our tour with the royal bedrooms?"

"That will be quite enough for tonight." Reggie reaches between us and jerks me away. I have to grab his arm to stay upright on my heels — with a *new* added hazard: Cal's breathtaking smile. "We need to find your friend and bid our *adieus*."

Reggie drags me away, but I can't resist a look back at the tall, slender fellow in the tuxedo. His arms are crossed, and he actually winks as he places one hand on his lips. *Is he sending me a kiss?*

I'm out the door and on the balcony, but my head's in a dreamy haze of MacCallam Lockwood Tate, brother of the crown prince, some kind of soldier, and duke of somethingorother.

Reggie steps away from me in a rush and begins talking fast French to a tall man with longish dark hair. I squint to try and see who it is. He's also wearing a black tuxedo jacket with medals and a sash across the front.

It takes me a moment to realize Ava is at my arm apologizing, and then, holy shit, it's him! Reggie's back, and I'm facing Crown Prince Rowan Something Something. I recognize him from the photographs Reggie showed me, and he's even hotter and more intimidating in person.

"Your royal highness Rowan Westringham Tate, I'd like to introduce you to Miss Zelda Benedict of Texas and Miss Ava Wilder."

"How do you do," the crown prince bows stiffly, but before anything more is said, he and

Reggie stalk away from us, again embroiled in a heated conversation I can't understand.

Ava drifts toward the ballroom, but I wait and watch the two men. With a chiseled jaw and simmering blue eyes, he's as handsome in person as he is in his pictures. From the way he holds himself, I'm sure he knows it, too.

He's very formal and controlled, and the way he moves and speaks to Reggie reminds me of one of those billionaires Ava's always stealing from. He's forceful and clearly used to getting his way in everything. I can't help wondering if he ever laughs.

They turn, and I snap out of my fantasies. Rowan apologizes for his rudeness (I don't remember him being rude to me). We agree to meet tomorrow, and with that, he stalks away from us.

"Okay," I whisper, watching the muscles in Reggie's jaw move as he looks back toward the ballroom.

The game is on.

Chapter 6: Duty

Rowan

The Technicolor-blue water of the Mediterranean is nearly blinding this morning. The salt in the air touches my tongue and fills my nose with scents of fish and days at sea. I imagine taking a boat and sailing far from this irritating place — a beautiful brunette stretched across the bow.

It's true, my mind is miles away, focused on emerald-green eyes, sweet olive skin, and pink lips that part to reveal a lovely white smile. I've been thinking about her all night, longing for her, if I'm honest. I escaped from the ball shortly after she left and returned to our estate at Occitan.

Relaxing under the warm spray of my shower, I slid my hand over my rigid cock, relieving my aching desire as I fantasized about the little dip where her collarbones meet at the base of her neck. I pictured tracing my tongue across the bead of her nipple, down to the curve of her waist.

My hand moved faster as I remembered her soft voice, imagined her cries as she came. The prospect of her long legs wrapped around me, being sunk deep into her clenching hot core, had me coming hard under the warm jets. Still, my hand is no comparison to what I imagine the real thing must be like.

I've stood here several minutes, indulging in the fantasy when I realize Cal is doing the same thing.

He's standing beside me quiet, looking at the water in a pensive manner—very unusual for him.

"I'm surprised you're not giving me shit about the ball," I say, interrupting his reverie.

Blinking out of it, he frowns up at me. "What's that? Oh." He nods. "I think you held up pretty well, considering the circumstances."

"Well, that's pretty lame of you."

"Should I call you Cindy? Or do you prefer Ella."

"There it is." Grasping his shoulder, I catch sight of Reginald headed our way. "And here he is." I straighten, all pleasurable thoughts gone.

Cal's voice is low. "What the hell do you think he's up to?"

"No telling, but I intend to keep my eye on him."

"I'll help with that."

My uncle stops in front of us and does an obligatory bow. "Your highness. Thank you for meeting me."

"You're not supposed to be alone." I'm only here because I had hoped to see Ava again.

"The ladies are behind me, but I wanted to come ahead to be sure we were on the same page with this."

"What the devil is this about, Reg?" Cal steps forward, arms crossed.

"The young lady I introduced you to last night is what you might call American royalty."

"Is that so?"

This makes me laugh. "America doesn't have royalty. They have reality TV."

"Either way, you'd do well to give her a chance. She could be the answer to your problem."

"She's not the answer to anything. My mother, the council, all the old crones and their husbands won't be satisfied unless I marry someone of noble birth, who will strengthen us politically and hopefully economically."

As I say the words, my insides feel like they're shriveling. I want to find Ava, spend more time with her. I want to know how she grew up, her favorite flowers, where she went to school, if she has a favorite movie...

Reggie interrupts my longings. "What Zelda Benedict brings to the table makes up for all that antiquated formality. Besides, your grandfather married an American."

"The country was healthy and prosperous at the time."

What Reggie knows about my problems is actually very little. My goal is to move the country away from oil dependence, and I've been working toward that goal since I was prematurely shoved into leadership. Still, if playing along with him means I'll get to see more of Ava, I'm happy to comply.

Crossing my arms, I feign interest in his scheme. "What exactly is your plan?"

"I said I'd show her the city. You can take over those duties for me today. Spend time together, and we can meet up for dinner at your estate this evening."

"What about her friend? Will she be joining us?"

My uncle glances at my brother. "Cal can take care of her. Give you and Zee some alone time."

"Right! Because I don't have any plans today." Cal's is sarcastic, but I'm right there with him. Last thing I want is to hand Ava over to him.

"I think we should all stay together."

Reginald shrugs. "It would be better if you had some time one-on-one, but perhaps starting out with doubles is a less threatening approach."

A flash of color behind him catches my eye, and I look up to see the ladies walking toward us. Ava is wearing a thin yellow dress that ripples in the breeze. She's like sunshine and fresh breezes, making my whole day feel brighter. Zelda is wearing something similar.

"Hello, my dears!" My uncle starts toward them, stopping to do the customary kiss on the cheek.

I glance over at Cal, and a peculiar expression is on his face. It's a mixture of satisfaction and desire, and I follow his eyes back to where my uncle is standing with the two women. I can't tell which one he's looking at, and I have to fight back the surge of possessiveness that it might be Ava.

"Meeting someone and marrying her are two vastly different things," I say to him quietly.

"I couldn't agree more." His reply is as forceful as mine.

"Despite what Reggie said, I'm not holding out hope for his plan to work."

"Neither am I." My brother starts toward the ladies, leaving me frowning after him.

I have no idea what he's thinking, but hell if I let him get the jump on me. Moving quickly, I join the group.

"Good morning," I say, smiling and giving the two ladies a nod. They each start to curtsey, but I interrupt. "I think we can dispense with the formalities at this point."

"Thank you," Zelda smiles, and her eyes are fixed on me, almost as if she's trying not to look at anyone else. "Reginald said you'd like to show us the Oceanographic Museum?"

A noise like a strangled laugh comes from Cal.

"The aquarium?" I ask. "It is on most tourists' To Do list when they first visit our country. We can actually walk there from here."

"That sounds lovely," Ava says softly, and my eyes drink in her beautiful face.

For a moment I can't find words. I want to say *Not as lovely as you*, but it's a cheesy line, and it definitely would not fit into Reggie's master plan, which for now I'm pretending to follow. Cal's eyes are on me, and I know he's waiting.

"Miss Wilder have you met my brother?"

Ava's eyes hold mine in a way that causes stirring below my belt. They glow like green embers, and I'll be lucky if I make it through the day without stealing a kiss.

"MacCallum Lockwood Tate, can you believe it?" My brother steps forward, turning on all the charm. I hate when her gaze moves from me to him.

"I like it," she says with a smile. "I'm Ava."

"Call me Cal."

She slips a hand into the crook of his arm, and with a sigh, I turn to Miss Benedict, who I notice is watching them with what seems to be equal disappointment. It's gone in a blink, however, and she gives me another forced smile.

"You're too kind to take time out of your busy schedule for us. I can't imagine what all goes into running a country."

"We're only a small nation-state," I say, allowing her to hold my arm. "I had several meetings yesterday before the ball, and I'll be in my office this afternoon. It's not such an inconvenience."

She nods, and I remember Reggie's last instructions. "I hope you and your friend will join us for dinner tonight at our estate in Occitan."

"Is it in the country?"

"It's just outside of town, down by the shore."

"We'd be honored. It sounds beautiful."

We're quiet again. Cal and Ava are ahead of us chatting away like old friends. He waves at one of the buildings ahead of us, and Ava's soft laughter floats back. It's like knives stabbing me in the chest. I tear my eyes away from them.

"I'll send a car to the Fontaine at seven."

"Great."

Her voice sounds less enthused, and I glance over to find her pink lips pressed into a thin line. She's watching the pair ahead of us, but suddenly, she blinks up at me as if remembering something. "Have you always lived here?"

"I was born in Monagasco, so yes. It's my home."

"Okay..." she nods, and her light blonde ponytail bouncing around her shoulders. Her heels click on the red brick pavement. "Do you have any favorite hobbies or anything?"

We're at the entrance to the large museum, and I hold the door for her. Cal and Ava are already inside chatting with the curator.

"I used to race, but I don't have much time for it anymore." *Much to my chagrin...*

"Race? As in horses?"

"Formula One. We have quite a famous competition here every spring. It's actually just a few weeks from now."

"That sounds exciting. Will you be in it?"

"No." Regret is a constant when it comes to my old pastime. It seems Miss Benedict is a quick study.

"I think you might rather be on the track than here with us." Blue eyes slant up at me.

"Nonsense. I'm happy spending time with you and your friend."

"Wow! Would you look at that!" She dashes ahead to the enormous, twenty-seven-foot octopus covering the ceiling in the main entrance of the museum. Its massive tentacles are spread all over the walls and around several of the pillars. I've seen it before, but it's still overwhelming. "It's incredible!"

I watch a moment as she turns in a circle looking up. Cal walks to her, hands in his pockets. "Pretty impressive, isn't it? My great uncle wanted this to be as much about art as about the underwater world. We have Jacques Cousteau's submarine further down in the great hall."

Zee reaches out to hold Cal's forearm, and he guides her down the vast hallway while she continues looking up at all the sights. A giant squid hangs behind the octopus, and an enormous whale skeleton is after that.

I'm confident they'll be occupied for a while, and I take my chance to find the beautiful Ava. As Cal led Zelda away, I noticed her disappearing into the dark hall labeled "Dangers of the Sea."

The exhibit twists around huge tanks of jellyfish, coral, and sea anemone. The space is dark except for the black lights illuminating the strange creatures.

"They're really beautiful, aren't they?" Ava speaks, and my stomach tightens.

"It's always been my favorite part of the museum."

"Look at that one!" She points a slim finger at a Portuguese man of war the size of my torso. Thick tentacles extend down as it floats in the current.

"They have no mouths, but they're able to consume entire fish."

"We used to get those in Florida. They have a horrible sting—much worse than jellyfish."

"When were you in Florida?" I lean on the wooden rail surrounding the tank, watching as the purple lights flicker in her eyes.

She hesitates a moment before continuing. "I grew up there. I guess that's something we have in common. Were you able to go to the beach a lot growing up?"

"All the time. Cal and I would spend every day playing in the surf when we were kids."

"So being royal isn't that much different from being any other kid on the beach?"

"I wouldn't say that. Most kids don't have guards lurking around the sand dunes."

She wrinkles her nose in an adorable way and starts to walk. I push off the rail and follow her. "I suppose they couldn't risk losing the two of you. Who would be the king?"

"We have that all worked out in our constitution."

That makes her stop. "You have a constitution?"

The surprise on her face makes me laugh. "How do you think our government is organized?"

"I don't know. I guess I thought you did whatever you wanted and told everyone what to do."

That makes me laugh more. "Our government hasn't operated that way in centuries, although, I think Cal wishes it still did."

"Still, you *can* do anything you want."

Watching her walk through the dark space, I can only wish that were true. "You might not believe it, but I probably have less freedom to do what I want than you do."

"Tell me about it." She turns and leans against the wooden railing.

Stepping up beside her, I watch the glowing orange clown fish swim along the coral reef. They dart in and out of the swaying pinkish-purple venomous plants without even hesitating.

I lean forward on the railing, and the warmth of Ava's body is right at my side. Without hesitation, I gently lift her hand in mine, threading our fingers like the swaying tentacles.

"Everything I do now is tied up in the good of Monagasco."

"How does that change what you can and can't do?" Her voice is soft, and I turn to find her green eyes round and full of concern.

"You're very beautiful."

Pink floods her cheeks, and her chin drops. Reaching out, I touch the soft skin of her jaw, lifting her face with my finger. Her soft lips part, and she blinks fast, gazing at my mouth. We're hidden in the darkness, only a breath apart. The slightest dip, and I'll have her. My lips ache for hers, and as I lean forward to have my first taste, Cal's fucking voice cuts through the silence.

"Now this is my all-time favorite part of the aquarium. It's dark and winding. Loads of places to make out."

Zelda laughs. "Somehow I get the feeling you know all the good make-out spots in all the historic places."

"How well you know me already, Miss Benedict."

"I met your kind in school."

"You probably drove them all crazy."

"I'm sorry," Ava whispers, slipping from my grasp and hurrying to where they're talking.

My head, shoulders, and hand drop, and for a moment, I grip the wooden rail with all the strength of my frustration. It makes a creaking noise, and I release it. No use destroying historic property. I follow slowly after them, thinking ahead to tonight, after dinner, walking through the garden maze or along the shore. We will finish what we started.

Chapter 7: Playing

Zelda

"You're going too fast!" I cry as Cal pulls me through the great hall under skeletons that make me feel the size of a toddler.

Today, he's dressed casually in khakis and a light blue shirt with a darker blazer on top. I want to say I'll just look at him. Instead I move too close as I pass him, or I hold his arm. I can't seem to stop touching him.

"I want to see the whale skeleton."

At that he stops and turns so suddenly, I run right into his chest. I actually let out an *Oof!*

"Hello, there!" He grins down at me as I hold his waist, his strong arms surrounding me, sending heat surging between my legs. "What interests you most in this moldy old building?"

I can barely think with his face so close to mine. That dimple is back, and his hazel eyes sparkle. *You?* No, can't say that.

"I-I don't know. I've never been here before."

"Hm… I see your point."

Remembering my job, I push myself out of his embrace and straighten my dress. "Like this!" I say, pointing up. "Can you believe how big that is? I could fit in that thing's stomach along with four other people."

He steps beside me and looks up at the whale bones. His body is warm, and I imagine leaning into him.

"Oh! And the jewelry—I want to see the Ocean tiara!"

"Hm... I saw that on my aunt's head. You need to see the deep sea room. It's the coolest thing in the place."

I meet his eyes, and his expression darkens. It makes me feel like a tiny fish is trapped in my chest, struggling to get out.

"Where is it?" I manage to say.

His hand covers mine again, and we start down the wide marble staircase to the floor below. Glancing out the impossibly wide windows, I see the sparkling turquoise waters of the Mediterranean and pull us to a stop.

"Wait!" I'm on the second step breathing hard, looking at the gorgeousness from this luxurious palace of a museum. "Look how beautiful."

He's looking at me, but he steps up beside me and looks out the window. "I grew up looking at that—"

"Lucky."

"You didn't let me finish," he laughs softly. "You make me see it for the first time."

Tearing my eyes away from the ocean, I meet his gaze. I don't have time to think before his long fingers thread in the back of my hair pulling my mouth roughly to his. A little noise aches from my throat as he pushes my lips apart and finds my tongue with his. Heat floods my pelvis, I taste fresh water and cinnamon, and my entire body is on fire. I don't think, I only respond, sliding a hand along the back of his neck and chasing his tongue with mine.

He holds me firmly against his body, and it's so good.

"Cal," I gasp as our lips part.

Our foreheads touch, and I can't open my eyes. I'm breathing so fast. His kiss singed my spine. It curled my toes. I haven't been kissed like that... possibly ever — by choice. I take a step back, holding his forearms out and away from me. My lips are throbbing.

When my eyes blink open, he's giving me that look again, like he's waiting for me to give him the signal. Instead I turn and continue walking down the steps, holding the wide, marble rail for balance.

"I thought we were going to see the deep sea room." My voice is only a little wobbly, not nearly as wobbly as my insides.

He lets out a little sigh and heads down ahead of me, quickly descending the staircase as if he's done it a hundred times. "Come on, then."

I get myself together and follow him. This prince seriously throws me off my game. I've got to remember who I am. I'm Zelda Wilder, professional con woman. This isn't my first rodeo. Still, that's one irresistible cowboy...

Inside the dark room, a woman with two small children is walking around. She lifts them, helping them touch the ceiling and watching as they squeal when the computer-generated fish swarm to where their hands land.

I'm frozen on the spot watching something so basic and wondering why a sight like this still has the power to shred me. Ava was too little to remember our mom, but I remember her taking us to the park, helping me climb the ladder of the small kiddie slide, squealing when I made it to the bottom.

I thought that slide was so huge, but looking back, I know it was probably shorter than I am now. Those days were golden... and then they were gone.

"You're a million miles away, beautiful." Cal is at my side. His voice is warm, and I notice his fingers lightly playing with mine. Everything in me wants to give in, but *dammit*, that's not why we're here. Our future, that promise I made to Ava, is on the line. I won't give it up for some weeklong fling with a sexy player.

"I'm a million miles under the sea!" I answer brightly, pulling my hand away and walking across the room. "How does it work?"

I reach up and touch the ceiling and the entire room shifts in my direction. Fish flock to me, circling my hand. The woman follows the children out, and we're alone again.

"It's some computer jazz. I have no idea."

"That's not your job?" I do a little wink, and his expression seems to falter. Is it possible I throw him off his game, too?

"Precisely," he says, reaching up to touch the low ceiling. The school moves in response to him.

"No fair! You stole my fish."

"Here, I'll bring them back." He walks slowly toward me, trailing long fingers along the smooth surface above us.

His expression grows darker with every step, and my heart beats faster the closer he gets. I can play it off, but my body betrays me. I feel the flush blooming over my chest, rising up my neck.

When he arrives at where I'm standing, he slides his hand forward, taking one last step that puts our bodies together. Our hands touch, our faces are a breath apart. His firm chest is warm against my tingling nipples. The space between us is electric. Neon-green fish circle us overhead, swimming forward to kiss our fingertips.

"I want to kiss you again." His dark eyes are on my heated lips.

"We can't." My breath is shallow. This is so messed up, but I can't pull away from him.

"How long will you be here, Zelda Benedict?"

"Umm... A week?"

"Are you not sure?"

"We're not on a deadline."

His breath touches my cheek. "About that kiss..."

Oh my god. "We'd better find Ava and Rowan."

"Are you afraid?"

Yes, very. "I... I didn't come here for this."

Jesus, I've never been good at seduction, but I'll be damned if his expression doesn't grow darker with every word. I lower my hand slowly, not wanting to leave our magic, undersea bubble.

"Why did you come here?"

My eyes travel around the undersea exhibit as I think of a good answer. "I'd never been to Monagasco." *At least it's not a lie.*

"Zee..." His voice aches in my chest, and the bargaining begins.

Would it *truly* mess up our deal if I give in to him? Would anybody even know? Would anybody even care? *Holy shit, Zelda Scott Wilder!* Of course they would! It would ruin everything!

Stepping back, I turn to the door and cover for my running from him in the most juvenile way possible: "Last one to the top's a rotten egg!"

What I don't count on is Cal being as competitive as I am. He's past me in a flash, and even catches my shoulder, pushing me backwards, almost making me fall.

"Cheater!" I squeal through my laughter as I try to keep up.

"Eat my dust!" He takes the wide stairs two at a time, while I'm still scampering like a duck.

"Damn these damn stupid steps!" I cry.

When I finally reach the top, he's leaning against a massive pillar with a giant bronze sea horse on top looking at his nails. "Hmm... what is that smell? Could it be you, Miss Rotten Egg?"

"You cheated!" I push hard against his chest. "You shoved me backwards!"

"I always win."

He catches my hands, and when our eyes meet we're right back where we were in the basement. MacCallam Lockwood Tate is going to ruin my life.

"Come on," I say, pulling away and heading in the direction I last saw Ava. "Dangers of the Sea" is what I think it said. It should be "Dangers of the Palace." Reggie didn't say anything about sexy younger brothers.

When we make it to the black-lit exhibit of jellyfish, sea anemones, and all other kinds of stinging fish, Ava gives me a look, and the worry in her eyes hits me like a sledgehammer. I am seriously screwing up everything.

She's probably been wondering where the hell I've been, and I just abandoned her to figure it out. As I approach, she hurries to me and catches my hand, holding me back as the guys walk on ahead of us.

"We should go back to the hotel." She sounds stressed, and I feel even worse. "It's after three, and we're supposed to have dinner with them at seven."

Nodding, I give her hand a reassuring squeeze, mentally noting how much it reassures me as well.

"Hey, guys?" I call out before I realize... Is it okay to address a crown prince as *guy?* Must be because they're all smiles strolling back to us. "We should probably head back if we're meeting for dinner. It's gotten late."

"Of course, I'm sorry." Rowan says, his eyes drifting to Ava. "I hope we didn't tire you too much for dinner?"

"I don't think so," I answer. "Just need time to freshen up."

His eyes remain on my sister, but she doesn't speak. She doesn't even make eye contact with him or Cal. It's because she's mad at me. I feel so guilty.

Although we walked to the museum, Rowan insists we take his car back. Less than ten minutes later we're in our luxury suite in the Fairmont. I walk straight through the sitting room and fall on my stomach on the sea-green sofa.

"Holy smokes, I'm dead!"

Ava perches on the edge of a chair facing me, and I watch as she pulls a delicate gold chain from her pocket. Dangling in evenly spaced increments are a tiny starfish, a seahorse, a sand dollar, a pirate's wheel.

"Let me see it!" I hop up and go to where she's sitting, examining the pretty bracelet. "Where did you get it?"

"Off the wrist of a tour guide," she says, turning it over in her hands. "I wanted something to remember this day."

"So it's a little something for you this time? How selfish!" I give her a wink and sit back on my knees beside her.

"You're right. I was very selfish." Her voice is quiet, almost sad.

"You'd also be off-balance. You still have to find someone special to give that herringbone bracelet."

Her pink lips press together, and she blinks down to the carpet. "I think I'll skip the dinner tonight."

"Skip dinner! Are you sick?" I press my palm against her forehead. "No fever."

She shakes her head. "I got a little dizzy at the aquarium. I think I just need to sleep."

"I'll text Reggie that we can't make it tonight."

"No!" Her hand shoots out, grabbing my phone. "You have to make the most of this. Get his attention, one on one."

I study her face. It's a mixture of happiness and misery, and again, I feel like a traitor.

"I'm sorry I left you so long. I kind of got... tied up with Cal in the deep sea room." Memories of his kiss, of his touch filter through my mind, and I do a little shiver.

"You need to get back on track with Rowan tonight. Take advantage of my absence."

She relaxes into one of the bucket chairs and picks up a magazine. I watch her for any signs of irritation or anger. I don't see any. She just seems... sad.

"You're right," I say, lying on the couch again. "I have to try harder. Be a better actress. All my jobs require a certain degree of acting. No reason this one should be different."

Her eyes fly to mine. "You have to *act*?"

"Yeah..." Now I feel uncomfortable. "I mean, he's gorgeous and built, and those blue eyes are stunning, but I don't know. He's just another spoiled elitist snob, don't you think?"

She flushes and looks away, not answering, and for a few moments we're quiet. Her eyes are fixed on the magazine, but she turns the pages too quickly. I wait a few minutes longer as she keeps flipping.

"Okay, then," I finally say. "I guess I should start getting ready."

With a sigh, she stands and goes to her bedroom. "Have fun tonight," she says softly before closing her door.

If I weren't committed to this job, I wouldn't go anywhere tonight. Ava's acting weird, and I don't know if she's really not feeling well or if it's something more. My phone chirps with a text, and I see it's Reggie.

Any progress with CPR?

Pressing my lips together, I study his question for a moment trying to think of how to answer. The short answer is no. As much as I try to get to know Rowan, he seems pretty stiff and disinterested. I have loads more fun hanging out with Cal, which of course is counterproductive.

I finally text back, *Not as much as I'd like.*

A nice walk on the beach at sunset will break the ice. Perhaps a damsel in distress act?

You want me to try drowning?

Nothing so dramatic. Think about it. See you in a bit.

Think about it. That's all I've been doing for the last twenty-four hours. I've got to do like Ava said and try to regain ground. Damsel in distress… Whatever the hell that's supposed to mean.

CHAPTER 8: CONFUSION

Rowan

When Reggie and Zee arrive for dinner, my chest caves. Ava's not with them. "Hello, Miss Benedict," I force a smile. "Welcome to my humble home."

Her eyes are wide as they circle the vast foyer. White marble floors are dotted with small, brown diamonds. Arches overhead with images of blue skies and clouds painted on the ceiling, and the Occitan cross sprinkled throughout.

"It's amazing," she whispers, looking around. Her eyes snap back to me when Cal appears at the top of the curved staircase.

"Hello, below!" He trots down the stairs, but when he reaches us, my uncle leaves his escort and walks toward him.

"Cal, would you mind showing me a map of the vineyards at Cote d'Azur?"

"What?" My brother's sunny disposition dims.

"Yes, I was telling a colleague the *folle noir* was outstanding. I want to see which vineyard he should visit."

"Right now?"

"Come, come, it will only take a moment."

The two of them set off in the direction of the library, and I'm left alone with Miss Benedict. She's wearing beige leggings and a pale grey tunic sweater made of a fuzzy yarn like Mohair. One shoulder is exposed, and her soft pale blonde hair is styled in large curls over it. Her eye makeup makes me think of that singer.

Zelda Benedict is actually quite lovely. I look down at my hands as we walk through the entryway into the left hall. Mother is at the spa in Marins, so it's up to me to play host.

"I hope your friend isn't ill." Yep, no getting away from where my mind is.

"She said she was tired. I'm sure it's nothing serious." Zelda's voice is soft. At times, it reminds me of Ava's, but I suppose it's because they're friends.

We're in the living room, and I'm looking at the wet bar in the far corner. "Would you like a glass of champagne?"

She glances up and smiles. "It would be the real thing here, wouldn't it?"

"It is from the Champagne appellation."

I pour us each a glass of Canard-Duchene and we do a little clink.

"Mmm," she sighs. "It's delicious. Not bitter or sweet."

"It's my mother's favorite."

She walks to the small fountain stationed in the center of the wall. It flows down to a small grate and provides ambient noise.

"Your life here is so lovely." Her thoughts seem to be miles away. "I can't imagine growing up like this, without a care in the world."

I wasn't prepared for her comment, and I pause a moment to think about how our lives here must appear. "Before my father died, I was quite selfish. I did whatever the hell I wanted to do without worrying about anyone."

"Are you saying you've changed?"

I exhale a laugh. "No, I'm still quite selfish. The only difference is now I lament the things I wish I could do while I work on the things I should."

"I suppose that's the definition of being noble."

"Something like that."

Cal's teasing voice cuts through our sudden solemnity. "Those are some seriously long faces to be sharing champagne. Pour me a glass, brother."

"I'll have one of those as well, Rowan." Reggie says. "Your mother has excellent taste in wine."

"Find what you were looking for back there?" I call, walking to the bar for two more glasses.

"Domaine de Toasc," Reggie answers.

Zee seems suddenly on edge. She moves from the fountain over to where my uncle is standing as if for protection. I've just finished pouring when James enters the room.

"If your graces are ready, dinner is served."

Zee takes Reggie's arm, and we proceed through double doors into a dining room off the side of the living area. I've always appreciated the interior design of this room. The walls are beige stone, and exposed beams line the ceiling. A heavy mahogany table is in the center, with heavy, red-upholstered chairs surrounding it. Heavy red drapes hang beside enormous French-door windows overlooking the sea. It's one of my favorite rooms in the house, strong and rugged.

Since it's only the four of us, I sit at the head with Zelda on my left and Reggie on my right. Cal takes the seat on Zelda's left.

"It's been a while since I've dined at this table," Reggie sighs. His observation pricks my annoyance at his return, but I let it pass.

"We don't normally open the house this early in the season," Cal says. "Mother wanted to come out. She missed being close enough to walk along the shore in the morning air."

"It must be lovely to walk along the shore in the sunrise."

"I wouldn't know," Cal laughs. "I'm more of a 'walk along the shore in the sunset' type."

Her cheeks pink, and she looks down. It's the softest I've seen Miss Benedict in the short time I've known her. I want to ask her about San Angelo, but the servers fill the room, setting gold-rimmed plates of dark green salads in front of each of us. Our champagne glasses are refilled, and I take a moment to do a little toast.

"To familiar places and new friends."

We all touch our crystal together and dig into the bitter greens softened by the balsamic vinaigrette, feta, and cranberries. I catch Miss Benedict checking out the tall bodyguard passing outside the windows. Our eyes meet, and she gives me a little smile.

"I suppose you don't even see them after a while."

"Not true," I say, returning her smile. "I'm actually very good friends with some of them. Comes with having them around everywhere."

"Is it hard knowing they might stop someone from trying to kill you?"

"I don't think about it that much. Thanks for reminding me."

"Oh! I'm so sorry." She blushes bright red, which makes me laugh.

"I was only teasing you," I say gently.

I reach out and cover her hand with mine. She starts to pull away, but at the same time, she checks herself and doesn't. *Strange.*

My brother's eyes are on our hands, and he breaks in. "Personally, I always feel better when ole Odd Job is behind the wheel."

"Odd job?" she laughs, removing her hand from mine. "Isn't that the guy from James Bond?"

"Are you still harassing poor Hajib?" Reggie says in mock disapproval. "You haven't called him his proper name since you were boys."

"He loves being called Odd Job," Cal argues. "He never stopped us from saying it."

"I'd like to see you correcting the future kings of Monagasco." Our uncle quirks an eyebrow, and I can't help remembering the days when my father was still alive.

We would come here in the late summers, and the three adults would congregate in the living room talking and laughing while Cal and I played chess or ran down to the shore to hunt for ghost crabs along the water line.

Our entrées are served — dried cod with tomato and spices — and a delicate pastry for dessert. The plates are removed, and Reggie stands and goes to the terrace doors, pulling them open. A warm breeze tipped with a hint of brine fills the air.

"That does it," Cal cries, jumping up. "We're taking a walk on the shore."

He catches Zee's hand and pulls her up. I chuckle and follow along, leaving my shoes on the smooth marble stones beside theirs and picking up a flashlight before following them down the long path to the water's edge.

The estate is situated on a little cove protected by an outcropping of rocks, and as such, the beach is calmer than elsewhere, more like a lake. The moon is just rising over the crystal waters, and Cal rolls up his khakis. Zee is ankle-deep in the water kicking small sprays at him.

"Stop," Cal says calmly, which only makes her do it more. "I'm going to dunk you if you don't stop."

Naturally, she does it again, and he makes a lunge. She screams and takes off running. I only laugh watching them, especially when Cal gives up after only a few steps.

"My stomach is too full to run," he complains.

I switch on the light, and a handful of ghostly white crabs scurry away. Zee's back at my side holding my arm and watching.

"I love chasing ghost crabs," she whispers. "Look how big yours are!"

"That's what she said," Cal whispers from my other side.

I shine the light on one, and it freezes in place for a moment, watching us before scampering away. Zee has my sleeve in a death grip.

"I thought you said you liked chasing them?" I tease.

"Just as long as they run away from us." She laughs, but it's fast and nervous. It makes me laugh.

"You're afraid of them."

"I am not," she says, jerking as my light hits another closer in our path.

I hear Cal sneaking up behind us, and suddenly Zee screams.

"Oh—OH!" It's so loud, I nearly drop the flashlight. "Oh! Ow!"

She tugs my arm on the way down, and now she's sitting on the sand, holding her foot, a pained look on her face.

"Are you okay?" I'm trying not to laugh.

"No..." She's not crying, and I shine the light all around looking for whatever caused her injury.

"Did you trip over something?"

"Are you bleeding?" Cal is on his knees beside her.

"No," she wails louder. "I'm such an idiot! I stepped on a crab, and when I jumped to get off of it, I twisted my ankle."

We both lift her under the arms, helping her scoot back out of the surf.

"Do you think you can walk on it?" I ask.

She nods. "I've hurt this ankle before. I think it'll be okay."

Cal takes the light from me and shines it on her ankle. "It's swollen. You'll have to spend the night."

"What!" Zee cries, trying to rise. "Oh!" She instantly drops to sitting again.

"You're staying the night. We have plenty of rooms and we can have a doctor here first thing in the morning to check you out."

"I'm not spending the night. I don't need a doctor!"

"No more arguments. Rowan?" My brother looks up at me. I've been frowning the entire time, unsure what to make of this.

"He's probably right. Better safe than sorry, and we've got more than enough room."

"But what about my s... sleepwear? Ava won't know what to think."

I feel pretty sure she wasn't about to say *sleepwear*, but I let it pass. "I'm sure we can find something for you to sleep in, either something of Mother's or —"

"Good heavens! Not a muumuu. I have T-shirts and things she can borrow."

Zee sits for a moment blinking back and forth between us, until at last she sighs. "As long as I can call Ava and let her know what's happening. She's probably already asleep, but I don't want her to worry."

I consider offering to make that call, but I don't. "Of course. We'll carry you back to the house."

We pull her up and start walking with her between us, one arm over each of our shoulders. She's quite a bit shorter than us, especially with her shoes off, and with every hop, she jerks our necks down.

"This isn't going to work," I growl, stepping forward and sweeping her into my arms. She lets out a little noise, but I start walking, holding her firmly against my chest. "Trust me, this is far more comfortable."

Cal seems a bit miffed, but he doesn't say anything. He follows behind us on the path.

"Now I really feel like Cinderella," Zee says softly, putting one hand on my shoulder.

She's warm in my arms, and I study her in the moonlight. Is Reggie right? Could this girl truly solve all my problems? She's energetic and fun, and she loves to laugh. She loves the ocean. All are traits I look for in a woman. She's light and free-spirited, and I'm just noticing in this light... she's beautiful.

Her cheeks are flushed from running on the beach, and her hair hangs in messy waves around her soft shoulders. Her lips are full and pink, and something about her reminds me of Ava. Ava. It all goes back to Ava.

Zee's watching me with equal intensity, and I realize I should say something. "I hope your foot doesn't hurt too much."

"It feels okay, actually." Her voice is quiet. "It really is an old injury. It'll probably be fine in the morning."

"Still, we should have it checked out."

"I'm afraid you're both overreacting."

"It's swollen, and you can't walk. We're not overreacting."

Her bottom lip goes between her teeth, and I wonder if I should try kissing her. Just to see if something happens. I haven't kissed Ava yet... My brow lines, and I almost growl. I can't get her out of my head.

Zee misinterprets my mental distress. "I'm sorry. I'm too heavy. You don't have to carry me."

"No... it's not that." Racking my brains... "I was just thinking I need to find a nightgown for you to wear."

"It's too much trouble. I can go back to the Fontaine."

"It's no trouble at all. You're staying here. That's an order."

Her eyebrows shoot up. "By order of the king?"

I exhale a laugh at the gruffness in my tone. "By request."

"In that case, how can I say no?"

Chapter 9: Damsel in Distress

Zelda

I didn't have to act too hard when Rowan swept me into his arms like some kind of swashbuckling hero. It was shocking and very sexy, and Reggie was right. A little damsel in distress helped get both of us on the right page, at least temporarily. In the moonlight, as he carried me, I was able to study him up close.

He's such a focused, brooding fellow. His dark hair is a little too long, but it hangs in attractive waves around his temple and collar. His square jaw and lowered brow give him a sexy-menacing look that I'm sure sends panties flying. I know my heart beat a little faster when he looked at me. He's strong and confident, and he's got the bossy king persona down pat. But what nails it all, the icing on the cake, are his gorgeous blue eyes. They glow like the turquoise waters we just left behind in all that dark deliciousness.

Inside the estate, he lowers me onto one of the cushioned loungers and kneels at the end, taking my injured foot in his large hands. I don't miss Cal lurking in the background, arms crossed and frowning. It makes me want to tease him. I want to ask him if he's jealous. *What the hell? Get it together, Zelda!*

"Does this hurt?" Rowan slides his hand up to the ball of my foot and gently pushes it toward me.

I'm so glad I opted for that paraffin pedicure. My foot's as soft as a baby's bottom right now, and my nails are painted shimmering coral.

"It's a little stiff," I answer, giving him a smile.

"And this?" His hand slides over the top of my foot, slowly pulling it toward his chest in a point.

"That feels okay."

Our eyes meet, and his lovely blue ones are warm. Suddenly my oversized rose-gold phone appears in my face. I jump back and glance up at Cal, who is giving me a perturbed look.

"You wanted to call your friend, remember?"

"My friend?" I'm confused. *Oh, shit!* "Ava! Of course."

"Hmm," he says and walks away.

"I'll give you some privacy," Rowan stands. "Let me know when you're ready to go up. I'll find something you can wear to sleep."

"Thank you."

I decide to send a text rather than call, since I'm pretty sure she's asleep. I'm partway through when Reggie peeks out onto the terrace. He looks quickly back in the room before hustling over to where I sit.

"Great work!" His eyes are shining. "That ankle injury is just what we needed."

"I didn't do it on purpose," I grumble, looking down at my stupid foot. "I was going to try drowning."

"This is better. Use it to your advantage. I'll check back later to see how it's going."

He pats my head and returns to the living room, where I hear him telling Rowan goodnight and to keep him posted on my status. I finish my text just as Rowan returns to my side.

"Ready to go up?" His low voice is warm, and I give him a smile.

"If I'd known you'd be carrying me all around the place tonight, I'd have eaten less dinner."

I'm in his arms in one quick sweep. "You're not heavy. I already told you."

We're back in that intimate embrace, his dark, square jaw and shimmering eyes mere inches from my face. I wonder if I should try to kiss him? Is that too fast? Reggie would probably suggest I get the party started, but I don't entirely get Crown Prince Rowan Westringham Tate. He's such a serious person. Instead, I put my hand behind his neck, allowing my fingers to lightly thread in his dark hair.

He stops to open a large, white door, and we step into a bedroom that almost makes my eyes bug out. It's similar to the dining room with beige stone walls and exposed wood beams lining the ceiling. A huge bed is at the back wall beside another enormous, arched window. It's covered in the softest-looking duvet, I know I'll sleep like a baby in it. A brass chandelier hangs from the ceiling, and six small pictures are arranged in a pattern beside an enormous flat-screen television, which hangs above the beige painted-brick fireplace.

Rowan carries me to an overstuffed loveseat with an oversized ottoman in front of it. A tray holding a crystal decanter of water topped by a matching crystal glass, a gold-rimmed saucer with two adorable, pale-purple cookies, and two discreet blue-gel capsules on a linen napkin is on one half of the ottoman. Rowan lowers me onto the small couch and props my injured foot on the other half.

"You thought of everything," I say as he sits beside me on the edge of the small sofa.

"I can't take credit. The kitchen sent that up."

His toned thigh is warm against my leg as I lean forward. "Ibuprofen, and... What are these little cookies?"

"Lavender macaroons. I highly recommend them." He smiles and waits a moment. "Will you be okay? I'll have one of the staff bring up a cane so you can get around."

"I'm sure I can walk on it. You don't have to carry me everywhere."

"You couldn't have walked up those stairs, but if you think you're fine, I'll say goodnight."

My lip is back under my teeth. *Should I go for a kiss?* Reggie is going to kick my ass if I don't at least get a kiss out of all this drama. I'm beginning to hate this con. Of all the jobs I've done, I never let emotions enter the picture. I feel like a dirty Cinderella, playing games with the handsome prince's heart. I don't believe he's as careless as Reggie makes him out to be, or as much of a threat to his country's security.

He starts to rise, and a heavy heart, I smile. "Doesn't the gallant prince deserve a kiss?"

Looking down at me, I see the hesitation in his eyes. I hold my smile, even tilting my head to the side in a playful way. Something changes in him. That intimidating focus returns, and he sits beside me, closer this time.

My heart beats faster as he reaches for my cheek and pulls my mouth to his. Our lips touch, but he doesn't push mine apart. He doesn't plunge his tongue inside, taking no prisoners the way his brother did at the museum. Instead he kisses me gently, a few times in quick succession. It's very tender and curious.

With a deep breath he leans back and looks into my eyes a moment. I don't say anything. It was a very nice kiss. *Nice.*

"Goodnight, then," he says and goes to the door, leaving the room without a look back.

I exhale a big sigh and lean forward to scoop up the pain relievers. My foot isn't really injured. I know from experience, it'll ache tonight and be fine tomorrow. I step gingerly on it and do a little skippy-walk to the bed where an enormous lavender silk gown is lying.

My mohair sweater and damp leggings are off, and I pull the giant thing over my head. It's luxurious, soft as whipped cream and clearly expensive. The bodice is a crisscross network of tucks and ruffles, and the silk belt is longer than my arms. I suppose it should be tied at the back, but I need to use it to lift the whole contraption up and tie it around my neck.

"I never sleep in a gown!" I whisper to myself as I limp over to the oval, full-length mirror in the corner. "I look like a little girl in her granny's clothes!"

It makes me giggle, when I hear a soft rap on the door. It's some maid bringing me a cane, I'm sure. *What an old grandpa Rowan is*, I think, shaking my head. A sexy old grandpa, I add.

I jump when I see Cal leaning against the doorjamb, dressed in loose pajama pants. His lined torso is easily visible through the thin button-up he's wearing. The moment he sees me, he explodes with laughter.

"What the hell are you wearing? A tent?"

My face flares red. "What are you doing here?"

"I brought you something to sleep in." He holds out a bottle of champagne. "And this to kill the pain."

"Leave it on the table." I turn and pull (and pull and pull) the sides of the nightgown up so I can skippy-trot back to the love seat.

"You're going to break your neck as well as your ankle in that thing." He follows me inside the room and closes the door. "If you don't drown in silk first."

"My ankle isn't broken. Anyway, your brother brought me ibuprofen and this gown to sleep in."

He shakes his head. "What a shocking lack of imagination."

"I think he must have a pretty great imagination if he thought this would fit me." I look down at all the silk pooling in my lap. "Or I really was incredibly heavy, and he was only being nice." *Nice.* Like that kiss.

"My brother's an idiot. Here," Cal drops a small stack of clothes in my lap. "You'll sleep in this. Go change."

"And where do you suggest I do that?"

"Around the side of the fireplace. I won't look." My eyes narrow, and he holds up both hands. "I promise."

"I haven't decided if you're honest."

"Smart girl."

Standing, I gather (and gather and gather) the sides of the gown so I can limp to the somewhat hidden corner beside the fireplace.

"You haven't eaten your macaroons!"

"Help yourself," I call, placing the navy tee and boxers he brought me on the edge of the fireplace.

"I'll wait for you," he says quietly.

I quickly pull the silk circus tent over my head. Cool air swirls around my bare breasts, tightening my nipples, but I'm only exposed long enough to toss the gown on the bed and whip his tee over my head. My senses flood with the deliciously spicy man-scent of Cal's shirt, and I'm stepping into the shorts when I glance up and catch his hazel eyes in the oval mirror.

I straighten fast, pulling up the boxers and then jamming my hands on my hips. "You watched me change."

He looks down, but the sides of his mouth curl in a grin. "It's true. I did. I couldn't help it. You have great tits."

"You are not a gentleman."

"True again. Sorry." He peeks up, humor lurking in those damn irresistible eyes. "But you already knew that part, didn't you? As smart as you are?"

My lips twist as I try not to smile. *I will not let him get to me this time.* It sounds like the cry of the defeated in my brain.

"You're a prince. You're supposed to be noble and all that shit."

"Lies, all lies. I blame Walt Disney for that propaganda." He leans forward to pour two glasses of champagne, and I limp to the sofa again, still doing my best to be angry.

"Princes are only noble because of our parents," he continues, handing me a glass. I take a sip of the sparkling wine. "Otherwise, we're just like every other male."

"How's that?"

"Looking to get laid."

I nearly choke. "Well... go look in some other room."

"Really?" He makes a sad-puppy face and my insides squeal. "I like this room. It's one of my new favorite rooms."

Shifting my position, I find the remote under my butt. I pull it out and turn on the television. "Then you have to watch TV."

A French-dubbed *Saved by the Bell* pops up, and I can't help thinking *perfect*. It's not romantic in any way.

Cal makes a little growly noise that makes me grin and shifts his position to watch. Our sides are touching now, from waist to hip to knee in a blazing line I fight to ignore. I take another sip of wine.

After a few minutes of watching a fuzzyheaded Screech follow the gang around wearing enormous goggles, he finally asks, "Are all American high schools like this?"

"This is as true to American high schools as Disney is to princes."

"*Touché.*"

We resume silently watching, when I notice two fingers wiggling beneath my palm. My eyes flicker down to where Cal is doing a not-so-sneaky job trying to hold my hand.

He sees me catch him and laughs. "Give me that remote." He puts his glass down before snatching the black rectangle from my hand. Channels flicker past like a kaleidoscope, until he stops on one. Woody Harrelson is at a craps table with a group of partying ladies. "This is more like it. Sexy."

It takes a moment to realize what it is. "*Indecent Proposal*?" My nose wrinkles as I finish my glass. "Gag."

"Don't tell me you hate movies."

"I love movies. I hate stupid ones that are totally unbelievable and rely on such obvious emotional pandering to attract viewers."

"Big words, Miss Benedict. I think you really love it."

"I do not!" I dive for the remote, but he laughs and leans back, putting us chest to chest, with me on top.

"Hmm..." He slides a hand under my tee and over the bare skin of my lower back. Chills skate across my arms, and my entire body heats. "I think you like this."

Lowering my forehead to his chest, I hesitate only a moment before pushing myself out of his arms and sitting on the opposite side of the small sofa. I'm flustered and horny, and my brain feels swirly.

We watch Demi Moore and Woody Harrelson lose round after round on the roulette table until all their money is gone, and Moore starts to cry.

"Idiots," I grumble. "Roulette is the worst game you can play in a casino. It has the highest odds in favor of the house, and they increase with every spin. Why didn't they quit and go back to craps?"

Cal chuckles from the other end of the sofa, and I look down to see him watching me. "You know a lot about gambling."

Whoops. I blink fast trying to find an excuse. "My dad liked to gamble."

"Liked?" He pushes to a sitting position and slides closer to where I'm perched.

"He died when I was really young."

Warm hands go around my waist, and Cal pulls me onto his lap, facing him in a straddle. Only, I won't meet his eyes. I keep my gaze fixed on the television.

"I'm sorry," he says, pressing a fiery kiss to the base of my neck.

Clearing my throat, my breath comes faster. "It was a long time ago," I manage to whisper.

His arms are at my waist, and his kisses move up the side of my neck until he's at my ear. "Still, I'm sorry you lost your dad. I know how that feels."

My whole body shivers, and I try to pull away. His arms only tighten around me. "Where are you going?"

"Cal…"

I feel his arousal hard against my thigh. My hands hold is biceps, and we're nose to nose, sharing our breath. He looks deep into my eyes.

"Let's say you and me do some good old-fashioned fucking, Zelda Benedict."

I blink fast, away from his gaze. "I can't," I whisper, even though my insides are liquid, and my lips heavy with desire.

"Sure you can," he whispers, leaning forward to cover my mouth with his.

Fingers thread into the sides of my hair, and his kiss is even more passionate than before. It's hungry and demanding, and I'm losing the fight this time.

Cal doesn't gently request, he invades, pillaging my senses. We lean back on the couch, and he's above me, moving my mouth with his. I'm not stopping him. I'm desperate with desire. My hands are on his neck, and I'm kissing him back, hungrily keeping time with his movements.

He pulls away, and a little noise of disappointment comes from my throat. It makes him smile as he reaches down and lifts me off the couch.

"Don't worry, sexy. I'm nowhere near finished with you tonight."

"Cal..." My brain is fighting with me to get control, but he tosses me onto the bed, pulling his shirt off in one swift move.

My protests die when I see his bare body. He's ripped and golden, beautiful, lean and muscular, and his light brown hair is tousled and tempting. My eyes trail down the lines of his stomach, getting tangled in the *V* at his hips, and all rational thought vanishes.

"Now you," he says, climbing on his knees beside me on the bed.

He takes the hem of the shirt I'm wearing and lifts it over my head. My instinct is to cover my bare breasts, but he catches my arms.

"No way," he grins, leaning us back on the bed. "Your tits are far too gorgeous for you to hide them."

My face heats, and I start to laugh. "Stop it."

He leans over me, then lowers gently until our bare bodies are stomach to stomach, skin against skin. We both exhale a groan.

"You feel so good," he murmurs, moving his lips over my shoulders.

I can only whimper, "So do you." I am *so* screwed right now.

I can't stop him as he slides lower, covering my left nipple with his mouth and swirling his tongue around the hardened peak before giving it a firm suck that registers straight between my legs.

"Oh, god!" I gasp as he moves to the other side to repeat. His hand is on me, giving my nipple a pinch before moving up. I meet his eyes as he pushes his thumb between my teeth.

Closing my lips around that thick digit, I give it a suck, and his eyes darken. "Fuck me," he groans, rising up fast to claim my mouth again.

I'm on fire. Energy hums up and down my thighs. I'm so close to coming, he only has to touch me once more, and I'll explode.

"I knew it would be like this," he breathes, cupping my lips with his. "You are so fucking passionate. I want to fuck you so hard."

"Cal, oh, god!" Those seem to be the only three words my obliterated brain can conjure.

I'm so ready for him to be inside me, and he's gone, sliding down my body, kissing my sternum, my navel, then jerking the boxers off my hips.

"Oh, shit, bare pussy," he groans before wrapping his forearms around my hips and pulling me to his mouth.

One slow sweep of his tongue across my clit, and I cry out. I'm trembling and exploding, pleasure snaking up my thighs like a vine. I can't remember the last time I had sex, but lord knows it wasn't with anyone like MacCallam Lockwood Tate.

"Jesus," he gasps.

"Please," I beg.

He hops off the bed so fast, I just barely see the large erection tenting his PJ pants before they're gone. A rip of foil, a quick roll of condom, and he's back above me.

"You are amazing," he says.

"If you don't fuck me now—"

A hard thrust, and we both cry out.

"Oh, yes!" I moan.

"Jesus, god," he grinds.

He's hard and huge and perfect, stretching and massaging me in the most erotic way. His hips speed up, moving fast and punishing, demanding, taking, holding my face as he kisses me hard. I can only grasp his shoulders and ride this out. I'm building to my second orgasm, and he's taking me there by delicious force.

Our bodies are covered in sweat. A bead rolls from his beautiful, messy hair to the scruff of his square jaw, and I lean up to lick it away. Salt fills my mouth just before he turns and covers it with his.

He's rocking, and I'm soaring. We're holding onto each other when the sky explodes. My hips buck and clench, and he groans my name. I feel him pulsing inside me, filling the condom, coming deep between my things as my muscles hold him, pulling more and more.

"So fucking good." He kisses my neck.

Our arms are around each other, and his forehead rests on my shoulder. We don't move for several moments as our breathing starts to calm, as our bodies start to come down.

I've never been fucked like that in my life, but it's more than that. I feel like I understand what the term *making love* means, which is insane. I'm not here to be Cal's girlfriend, and lord knows this "playboy prince" has a reputation for getting around. Reggie somehow worked that into a previous conversation.

"Zelda," he murmurs, pressing his lips against my skin, cutting off my spiraling thoughts. "You are amazing."

I exhale a laugh. "High praise, I'm sure."

His head pops up and he grins, resting it on his hand. "It is, actually, but I mean it. You're as good as you look. Better."

"Maybe we should stop talking about it."

That makes him laugh, and he leans down to give me a firm kiss. It lingers a bit longer, warm and delicious until he breaks away.

"I swear that mouth drives me crazy."

"You're not too shabby with yours." Reaching out, I touch his bottom lip with my thumb. He drops his chin and bites me, sending a little thrill through my midsection.

"I'd barely even started." He cocks an eyebrow. "Just wait until Round 2."

A shiver passes through me, and his eyes darken. "You like that, don't you, little slut. I've been trying to get in your pants since that night at the ball."

"And now you have." I pretend to pout. "You've lost all respect for me."

"Just the opposite. I have very high respect for women who are dynamite in the sack. I plan to take advantage of you several more times tonight."

I can't help laughing. "Several?"

"How is your ankle?"

"I don't even feel it."

"That's good, although I suppose your riding me tonight is out of the question."

Pressing my lips together, I do a little frown. "I probably shouldn't sit on it, which means I probably shouldn't sit on you."

"Shit." He props his head on his hand and traces a finger along my lips. "I have this fantasy of you on top of me, straight up, bucking those hips, this gorgeous hair falling all around your tits." He leans down and kisses me again. "I'm getting a semi just thinking about it."

"You're insatiable. Give me a chance to breathe."

"Come here," he rolls onto his back and pulls my cheek to his chest. I listen to his heartbeat as he threads his fingers into the back of my hair. "I wanted to punch Rowan in the nuts tonight when he swept you up in his arms like some kind of fucking superhero."

"Hmm," I say, feeling my eyes growing heavy. "That was a great moment. You should try it sometime."

"I fucking would've if he hadn't. Show off. I saw you first."

"Mm-hm." I say through an exhale, my cheek blissfully pressed to his toned chest.

On the television, I watch as Demi Moore takes a dollar coin from Robert Redford that has tails on both sides and gets out of his limo.

"Dumb movie," I grumble, and I feel Cal chuckle.

"It's my favorite part."

"I hope you're teasing. She should've stayed with him. Who lets their wife have sex with another man for money?"

Cal's fingers slide across the back of my neck. "They did a pretty good job of making them out to be desperate. I don't know from personal experience, but I don't think desperate people always make smart decisions."

A lump forms in my throat as I think about his words. I think about my situation, and the decisions I've made. I know what it's like to be desperate. Closing my eyes, I try to push away the guilt of what I've done, but I'm not sure I can.

His fingers still. "Are you falling asleep?"

I barely nod. I don't want to think about personal experience and wrong choices. I want to sleep in Cal's arms and pretend nothing else is waiting outside this room.

"I think I'm feeling the wine," I say softly.

"And all the strenuous activity."

"Mm… that too."

He gently moves me to the side, curling his body around my back. I slide my palm down his forearm and lace our fingers together as I allow his warmth to comfort me. It only takes a few moments for me to slip into unconsciousness.

My eyes pop open as the sun is just lighting the horizon. The sound of heavy breathing is at my back, and my heart sinks. Oh god, I've ruined everything!

Without even looking back, I slowly move to the edge of the bed and slip my legs out, rising as gently as I can without shaking the mattress. It's one of those foam mattresses, and Cal doesn't even stir.

He's lying on his back sleeping soundly, and I take a moment to admire his beautiful body. The white sheet is draped across his waist, and in the dim light, the lines of his muscles are deep and defined. Everything in me wants to crawl back in bed, wake him, and take care of that morning wood, but I know that would be a huge mistake. Even bigger than the one I made last night.

As quietly as possible, I step into my leggings and pull them on. My ankle is stiff, but as I predicted, it's much better this morning. I think about Cal's fantasy and my body warms. I could ride him today… *Ugh! Fuck my life.*

Shaking that away, I pick up my sweater, but instead of wearing it, I pull on Cal's navy tee. It smells like him, and I bury my nose in the collar as I watch him sleeping. My chest aches, but I know what I have to do. Picking up my purse, I creep to the door, and with one last look, I disappear.

CHAPTER 10: REGROUPING

Rowan

The noise of footsteps overhead causes me to minimize the browser on my laptop. Cal appears at the living room entrance, and for a moment he only stands there, looking around the room.

"Coffee?" I say, nodding toward the tray on the low table holding a carafe and two additional cups.

His shoulders drop, and he stalks forward to the coffee service. He appears well rested, but he's scowling and clearly pissed. I watch as he yanks up the carafe and roughly pours a small cup of espresso.

My brow lines. "What's the matter with you?"

He only takes a long drink, shakes his head, and walks to the French doors, looking out at the water.

"Shall I call Doctor Hebert now or wait a little longer."

"Why would you call him?" He's still standing at the window looking out.

"Our house guest?" I'm starting to get annoyed. I didn't want to call him too early in case she slept in, but it's after ten. I'm sure he has other patients."

"Don't bother." He turns and walks back to the table, depositing his cup before starting for the exit.

"What do you mean? We said we'd have the doctor look at her ankle—"

"She's gone. She isn't here. She must have left some time in the night."

For a moment I sit looking at the empty fireplace, trying to understand. "Why would she do that? Did something happen to make her feel uncomfortable?"

"I wouldn't know." He's about to exit, but I stop him.

"I considered inviting them to the casino tonight, if they're both well enough. Will you be around?"

He turns halfway back and for several moments seems to think about what I just said. "You're inviting Zee to the casino?"

"And Ava. I thought you might join us to sort of... round out the numbers." It suddenly dawns on me what might be wrong. "Unless you have other plans. I realize I've been monopolizing your personal time lately."

He continues in that spot, thinking. I'm starting to wonder if I should call the doctor in to check him out, when he seems to reach a decision.

"Yes," he says solidly. "I'll go with you tonight. That's a good way to get some answers."

Whatever the hell that means.

"I'll give them a call."

* * *

Zelda

I'm deep under the covers when Ava bursts through the door and jumps on my bed. "What time did you get home? I just saw your text, and I wasn't expecting you for hours!"

"Mm," I groan. "Go away, Ava."

She only jumps harder on the bed. "Wake up and tell me what happened! You twisted your ankle? Is it the same ankle you sprained trying to play basketball?"

I push the covers up and burrow down further into the plush duvet. The last thing I want is to rehash last night or confess my Super Colossal Screw-up. Lucky for me the doorbell rings, and Ava takes off to see who it is. I hear her voice in the other room.

"Oh my goodness!" she whisper-cries. "They're absolutely gorgeous! Zee, you have to see this!"

My curiosity is piqued, but not enough to make me emerge from my protective cocoon. The noise of voices is followed by the sound of the door closing. Everything is quiet for a few moments, then Ava returns.

"You're not going to believe the bouquet Rowan sent!"

"Rowan?" I crawl a little closer to the light, still unsure if I want to emerge.

"It says, 'Sorry you've been ill. I hope you'll be well enough to join us tonight. Yours truly, Rowan W.T.' and it's the most enormous bouquet of roses I've ever seen! It fills the entire front table!"

"Rowan sent you flowers?" My voice is muffled coming from under the blankets. *He didn't send me flowers*. Then again, he probably thinks I'm upstairs in his guest room right now.

"You should come out and look at them. Or just come out and stop being a weirdo."

I can't hold it in anymore. I press my face into the pillow and yell it out: "*Fuuuuuuuck!*" I feel the little tears in the corner of my eyes. "Oh, fuck." I whisper, pushing them away.

The bed depresses, and I know she's sitting beside my back now. "That's a word I haven't heard out of your mouth in ages. What happened last night?"

I can't breathe. I'm not sure if I should even tell her, but I know I have to. What I've done impacts her future as much as it does mine. Oh, god, I've never done something so careless in all the time I've been taking care of us. I've always been the dependable one, the one who finds the jobs and then sees them through to the end. I've never been the one who screws them up. It's not who I am.

Taking a deep breath, I force myself to climb out from the covers. It's time to stop acting like a child and face the consequences. I sit up and push the blankets off my head, down to my lap. Ava's eyes are round, but she starts to laugh.

"Your hair is crazy!" Reaching forward she smooths it around my head. I almost can't take it.

"I've messed up, Ava-bug." I finally say, looking at my lap. "I might have cost us the whole job, our future, everything."

Her round eyes narrow with a frown. "What did you do?"

I push my face against my bent knees and say it fast. "I slept with Cal. Last night. I slept with him... as in we had sex."

It's so quiet in the room, the noise of the second hand seems as loud as a hammer. Ava's lips are parted, and she only stares at me.

"Time out," she says softly. "Did you just tell me you slept with Cal last night? Rowan's brother Cal?"

"Do you know any other princes named Cal?"

I confess, despite my external misery over what I've done, that damn little fish is still flipping around inside my stomach when I think about last night. FML.

"I don't know any other princes period." She rises off the bed and walks around the room.

"I don't know how I'm going to do the deal with Rowan now. How can I go after him when I've slept with his brother? I've ruined everything. We might as well start packing."

She pauses, and holds her fingers to her lips. Judging by her profile, she doesn't appear angry or even upset. I'm not sure what to make of how she's reacting — or underreacting.

"I have to tell Reggie what I did," I continue. "He's going to flip his lid."

"Is your ankle okay?" She returns to the bed and sits beside me, digging in the blankets and sheets for my foot.

I reach down and stop her search. "Ava! Did you hear what I said? I've killed the deal. Rowan isn't going to look twice at me when he finds out what I did!"

"It's true." She's smiling now, and I'm starting to wonder if her illness last night might have been mental. "Is it possible he won't find out?"

"I don't know. Cal will probably say something." I push the covers back and stand. "Anyway, there's no point in staying here now."

My chest aches saying the words. The only reason I messed up like this is because I really like Cal. MacCallam Lockwood Tate sneaked his way into my heart, and now the thought of leaving here, of never seeing him again... of never getting that ride...

"It's going to take a while to get over," I say quietly.

"Why do we have to leave?" Ava jumps forward, catching my hands. "Why can't we just wait and see what happens?"

"What are you talking about, 'Wait and see'? I can tell you what's going to happen. We're going to be exposed as frauds, and that will be the end of it. No exposed prince taking advantage of his country, no vindication for Reggie. We're all out, and you and I have nothing."

Her lips press into a tight frown. "We still have the Ten-K, yes?"

Nodding, I walk over to my bag to fish out the black Amex card. It's sitting in my wallet like an old fashioned insurance policy. "Yes," I say, sadly. "We still have this. I guess we can keep it."

The phone rings, but I'm not in the mood to talk. I want to crawl back under the blankets. I'd been hiding from the world under there, but also, secretly, I'd been reliving one of the best nights of my life, although I'd never admit it out loud.

Under the blankets, with my eyes shut tight, I revisit every kiss, every touch, every shiver and moan...

I can still feel his hard body against mine. I can still feel his warm skin as I trace my fingers along the lines of his chest, down his stomach, along the V of his obliques. I can still feel his rough kisses, and if I close my eyes, I can still see him sleeping just before I left him.

No one has ever made me laugh as much as he does. No one has ever helped me forget all the shit and simply let go. I'll take him with me from this job, and no matter how much we've lost, I'll always have him in my memories.

"It's for you." Ava holds the cordless room phone. "Reggie."

I make a face and take it from her, my stomach in knots. "Good morning, Reggie."

"Hello, there." His voice isn't as angry as I expected. "I have to say, you are the most unpredictable girl."

"How so?" Maybe I'll play dumb just a little bit longer. Ava wants to see what might happen.

"While I thought you'd spend the night, make a play for the king, have breakfast and possibly spend the day with him, you sneak off in the night, leaving him intrigued and wanting more."

My cheeks flash with shock. "I don't know what you mean."

"Don't play games with me. We're on the same side." His voice is somewhere between agitated and amused. "I just got off the phone with his royal highness, and he plans to invite you to the Royal Casino this evening."

"He's not angry? He still wants to see me?"

"Apparently no, and yes, respectively." Reggie pauses for a breath. "Clearly you know what you're doing when it comes to Rowan. No one else ever does."

"You're wrong..." I replay all my interactions with the broody crown prince last night. "I don't think he's interested in me at all."

"Didn't you hear what I just said? He's calling to ask you out. He's pursuing you."

I walk around the room thinking. He brought me water and ibuprofen. He brought me a gown that would fit an elephant. He gave me the lamest kiss goodnight, and I didn't hear from him again. Could he have had a change of heart while he slept?

"We kissed last night..." I say.

"You what?" Reggie is ecstatic, but a sharp banging sound across the room snaps my attention.

Ava has knocked over a vase. Thankfully it didn't break, and she hastily picks it up along with the fake flowers it held. I notice her frustrated expression and cover the receiver with my hand.

"It's okay, Ava-bug!" I whisper, giving her a reassuring smile. "No damage done."

She doesn't smile back. She only blinks quickly and leaves the room. Not sure what to make of that behavior.

"Build on that!" Reggie is saying in my ear. "Relationships take time. Get to know one another, find a reason to be alone tonight and talk. Once his emotions are involved, you'll have him."

"Ugh," I groan. "I don't like this, Reggie. I think you're wrong about Rowan. He's kind and thoughtful. I don't think he's a danger to your country. I think you're just pissed he doesn't like you."

"Are you near your computer?"

Glancing around the room, I see my Mac sitting closed on the desk. "Yes..."

I walk over to it and lift the cover. It springs to life, and I wait for instructions.

"I'm sending you an email right now. I want you to take a look at the photo attached and the article."

"Give me a second." I open my browser and go through all the steps to activate the in-room wifi. A few more clicks and I'm in the email account Reggie set up for me for this job. "What am I looking for? Never mind, here it is."

"Tell me what you see, Zelda."

Opening my one new message, I scan the text in the body:

The sovereign acts as a focus for national identity, unity and pride; gives a sense of stability and continuity; officially recognizes success and excellence; and supports the ideal of voluntary service.

"That's a mouthful," I say before double-clicking the first attachment.

My screen fills with a grainy photograph. It's a dark room, and I have to squint to make out the profile of Rowan, leaning against a wall, his head tilted back. A blonde woman is kneeling in front of him, and it looks suspiciously like he's getting a blowjob. I close the image at once.

"Was that what I think it was?" I snap.

"I can tell you what it wasn't." His tone irritates me.

"Doesn't change my feelings," I say. "The paparazzi are everywhere, and they have telephoto lenses. Rowan's a grown man. As long as that was consensual—"

"Look at the next one."

"Listen, Reg, I really don't want to see Rowan's peen again."

"That's part of your problem right there."

Behind me I hear the fast shush of feet on carpet, and I know Ava's back.

"What will I see if I open it?" Squinting my eyes, I click on the image. On my screen is a shot of him in a red nylon suit. His brow is lowered, and he's standing next to one of those weird-looking racecars. He actually looks hot.

"I don't understand," I say.

"Formula One racing is his other pastime."

"That's right... He told me he loves racing." I move back when Ava sticks her head in front of my computer. Pushing off the floor, I walk to the bedside table. "So he likes hummers and fast cars. Sounds like a typical guy to me."

"Precisely."

"How is that bad for the country? You're making a mountain out of a molehill."

"He's destabilizing our economy. He's shutting down our oil leases and meeting with experimental startup companies that would bankrupt the nation. He kicked out the existing cabinet, men with experience. I was in the middle of closing a deal with our neighboring country that would establish free trade routes—"

"*That's* what you're pissed about! You want control."

"I want what's best for Monagasco."

We're quiet again. I don't know how to argue with him.

"I didn't hire you to figure out our problems. I hired you to do a job." Reggie's accent gets thicker when he's ticked. "Are you going to do it or not?"

As I think about his question, my eyes travel around the luxurious room. Funny how fast a person can get used to the finer things. All this started with a thousand-dollar plaque down my dress, and my overwhelming desire to secure our future. With a long exhale, I relent.

"I'll do it, but I'm not lying when I say he's not into me. Attraction is something money can't buy."

"You can't be that naive. Rowan is attracted to your inheritance."

"Fake inheritance."

"I'll put another ten in your online account. Buy something nice to wear tonight. The casino has a strict dress code."

We disconnect, and I glance back to where Ava is sitting at my laptop. The first photo is open again, and her lips are pressed into a thin line.

"Don't look at that, Ave. It's not fair."

With a huff, she slaps the laptop closed before storming out of my room. Now I'm suspicious. I'm about to go after her when the phone rings again, stopping me.

"Grand central around here," I mutter, lifting the black receiver.

A deep male voice is on the line. "Zelda? It's Rowan."

My heart jumps, and I snap back into character. "Rowan! Hello..." Scrubbing my fingers over my eyes, I try not to remember his expression in that first photo.

"Why did you leave in the night like that? Are you okay?"

"I... umm, Oh, you know. Strange room and all. I couldn't sleep. Who knew my Uber app worked in Europe?"

"How is your ankle today?" His tone is stern, and I can't tell if he's concerned or angry.

"It's totally better. I told you it would be. I'm sorry, I should have left a note—"

"And Ava? Is she feeling better today as well?"

"Yep, all good. She loves the roses you sent."

"I'm glad." He pauses only briefly. "The royal casino is something of a tourist attraction. I thought you might like to see it. Tonight. With me."

My eyes narrow, and I pause. *Is he asking me out?* Maybe I'll have to revise my statement to Reggie.

Maybe our little clutch last night on the way up from the beach carried more weight than I thought. Then again there was that kiss... Not great.

"Ava is also welcome to join us," he continues, and I know I'm right. It's another group activity. "Cal will be with us."

Panic fills my stomach. "Cal?" *Shit*, and I already said my ankle was better. No getting out of this one. "That sounds great. We'd love to go."

"Excellent. I'll pick you up at eight. You don't have to gamble, although I usually play a few hands of Baccarat."

"Sure." I feel slightly nauseated as we disconnect.

I'm not sure what will happen when I see Cal again, and on top of everything, we'll be at a casino. Is it okay if I know how to gamble? Should I pretend to be clueless?

Picking up my phone, I shoot Reggie a text. *Casino date tonight is a go. Can I know how to gamble?*

Carrying my phone with me, I decide to check on my little sister. I have to pause in shock at the enormous bouquet of red roses now filling the entryway. The card is gone, so I have no idea what he wrote to her.

"Damn," I hiss under my breath, shaking my head as I head to her door. I shouldn't be miffed. So he bought her a florist's worth of flowers. He did offer to call me a whole doctor for an ankle sprain.

I'm just about to knock when Reggie's reply vibrates my phone. *Your call, although probably not wise to be a card shark. Don't be shy around CPR. Make your move. I'm counting on you.*

"My move," I mutter. "My move is falling for the wrong prince."

Ava doesn't answer when I knock, so I turn the doorknob slowly and peek in. She's dressed in one of the designer outfits Reggie bought us—tight white capris that show off her long, slim legs, with a flared black sleeveless jacket-top. She's brushing her hair a little too hard. Her pilfered aquarium bracelet shakes and sparkles on her wrist.

"Going out?" I walk over to her and put my hand on the brush.

Her rapid movements still, and our eyes meet in the mirror. "I need something to wear tonight. The casino is very formal."

"I'm sure Reggie's got it covered."

"Then I want to shop." She begins brushing again, flipping her long, dark hair over her shoulder.

"Everything okay?" I've never seen her this way. "You know, it's possible I haven't blown this job. Reggie thinks I still have a chance." *As much as I hate it.*

"You kissed Rowan, and you slept with Cal?" Her question is clipped, and embarrassment tightens my stomach. Of course, she's mad.

"You're right," I say, looking down. "I have to get my head in the game. I have to stop screwing around and focus on the prize."

She puts the brush down and faces me. She's a little softer, but I can tell she's still not happy. "I think you're doing the best you can. Don't be so hard on yourself." She picks up her clutch. "I'll be back after lunch."

"Really? We're not going to do anything together?"

"We'll catch up tomorrow. Or tonight at the casino. Mind if I take the card?"

"Of course not. The money is for both of us."

She's gone before I can say another word, and I look at myself in the mirror. My hair is still a rat's nest from hiding under the covers, so I take the brush and pull it through until it's smooth. Then I walk slowly to the tower of roses, pulling one from the throng and pressing it to my nose. Sweet perfume.

I'm back on with Rowan, but that only solves one problem. How do I pretend to care about the crown prince, when all my thoughts keep flying to his brother? How can I pretend like nothing happened last night?

I drop onto the soft green sofa and look out at the turquoise blue waters, fighting the memories of last night trying to filter into my brain. I've never failed at a job before, and I'm not going to start now. I won't choke in the biggest game of my career. I'll regroup and see this one through to the end.

CHAPTER 11: PREFERENCE

Rowan

Cal is unusually quiet on the limo ride into town. We're both wearing requisite black tuxedos, and while his hair is combed back and smooth, mine is all around my ears.

"I should have had a hair cut today," I grumble, tilting the scotch back and forth in my crystal tumbler.

He continues looking out the window, not answering. His elbow is bent, and he's pinching his top lip. It's one of his tells.

"You're going to have to loosen up if you expect to win tonight. I can tell you've been dealt a tough hand."

That brings him around. "What?"

"Why are you so distracted?"

His brow quirks, and he shifts in the seat, sliding his palms down his thighs. "Rode over to Longines this morning. That gelding has to be put down."

"Pierre?"

"He never fully recovered from his injury last fall. The vet says it's getting worse. He's in pain."

Leaning forward, I touch his knee. "Sorry, brother."

Cal shrugs. "He's twenty-five. It's time."

"Still, he was your first horse."

He leans back and polishes off his scotch. "I'll try not to let it ruin the evening."

We're at the hotel, and I give him a tight smile before sliding forward. Hajib holds the door, and the moment I look out, I call back to Cal.

"We have to hustle." A cadre of photographers is already swarming in our direction.

With a push off the plush leather, I'm across the space between the car and the front doors before they're able to catch me. Cal is right on my heels. The doormen keep them outside while I step to the house phone and call our dates.

"They're on the way down," I say. Standing beside my brother, I look through the glass at the waiting paparazzi. I can almost see their fangs gleaming. "We should have planned an escape route. I didn't expect them to be so interested."

"The word's out. You're looking for a bride, and you've been spotted with the same woman three times now."

"Zee?" I think about last night, me carrying her up from the shore in my arms, rotating her bare foot. "We need to flush out the rat at Occitan."

"I couldn't agree… more." His unexpected stutter causes me to look up. His expression is stunned, and I turn to see the ladies exiting the lift.

My own stomach tightens at the sight. Ava is wearing a two-piece long black dress with a V-neck, midriff top. I can't decide whether to focus on the soft swell of her breasts or her lined torso. Both are causing a sudden rush of blood from my head to my cock.

I have to tear my eyes away from her sexy body to greet Zelda, who's leading the two. She's equally stunning in a white dress that stops mid-thigh. Her toned legs are lined, and the bronze heels she wears are amazing. Her dress is cut out at the back, and almost appears two-piece as well, except for the small bit of fabric covering her stomach.

"Wow," I meet Zelda in the middle and take her hand. "You both look very beautiful."

She's doing that thing again, where her eyes are fixed solely on me as if she's trying not to see anyone or anything else. I don't know what it means other than I can't look at Ava.

"Thank you," she takes my hand. "Always the perfect date."

Ava makes a soft noise, and I take advantage of it to look in her direction. "I'm glad to see you're feeling better."

She blinks up at me, and once again, I'm hit with a jolt of emerald green. Her soft hair is pulled away from her face in a smooth sweep down her back, and her lips are a pale shade of pink. *I must have her tonight.* The thought stampedes in my brain.

"I can't wait to see the casino," Zelda says, taking my arm and breaking the moment. "I looked it up online, and it's gorgeous! So historic."

"It was built more than a century ago." We walk slowly to the door, and I do my best to fight my irritation when Cal takes Ava's arm. "It was one of our great-great grandmothers' ideas."

"The family was in financial ruin, and she saved us all by starting this massive enterprise," Cal says.

Zelda tenses at his voice, and I glance down to catch a hint of pink in her cheeks. "It's enormous."

"That's what she said," my brother mutters behind us, and Ava laughs.

Zee doesn't respond, but her cheeks redden more.

161

"You said you like to play Baccarat?" she says. "Is that like poker?"

"More like blackjack." I pause at the hotel entrance. "I'm afraid we've attracted the paparazzi. We'll have to dash to the car, but I'll shield you from them."

"It's like running the gauntlet." Zee mutters looking out at them.

As soon as we leave the building, the shouting begins. They call my name, they call Cal's. They ask who the women are. One bastard makes a shitty crack about me getting a hummer.

Hajib is efficient as always getting the doors open and closed and leaving the premises without killing anyone. We're all quiet inside, recovering. I'm infuriated by the blowjob remark in front of our guests, particularly Ava.

"Is that something you deal with a lot?" Zelda's eyes meet mine, and a touch of compassion is in them. "It must be miserable."

"It goes with the territory."

"Escorting beautiful women makes it worse," Cal adds quietly.

"So it's Ava's fault?" Zee laughs.

For a moment I study her. She's serious, and I confess, her humility softens me. "Don't be so quick to let yourself off the hook."

She shakes her head, and we've arrived at the casino. We're as close to the entrance as possible, as several of the photographers have followed us. We'll be safe enough once we're inside.

Another brisk run, and we're pushing through the entrance of the palatial casino, the screaming paparazzi blocked outside. Again, we pause to catch our breath and straighten our clothes.

Zelda runs her hands over her pale blonde hair and lifts her chin to look all around the grand salon. "It's enormous!" She walks across the Persian carpets to gaze at a larger than life oil painting in an ornate golden frame.

The three of us follow a few steps behind her, and while I've been in the building more times than I can remember, it's like seeing the thick, red-velvet drapes and sparkling gold leaf Corinthian accents anew.

"I love this one," Ava says.

She's looking up at a huge portrait of a woman in a field of heather that's being swept forward by the wind.

"Most of these have been here for centuries," I say. "I'm not sure who painted that one."

She looks up at me. "It's very fine. All of it is so... noble."

"Have you been to many casinos?" I know I should be with Zee, but I notice Cal is with her. They appear to be having a lively conversation, and I'll steal my moments with this beautiful lady when I can.

"I-I've been inside a few," she says hesitantly, "but only out of curiosity. I'm not allowed to gamble."

"Not allowed?" I smile, and she blinks away from my eyes.

"I don't have a poker face."

"Ah," I reach for her hand, pulling it into the crook of my arm. "That is a liability."

"So I've been told."

We start to walk, and in this position, her luscious body is very close to mine. I feel her heat, and I have to fight my primitive desire to take her. Everything in me aches for her.

"Tell me about growing up in Florida," I say in an effort to redirect. "Were you close to the coast?"

"Yes! We practically lived in the ocean, sometimes we even slept on the beach at night." Her enthusiasm is adorable.

"We?" My brow lines, and she looks startled.

"Oh..." She looks away, over her shoulder, before turning back. "My older sister... and me."

"You have a sister? What is her name?" She laughs in a way that sounds a little strangled. I stop and look at her. "Are you feeling ill?"

"Would it be possible to get a drink?" Her hand tightens on my arm, and I cover it with my hand.

"What would you like? Champagne? A cocktail?"

"Whiskey sour?"

"Whiskey?" I grin, and she looks embarrassed. "No, I'm impressed by the contradiction."

"What do you mean?" She flashes me a look, and I notice something I missed before. Ava Wilder is secretly feisty. I'm intrigued.

Stepping to her, I touch her chin with my thumb. "I'd like to know this side of you better."

Her full lips part, and my dick stirs. I have to grab the reins on my lust. We're in a public place for god's sake.

"Come," I take her hand and escort her to the elaborate bar. Like everything else, it's adorned in oil paintings, sculptures, and heavy golden accents.

The bartender is with me at once, and I place our orders. Ava stands beside me looking at the frescos on the ceiling. I take the opportunity to look at her beautiful throat and shoulders.

"Your grace." The bartender places a tall, slender whiskey sour, accented with a cherry and an orange wedge in front of me.

She nods to my plain tumbler of scotch. "It's so fancy compared to yours."

I lift it and give her a toast. "To garnish."

"You don't have to pay?" she whispers. Her lips lightly touch my ear, and fuck me.

"We have a tab," I say as I lead her through the salons, through the French doors, and out to the patio. She lifts the cherry out of her glass and slips it between her full lips. Everything this woman does is pure sex.

"If you're hungry, there are several restaurants..."

"I'm not." She smiles, turning to scan the garden. "I hope we can see the fountain. Do you think the photographers will be there screaming at us again?"

"I'll be sure you see the fountain in peace."

She glances over my shoulder at my omnipresent bodyguards. "I noticed we have company. Can't they do anything about the paparazzi?"

"Engaging with them only makes it worse, I'm afraid. We do our best to ignore them."

"In America they hide behind 'freedom of the press' laws." Her voice is angry. "Freedom of the press means we're prisoners of print."

"You're very smart." She leans against the stone archway of the balcony, and I slide the backs of my fingers down the soft skin of her arm. A gratifying sprinkle of tiny bumps appears in its wake.

"So I've been told."

"And you have no poker face." I'm reading her hand. Her soft breasts are flushed, and her breathing fast. Leaning closer, I touch her chin. "I've wanted to kiss you since we were at the aquarium."

"I know." Her eyes are focused on my shirtfront.

"Look at me," I order.

She obeys, and when I see the heat in her eyes, it's all the encouragement I need. I cover her mouth with mine, sliding my hands over her exposed back. With a soft moan, her gorgeous body melts into mine. Her shoulders rise, and the tips of her fingers touch my face. I push her lips apart, tasting her sweet mouth. She's mint laced with cherries, and every touch, every stroke of our tongues curling together fuels the fire in me.

"I want to make love to you." My voice is rough and hungry.

"Rowan," she gasps. "We need to stop. We should talk more."

I'm chasing her mouth, capturing her full lips, threading my fingers in her silky hair. I'm a junkie, and I'm finally getting the hit I've been craving for days. "We can talk later," I say, claiming her mouth again.

She moans a response, and I know she can feel my arousal. I don't care. I feel hers in every kiss, every touch. I would take her right here against this stone archway if it weren't for those fucking bodyguards.

"Let's go across the street." I glance up at the guards on duty, pretending not to watch.

"What's across the street?" she pants, one hand on my neck, the other holding my arm tightly, as if for balance.

My palm is flat against her lower back, holding her securely to me. "The Paris Hotel."

"Mm," she struggles, and I allow her to move.

She steps to the side, smoothing her hands over her dress, touching her lips lightly. I watch in frustration. I don't want her pulling away from me.

"I only meant it would give us more privacy," I say. "The guards don't have to be with us there."

Her eyes widen and she looks around. At once her cheeks flame red, and she covers them with her hands. "Oh my god, I forgot about the guards."

Stepping forward, I take her in my arms. "Please don't pull away. They're an unfortunate byproduct of who I am, but I want to know you better."

"What about Cal... and Zee? We should find them. We can't just leave without a word."

I hate that she has a point. "Cal will look out for your friend. She seems to enjoy his company better anyway."

Emerald eyes flash to mine, so beautiful. "She thought she was coming here with you tonight. I'm ruining your plans."

"The only plan I had for tonight was you."

Pushing away, she shakes her dark head as she walks across the patio to the heavy stone rail. Her black skirt swirls around her legs, and the lines in her torso deepen as she walks. She's so fucking gorgeous.

"I thought Cal was the playboy prince." It's a sharp accusation, and I'm taken aback.

"What does that mean?"

"It seems you get hummers from anonymous women, last night you kissed my sister, and tonight you want *me* to go to bed with you?"

I'm at a loss. My brain swiftly catalogs her complaints, searching for a rebuttal. "Your sister?"

"I... I mean... Yes!" She's momentarily flustered. "Zee is like a sister to me. Sometimes we even call each other *sister*. Is that all you got from what I said?"

"No, I'm sorry, I just wasn't following you for a moment." I look away. The top of the enormous fountain is just visible over the hedges. "I don't know what to say. Yes, I kissed Zelda last night. She had hurt her ankle, and I carried her to the house. It was a thank you kiss, nothing more."

Her back is to me, and I want to break down these barriers. I want to have her. Perhaps that does make me a playboy prince, but I don't think in those terms.

I touch her soft shoulder. "The first night I saw you, you quoted Robert Frost. *Passionate preference; love at first sight.* Why did you say those lines?"

Shanking her head, she does a little shrug. "It came into my mind. I don't know why." She walks away, crossing the space to the stone arch.

I'm right behind her, making her face me. "I'm not playing games, Ava. I want to know your mind. We can go back inside and find your friend, but after this night, I want to know you in every way. I don't want anyone else."

Her eyes move to my lips, and I know she isn't offended by my words. I know she wants the same thing as me. I can feel it in her kiss.

"I should say no," she answers. "I don't want to be just a nameless face to you, another random woman who satisfies your needs and is later forgotten."

"You're so much more than that. Let me show you."

She only hesitates a moment before surrendering to my request.

Chapter 12: Focus

Zelda

Cal steps between me and looking for Ava. "You walked out on me last night." His full lips narrow into that sexy grin. "I want to be angry, but... Damn. Look at you."

Not going there with him. "I like your coat," I deflect, flicking a finger over his black sleeve. "Interesting detail. Is that paisley?"

"Who gives a fuck?" He lifts his arm, and in the bright light, the faintest design appears in the fabric. "It's Ming dynasty, I think. Pretty basic for Balmain."

"Is he the royal designer?"

"If he is, he wouldn't work with me. I picked this out at a show last spring."

"Wearing a year-old tux? Shocking! No wonder he skipped you," I tease, walking slowly across the polished marble floor. An enormous black star is in the center. "You know, they have a replica of this place in Vegas? They have replicas of all the great casinos there."

"Have you been?"

I shake my head. "Now I never will. It would be too depressing."

"No arrogant princes following you around?"

Glancing to the side, I smile. "You're not so arrogant."

"I must be. I'm convinced you should choose me over him."

The tone in his voice is serious, and a little charge moves through my stomach. It makes me miserable. I've already chosen him over Rowan, but I can't let it happen. As much as I prefer spending time with him, I can't blow this opportunity for Ava and me.

"Speaking of *him*, where is his royal majesty?"

"Probably playing Baccarat. Are you asking me to take you there?"

I can't tell if he's angry or not. He has an impeccable poker face. "You can get me a drink."

"Your wish is my command. Champagne?"

"I think I had enough champagne last night. Gin and tonic."

"Shit. I was hoping to cloud your judgment again." He gives me a wink and saunters off to the elaborate bar.

I look down at my fingers twisting together. I've got to find Rowan. I've got to get my head out of the clouds and my ass with the crown prince. I wore this dress, these heels, all of it to entice him. Here I am reveling in the attentions of the wrong man.

Only a few moments pass, and he's back. "Speaking of Balmain, you should go with me to the spring show. They're one of the few houses that uses live orchestration."

"I've never been to a fashion show."

"That settles it, then." He leans forward and whispers, "I'll get that cherry."

My heart beats faster. "Were you expecting to get another one?"

"No." He stops and catches my chin, stealing a brief kiss along with my breath. "I'm not such a sexist prig to think if you're not *my* first, I should be yours."

"You're the very model of a modern playboy prince."

"*Pirates of Penzance?*"

Exhaling a laugh, I shake my head. "I've never seen it. I got that from that god-awful *Pirate Movie.*"

We've been walking since we got our drinks, and now we're at the back entrance to the casino. He leads me out the ornate doors onto a long terrace overlooking the sea. The moon is just rising, touching the water with silvery tips. It's gorgeous.

"You hate every movie," he says.

"I do not. I just have a low tolerance for crap."

Cal sits on the stone railing in front of me, and his warm hands cover the exposed skin on my hips as he pulls me close to his body.

"Where did you acquire such a refined taste in film?" He leans forward to kiss the side of my neck, and that little fish in my middle is flipping all over the place.

"Cal..." Setting my drink down, I push against his shoulders.

He only tightens his hold. "I'm not letting you go, so stop struggling. Now answer my question."

My entire body is on fire. "My parents loved classic films. It's where Ava..." *Shit!* "I mean, um... It's *why* Ava and I became friends."

"You have parents in common?" Another burning kiss.

"Our parents were a lot alike."

"Interesting," he murmurs, moving higher into my hair. My knees go liquid, and I almost collapse. "You smell delicious."

His kisses travel to my jaw. Somehow I manage to bend my elbows and push myself out of his arms.

"Seriously, Cal, we're not doing this."

"Why the devil not? We did a damn good job of it last night."

"I'd had too much champagne last night."

His hazel eyes flash. "I'm calling bullshit on that, Miss Benedict, you were *not* drunk last night."

I start to walk away, but he's right behind me, catching my arm. "Wait. I'm sorry. Don't go. Let's talk some more."

It's a mistake. I know it with every fiber of my being, but I don't leave. "It's really beautiful here. I love the water."

"We can walk down to the shore and look for ghost crabs," he says, sliding my hair off my cheek with his finger. "If you twist your ankle, I'll carry you this time."

"Cal—" My argument is lost in his mouth covering mine.

He kisses me the way he always does, passionate and consuming. Our lips part, his tongue finds mine, and my panties flood with heat. Warm hands slide over my bare back, dipping lower, into the back of my dress. I push my fingers into his hair and pull him closer to me. Oh, god, I should stop this, but I want it so much.

"I love this dress," he murmurs against my cheek, and pleasure snakes up my thighs along with his fingers.

He's lifting my skirt, making his way to the center. I hold my breath, waiting for him to discover…

"Fuck me," he hisses, and our eyes lock. That naughty grin splits his cheeks. "Somebody forgot her panties tonight."

Laughter explodes from my lips, and I drop my forehead against his shoulder. "Oh my god," I groan as his finger slides over my clit, making me jump. "Oh, god, Cal." I'm not arguing anymore, I'm begging.

"You don't have to beg, beautiful, I'll make you come." Husky words, lost in our mouths as he kisses me again, deeper, taking what he wants. It's what we both want.

Instinctively, my knee rises, allowing my skirt to go higher on my legs. Cal never stops touching me, sliding his fingers rapidly over that rigid little button until my thighs begin to tremble.

A strangled moan is lost in his mouth. He rotates his hand and plunges two thick fingers deep inside me, while still massaging my clit. My grip tightens on his arms, my nails cut into the fabric of his coat as I start to come.

"Oh, god... Oh, Oh, Cal!" I'm gasping, shamelessly riding his hand.

"Yes, fuck it out, sexy." His voice is hot in my ear, his lips touching the skin just behind it. Chills fly down my arms, and the muscles deep in my core spasm again. "Damn, I wish my dick were in there."

"Cal," I whisper. He's so dirty. Who knew I'd be so turned on by his wicked mouth?

"What do you want, sexy?" His face hovers over mine. My eyes are still closed, and through the haze, I feel him kiss them gently. He kisses my nose. "You want more?"

Hell, yes, I want more. Blinking up at him, I can't say it. He's so fucking gorgeous here in the moonlight. I'm slowly coming down. My breath is becoming calmer, and all I want is him. I want all of him.

"What am I going to do?" I don't mean to say it out loud, but too late.

"You're going to come with me across the street to the Paris Hotel, and we're going to spend the night together in one of their penthouse suites. I have a fantasy to act out."

He pulls his hand out of my dress, and steps back. I'm frozen in place watching him. Our eyes are locked as he slips those two amazing fingers into his mouth, tasting me on them.

"Delicious," he says, giving me a wink.

I almost collapse. He pulls a handkerchief out of his back pocket, and uses it to finish cleaning up. I push my skirt lower on my hips, feeling the remnants of what we did slick on my thighs.

"I've got to visit the powder room." I hold the wall behind me until I'm sure I have my balance. "Then I'm going to find Ava."

My brain might be scrambled by this sexy player, but I'm not going anywhere without knowing where she is and talking to her. It's what we do, and nothing can make me forget about my responsibility to her.

Cal's lips twist. I know by the tent in his slacks he wants more now. Hell, I want more now, but I'm not the type who forgets everything important the minute she orgasms, no matter how fantastic it is. I've never been that person.

"You're going to kill me, Zelda Benedict," he sighs, placing a palm on the stone wall beside my head and leaning forward.

I step to the side and turn quickly into the casino. "I'll meet you inside, then you can take me to that Baccarat room."

* * *

176

Rowan

As I wait for Ava to emerge from the powder room, I speak to the head of my security team. "I want you to sweep the area by the fountain. We're headed that way, and I don't want a single fucking photographer in the area."

"Yes, sir," the man says, and he signals two of the guards. They leave us with still two more men in dark suits lingering in the periphery.

Ava walks out, and as soon as our eyes meet, my stomach tightens. She's reapplied her lipstick, and her hair is smoother.

"I didn't mean to muss you," I say when she returns to my side. I don't hesitate to take her hand in mine, and she doesn't pull away. It's a small sign of progress.

"Occupational hazard?" She slants her eyes at me.

"If only my occupation were so enjoyable."

"Didn't you want to play Baccarat? Zee's probably looking for us there."

"I've told security our plans. I'd like to show you the fountain... if you still want to see it?"

Her beautiful smile appears. "I would love to see it."

I lift her small hand to my lips and kiss the tops of her fingers. "I want to give you the things you love."

The softness in her eyes is very encouraging. I lead her out the side doors and down the wide, stone staircase. We follow a curved sidewalk lined with different varieties of palms.

A small crowd has gathered to watch the water show. I scan the area and see my men stationed near the entrances. I intentionally wore a plain black tux, no insignia, hoping to blend in. Still the word gets out. My hope is we can make it through the four-minute show without attracting attention.

Instead of staying apart, I lead us into the middle of the group to use them as camouflage. My back is to the low, stone railing, and I position Ava in front of me, her back against my chest. Her head is just at my jaw, and I slide my palm over the skin of her flat stomach. She flinches slightly, but her hand finds mine, and our fingers lace just as the show begins.

Rainbow lights fill the streams of water, and they swirl and dance to the music of a Bach suite for cello. The way I'm holding her, I feel her every response to the display. The music swells, and her breath quickens. I can't resist, I lean down and press my lips to the side of her neck, just behind her hair. Her grip on my hand tightens, and I know she's mine. It's the finale, and all that's left is to take her the short distance across the street to the Paris Hotel.

The final drops of water descend into the pool. The crowd claps softly before beginning to disperse, and she turns to face me. Our fingers are still entwined, and she's smiling. Her eyes sparkle, and the moon highlights the tips of her hair.

"What now?" she says softly.

"Let's walk." Then I hesitate. "Unless your shoes—"

"I came prepared," she laughs, moving her skirt aside to show me the bronze leather sandals she's wearing. "I'd love to walk."

"You're tall," I say, without thinking. "I like that."

She grins. "It's okay. I've gotten used to being the tall girl. Apparently, my tall father married my short mother, and I took after Dad."

"Tell me about your parents."

Her hand is in my arm, and we're walking down the beige stones, under black lanterns topped with white globes.

"I only know them through what my sister's told me. I was so young when they died."

"You lived with relatives?"

She shakes her head, and I don't miss the shadow that clouds her expression. "We were orphans. I guess we still are."

"I'm sorry." Sliding my fingers over the back of her hand, I try to imagine how her life has been. "Were you alone?"

"We were put in the foster care system." She says no more, but I can infer the rest from her tone.

"It was a bad experience?"

"We ultimately ran away. I spent a few years hiding under bridges and sneaking into boat houses until we started making enough money to afford a room."

I'm surprised by the tightness in my chest at this revelation. I haven't known her long enough to feel this burn of protectiveness toward her.

"We're so far removed from the States. We have a fairytale notion someone like you would naturally have a safe place to live and plenty of food to eat."

"They should..." her voice trails off, and I'm sorry I led us down this dark train of thought. She breaks it, however. "Enough of that. Tell me about your family. What is it like growing up as the future king of Monagasco?"

Smoothing the back of her hand with mine, I think about my childhood. "I wasn't spoiled. My parents tried to give Cal and me as normal a life as possible."

"Considering you had everything you wanted?" She laughs, and I know she's teasing.

"It's true, but they made us do chores, pick up after ourselves. We weren't allowed to be wasteful or selfish. We had to go with them to charity events, serve at soup kitchens, all that sort of thing."

She stops walking and faces me. The white streetlights glow golden in her hair. "It's why you're kind. I've felt it from the start."

A breeze whispers around us, sending a lock of her dark hair across her cheek. I catch it and move it away. Her green eyes are stunning against her tanned skin.

"I confess, my thoughts haven't been kind since I've met you." I exhale a laugh. "All I can think of is seeing you naked."

Her lips press into a grin and she starts to laugh. "You certainly have a one-track mind."

"I feel like I should apologize, but dammit. I won't."

It's her turn to surprise me. She presses that gorgeous body into my chest and slides back the lock of too-long hair that's fallen across my forehead.

"I won't apologize either, then. I've wanted to see you naked since that first night on the balcony."

"Are you saying you'll go with me to the hotel?"

"Will I get my wish?" Her fingers have moved to the base of my neck, and I grasp her bare torso, pulling her hard against me.

"How fast can you walk?"

Her nose wrinkles. "I'm pretty fast when I need to be."

"I feel the need to move quickly."

She laughs softly, as I kiss her teasing lips.

Chapter 13: Evening

Zelda

Cal wears a satisfied grin walking back from checking in with the royal guards. I can only imagine what he's about to say.

"His royal majesty and Miss Wilder left an hour ago. You know what that means?" The look on his face makes my stomach squirm.

"What? Where did they go?" I want to be angry at Ava for doing what I wouldn't, but at the same time, I disappeared on her again. At least she's with the crown prince and his team of bodyguards.

"The Paris Hotel was their ultimate destination. It means they're off to do some royal fucking." His hand snakes around my waist, pulling me close. "We should follow their lead."

My chest clenches unexpectedly. "What?" Ava and Rowan? "That's impossible. Why would you say that?"

"Perhaps because he's obsessed with her. He sent her flowers, he can't keep his eyes off her, and he looks like he wants to punch me in the face whenever I touch her."

"What the hell?" I walk slowly to one of the blackjack tables where only two men in tuxedoes are playing. Cal is behind me, but I'm too distracted to notice.

How did I miss this? Would Ava throw the job? I suppose I've already thrown it telling her I slept with Cal.

"Miss?" The dealer looks at me expectantly, and I scan the rules for the table.

Twenty Euro minimum. I take one of the colorful chips from my bag and place it on the table to start my hand. The dealer nods and passes me two cards.

Facing up is a six of hearts, and my lips twist. *Not very good.* We turn over the other card, and it's a five spades. I cast a quick glance at what he's got, an Ace of diamonds.

"Double down," I say automatically.

Next round, I get an eleven, dealer a queen of hearts. The men beside me make noises of approval. I now have eighty Euro.

"One more," I say, tapping my finger in front of me.

Two kings.

"Split," I say, feeling my insides start to relax.

Cards are easy. Blackjack makes sense. People are hard. I reach into my bag and place four twenty-Euro chips on the table. Cards go around, I'm dealt a ten of hearts and an Ace of spades. The two men playing with me make louder noises.

Cal leans down and speaks in my ear. "Someone knows her way around the blackjack table."

At once I snap out of it, realizing what I'm doing. "Must be beginner's luck," I laugh as the dealer passes me eight twenty-Euro stacks. "Would you change those to fifties, please?"

He pulls them back and slides three white chips across the table along with one twenty chip. I slip them along with the remaining two chips in my bag, and when I stand, I can't miss Cal's expression.

"I feel like there's something you're not telling me," he says with a grin.

"I told you my dad liked to gamble."

"You didn't tell me you did."

Shrugging, I walk slowly away from the table. "We would play blackjack when it rained."

"Must've rained a lot."

"We were in Florida, so you know."

"Florida? I thought you grew up in Texas?"

Jesus! This revelation about Ava has me completely floored. I'm forgetting everything! "He lived in Florida... after my parents divorced." Blinking fast, I keep spinning the lie. "It's how I met Ava."

I glance up, and Cal's eyes narrow. I'm not sure he believes me, but I can't worry about that now. Now all I can think about is Reggie and what's going to happen when he finds out. If Rowan's security guards know, what's to stop them from telling the grand duke? I stop when we reach the small gallery of couches and plush chairs. Cal stops in front of me, and he's frowning, arms crossed.

"What?" I say, hesitantly.

"I'm trying to figure out what's got you so thrown. The fact that Rowan's with Ava or vice versa."

Taking a deep breath, I give just a little. "I'm worried about her. She's younger than me, and... inexperienced."

"You're worried because she's a virgin?"

My eyes flash. "That's none of your business."

Both his hands go up. "You said it."

Now I feel even worse. I'm moving fast, and Cal's right with me, waiting as I exchange my chips at the cashier and following as I go through the doors. I skip down the stairs, past the line of exotic, ultra-expensive sports cars parked out front, past the large, mirrored sculpture, to the line of fountains.

Only then I stop, stepping forward to the low wall surrounding the arched spray. Cal is beside me, hands in his pockets, and I'm sure he's waiting for what the hell I'll do next. I don't even know.

Wrapping one arm over my stomach, I glance up at him. "I'm sorry, I just... I feel responsible for her."

He smiles and steps to me, putting a hand on my waist and pulling me to his side. I don't fight him. I kind of like the comfort of Cal's arms. It's the first time I've been with a man who didn't make me feel defensive or protective in a long time.

"I think it's nice you worry about your friend. It means you have a good heart."

I look at my pewter nails, thinking about the reason we're even in Monagasco. "I'm not so sure about that."

He turns me to face him, and warm fingers catch my chin, forcing my eyes to his. "I'm sure."

This time when he smiles, it's different. He's not teasing me, he's not flirting. It's genuine concern, and I feel a little shift in my chest, like something changed.

He leans forward and rests his forehead against mine. My eyes close, and I feel his lips touch my nose. It makes me smile. It makes my insides unclench.

"Thanks," I say, leaning back. "I guess I had a moment. She is a grown woman, right?" *As much as I hate not having a plan for this.*

My lip catches in my teeth. I think about what I know of Rowan, how he helped me after I twisted my ankle, carrying me to my room, the ibuprofen and water, the gown the size of a circus tent. Then I think about my other concern. "You don't think the guards will tell everyone, do you? That's she's with him?"

"They only told me because I asked, because of you."

I feel a distinct sense of relief at those words. Cal's fingers lace with mine as we approach the next fountain, and I step closer to his side. The arched water is lit with bright yellow lights, and for a moment we pause to watch it.

"You shouldn't worry," he says. "Rowan is pretty decent when it comes to women. He's not an asshole like me."

That makes me laugh. "How are you an asshole?"

A little shrug and we're walking again. My heels make clicking noises on the beige stone pavers.

"It's what the media calls me, the Playboy Prince."

"What makes you a playboy?" I squint up at him, and he's studying the path ahead of us.

"I don't know," he says quietly. "I've been caught in a few interesting situations."

"Is that so?"

He clears his throat. "I think it's more because I rarely date the same person twice. I get bored easily."

"Hmm... I guess I've been warned."

187

"Not you," he says, with a laugh. "I can't tell what you're going to do from one moment to the next."

We've rounded the last fountain, and beyond a stand of banana trees, I see the Paris Hotel rising into the sky. His proposal from earlier in the evening crosses my mind. I'm feeling less worried and more playful now that I know Ava's safe and we're not likely to be caught. At least not tonight.

"So about the Paris Hotel... Do you have a standing reservation? Should I ask for The Playboy Prince Suite?"

"I wish. It's more a byproduct of having an owner's share. We have standing reservations."

"Your family owns the hotel?" We emerge from the garden path, and the full façade of the enormous building comes into view. My mouth drops open, and I stop walking.

"Wow," I whisper.

"Pretty impressive, isn't it?"

I follow him up the stairs to the ornate, dark-wood entrance of the elaborate hotel. Inside it's decorated to match the casino, with blue Persian rugs and tall, white ceilings covered in statues and scrollwork.

Cal goes straight to the desk, where the attendant recognizes him at once. "Your majesty." He does a little bow, and Cal only waves.

"Is the Garnier suite available?"

"Ahh," the man whispers, leaning forward, "I'm afraid not. Your brother —"

"Right, nevermind. How about 3-2-1?"

"Of course. One moment, sir."

The card is passed across the desk, and Cal pulls me to him, wrapping an arm around my shoulder as

188

we walk to the elevator. "You'll like this one. It's all the way at the top and *lots* of champagne."

He kisses my temple, and I laugh.

"How is it at the top when it's numbered 321?"

A momentary pause, then he seems to understand. "No, it's a countdown. Three, two, one. The theme actually changes quarterly, depending on the sponsor."

"Sounds like you stay here a lot."

"When Rowan is in the Grand Prix, it's the best place for watching the race. Otherwise the traffic is prohibitive."

The elevator is all mirrors and gleaming, dark wood. Once we're inside, he slides his card before hitting the button for the top floor. The doors close, and he pulls my arm, positioning me between his body and the mirrored wall.

"Feeling better?" Hazel eyes hold mine a moment.

I trace a finger along the line of his jaw, thinking how this might be the last time we're together. It's a sad thought, I decide to put out of my head.

"Yes," I say softly, and in that moment, the space between us disappears.

His mouth is on mine, pushing my lips apart. A little whimper squeaks from my throat as our tongues curl against each other's. I have to hold the lapels of his coat to keep from sliding down the cool wall in a puddle. Warm hands are again on the bare skin of my waist, but this time, his thumbs slide to the front of my dress, teasing the skin on my stomach. I groan as the bell rings, and the elevator stops.

"I'm ready to get you out of that dress," he says, taking my hand and pulling me out of the shiny, mirrored box to the gleaming entrance of the suite.

"Dom Pérignon?" I read on the plaque above the numbers *3-2-1!*

"I told you," he slides the card and the door opens. "*Lots* of champagne."

We stop just inside the door for another kiss, and as it closes, I feel his fingers working behind my neck, sliding the zipper down the back of my dress. His lips chase mine, and my top falls to my waist, revealing the pink satin demi-bra that only covers the lower half of my breasts. My nipples play peek-a-boo over the tops of the lace edges.

"Jesus, it just gets better," he groans deeply, leaning down to cup the bottom of one and pull my beaded nipple between his lips, soaking the lace.

The sensation registers directly between my thighs, and I let out a little moan, threading my fingers into the sides of his hair.

"Cal," I gasp. "You're getting my bra all wet."

"To match those panties... Oh, right," he teases, with a wink.

With a flick of his wrist, his bow tie undone. Coat off, he unbuttons his top two buttons followed by his cuffs, never taking his eyes off me. I shiver at the darkness brimming there.

"Take off that dress," he says in a low voice, as he pulls his shirt over his head, exposing his lined torso.

I reach down to unfasten my heels, and he stops me. "No, leave those on. Just the dress."

Straightening, my back is still against the wall, I hook my thumbs in the sides of my skirt and shimmy it over my hips. It lands on the floor in a soft thump around my heels, and I step out. Cal stops moving, and I'm sure I'll burst into flames at his expression. His gaze moves from my breasts, down the line of my stomach to my bare pussy, down my legs to the gold, strappy heels. I see his Adam's apple move once before he steps forward, catching my face roughly in his grip and pulling my mouth to his.

Once our lips collide, his other hand moves straight between my legs, cupping me, plunging two fingers deep inside. My gasp of shock and passion disappears in his mouth. I'm grasping at his arms, his shoulders, my nails scratching his skin.

"Come with me," he says, his voice low and thick.

He takes my hand and pulls me through the suite to the small bedroom. Windows are all around overlooking the lights of the night, but I don't see them. All I see is him. I'm on the bed in a toss, and his hands move along the waist of his black pants. They're off, and he's with me, holding my shoulder as he finds my mouth. He lies back on the bed, and I know what he wants. I'm across him in a straddle, reaching around for his hard length, positioning it before I drop down, taking him all the way, balls deep.

"Fuck me," he hisses, as I sit up straight. He's lying back against the pillows, eyes sparkling, and I roll my hips, rocking him into me.

I pull the band out of my hair, and it falls around my shoulders. Reaching behind me, I unfasten my bra and toss it aside so the curling tips of my hair tickle just beneath my hardened nipples. I rise up on my knees and drop down, rotating my hips again.

"Fuck—it's so much better than my fantasy," he gasps.

I feel powerful. I've never felt this way before. Leaning forward, I put my hands on either side of his head and kiss him deeply. He's thrusting, still moving inside me, stretching and massaging me in the most erotic way. In this position, my clit is pressed against his skin, and the friction of our bodies sends waves of pleasure snaking down my legs.

Now I'm pushing his lips apart, finding his tongue. His fingers cut into my ass as he grips me. I'm panting and gasping, chasing the orgasm just within my reach. We're moving faster. He's hitting me hard, rocking into me, when *SLAP!* I jump at the sting of his palm against my ass.

"Oh!" I cry from the surprise, pleasure mixed with stinging pain.

His hands rub and knead my flesh and again *SLAP!* another hard strike against my ass.

"Oh, god..." I start to tremble. My thighs shake as I start to come.

I'm rocking my hips against him faster, grinding out my orgasm, and he's gripping me, moving me over him. The pleasure tightens in my pelvis. My teeth clench and my eyes squeeze shut as the most powerful orgasm rockets through my body. I make noises I don't recognize, animalistic and wild. He groans deeply, holding me, riding out this explosion with me.

We roll together so I'm on my back, and he finishes, thrusting hard and then tapering off, rocking in a rhythm that brings us down from a high I never imagined.

Our lips meet, kissing softer, tasting each other gently. I reach up to cup his cheeks as our lips follow each other's again and again while we slow to a long embrace.

Cal's large hand smooths my hair away before sliding down the length of my body. He's over me, propped on his elbows, and our eyes meet. We hold each other in that gaze a few moments. I feel like I'm in a place I never knew existed.

"We haven't even gotten to the champagne yet," he says with that trademark naughty grin.

My eyes close, and I exhale a laugh. His hands are near my face, and I feel him touching my skin, sliding his thumb across my lips before he leans down and kisses me again, a little rougher this time. My mouth opens automatically, and our tongues embrace. I reach up to hold him, sliding my fingers over the lines of his neck and shoulders.

"Shit, Zee," he groans, dropping beside me on the mattress and pulling me to him without a moment's hesitation. "You have to stay longer than a week. You have to stay through the race. I need you here for that."

Laughing, I trace my finger along the lines in his stomach, back and forth over the six-pack of his abs. "You need me here for a race?"

"It'll be boring without you. The same old crowd doing the same old shit."

I prop my head on my hand so our eyes can meet. "We can talk about it tomorrow."

"Tomorrow?" he looks over his shoulder at the clock. "I'll unplug the clock and order room service."

I laugh as he scoots off the bed, his perfectly chiseled muscles flexing as he moves around the room. He takes a black binder off the desk and returns to me in the bed, leaning against the headboard as he opens it to the food menu.

"Give me that," I say, taking it from him.

"Order carbs." He kisses my shoulder, sliding down to rest his head in my lap. "We're going to be burning a lot of calories tonight."

Flipping the pages, I land on a Mediterranean pizza that sounds delicious. "I found it! Pizza and champagne." Leaning forward, I reach for the room phone while he coils around my waist.

I'm just pressing the buttons as he playfully bites my hip. The server thinks I'm insane, but I manage to say what we want between being bitten and Cal's insistence on leaving a hickey on my breast.

"She said twenty minutes." I drop the phone on the base.

"Just enough time for Round 2!" He tosses the binder on the floor and pulls my body back to his. I'm powerless to resist as he kisses his way down the length of my torso.

CHAPTER 14: FANTASIES

Rowan

The Garnier suite balcony overlooks the fountains and the gardens spreading out in front of the Royal Casino. I've opened a bottle of champagne, and I stand with Ava watching the glowing orange fountains and the tourists strolling in the moonlight.

"No matter what happens, I can never forget this night," she says softly, looking over the grounds below.

"A rather ominous thought, yes?" I reach up and smooth a lock of dark hair off her shoulder.

She blinks to me and smiles. "It's only accurate. The last few weeks have been so unexpected. I can't imagine what's next."

"I agree with you on that." I think about everything that's happened since that ridiculous photo hit the tabloids. "I thought my life was torture enough, and then it got worse. Then I found you."

Setting her glass down, she places both hands on my shoulders. "I wasn't supposed to meet you. None of this was supposed to happen."

I set my wine glass aside as well and cup her cheeks. "Who decides what's supposed to happen? We *did* meet, and I haven't been able to stop thinking about you since."

Pulling her close, I capture her mouth in a passionate kiss. Her soft lips open to me, and as our tongues slide together, heat floods my pelvis. My erection strains against my zipper. I want to be inside her. I want to ease this prolonged tension in her warm body.

She steps back, placing her palm against my cheek and sliding her thumb down my lips. She hesitates, and her eyes lock on mine as she nudges it into my mouth. I give it a firm suck, and I'm rewarded with a sharp gasp. Her lips part.

"Ava," I say in a voice just a notch above a groan. "I need to be inside you."

She nods, turning her back to me. In a sweep, her long hair is over her shoulder. "Help me with my top."

A small silver zipper is exposed, and I carefully slide it down, watching the fabric fall away until only her black bra is left. She turns to face me, and my breath skips at the unforgettable sight of her breasts covered in sheer black lace. Her dark nipples tease me through the thin fabric, and my body aches for her.

"You're so beautiful," I whisper. "I want you so badly."

"I want you," she whispers in response.

I watch, mesmerized as she reaches behind her, and her bra falls away. Her breasts are bare, nipples tight. I reach up to grasp one, rolling the tight bud between my fingers as she moans. She's still wearing her skirt, and I'm still in my tux.

"Give me just a moment." I swiftly undo my tie, shrug off my jacket, and unbutton my shirt enough so I can pull it over my head.

She watches, biting her lip as I swiftly remove my clothes. Once my chest is bare, I pull her to me, pressing her gorgeous breasts against my chest. It feels so good.

"Let me do the biting tonight," I say, kissing the side of her jaw before giving it a little nip.

She exhales a moan and pushes her arms around my neck, pulling us closer together. We're still on the balcony, under the gorgeous moonlight with the beautiful view of the fountain and gardens below, the sea just behind them. The night air is cool, and I reach down to remove my pants quickly.

My erection is pointed right at her, and her eyes darken as she leans down to remove her skirt. I imagine her taking me between those pillow lips, sucking me to ecstasy—but not before I've come between her thighs.

I sit in the chair, and she moves to me. My hands are on her waist, and I pull her onto my lap in a straddle. She holds a square condom packet, and I wait as she tears it open, positioning it over my tip and rolling it down my length, leaving room for the massive orgasm that's been building all night.

Grasping her hips, I'm ready to plunge deep into her hot core, but she tenses. I hesitate a moment. "Is something wrong?"

She blinks down and shakes her head. "I'm sorry." Her voice is quiet. "I'm not a virgin, but..."

Straightening, I pull her to me, smoothing her dark hair off her face. "What is it, Ava?"

Her chin drops, and her cheeks flame red. My brow lines in confusion, and I lift her in my arms, carrying her inside to the enormous king-sized bed. I move the thick blankets aside and ease us to the center, her on her back and me beside her.

"Tell me," I say gently. "Why are you afraid?"

"I'm embarrassed," she whispers, her beautiful green eyes fixed on my shoulders.

I touch her so lightly along her face, down her cheek. "You don't have to be embarrassed with me. I want to know everything about you."

She clears her throat softly. "Just... please be gentle. I've never been with someone because I wanted to."

My brow lines as I try to understand. "Do you mean—?"

"Don't," she whispers, reaching up to touch my lips. "I want this to be perfect."

The meaning of what she said twists in my stomach. That protectiveness I felt earlier roars to life in my chest, now along with a knot of anger. I pull her to me, burying my face in her sweet smelling hair and inhaling deeply as I hold her. Her small hands are around me, holding me just as close. She's not fighting me; she's not pulling away. She's trusting me with knowledge I hate knowing.

Lifting my head, I look deep into her eyes. "I will never hurt you, Ava," I say, infusing the words with all the conviction I feel in my chest.

She only studies my face a moment before she smiles. "I know. It's why I'm here."

Reaching for her neck, I gently pull her beautiful mouth to mine. Her hands are on my neck, my shoulders, and I take her lips gently, then with a little more force. She meets me with equal intensity, and it's what I need to know.

I push her lips apart with my mouth, and as our tongues connect and curl together, my erection surges back. She exhales a soft moan, and my kisses move to her chin, down to her beautiful breasts. I slide my palms over one, covering a nipple with my mouth and giving it a firm suck, a little bite.

Her back arches, and she moans louder. I'm moving lower, to the strip of lace across her hips. Clasping both sides, I jerk them off her, and sigh at the sight of her bare pussy, a bit of cream hiding inside.

She makes a little cry when I pull her to my mouth, tasting her, sliding my tongue up and down the length of her slit. Her hips jump, and she moans. Her flat stomach quivers, and I'm determined to make her come hard.

"You want this," I say, nipping the inside of her thigh, rising higher to kiss the crease in her leg.

"Yes... oh, god, yes!" she gasps, gripping in the sheets.

I'm back on her, running my tongue up and around her slick folds not stopping until I feel her break. I kiss her clit, pulling the tight little bud again and again until she's no longer shaking, she's crying out, trying to wriggle away.

"Okay," I say with a grin, releasing her thighs and kissing her stomach, sliding my tongue up the length of her body until I'm over her, looking deep into her sexy eyes, shining with satisfaction.

"My turn," I whisper, kissing her full lips.

She holds my face, kissing me back hard as I plunge deep into her swollen depths. She's hot and soft and so fucking tight.

"Oh, god!" she gasps, her nails cutting into my skin.

I instantly slow my pace, finding her eyes. "Are you okay?" I whisper, stroking her cheek with my thumb.

"You're so big," she gasps. "I feel so... full."

"Am I hurting you?" My brow tightens. I'm so fucking gone, I don't know what I'll do if she says yes.

She pauses a moment that feels like an eternity before shaking her head. "No, it-it feels... *good.*" Her cheeks flood with pink, and I kiss her again, holding her face as I begin to rock her. I couldn't stop if I tried.

Her body is so sexy, so hot and tight, and now she's moving with me, bucking her hips and working my dick like we've been here before. My ass tightens, and I feel my orgasm mounting. A bead of sweat rolls down my cheek, and I lean up to pull the soft skin of her jaw between my teeth.

"Oh, Rowan," she whispers, moving her hips faster. "Oh, god!" she gasps, and I reach down between us, searching for that place between her thighs.

I fumble for her clit, covering the top of her mound and massaging the sides as my hips move faster. When I touch her center, she gasps, and her insides clench just before breaking into spasms. Tightness explodes through my pelvis. I'm pulsing, filling that fucking condom, blacking out from intense pleasure.

"Oh fuck," I gasp, holding her, my eyes squeezed shut. My dick pulses deep inside her, and her muscles continue working me, pulling and milking.

"Ava." It's a ragged groan through the waves of orgasm.

We're holding each other. She holds my shoulders, clinging to me as much as I am to her. I lift my head and find her mouth, kissing her like she's water in the desert. Our lips part, tongues collide, and we consume again and again.

She's sweet and innocent and sexy and intoxicating. I'm not sure how I'll ever get enough of her passionate soul.

"Ava," I whisper her name, sliding my fingers up to her soft hair and down the side of her beautiful face.

She reaches up and cups my cheeks, holding me as she kisses my face. I turn and kiss her palm.

"Your majesty," she whispers then exhales a small laugh. Her green eyes roll and she shakes her head.

"What?" I can't stand to think she's second-guessing this.

"A king," she says, with another little laugh. "How can I have fallen for a king?"

Satisfaction floods my chest. I lean up and prop my head on my hand. Running my other down the length of her body. I pause at her soft breast, circling my thumb over her nipple and watching it harden in response. I flatten my palm against her stomach then wrap it around to cup her gorgeous ass. Glancing up, I meet her eyes studying me, watching my reaction to her body's responses.

"Have you fallen for me?" I ask. I want to hear her say it again.

A playful smile curls her lips. "Did I say that out loud?"

I laugh as I lean down, pressing our smiles together just before they melt into a passionate kiss. How is it possible? I've fallen for her as well.

* * *

201

I'm lying on my side on the brown sectional sofa. Cal sits on the floor with his back leaning where my face is propped on my hand. On his lap is a plate of the best pizza I've ever eaten in my life.

"It's crack pizza," I announce, as he holds up another slice for me to bite. "I've never tasted anything this delicious, and it's only cheese."

"We take our cheese very seriously," he says, leaning his head back to look at me.

I lean forward and kiss him. I haven't stopped kissing him since we made love. I don't want to stop as long as we still have time together. I'm so fucking afraid of what's going to happen tomorrow, I refuse to let myself even think about it. Instead, I'll soak up as many memories of MacCallam Lockwood Tate while I still can.

"Mm," he says, swallowing his bite and changing the channels on the enormous flat screen television. "You must love this one. It's black and white."

I look up to see he's stopped on a scene in which Woody Allen is walking beside a very young Meryl Streep.

"*Manhattan*! I do love this one!" I give his shoulder a brief shake and he laughs.

"Finally, something we can agree on."

Falling back against the cushions I close my eyes. "Just listen to that Gershwin soundtrack." I sit up quickly, just in time to see Meryl Streep slide the weight of her long blonde hair over her shoulder. "Look how beautiful she is."

"She reminds me of someone."

"Jennifer Lawrence. I've always thought that. Statuesque, blonde, amazing actress..."

"Hmm," I can see his brow line in the flickering light. "I was thinking about you."

"Me?" The way he says it makes me feel self-conscious. "Our noses are different."

"Your hair is the same, your eyes..." He shifts, facing me. "You're equally captivating."

He's looking at me too intently. I turn away and take another bite of crack pizza while the characters onscreen argue about the nature of politics in Ingmar Bergman films.

"Pseudo-intellectuals," I say, hoping to break the sudden awkwardness.

With a quiet laugh, he pushes off the floor. "I think we should move this party to the bedroom."

"Really?" I give the room service cart a quick survey. Half the pizza remains on the silver platter. "We'll have to leave our drugs out here unguarded."

"I'll save the champagne. You cover the crack." He motions with the dark green bottle. "It'll keep until morning."

With a sigh, I push off the couch and step over to place the silver lid over the remaining food. I'm just turning back when I catch sight of his tight, naked ass disappearing into the bedroom, and chase after him to grab it.

Cal tackles me at once, and we fall onto the bed laughing. He holds me down and kisses me firmly on the mouth. I kiss him back, and when he rolls onto his back, I pop up.

"Are you tired?"

"Hell, no. I'm just warming up. I plan on fucking you three point seven more times tonight."

"Point seven. You're very precise in your measurements."

"It's possible the last time will run over into tomorrow."

Turning my head, I strain to look at the clock. "I think we've already made it to tomorrow."

Catching my chin, he pulls my face back around. "Quit being a party pooper. You pooped out on me last night."

"I was really tired last night!"

We scoot around so we're side by side, resting against the pillows. I lean forward to put my cheek against his bare chest. I love hearing the sound of his breath, his heart beating.

"I'm just the opposite," he says, thoughtfully, threading his fingers in the back of my hair. "I sprained my wrist playing tennis once, and I was so adrenalized, it took me forever to fall asleep."

"Is that why you brought me a bottle of champagne?"

"Partly." His fingers find the back of my neck, giving it a stroke before threading into my hair again. I snuggle deeper into his side, loving the feeling of him touching me. "It's possible I had ulterior motives."

"Well, you got what you came for." I lift my head and press a kiss against his heated skin. "Still, I was exhausted. We ran all over that museum, then we ran all over the beach."

He chuckles, causing my head to bounce. "I told you my uncle would take you to that damn aquarium."

"I loved the aquarium." We're quiet a moment, and I think about what he said. "You were right, though. About your uncle."

"I know that old fellow pretty well. Grew up with him."

Pushing up to a sitting position, I lean beside him. His eyes are on the television, and I study his profile, his straight nose and full lips, the little line in his chin.

"So what happened with him?" I ask quietly, internally holding my breath.

Hazel eyes meet mine. "What do you mean?"

Blinking down, I run my finger along the top of his shoulder. "I mean, why are you on the outs with him? Why is Rowan so angry?"

He does a little frown before answering. "It's matters of state."

"You mean it's classified or something? Like you could tell me, but then you'd have to kill me?"

That makes him grin. "Hardly. More like you'll find it so boring you'll fall asleep on me again."

"I don't think I will. I really want to know."

He shifts to the side. "Why?"

Shrugging, I glance down. "Reggie is the reason I met you. I guess, I want to know why you're so angry with him. I wouldn't know you if it weren't for him."

He catches my chin and lifts my face. "That is definitely a point in his favor." A quick kiss, and he gathers me to his chest. "About six years ago, right before our father died, Rowan overheard Reggie plotting with Hubert Farbridge, a member of the cabinet. I don't know what was said, but Rowan took it to mean they were conspiring to cause our father's death.

"Cause his death? But how? Did they shoot him?"

"His heart was bad. He had a terrible temper, and they knew how to get him worked up into a rage. The night he died they'd had a terrible fight about joining forces with Twatrington."

My head pops up. "Twatrington? What's that?"

He grins and runs his thumb along my jawline. "Our neighbor to the southwest. They've attacked farmers along our border for years. Their ultimate goal is to combine the two countries into one — under their rule."

"Why would they do that?"

"Better access to the sea, tourism dollars. We've spent a lot of time cultivating relationships with the nobility. Most of our visitors spend large amounts of money here because they have deep pockets, and we're thought of as something of a high-end destination."

"I definitely agree with that. Everything is so beautiful and refined — the architecture, the sea. It's like an elegant paradise."

He shifts to the side and puts his palm on my face, softly running his fingers over my lips. The depth of his gaze makes my stomach squirm.

"Are you saying you might want to stay here? Longer than a week?"

That little fish is back, flipping all around my insides. "I think it would be amazing to stay here."

He pulls me closer, rolling me onto my back and leaning down to kiss my neck, gradually working his way up to my jaw, sending heat rising under my skin, chasing after his luscious lips. We kiss long and passionately. I pull his bottom lip between mine; he catches my top. I'm completely turned on by the time we come up for air.

"Then we'll have to figure out a reason for you to stay, won't we?"

Exhaling a laugh, I shake my head. "If only it were that easy."

"Maybe it can be." He covers my mouth again, pulling me onto his lap in a straddle. I lift my hips, and he moves into position to plunge deep inside me, drowning my doubts in the flood of our desire.

Chapter 15: Afterglow

Rowan

Opening my eyes in the bright, blue suite with Ava snuggled soft and warm at my side is like waking up in the clouds, no longer on Earth, just this side of heaven. Stretching gently, I do my best not to wake her. I shift to my side and look down at her.

Her knees are bent, and one hand is under her cheek. Her long lashes rest on the tops of her cheeks, and her pink lips are slightly parted. Dark hair fans out behind her, and my fingers ache to touch her. She's so incredibly beautiful.

I think about last night, what she told me, and I have to wrestle down the fury threatening to rise in my chest again. She didn't say the words, but from the implication... *Was she raped?*

I can't even think it without thoughts of murder filling my mind. I don't want to make her relive a painful time from her past, but if someone hurt my Ava in that way, I will find out who did it. That bastard's days are numbered.

She stirs, exhaling a soft noise, and my chest tightens with joy. In spite of her past, she made love so passionately last night. She went with me wherever I wanted to take her. She stole my heart. I don't know how I'll let her leave at the end of her visit.

Her eyelids flutter, and the hand under her cheek reaches out. I catch it in my larger one, and pull it to my lips, causing her eyes to spring open.

"Rowan," she says softly. I love sound of her voice saying my name. "Were you watching me sleep?"

"Yes." I slide the back of my fingers down the smooth skin of her arm.

Her shoulder rises and she exhales a laugh. "That tickles."

"Ava," I groan. Yep, my morning wood is aching, and it didn't take more than that to push me over the edge.

Pulling her to me, I slide down to kiss her soft breasts, running my tongue over her tightening nipple before sucking it firmly into my mouth. She arches her back, softly laughing as her fingers thread into the sides of my hair.

"You didn't get enough last night?" her voice taunts me. Still, she squirms around to press a kiss against my temple.

"No." I move lower, kissing the curve of her hip before moving to the center, circling my tongue around her navel.

"Ooo, yes," she gasps as I keep moving lower.

It's possible I might never get enough of her beautiful body. Wrapping my arms around her thighs I spread her open so I can focus my attention directly on her clit. Her hips jerk and her hands fly to grasp my hair.

I need to be deep inside her, but I won't take her without making her come, especially not after what she revealed to me. I want to show her how good this can be. I want all her orgasms. It only takes a few more concentrated passes before her hips are flexing, and she's trying to squirm away.

"Rowan! Oh, god! I can't... Stop!" She's gasping and shaking, and I release her, kissing her lower stomach, just above that sensitive spot, rising up to her breasts, and finally arriving at her luscious lips.

She holds the back of my neck, kissing me hard, pulling me closer. It's only a moment before we're in position, and I plunge deep into her clenching insides. She's so tight and hot, and I'm on the razor's edge. It only takes a few hard thrusts before I'm shooting over the moon, releasing the tension that somehow seems to build up every night.

We're entwined like contortionists, lying on our sides, easing down from another incredible high. Her face is pressed into my shoulder, and I hold her under the ass. Her long legs are wrapped around my waist, her arms around my neck.

"Didn't think we could do it again?" I tease as I kiss her.

Her head tilts back, and she smiles. "I think I can sleep a little longer."

"Go right ahead," I say, running my fingers over her ear, pushing her silky hair off her flushed cheeks. "I'll be right here when you wake."

She exhales a laugh and her dreamy eyes meet mine. "I was thinking about the night we met. You never told me your favorite Robert Frost poem."

"Since that night, it's become 'In the Clearing.'"

"And before that night?"

We shift in the bed, and I move to my back, holding her securely against my chest. I hadn't thought about things like poetry or love in years before that night. "It would have been before my father died."

211

I feel her tracing her fingers along the lines of my chest, and I try to remember ever feeling this level of contentment.

Her voice is a smooth vibration. "I always liked the little horse in 'Stopping by the Woods on a Snowy Evening.'"

"His impatient little horse, wondering why he's feeling so contemplative." It only takes a moment longer before I know my favorite. "'Fire and Ice.'"

"Oh, I love that one." Her head pops up, and a little grin is on her lips. "'From what I've tasted of desire, I hold with those who favor fire'?"

I touch her lovely face again. "Especially now."

She leans her cheek into my hand. "What are we going to do today?"

Thinking over my agenda, I decide to clear my schedule and spend the entire day with her. "Whatever you want. Name it."

"Really?" Her brow lines, and I lean forward to kiss the frown away.

"Really. What would you like more than anything?"

"Hmm…" She slants her eyes as she thinks, and I can't imagine what she's going to say. "I want to see you race. Will you take me to the track and show me?"

It's not what I expected, but it's not an unwelcome suggestion. I only think about it a moment before I concede. "Yes, but I need to change. I guess you do as well. I'll take you to your hotel, then I'll pick you up at two and we'll head to the track. Sound good?"

"I love it! I can't wait." She does a little bounce, and I can't resist. I grab her around the waist and kiss her again.

Zelda

Cal drops me off at the Fairmont with a kiss and a plan to meet for lunch. I'm supposed to be showering and changing into something fresh, but instead I'm back in my bed, deep beneath the covers reliving last night.

We didn't make love three point seven more times. It was a full four more times. My entire body heats as I remember the last, him taking me from behind. He gripped my breasts and bit the back of my neck as he plunged so deep between my thighs. It's a hot memory, and my hand slides down between my legs when I hear the door open and then slam shut. I freeze for a half second when the sudden jolt of a body landing on my bed causes me to crawl to the surface.

"Ava?" My head pokes out from under the blankets, and I see my sister lying on her back, her arms and legs sprawled out like a starfish.

She sighs as if she's fallen into a vat of cotton candy. "I had sex with a king." Then she laughs. "Correction, I had sex with *the* king. I pretty much spent the entire night last night having orgasms. Can you believe it?"

I sit up and start to laugh. "I'm not sure you believe it. Do you need me to pinch you and be sure you're awake?"

Rolling onto her stomach she looks up at me, and I confess. Something about her is different. I can't put my finger on it, but she seems calmer somehow. She's definitely glowing.

"He's amazing, Zee. He's strong and sexy and massive, and oh my god. His dick is so big—"

"Whoa! Hold it right there!" I wave my hand between us. "I don't need to hear about his massive peen. It's all I'll be thinking about next time I see him. Back it up to the part about how he's the king."

She starts to laugh, and I do too. I'm only partly teasing about the penis size—apparently the brothers have something in common. I'm mostly happy and relieved and so glad she was with someone who took care of her.

"So you already knew he was strong and all that," she says, then she falls back on the bed again. "He's also so gentle and attentive and... possessive and demanding."

Dropping onto my side, I prop my head on my hand, threading my fingers in her hair. "That's awesome, Ava-bug!" She smiles, and her eyes drift around the room. I can tell she's remembering something, but she suddenly snaps her attention back to me.

"Were you with Cal?" Pushing against the bed, she moves to a sitting position. "I didn't want to leave without talking to you, but I remembered last time... I figured you and he were together. I know you care about him."

Twining my finger around a long lock of dark hair, I give it a little tug. "I was a little freaked out when I heard you'd left with Rowan. I don't like us not having a plan in case something goes wrong..."

"I know. I'm sorry, but it was Rowan. You've spent the night at his house. You know what a wonderful person he is. He's the whole reason we're here!"

I take a deep breath. She's right, and I can't argue with her. "In the future, we'll be more careful."

Her eyes drop to her lap. "I can't seem to think about a future without him in it. What am I going to do, Zee?"

My brow lines, and I study her face. "I've been thinking about that question all night. Or trying not to think about it."

Green eyes meet mine, and they're flooded with worry. "You know Reggie lied to us. There's no way Rowan is all those bad things he said."

"I know." I nod, looking down, thinking about my conversation with Cal. "I don't know what we're going to do."

"What if we tell them? We can just be honest and say Reggie lied to us. They might understand."

"Yeah, but we lied to them. Over and over..." My stomach knots, and I want to cry when I think of what Cal will say when he learns the extent of my deception. How many times I lied to him and all the different ways. I feel that little fish in my insides dying.

Ava lunges forward, hugging my waist as she presses her cheek to my stomach. Her voice is a cracked whisper. "I can't bear the thought of losing him. It hurts so much!"

I wrap my arms over her shoulder and lean down, hugging her to me. For several moments we stay that way, and I know the only way out of this is the hardest way possible.

"How did you leave it with Rowan today?"

She sits up, and her eyes glisten with unshed tears. "He's picking me up after lunch. We're going to the track, and he's going to show me his race car."

I'm about to answer her when my phone buzzes with a text. I look over at it, and I see it's from Cal. *Rowan is taking Ava to the track. Let's go with them?*

A lump is lodged at the base of my throat. I take a deep breath and let it out slowly, glancing up at my sister. "Maybe we can put it off just a little longer? Hide from the truth and steal a few more hours?"

"Do you think we can?" She's blinking back tears.

"It's going to hurt like hell sooner or later." I take her hand, and a shiver moves through her body. I'm trembling on the inside as well. "Maybe we can delay the pain just a little bit longer."

Chapter 16: Snake

Zelda

In a roar as loud as a jet engine, Rowan's red Formula 1 car soars past us on the practice track outside of town. It moves so fast, it's hard to believe, and Ava's on the edge of her seat, her hands clasped tightly in her lap. Cal's watching his phone's timer.

"One minute eight," he says, touching the face. "He's so fucking fast. Too bad he can never hit those speeds on the course."

"It seems dangerous," Ava says, looking nervously up at him.

Cal's right beside me, an arm draped around my waist, smiling so big. "Nah, Ro's an incredible racer. He's been doing it for years." Sitting a little straighter, he hands Ava his binoculars. "Watch as he comes through that set of curves. He'll ease off a little on the first one then let it rip as he pulls into the straight. It's how he's able to clock such a great time. He's fearless."

I can't help a grin watching the enthusiasm in his eyes. "You're really proud of him," I say, kissing his cheek.

He leans back and gives me a smug grin. "It's not very sexy, I know. I should be more brooding and competitive. Loki."

Snorting a laugh, I press my face against his shoulder. "I think it's very endearing."

Rowan's car flies past in another blast of noise and blaze of red, and Cal stands. "Come, let's walk down. It's his last lap. We can meet him at the finish line."

Ava's on her feet at once, and we follow him along the silver bleachers to the steps leading down to the tarmac.

"It's too bad he doesn't compete anymore," he continues.

We're holding hands, and Ava strolls beside us. It's a sunny day, and she's wearing a white halter dress that ripples in the breeze. She topped it off with a wide-brimmed straw hat, and I swear she looks like she just stepped out of *Vogue* magazine. I look like I'm headed to a racetrack in cropped khaki cargo pants and a thin sleeveless tank. Cal's more my speed in jeans and a thin V-neck sweater.

"Why doesn't he compete anymore?" she asks, placing a hand on the top of her hat.

We step out onto the track, and the wind gusts around us. The sound of Rowan's car echoes from the other side of the track.

"Too dangerous," Cal says. "When these guys crash... well, not much is left."

Ava's eyes go round, and her cheeks go completely pale.

"But don't worry!" he hastily adds. "Rowan's done this so long, the chances of him having an accident alone on the track are slim to none."

She does a little nervous nod and looks back out to where a streak of red races toward us at blinding speed.

"I've seen some of those wrecks," I whisper in Cal's ear. "They're pretty scary."

"You'd be surprised how far they've come with safety on these things. From the suit he wears down to the cockpit design. They've got it to where drivers can be out of the vehicle in five seconds."

"Five? Out of that tiny thing?"

"Yeah, it's pretty impressive. They call it a 'survival cell,' and no fuel, oil, or water lines run through it. No more sitting, trapped in a fiery inferno, like Niki Lauda."

My heart lurches. "The guy in that Ron Howard movie?"

He exhales a laugh and pulls my head to his lips, giving me a kiss. "Yes, the Ron Howard movie."

I struggle to push the image out of my head. I can't even think of Rowan burned beyond recognition. Ava's up ahead waiting with the pit crew as Rowan coasts in to a stop. He slides out quickly, removing the helmet and giving her a smile. She's less enthusiastic than when we arrived, and I can't say I blame her.

"I'm sure your mother's glad he doesn't compete anymore," I whisper.

Cal's arm moves from around my shoulders to holding my waist, and despite the horrible "what ifs," I can't help a smile as I watch Rowan lean back against the car and pull Ava to him, kissing her lips. A deep, accented voice from behind us makes me jump out of Cal's embrace.

"Yes," Reggie says, irritation clear in his tone. "Her majesty is very glad he's not racing anymore. Although, the crown prince seems to have a mind of his own these days."

"Reggie!" My voice is too high, and I know he knows I know we're busted. I could die. "What are you doing here?"

Cal's eyes move from his uncle to me and back again. "Hello, Reg, what are you doing here?" He reaches out and takes my hand again, and Reggie's eyes move to the connection between us.

I can't pull my hand away without hurting Cal, but now it's impossible to hide what's happening. Ava's blissfully ignorant of her audience, and when I glance back, she and Rowan are smiling at each other. He leans forward and says something in her ear, and she shakes her head. They're so clearly new lovers with the way they touch each other, and while I'm dying standing here knowing Reggie's watching them, deep down, I'm so happy to see her so blissed out.

"I actually came for Zelda," he says, giving me a pointed look. "I received a call from the executor of your uncle's estate, and I wonder if you might ride back with me to the hotel so we can discuss what he said."

"Why didn't he call me?" I say, trying to escape what's coming.

He gives me a pointed glare. "Probably because he couldn't reach you."

"We were planning to go for dinner, Reg," Cal interrupts. "Can't whatever it is wait?"

"Is that so?" he says, still watching my expression.

My heart is beating so fast, it hurts. "Yes," I say softly. "We were."

"Then perhaps I can drop her at the restaurant. This shouldn't take long. Where are you going?"

Cal pauses, and I can tell he's searching for an argument.

"It's okay," I say giving him a confident smile. It is so, *so* fake. "I'll meet you at the restaurant."

"The Brasserie at Columbus," he says, glancing at his uncle. "I'll be there in ten."

"We're right behind you," Reggie says, taking my arm.

Cal steps forward and kisses my cheek. "See you in a bit."

"Tell Rowan his race was thrilling."

He does a little smile, and we part, me headed to face the consequences, him completely ignorant.

We walk quickly through the breezeway under the metal bleachers out to the parking area where Reggie's town car waits. The driver holds the door as we climb in, and it isn't until the doors are shut and we're driving away with the security glass firmly in place that he turns to me.

At first he doesn't speak, he only studies my expression. I swallow the knot in my throat. I don't have a leg to stand on, and I know it.

"It appears your sister has won the heart of the crown prince," he finally says. "While you were off playing with his brother."

"I tried, Reggie." My voice is too soft, too weak. "I really did."

"I set it all up. I gave you multiple opportunities. Then you sneaked away in the night after you twisted your ankle? You were supposed to have breakfast with the future king!"

After I'd just spent the night with his brother. "He wasn't interested in me."

"He never had a chance to know."

With a sigh, I look out the window at the passing trees and flowers. "Can't we change the plan? Ava's not a member of the nobility or anything. Can't she be the one to help you out?"

Reggie's eyes narrow. "The plan wasn't for him to fall in love with a beautiful orphaned girl from America. That's romantic enough to enchant the nation!" His voice rises a bit, and I flinch. "The plan was for him to fall for *you*, a phony heiress he thinks would secure Monagasco's economic future. It would show he's too inexperienced, too shallow to be our leader. He was to be led around by his cock and duped by someone like *you*!"

My chin drops, and embarrassment burns in my cheeks. *Why did I ever agree to this job?*

"That's not Rowan at all. He's none of those things," I say quietly. "He's very serious about his position. Every time we're together, he's reading something or taking a phone call. He's very fit to be king."

"Even when he's planning to race the Grand Prix next week?"

"What?" My eyes widen. "Why would he do that? It's too dangerous!"

"Because despite what you think, Rowan is irresponsible. Apparently, he thinks national security is less important than the pursuit of his hobbies."

He turns his phone to me. On the screen is the headline, **CROWN PRINCE TO RACE IN GRAND PRIX**. My jaw drops. I can't believe what Reggie is saying.

"He wouldn't..."

"It seems he already has. Even better, he's done it with the race only days away."

"How does that change—"

"No one has time to prevent him or talk him out of it."

I think about what Cal said, all the safety precautions. I can only believe Rowan has weighed the odds and decided it's safe. I know Rowan... sort of. At least, I've been around him, and I've talked to him about his country. I still believe in him.

Reggie is frowning at me, and the bigger question is *what now?* I'm not foolish enough to think Reggie will continue bankrolling our presence here, and I'm also smart enough to know ten thousand dollars will last maybe three days in this pricey little kingdom. I've still got to get us home.

"So is it over? You're done with Ava and me?"

Reggie's lips press into a line, and he crosses an ankle over his knee. "In a word? No. You two have become unexpectedly useful."

"How so?" The last thing I want is to be pulled into another plot against Rowan — or Cal.

Now that I've seen how close they are, I know anything that hurts Rowan, Cal will take as a personal injury as well. I sort-of love him for that. It's so much how I feel about Ava. At the same time, that puts me in a very bad place with the man for whom I've developed such strong feelings.

"The two of you have both princes by the balls, to use a tacky expression. Just keep doing what you're doing, and keep me in the loop on the crown prince. As long as you do that, I'll keep your account filled."

This new plan makes me feel even slimier than the first. I hate it, and I don't want to do it. "You're wrong. I didn't even know Rowan was going to race the Grand Prix."

"They have a security breach at Occitan. It's possible not even his brother knew what he did today."

"If there's already a breach, you don't need me."

"*Au contraire*, Miss Wilder. I don't know the rat. I don't know who he or she works for. You'll stay right where you are and answer any questions I have."

The car pulls to a stop, and glancing out the window, I see we're at the Brasserie where I'm meeting the other three for dinner.

"Or what?" My voice it a bit sharper than I feel inside, which is really sort of trapped and miserable.

Reggie's eyes flash in response. "Or I'll expose you for the lying little cunt you are."

My stomach plunges, but I swallow back my tears. He couldn't have been crueler if he'd slapped me across the face. Still, as much as I hate him, as much as he's a miserable old fuck, he's right. I lied.

I lied in a big, awful way, and when Cal finds out what I've done, my beautiful dream will be over. The most I can hope for now is damage control. I've got to find out what this snake is after and do my best to derail his plans.

CHAPTER 17: RELEVANCE

Rowan

As we wait for a table at the Brasserie, Cal is distracted watching for Zelda to appear. I want to be empathetic, but I can't really think about anything but Ava.

When she ran up to the car this afternoon on the track, I felt for the first time like I had everything I wanted. The American conglomerate I've been working with emailed me this morning to give us the green light. We'll start building clean-energy electric storage facilities by fall—funneling both a new stream of revenue and a new source of jobs into the nation.

Standing on the track, I had my new deal, my favorite pastime, and my beautiful girl all together. The only thing remaining is announcing my decision from this morning.

With the economic pressure leveling off, I want to celebrate. Reaching for Ava, I pull her against my chest at the bar as we wait for Zee to join us. She lifts the enormous hat off her head and smooths her hair back, smiling up at me. I can only smile back. I don't give a shit if I'm wrapped around her delicate little finger.

"I want to take you back to Occitan and spend the rest of the day at the beach." I don't mention *clothing optional*.

"I would love that. I didn't get to see it the other night." Her green eyes sparkle, and my hold on her waist tightens. She turns to my brother. "Cal, where is Zee?"

My brother is distracted as he answers her. "She caught a ride with Reggie. Something about needing to discuss her uncle's estate."

Ava stiffens in my arms. "She what?"

Her voice is worried, and I can't help wondering why she's disturbed by Zelda's being with Reggie. Personally, I'm still mildly furious at my uncle's return. My mother tries to smooth it over, reminding me how I grew up with him and how at one point in time, my father trusted him.

She doesn't know the conspiracy I overheard all those years ago. I don't have proof of Reggie's involvement, but I'm keeping him in my sights. The only thing holding me back from kicking him out again is the fact he brought Ava to me. She gives me the ability to tolerate his presence.

"Hmm," Cal's brow lowers, and he's looking at his damn phone again. "That's getting it in under the wire."

"I swear, MacCallam, if you could detach from social media for five minutes—"

"You wouldn't know what the hell you were up to," he finishes, turning the oversized titanium phone to me. "I guess this means I'm captain of your pit crew."

CROWN PRINCE TO RACE IN GRAND PRIX is blasted big as the screen. Ava does a little gasp. My jaw tightens and fury burns in my chest. "How the fuck did they get that already?"

Ava's voice is soft in my ear, and I don't miss the tremor there. "I thought you couldn't race anymore?"

I made the decision this morning in the high of learning our tech deal had gone through. The entry forms come every year like clockwork, and for the last six years, I've simply thrown them away. Not this year. I held them until today, the absolute last day to throw my hat in the ring.

"I only decided this morning."

The muscle in my brother's jaw moves. "We've got to find that fucking rat at Occitan. In the meantime, are you serious about this?"

"I was this morning. Obviously, I haven't discussed it with anyone."

"But you returned the forms."

"I want a place in qualifications."

Cal laughs and braces my shoulder. "Mother is going to have a shit fit, and I can't wait. You're bound to win it this time."

"We'll see." I'm smiling, though. He's right, and it is so good. "I've clocked my best times these last two practice sessions."

"I was there." His response boosts my mood. I'm lucky to have him on my team.

When I look back at Ava, she's watching me, her green eyes round with worry. I pull her close and give her a reassuring grin. "Don't worry, gorgeous, I'll be okay."

My hand slides over the curve of her ass to her lower back, and I lean forward to kiss her lips briefly. Cal's ordering champagne, and I notice a throat clearing somewhat obviously behind us.

Glancing up, I meet olive drab. "Felicity!" Stepping forward, I shake her hand firmly. "Good to see you, old chap!"

"Rowan!" She laughs loudly, moving her eyes and head over her shoulder. "You do always have the queerist greetings."

Frowning, I look behind her to see, of all people, Lara Westingroot. Straightening, I move Ava to the side from where she was pretty much sitting on my lap. I'm not hiding her—I still hold her hand, lacing our fingers. I'm only more formal now.

"Miss Westingroot, how are you?" I do a slight nod.

"Rowan." Lara moves in too close and touches my hand. "You should know we don't have to be so formal now."

My shoulders tense as Ava leaves me to stand beside Cal at the bar. *Shit.*

"Are you in good health?" I ask.

Lara laughs and blinks up at me. *Is she attempting to flirt?* "As good as can be expected with this latest news."

"Damn tabloids," I grumble. "I hadn't told anyone when they smeared it all over the Internet."

"At least she's very beautiful." Lara glances at Ava in an obviously appraising manner. "For a commoner, of course. But honestly, another American? Surely you could find a conquest from among our own ranks."

For a moment, I'm confused. "I'm sorry, I thought you were talking about the race."

"I'm talking about this person you've taken up with as of late." Criticism is in her tone, and it sets my jaw. Miss Westingroot will not appraise my behavior if she knows whats best for her.

"I enjoy Ava's company. She's fresh and interesting."

"Fresh and interesting? What's that supposed to mean?"

For a moment, I study this beautiful ice queen's face, and all the reasons my fifteen year-old infatuation didn't survive into maturity are clear. Lara and I have never spoken the same language.

"If we're going to stay relevant, we need to meet people outside our insulated group."

"Stay relevant?" Her mocking laugh irritates me. "We're relevant because of who we are, Rowan. We are Monagasco. Our country has existed for eight hundred years! We're legendary."

"I haven't existed for eight hundred years. It's important for our leaders to keep up with the times. Can you not understand that?"

She rolls her eyes and does a little wave. "You have always had peculiar notions, Rowan. It's because you read too much."

"Is that so?" I might have had too much wine when I let her go down on me before, but I won't be duplicating that mistake.

"Stick with what works." She glances to where Cal is making some joke, doing his best to distract Ava. "Shall I expect you to call me about the gala?"

"I'm pretty confident I already have an escort."

That earns me a glare. "Then I suppose I should take my leave. Good afternoon, Rowan. Enjoy your dinner."

Lara strides away, but Felicity lingers a moment longer. "She's furious. Nice work."

"It wasn't intentional."

Felicity does a little wave in Cal's direction. "Is this for show or are you being serious?"

Her blunt style relaxes me. "I hope it becomes very serious."

"But she's not wealthy or connected," Felicity's thin lips grow even thinner as she presses them down. "And now you're racing again."

"What of it?" I'm curious as to what she might say.

She only holds up both hands. "I'm on your side. It's the old guard you have to appease. They're only happy making us young ones suffer through the same rules and regulations that made them miserable when they were our age."

"I'm not interested in appeasing anyone." It's not entirely true, considering how hard I've been working to make peace since Hummergate.

"Clearly," Felicity laughs. "So... Need another member for your pit crew?"

"Have you ever been on a pit crew?"

"No." Her smile fades, and I shake my head.

"It's a brutal course. I'll need an experienced team."

"You're right." Felicity nods, and for a moment, we're quiet.

It gives me a second to remember that night at the ball and how she rescued me from the barrage of single females of a certain age. I do owe her one.

"Tell you what. I'll get you a pass so you can come down, hang with the guys, watch the race up close."

Her eyes light. "Thanks! You're amazing!" She does a little clap. "And I'll look out for your new lady. Lord knows she'll need a buffer in this crowd."

"You're a sport." I pat her shoulder and take a step toward the bar.

"I'm betting on you, Rowan Westringham Tate," she calls. "Don't get killed."

"I don't intend to."

With a little salute, she's gone, and I continue to where Ava stands with Cal. He hands her a whiskey sour, and her expression isn't as sunny as before. She's not smiling, and I want to take her away from here where I can reassure her she's the only female I want in my bed.

"Are we still waiting on Zelda?" I look to my brother.

"She just texted she's almost here." Cal slips his phone in his pocket, and I understand his reason for checking it so often now.

I've never seen Cal worry this much about the whereabouts of a conquest. It's a nice change for him, and I'd give him a little good-natured teasing. Only I notice how quiet Ava is being.

I place my hand on her arm, and when she glances up, my chest tightens. "We're going to rain-check dinner," I tell Cal. "I'm taking Ava back to Occitan."

A loud shuffling noise draws all our attention. Two men are struggling in the hedge, both holding cameras with telephoto lenses.

Cal's voice is low and urgent. "You'd better go now."

Ava places her glass on the bar and takes my arm as we make a quick escape through the small restaurant. We're in the car as more photographers flood into the public space. Hajib closes the door with a solid slam, and we're off.

Leaning forward in the seat, I place my forearms on my thighs frustrated by my inability to control the flow of information about me.

"It's too bad," Ava says with a little sigh. "I wanted to try that place."

This is not what I expected or want to hear. "Are you sorry we're leaving?"

She reaches out and takes my hand. "I'm not sorry to be with you or to be away from those reporters. You joining the race must be big news."

I cover her slim hand with both of mine and lean back so I can meet her eyes. I remember how afraid she looked when Cal dropped the bomb. "I'm sorry I didn't tell you about the race."

Shaking her head, she lets out a sad little laugh. "You don't have to tell me about anything you do. Our time together is lovely, but I know my place. This isn't forever."

Those words twist my stomach. I study her small hand in mine, thinking about my conversation with Lara. I think about everything happening now, all the good things, and how my lack of freedom might change as a result. Before the deal, I had to keep in mind the future, our political situation, and economic growth. With the deal I've hammered out, two of these issues are somewhat resolved.

"I was only thinking..." she hesitates, drawing my full attention. "Cal said competitive racing is so dangerous. He said you shouldn't do it because you're the future king."

It's a fair assessment, and the reason I've held back up to now. "The race is on a slow track. It's almost impossible to pass other cars, which is how most of the wrecks occur."

"What happens if you *do* crash?"

"Are you worried?"

Her pretty lips press together, and her gaze flickers to her lap. "Yes, I am. Very much."

Warmth spreads through my stomach, making me smile. Now we're back to where I want us to be. "Then you'll have to give me something for luck."

She blinks a few times before looking up again. She seems to be thinking of something, and with a little nod, she smiles. "I have something."

"I can't wait to see it."

We're at the country house, exiting the vehicle, and I look up at the clear sky. It's warm and inviting, and I intend for us to have an easy time, a late dinner, a swim, and then a seductive night. Mother is still in Marins, giving us the place to ourselves. Taking her hand, I lead Ava up the long, white steps, but when we get to the top, I follow the wrap-around porch to the back where we have a clear view of the calm waters of our little cove.

"It's so beautiful!" she sighs.

Looking out at the sapphire blue water, I pull her against my chest, sliding my hands up the soft fabric of her dress. Her palms rest on my shirtfront, and I lean forward to kiss her cheek, moving to her ear.

"Let's go for a swim."

A shiver moves through her, and it registers straight to my cock. "I don't have a swimsuit," she replies in a sultry tone.

"Even better." Heat is in my voice.

Our eyes meet, and hers are darker. I slide my hands to her cheeks, holding her face as my jaw tightens. "Cal thinks we have a mole on the estate taking pictures. Possibly someone on staff."

Her hands slide up to cup my cheeks, mirroring my gesture. "Then we'll have to be discreet." She rises on tiptoe and kisses me quickly, catching my lip between her teeth.

My semi goes to full hard-on at once, but she twirls out of my arms. "Meet you at the beach!"

She runs down the narrow boardwalk to the pier, laughing and waving for me to follow her. I stand for a moment watching, thinking how calm and satisfied I feel right now. This is how it should be.

Once Ava reaches the shoreline, her white dress flies over her head in a swift movement. Her long, tanned body disappears in the blue waves, and I'm right behind her, covering the distance in record time.

Chapter 18: Searching

Zelda

When I arrive at the Brasserie, I only find Cal inside. He's at the bar, standing beside a vacant barstool with a gin and tonic waiting. I can't begin to tell him how much I appreciate it. At the same time, the closer I get, the worse I ache. Was it only last night we were so happy together, laughing and watching movies in the Paris Hotel?

"Hello, beautiful." Cal kisses my cheek as I climb onto the barstool.

"Thanks for this." I lift the skinny glass and take a sip. "You knew just what I needed."

"I aim to please," he grins, placing a hand on my waist. "You just missed Ro and Ava. I won't lie to you, I'm pretty sure the crown prince is in deep smit."

That helps me smile. "I've never seen Ava so happy. It's like a fairytale."

"There you go again with the fairytales. I warned you about those." My stomach sinks, but he can't possibly begin to know how true his statement is.

I fight it off. "Still, I'm happy to see them both so happy."

"It is rather inspiring, isn't it? Give you any ideas? Sudden cravings?" He leans in and gives me a little eyebrow twitch. As usual, my stomach flips.

Bad feelings aside, I love sitting here with him, exchanging sexual innuendo. He's so casual in his jeans and light sweater. His brown hair is messy from the wind on the track, and his hazel eyes glow. I know from experience under that blue sweater are the lines and muscles that make me swoon. I almost wish we could blow off dinner as well.

"I'm sorry the ambience isn't what it used to be here," he says, misinterpreting my quiet observation. "We should've gone to the Buddha bar."

"The Buddha bar! What's that?"

"Sushi, Chinese, and Thai food."

"Mm, I love Thai food!"

His eyes darken, and he steps forward, pulling me against his chest. "I like the full-body orgasm you had saying that."

Reaching up, I pinch his side. "I did not." Feeling naughty, I add, "If I had an orgasm it was looking at you."

He releases me and shakes his head. "Shit, I'm not hungry anymore." With a wink, he adds, "At least not for food."

I laugh as I take another sip of my drink. How is it possible this man erases all the heaviness I feel?

"We need to eat. We have to keep our strength up for all that fucking."

He laughs more. "Dammit, Zee. You're killing me."

My eyes narrow, and he takes another sip of champagne. Taking the menu, I scan the unusual selection—*Mediterranean with Asian accents?*

"What did my uncle want?" Cal says, and just like that, my happiness bursts like a bubble. He sees the change, and concern fills his voice. "Is something wrong?"

My conversation in the limo, my reason for being here, all of it races back to the forefront of my mind. So many secrets I'm keeping from him, so many lies. How could I ever tell him the truth and expect him to understand? Reggie's voice is in my head, *I'll expose you for the lying little cunt you are...* God, that stings so much.

Finally, I answer him the only way I know how. "I have to leave soon."

Silence fills the space between us like a sudden rainstorm, extinguishing our banter. The noise of the restaurant seems to grow louder, and when I look up, I see Cal's expression has darkened.

"Why?" He moves closer. "I thought you liked it here."

His presence is so soothing, but it's time for reality. I have to let him go. A flash of pain tightens my chest.

"I'm not as free as I'd hoped," I say quietly.

Our eyes don't meet. I watch as Cal traces his finger through the condensation on my glass. "Do you have a departure date?"

I shake my head. "Reggie's working out the details. It will probably be in the next few days. Maybe a week."

Unable to stop myself, I look up for his warm hazel eyes. My sadness is reflected back at me, and I want to step forward into his arms, hold onto him — as if I have the right to keep him.

"Do you think you can stick around for the race?" he asks "It's only a few days away."

"I don't know." *I don't know what's coming next.*

"You can definitely stay for the gala. It's tomorrow night, and I need a date."

"I'm sure you can find a date."

A hint of that smile plays around his lips. "Of course, I can find a date, but I want to go with you."

This time I do move forward into his arms. They tighten around me at once, and my cheek is pressed against his chest. He holds me, and I inhale deeply the spicy-citrusy scent of his clothes. It takes me back to the first night when he loaned me his shirt, which I never plan to return. Ever. The thought of letting him go forms an aching hole in my chest.

His hand moves up, sliding over the back of my neck. His fingers thread in my hair. "Maybe I'll visit you in Texas. It's close to Vegas, right?"

That makes me laugh, and I pull back to meet his eyes. "Compared to what? Here?"

"I think I'd like Vegas."

"I'm sure you would. It's perfect for playboys."

The hostess comes to lead us to our table. Cal gives me a tight smile and steps back, catching my hand and threading our fingers. I study his perfect ass in those jeans as we walk, and my mind is frantic trying to think of something, anything I can do to change my situation. I'm so far out of my league in this place. I have been since the first night I attended that charity ball.

Our table is outdoors on a small patio overlooking the sea. Only a few other diners share the space, and a blonde waitress quickly appears.

"I'll have the burger and chips," Cal says, handing her the oversized menu.

"To drink, Monsieur?"

"What are you having?" Cal asks me.

"I'll try the sushi."

"Good choice." He glances up at the waitress. "Vinho Verde."

She nods and takes down my order before disappearing into the restaurant.

"Green wine?" I say, taking a sip of my water.

"Look at you! Picking up the language." He smiles, and gives me a wink. "It's not actually green, but it is effervescent. I think you'll like it."

"So it's like champagne?"

"Hm," he looks out over the sea. "It's lighter. Better for summer."

Our waiter returns with two white wine glasses, and a tall, skinny bottle. She serves us both, and places the bottle in an ice bucket.

Cal holds his glass out to me. "To memorable days."

I give him a little clink and take a sip. It's crisp with mineral notes, and the fizz is so delicate. "It tastes like a day at the beach."

"Which is what we should be doing right now. Rowan has the right idea."

"Right." I've been so distracted since the car ride. "Where did Rowan and Ava go?"

"Paparazzi showed up. They'll hound him until the race, I'm sure. Anyway, they took off for Occitan just before you arrived."

I have to remember to act surprised about the race, even though Reggie told me about it in the car. "What race?"

"Apparently my older brother signed up for the Grand Prix this morning. I do hope you stick around for it. I'd like you to see it."

Taking another sip of my wine, I think about all of it—time, Reggie, the race. "Remember how you told me Rowan kicked your uncle out of the kingdom?"

"He tried, anyway. Guess who's back?"

"He came with us," I say, thinking as the server places an artistically arranged platter of sushi in front of me.

"Nigiri, shrimp tempura, tuna..." he points out the different items on my plate, and I smile up at him in thanks.

Cal grabs a knife and cuts his burger. I lift the chopsticks and hope I remember how to use them. It's been years since Seth showed me how. Thinking that name makes my old life feel so far away. I can't imagine going back to it and ever feeling the same. *Come on, Zelda, you're smarter than this! You've out-conned Reggie once before; you can do it again.*

"You said Rowan didn't tell you exactly what made him do it... Did he at least give you the gist?" *Anything I can use?* I don't say.

Cal leans back in his chair, chewing a bite of burger watching me. I mix a pinch of Wasabi into the small pool of soy sauce and go for a rich, pink slice of tuna. Holding my breath, I position the sticks in my hand and pick it up. *Balance...* it manages to ride from the sauce to my mouth without falling in my lap. The fresh flavor of good fish fills my mouth.

"Good work." He grins. "I saw you sweating that bite."

"I wasn't sweating! It's just been a while..."

He shakes his head and picks up a French fry. "Let me think... it was something about Hubert and forming an alliance with Twatrington that would essentially unite the two countries under a new government."

"Can he do that?" My brow lines, and I look up at Cal still watching me.

He does a little shrug. "With a majority of votes he could. The economy was bad. Hubert was head of the Parliament at the time, and while the king is the titular leader, he doesn't have total control."

"It's not a true monarchy?" I actually sound like I know what I'm talking about.

He takes another bite of lunch. "Constitutional."

I go for the pink and green shrimp roll. It's covered in a layer of rice with salty seaweed on top.

"Could something like that still work today?"

Cal's eyes narrow, and he lifts his wine glass, taking a sip. "If Hubert were still in power it's conceivable. Still, he'd have to change Rowan's mind about such a unification, and my brother would die before he'd sell out Monagasco."

Distracted, I stare at my colorful plate. My mind is desperate for a solution. Is it possible Reggie's found a way around these obstacles — or he's working on one?

"Is that why you rode with him today?" Cal's voice has changed. It sounds harder. "Are you in league with my uncle to overthrow the government?"

My eyes fly to his. He's watching me closely, and my forehead tightens. What would he say if I told him that's exactly what brought me to his country? I was in league with Reggie to prevent Rowan being crowned king, thereby assuring his enemies control of the government.

Oh god. My insides die.

"What?" I manage a laugh, but it sounds off, even to me. "Why would you say something so crazy?"

Cal's eyebrows lower, and for the first time since I've known him, a fierce light enters his eyes. MacCallam Lockwood Tate is an ass-kicker.

241

"You're asking a strange line of questions, Zee. What's this about?"

Sitting up straight, I place the chopsticks on the side of my plate, forcing my practiced brain to calm. It's not the first time I've been in a tough situation. Poker face returned, I find a believable cover story.

"I was only thinking... if I leave, your uncle will be kicked out again." Reaching for my glass, I take a slow sip of wine, careful to keep my hands from trembling. Focus on the story. "He doesn't want to leave his home. I guess I was trying to help him find a way to stay. If whatever he was trying to do before is impossible now, then Rowan can allow him to come back. Right?"

Cal's muscles visibly relax. He gives me a half-smile as he returns to how we've always been with each other. I let out a controlled breath. That was too fucking close. I can't let Cal figure out why I'm really here before I have something to make up for what I've done. I've got to find my gift of atonement before he ever uncovers the truth about Ava and me, or he'll never forgive me.

It's a long shot he'll forgive me, period, but I can't think that way. I can't let him go without a fight.

"I don't know if Rowan will ever forgive our uncle for what he did." His voice is quiet, controlled. "If Reggie wants to stay in Monagasco, you should let him work it out on his own."

"You're right," I say, happy to move away from the subject. "We don't have to talk about it anymore."

He does a little wave. "I'll sign the bill, and we can head back to the estate. There are still a few hours of sunlight left."

Our eyes meet, and I reach across to hold his hand briefly. "I'm sorry if I spoiled our dinner with all my questions."

"You can make it up to my by going to the gala tomorrow night."

He turns his hand over so our palms touch, our fingers lace. It's so warm and perfect. All I can think about is our bodies meeting in the same way and how good it always feels.

"I'll go." I can't tell him no, and I will do everything in my power to make this right. After that, I know what I have to do.

* * *

Rowan

Ava is in my arms, her soft breasts flat against my chest. Her slim arms are around my neck, and her eyes close as I rock into her. Her dark hair swirls around us in the water like a cape. She's so beautiful, and my cock is deep between her thighs. I can only let go as waves of pleasure roll over us.

With every thrust of my hips, her inner muscles clench, and she exhales a soft moan. I'm so close to finishing, my balls ache. A tilt of her chin, and our mouths unite, tongues sliding together. She tastes like the strawberries I fed her along with our champagne, and she feels like fucking heaven — hot, clenching, dick-massaging heaven.

"Rowan," she whispers softly. "Please."

"Please?" I take another hit off her luscious lips.

"Move me," she sighs, and I slide my hands down to her ass, gripping it and pulling her harder against my hips, scrubbing her clit against my body.

I'm rewarded with a renewed eruption of clenching muscles around my shaft, and I have to grind my teeth to keep from coming. I continue moving her, harder, faster until her thighs flex at my waist. Her nails grip into the skin of my shoulder, and I'm no longer setting the pace. She's riding me, getting off on my cock. It's so damn good, I can't hold back anymore.

"Fuck, Ava," I groan, holding her upper back, trying to keep myself anchored on this planet with only her for support.

My dick pulses again and again, filling her, and she's riding, trembling until she breaks. I feel her entire body tense, and a low moan cracks with her voice.

"Yes," she gasps, bucking against my hips. "That's it."

She's smiling, but her eyes are still closed. Her arms are tight around my neck, and her body moves slower, coming down as a beautiful flush spreads across her breasts.

"Look at me," I say, catching her chin as I give the low command.

"Hm," she smiles, blinking those beautiful eyes open.

I can't help it, I kiss her again, pulling her tongue into my mouth. Devouring her sweetness, causing her to moan again, another little spasm around my dick. Pulling back, I give her lip a teasing nibble, and she sighs.

"So good," she says, leaning her head against her arms, which are still tight around my neck.

My thoughts move to what we've done several times over the last few days. Her body is fantastic, and I've become somewhat obsessed with her. I haven't been as careful as I normally would.

"I'm sorry I haven't been more vigilant about protection."

Her brow lines, and her head rises. "I hadn't really thought about it either. But you don't have to worry. Technically, you're my first real lover."

I touch her chin and the warmth in my chest could only be tempered by my determination to avenge her past.

"You don't have to explain. I trust you." *Or, more accurately, I'm so fucking horny for this woman, I've become completely reckless.*

I think about the other possibility of what we've done, and strangely it doesn't bother me. An unexpected wave of satisfaction fills me at the idea of Ava's belly round with my child.

"I'm on the pill," she adds, killing that fantasy.

It's a good thing. I need to get my head straight about this woman. We've only known each other a short time. As future king, I have to be more deliberate and responsible about my decisions.

Still, Ava is something special. I love every conversation we've had. I love how well our bodies work together, and I can't forget my feelings on the track today seeing her walking out to greet me.

"*You* don't have to worry." I hold her a little closer to my chest. "I'm clean. I haven't been with anyone in a long time."

Those last words, added as an afterthought, cause me to remember my lonely existence before this beautiful creature appeared. I didn't even realize what I was missing.

"Why were you alone?" Her voice is soft, and her legs are loose around my waist.

We're floating in the pleasant water, luxuriating in the calm of afterglow.

I think about her question. "I don't know exactly. My father died, and I felt I had to focus on getting up to speed, proving I was ready to take his place."

"Does running the country mean you can't have a girlfriend?"

"No." I smile and touch her beautiful face. "It just means people always want something. Everyone has an agenda. It's hard to know who to trust."

She leans her cheek into my hand. "I tried to stay away from you, you know."

"I suppose that's what made me want you more."

"Is it?"

"No." I can't lie to her now. "That night in the moonlight, when you were alone, watching the waves and quoting Robert Frost. It was exactly what I was doing in my mind. Looking at the waves and wishing I could run away."

Her expression changes, and she places her slim fingers along my jawline. "We both want freedom? Shouldn't you already have it?"

My arms tighten around her. "I'm pretty sure I know what I want."

"Me too."

Our eyes mix and mingle, emerald green and ocean blue. I can't help feeling we were meant to find each other. Our paths were destined to cross. *Passionate preference, such as love at first sight…*

She kisses me roughly, holding her body to mine as if she's afraid I'll disappear. "I always want to remember this," she says.

I'll never forget it.

"Go with me to the gala tomorrow. It's the kickoff to all the race events. After it, I'll be slammed with time trials and practice runs. I'll have to keep things going with the cabinet. I'm afraid for a few days, I won't be able to see you like this."

She doesn't hesitate. "I would love to go with you."

"We might be hounded by photographers. I hope you don't mind having your photograph plastered all over the damn place."

"I don't mind. I don't really notice them anymore when we're together."

Sliding my fingers along her hairline, I think about my decisions, about what my mother wants, about what's good for the country. I think about Ava being here on a holiday, the possibility that her visit will end and she'll leave. A hollow feeling burns in my stomach.

"After the race, I'd like to talk to you about something."

She smiles. "You could talk to me now. I'm here."

Turning her body, I pull her back to my chest and wrap my arms around her waist. My chin is on her shoulder, and I look out at the horizon. I think about the future and what I want.

"After the race," I say.

Her fingers thread with mine, and I know what I want. I know for the first time, and I feel complete.

CHAPTER 19: COMPLICATIONS

Zelda

It's after ten when Ava and I return to our suite at the Fontaine. It's been several days since we slept in our own beds alone, but I'm thankful for the break and the chance to strategize. She's worried.

"What happened today, Zee? What is Reggie going to do?"

I go quickly to the television and turn it on, but it's no help. The local news is in French. I recognize locations. Many streets will begin closing tomorrow to prepare for the race. The gala is tomorrow night, and locals will be out to watch the racers and the nobility and to cheer for their favorites.

Walking quickly to the door, I pick up the newspaper still rolled from this morning. Again, I can't read it.

"If only I'd learned French," I say through an exasperated exhale.

"What are you thinking?" Ava's right with me, following me through the room.

I walk back to the sofa and drop into the cushions, thinking.

"Oh! I wish you'd tell me something!" Ava's shouting now, and I look up at her. Her dark hair is in beachy waves, and she's still in that white dress from earlier at the track.

"What did you say?" I confess, I've been too distracted to listen.

"What happened today? What did Reggie say? What are you planning to do?!"

Holding out my hand, I reach for her to sit beside me on the sofa. "It's not good." I feel her tense, and I know this is hard for her to hear.

"Reggie was at the track today. He knows you and Rowan are seeing each other. He probably knew before—hell, it's probably why he even showed up today. To bust us."

"What's he going to do?" Her voice wavers, and I know she's feeling that same sickening fear I felt earlier at the thought of Cal finding out what I'd done. Only her fears are for Rowan.

"He wants us to keep him posted about the prince. He wants to know what he's doing, where he's going, then he'll allow us to stay here."

"But I never know what he's doing or where he's going. He doesn't tell me those things!" I can see the panic in her eyes, and I want to soothe her.

At the same time, I know how swift Rowan's judgment can be. She's right to be afraid.

"It's going to be okay, Ava-bug. Do you trust me?" I expect her to say *yes* like she always does, like we've always been in the past.

Instead she says one word, "How?"

Pushing off the couch, I start to pace. "I don't know."

"Oh, Jesus!" She leans forward pushing her face in her hands. "He's going to hate me. He'll never look at me again! And after everything we've said... Everything we've done!"

That does it. I rush to kneel in front of her, pulling her hands into mine. "Look at me! I'm not going to let that happen. I've seen Rowan with you.

He's in love with you. He'll give you the kind of life you deserve."

Her eyes go round. "He's not in love with me. We've never said —"

"Feelings like that don't have to be said. They're apparent for everyone with eyes to see them. He cares about you, and I won't let my mistake spoil that for you. If anyone deserves a fairytale ending, it's you."

"But what about you? What about Cal?" She's blinking fast. "I've never seen you so happy. Not ever! It's the first time you haven't always been planning and calculating and looking for the next job. It's the first time you've smiled!"

Standing, I force myself to calm. This isn't about me. "We've had money, Ava. Money is why I'm smiling."

"That's bullshit!" she shouts, and I feel my jaw hit the floor.

"Ava!" I've never heard her lose it this way.

"I'm not going to let you sit here and say these things. You're happy here. It's not just me!"

"You'd have to be an idiot not to be happy here! Of course I'm happy here, but that's not the point!"

"Then what is the point?"

Clearing my throat, I walk over to the wet bar for a bottle of water. "The point is I took this job. I sat on that boat and shook hands with the devil. You're here because I never leave you behind."

She's listening, but her dark brows are pulled together. She's looking for any chance to argue with me on this, but I won't let her. I twist the top off the water bottle and take a sip, calming my thoughts as well as my voice.

"I'm going to find out what Reggie's up to," I continue. "I'm going to see if there's any way to redeem what I've done. There probably isn't. I'm going to have to be the villain in this story."

"You're not!" Her voice breaks, and unshed tears are in her eyes.

"I am, Ava-bug. I agreed to come here and lie to Rowan. I didn't expect to meet Cal, but I definitely came here intending to hurt Rowan."

She's off the sofa now, crossing the room to stand in front of me. "From the start, we said we would stop it, we'd walk away if we found out Reggie was tricking us. We can just walk away!"

"Yes, but walking away means walking all the way away—all the way back to Florida." Her chin drops, and I know her heart is breaking. My heart is breaking for both of us. "I'll walk away," I say. "I'm doing my best to find any way for you to stay."

Her face snaps up, and again her forehead is lined. "What are you saying?"

"I'm going to figure out what Reggie wants. I'm convinced he's here to finish what he started when Rowan kicked him out..."

"And?"

"And if I can beat him to it, whatever it is—if I can warn Cal or Rowan, maybe they'll feel... A little less like punishing and more like forgiving."

Her breathing picks up, and I can see that tiny glimmer of hope growing in her eyes. She'll always trust me, and I take that responsibility very seriously.

"Then we can stay?" she whispers.

"I hope so." I nod as I start to pace again, thinking. "I hope Rowan will believe me when I tell him you had nothing to do with this scheme. You were only here because I wouldn't leave you behind."

"I'm sure he will—he'll forgive you. Rowan is really kind and gentle."

Glancing up at her, I can't help a skeptical grin. "Rowan is not kind and gentle. He's powerful and tough, and from what I've heard, he's pretty ruthless when it comes to handling people who cross him."

She frowns as if I'm describing someone she doesn't know. "He's focused, and he takes his position very seriously, but he's not ruthless."

Walking back to her, I put an arm around her shoulders. "That right there is why I'm doing this. If that man is so sweet to you that you don't even notice what a badass he is, I'm going to find a way for you to stay together. I promise I will."

Her shoulders fall, and she lets out a slow exhale. "I can't argue with you anymore. I'm too tired."

I laugh and give her side a little poke. "Somebody's been having sex all evening."

"Shut up. I'm going to take a shower."

"No more gushing about having sex with a king?"

"Goodnight, Zelda!" she calls waving over her shoulder at me.

"That's a switch!" I call after her. My phone buzzes on the counter, and I laugh as I walk over to pick it up.

Wish you were here. No one to criticize the horrifying movie choices I'm making.

"MacCallam Lockwood Tate," I whisper, unable to stop a smile.

What are you watching? I text back.

Come back and I'll show you.

Have work to do. Tell me.

Work? You're on a holiday.

Chewing my lip, I decide to give him a little insight into my plans. *Trying to find a way to stay longer.*

In that case, I'll survive my poor entertainment choices.

Smiling, I walk over to sit on the sofa. Resting my head on my hand, I wipe the stubborn tear from my eye and force myself to have hope. Touching the screen quickly, I text, *What have you chosen this time?*

You've Got Mail.

Grow a dick, MacCallam.

I love it when you use my full name.

Snorting a laugh, I roll my eyes. *You're not watching that.*

Come make me turn it off.

Not tonight.

A few seconds tick by, and I look over at the television. Picking up the remote, I change the channel until stupid Meg Ryan appears. *This movie is so dumb*, I text.

Gotcha. What are you wearing?

Slanting my eyes, I think of our first night. *Changing clothes.*

Send me a tit pic.

No!

Smart girl. I'd make that shit my wallpaper.

Still no Prince Charming, I reply.

It's Playboy Prince, sugar tits.

I laugh again, rolling my eyes. *Goodnight, MacCallam.*

Goodnight, beautiful.

With a sigh, I push off the couch, switch off the television, and walk slowly to my bedroom. I consider calling Reggie, but I have no idea what to say. It's not like I can ask him straight out what he's got up his sleeve. Instead, I pull up our last text exchange searching for any clues. It's only questions about how it's going with Rowan, or "CPR," and me.

"I've got to get something on him. I've just got to," I whisper, plugging my phone into its charger and walking into the bathroom to get ready for bed.

* * *

Our pickup time for the ball is an early six thirty, but Cal says it's because the spectators like to cheer and watch as the racers board the yacht.

"It's going to be on a yacht!" I call to Ava as I stand by the wet bar waiting.

I'm having a glass of champagne, careful not to spill it on my filmy red designer gown. It's knee length, and the halter-top shows off my shoulders. It also has a large, upside-down triangle cutout ending at my lower back. I seem to recall Cal liking such details, and I confess, I like his hands on my skin.

True to his word, Reggie is keeping us bankrolled. I can only suppose that means we're still "useful" to him. I feel like a shit taking his money, but it's the only way I can continue working on my own agenda. We have to look the part, and at least I haven't been able to tell him anything he doesn't already know about the guys.

"Will it set sail?" Ava walks out in a strapless beige dress. It's knee-length, and the scalloped top just covers her breasts. Her hair is styled over her shoulder so that one long lock ripples down, the bottom just curling where her nipple is hidden.

"Damn. Ro is going to tent his trousers when he sees you in that."

She laughs, her cheeks flaming, and I give her a hug. "You look beautiful."

"What about you? I love that dress! The color is gorgeous, and the back is a total tease."

My phone buzzes, and I pull it out. "It's show time."

Rowan sent a decoy limo to the front of our hotel so we can escape through the kitchen entrance. The manager escorts us to the door, where outside Cal is leaning against the actual limo.

"Sorry for the alley pickup..." His words drift away when our eyes meet, and that little fish is alive and well in my stomach, flipping all over the place. "You look incredible."

I push a lock of pale blonde behind my ear doing my best not to blush as hard as Ava. "Yet another reason I needed to be here last night," I say in a tone that's far more carefree than I feel. "We had to shop today, get our hair done."

He catches my forearms and leans down to kiss my cheek. "The entire miserable night was worth it for this." Warm hazel darkens, and I'm squealing on the inside.

Ava walks up behind us. "Where's Rowan?"

"He thought it would cause less of a problem if he met us at the pier." She makes a little sad noise, and he tears his eyes from mine. "Oh, wow! He probably should have come with me. That dress will definitely provoke a response."

"That's just what I said!" Moving to his side, I slip my hand in the crook of Cal's arm.

"I'm sure the crown prince knows how to conduct himself in public," Ava says, but I don't miss her smug tone.

"When the two of you go missing, we'll know to search the bedrooms," Cal teases.

"No way!" I cry. "If the boat's a-rockin, *don't* come a-knockin!"

Cal slides a hand over my lower back, hitting me with a cascade of chills. "Mm, if we go missing..." he rumbles in my ear.

"Come on," Ava climbs into the limo with the help of Hajib.

It's only a short drive to the dock. We're pulling into the parking area and stepping out to meet Rowan in no time. As predicted, his eyes fix on Ava's, and I see the muscle in his jaw move when she crosses the space to him.

"You're beautiful," I hear him say in a low voice, and her skin flushes a pretty color.

His large hand takes hers, lifting it to his lips, and her eyes gleam as she watches him. Protecting her future, knowing how perfectly safe and happy she would be here with him dominates my thoughts.

"What are you thinking?" Cal's voice is low beside my cheek, and he places his hand around my waist.

Turning my head just slightly, I don't take my eyes off them as they walk the short distance to the gangplank. Cheers and shouts come from the crowd, flashes go off in a strobe of white, and Rowan waves discreetly, smiling to his subjects. He holds Ava's hand tightly in his, and she follows, watching him and smiling.

"She's so happy," I whisper.

It's all I've ever wanted for her. She's found a tall, dark, and handsome prince to carry her away to her happily ever after.

"You're such a good friend," Cal says, and just like that, I'm pulled from my fairytale and back to our lies.

"Right," I say, clearing my throat, hating this so much.

"I hope you're so happy."

You have no idea how happy, I think, with a sad little exhale. His hazel eyes have a rare earnestness as he lifts my fingers to his lips. It's a feather-light kiss, a brush of skin I feel it straight between my thighs. *Damn, MacCallam Lockwood Tate is so irresistible to me.*

I answer him honestly. "I had no idea this vacation would go this way."

It's a short walk to the boat, and Cal has his share of screaming fans. He waves, and I wish I could be like my sister—so completely enraptured with my date that I don't even notice all the death glares shooting at me from the crowd. Too bad, I see all the bitches that want to take my place. I can't think about them. I have enough complications on my plate.

Once onboard the super yacht, it's like my first night at the charity ball, only this time, I'm far more comfortable in my dress and heels, and the entire plan has fallen apart. I have nothing and everything to lose.

"MacCallam! Introduce me to your lovely date." The same woman who cornered me with Reggie that first night approaches us, and while I remember her, I'm pretty sure she has no recollection of me.

"Mother," he says, leaning forward to kiss her cheek.

Her majesty gives me a more focused examination tonight, and I can feel her sizing me up.

"Miss Zelda Benedict of Texas," Cal says.

Inside I cringe hearing him repeat our lies, still I hold my poker face intact. "Your majesty," I say, doing a slow curtsey.

"Benedict? We've met before," she says, clearly not connecting me with Reggie.

"Yes, ma'am. At the charity ball."

She waves a hand dismissively. "A legion of young ladies attended that ball."

"And out of them all, I found Zee," Cal says, taking her hand and stepping forward to kiss her cheek again. "We're just making the rounds."

I can tell he's trying to disengage, but his mother isn't finished. "Who is this young woman who has Rowan so infatuated?"

"She's a friend of Zelda's," he says, nodding to me, which gets me a more pointed inspection from the queen.

"From Texas?" Her eyes are on me, but I'm not sure she's actually addressing me.

"Florida, mother," Cal says, releasing her hand and stepping back. "Lovely girl. We've spent the last several days together."

The old crone's about to launch into some complaint, I can see it in her eyes, and my hackles start to rise. I might not be Ava's mother, but I've been the closest thing for the last ten years. Lucky for both of us, Cal makes some excuse and leads us away, further into the crowd toward the deck of the enormous yacht.

We're walking slowly under white canopies and Cal speaks briefly to couples sitting on round, wicker love seats and long, flat deck chairs.

Once we're somewhat alone, he assesses my cooling temper. "Mother has very definite ideas about what the future queen should be like."

I have to remind myself she's his mother, but it's difficult. "I'm sure she does," is all I'll say.

I'd like to see that old bat find anyone sweeter than my little sister, even if Ava might steal your watch.

"We all should have friends as loyal as you," he chuckles and leans in to kiss my cheek. "I'll get us a glass of wine. Don't move."

I give him a little smile and walk over to the rail of the yacht, looking out at the breathtaking view. It's a clear night, a light breeze is blowing, and the air is a little salty. Turquoise water stretches away, turning slowly deeper blue, and it's so beautiful, I dream of what it would be like if we could just run away.

"It won't work," I whisper to myself. I'll have to be honest with him at some point.

"What won't work, Zelda Wilder?" I jump at the exaggerated country twang, and just as fast, fear shoots through my stomach.

I turn slowly to face… "Seth." A tremor is in my voice. "What are you doing here?"

"Well, you could've knocked me over with a cotton ball when I saw your sister Ava's picture on the arm of the Crown Prince of Monagasco!" He's doing the casino act, and I am *freaking out*. "I hopped the first flight over to come check on my girls."

"Stop it," I hiss, grabbing his arm and my composure as fast as possible. "You can't act like that here."

Seth's eyes narrow, and his smooth Kansas is back. "How should I act, my old partner in crime? What kind of a con are you running, Zelda Wilder?"

I frantically scan the crowd looking for Cal. He'll be back any moment. "It's *Benedict*, and Ava is *not* my sister. I'll explain it all to you later. You've got to go."

In a swirl of ice-blue chiffon a woman joins us. She's very beautiful and clearly noble. Her pale blonde hair is styled in a French twist, and an ornate necklace with brilliant blue sapphires is around her neck.

"There you are, Colonel," she says, taking his arm. "Felicity wanted to stop and speak to the crown prince."

"Colonel?" My brow arches.

"Oh, I just told Miss Westingroot I was a little ole Kentucky Colonel."

It's then I notice he's wearing a gold pin on his black tuxedo jacket. Sure enough it has *Kentucky Colonel* stamped on a blue background under a bald eagle.

"Did that come with the coat?" I snark under my breath.

"It's just an honorary title, of course, but Lara here seems to think it's worth a damn."

"Who knew America had such things?" Lara says, but I don't care for her snotty tone.

My heart jumps again at the sound of Cal's voice. "Hello, what do we have here?"

Locking my eyes on Seth's, I mentally order him, *Don't fuck this up...*

"MacCallam," Lara steps forward to kiss my escort's cheek. "How is your health?"

"Good as yours, I imagine, who do we have here?"

He touches my lower back, and Seth's eyes narrow. My jaw tightens in response.

Lara gestures toward Seth. "I'd like to present Mister Seth Hines. A real Kentucky Colonel."

Her tone is still mocking, and I break my staring battle with Seth to evaluate this Westingroot chick.

"As in the chicken franchise?" Cal actually sounds impressed. "Incredible business model. All built around fried chicken."

"Yes, the Colonel was a smart man," Seth continues in that ridiculous accent, "Our honorable order lost a real gem when he passed."

My eyes are back on Seth now, and I'm speechless. Is he actually attempting to be some fried chicken heir? I guess I have no right to judge. I'm supposed to be an oil baron's niece.

"I'm sorry," Cal speaks to me. "Zelda, do you know Miss Westingroot? Mister Hines?"

"We've only just met," I say, doing my best to keep it together.

Seth is right on it. "I didn't get your name, Miss…?"

"Benedict," Cal answers for me. "Lux Benedict is her uncle. Of Texas?"

"Well, cotton and fiddles," Seth says, and I cringe. "Texas is a mighty big state, but I've still heard of the mighty Lux Benedict."

"That's right!" Lara Westingroot is addressing me now, and her tone has turned to solid ice. "*You're* the one we have to thank for the lovely Miss Wilder's presence."

"Miss Wilder?" Seth asks, his eyes round with fake curiosity.

"The young lady attached to the crown prince like a remora."

"Excuse me?" My voice is sharp. "She happens to be one of my best friends."

Seth's eyes widen, and my fear at what he could say to expose us is the only thing keeping me in check.

"I declare, Miss Benedict, have you known the crown prince long?" A wicked gleam is in his eyes, and I start to sweat.

"Yes, Miss Benedict," Westingbitch chimes in. "How long have you known his royal majesty? Or better yet, *how* do you know him at all?"

My shoulders are tight. I don't want Seth knowing anything about our arrangement or why we're here. "I... We... We met the grand duke."

"A Grand Duke!" Seth exclaims. "Now that is a fancy moniker. Did you meet him in Texas?"

I'm fumbling, searching for anything to deflect these questions. Thankfully, Cal takes my hand. "I'm pretty sure you promised me a dance, Zelda."

Glancing up, he gives me a reassuring smile, and I want to kiss him. "Yes, you're right, I did."

"If you'll excuse us." He does a little nod to Seth and the Ice Queen.

After securing our glasses on a low table, he leads me away from the grand inquisition to an area at the back of the enormous deck. An acoustic band is playing softly, some kind of yacht rock, and Cal pulls me against his chest. My forehead touches his jawline, and he speaks in my ear.

"Lara is an elitist prig. I'm sorry if she embarrassed you." His arms are warm and strong around me. I hold him, fumbling my way back to calm.

"She really hates Ava," I think out loud, scanning the area for my sister. I haven't seen her since we boarded, and I know she's going to panic if she sees Seth. "We should probably find them."

"Don't worry. Ro can take care of her." He kisses the side of my ear. "I'll take care of you."

A shimmer of longing moves low in my pelvis. It's followed quickly by sadness. I would stay with Cal forever if I could. The song ends, and our eyes meet. He reaches up to touch my chin.

"Why so sad, beautiful?" I love his smile, that light in his brownish-green eyes.

"It's nothing." I force myself to smile. "I don't want to spoil our night."

"Thinking about home?"

Reaching up, I run my finger down the lapel of his elegant tuxedo coat. "I'm thinking about a lot of things."

The band starts on another song, and I want to scream when fucking Seth appears at my side. "Mind if I cut in?"

Neither of us has a chance to respond before Seth grabs my waist and turns me away onto the floor. His face is at my ear now, and panic is in my heart.

"I confess, Zelda Wilder, you make me proud out here among all these aristocrats. Who would believe you're the same little bruised-kneed hick I found in Tampa?"

"What do you want, Seth." My jaw is tight. An edge is in my voice. I don't like being cornered, and this asshole will not intimidate me.

He leans back to meet my eyes, street-smart hardness flashing in his. "I want to know what you're doing here. I know you weren't hired for your looks."

My lips tighten, but I'm aware we're being watched. I move closer to his ear. "It's over. We botched the deal. I'm leaving."

"I've worked with you a long time, Zee. You think I'm buying you threw a job?"

"It's true! I was supposed to be with the crown prince. It didn't work out, and now he's with Ava."

"Of course, he's with Ava. She's a fucking supermodel." We turn, and I blink around the room, holding my hand at the top of his shoulder so it blocks my lips.

"Right. She's a liability. You've always said that." I've got to keep him away from her.

"What were you supposed to do with that guy? Tell me the plan, and maybe we can salvage it."

No. I don't want Seth knowing anything. "I've got it under control. Ava's going to stay here. I'll be back in Miami in a week. You're not losing out. You never wanted her on our team anyway."

"You let me be the judge of that. Is it a full loss? What's your take?"

"Only ten thousand."

I feel his body tense. "*Only* ten thousand?" His hard laugh is in my ear. "*Only*? You have a fucking distorted sense of the world if you can say only ten thousand."

"It was supposed to be a lot more, but now it's over."

He's quiet, and we turn again to the slow rhythm. My heart is beating so fast. Desperation is making it difficult to breathe. I've got to keep Seth at bay.

My eyes meet Cal's, and his brow lowers. Dammit, he knows something is wrong, and I watch as he sets his glass down and moves through the crowd to where we're dancing. I love how protective he is, but I'm panicking because I only have seconds left to appease Seth.

"I'll split it with you, fifty-fifty," I hiss in his ear, teeth clenched. "Just don't fucking ruin this."

"Fifty-fifty?"

It's the last words Seth says before Cal is with us.

His strong arm goes around my waist, and I'm back at his side. "That's enough, Mr. Chicken. I'll have her back now."

Seth does a little nod. "I meant no disrespect, sir. Disrespect is not very Kentucky. I'll just say *adieu*. Is that correct?"

"That's right." Cal's eyes are leveled on him, and the overprotective glare he's shooting at Seth turns me on even more than his sexy mouth.

Seth nods and steps forward again, kissing my cheek and speaking directly in my ear. "Text me."

I flinch, and Cal feels it. He starts to make a move toward Seth, but I step between them. Facing Cal, I resume our slow dance in time with the music. Cal's eyes are focused over my shoulder watching Seth disappear through the bodies. The muscle in his jaw moves, and he looks down at me. My heart melts at his expression.

"You okay? Was that asshole making you uncomfortable?"

"I don't like fried chicken." I say with a little laugh.

I'm not sure how much more of this emotional roller coaster I can take. Cal pulls me close, and his hand moves slowly across the skin of my lower back as we sway to the remainder of the song. I rest my cheek against his shoulder, allowing his strength to soothe me.

I'm still a little trembly inside, but Seth is appeased for the moment. I didn't tell him about the additional ten thousand Reggie put in our account, and my hope is I can keep that to myself. I'm going to need it if I ever expect to get away from him for good. The song ends, and I exhale the last of my nerves.

"What now?" Cal says, looking down.

"Would you mind if we find Ava? I need to tell her something." She needs to know Seth is here, and I've got him under control.

"Sure." He pulls my hand to his lips and kisses the tops of my fingers before leading me slowly through the elegant bodies.

I think about what I told Seth, my exit strategy. My eyes drift down to my small hand so firmly in Cal's grip, and I take a shaky breath. It's going to hurt like hell when I have to leave him.

Chapter 20: Playing Politics

Rowan

The Rose Gala is the official kick off to racing season, and as such, my decision to enter the fray dominates conversation. The queen is livid, but I've managed to avoid her lectures since she suddenly returned from Marins. I'm fully committed, and nothing she can say will change my mind.

"I like your strategy, Rowan." Prince Fayed Patel of Tunis crosses the upper deck to greet me. "Enter on the last day and cause an upset. It won't win you the race."

My former rival's eyes shine with humor. On his arm is his wife Paridhi, a dark-haired beauty in a pink lace sari.

"I love your dress," she says, reaching for Ava's hand. "Will you tell me where you got it?"

With a quick glance at me, Ava goes with her to the railing overlooking the emerald waters leaving Fayed and me alone to talk.

"I heard your deal with the Americans went through," he says.

"All that's left is the approval of parliament and signing the contracts."

"Your decision to scale back your holdings in our country isn't a popular one." His tone is gentle, but I have to handle this situation diplomatically. Fayed is a close ally.

"Increasing our dependence on oil is not on my agenda. You see what it's doing to the economy in Saudi."

My friend nods. "This clean energy proposal is very new. You think it is more stable?"

"It might be. It has a large number of strong backers." A glance around the room, and I nod to a few members of the old guard watching us. "It only needs to be presented in the right way. The research is sound, and I'm confident introducing a revenue stream more stable than oil and tourism is the best course for our future."

"I am acquainted with your attention to detail. I'm sure this proposal has merit." Fayed tilts his glass side to side. "Still, I hate to lose an ally."

I'm quick to stop that presumption. "Nothing will be lost. We're not divesting; we're simply reinvesting in something new."

"Ah," he nods. "We can discuss this further at another time. I noticed technology isn't the only *new* thing occupying your thoughts."

My eyes follow his to where Ava stands talking to Paridhi. She's so natural with the princess, admiring her dress and hair. "After the race I intend to announce the deal, and depending on how it goes, my choice of a bride."

Fayed's dark brow rises. "She's very beautiful. Who is she?"

"A friend of my uncle's." I think about the answer. "She's American, but she has a way about her..." I can't think of how to finish without sounding like a lovesick fool.

Fayed chuckles and pats my shoulder. "It's a love match. The best kind." The women are slowly walking back to where we stand. "Good luck to you.

I'm going to win on Sunday, but I'll share the magnum."

That makes me laugh. "Don't claim that magnum prematurely. I'll see you at qualifications tomorrow."

Paridhi takes her husband's arm, and Ava holds mine. We watch as they stroll away, disappearing into the crowd. I glance down at my beautiful date, thinking how she changes the tone of the entire evening.

In the past, these events and functions have always felt like a chore for me. Tonight, I want everyone to see the gorgeous woman on my arm. I want them to become accustomed to seeing her with me.

"You love this," she says, looking up at me and smiling. "You're the most relaxed and happy I've seen you in public."

Putting both my hands on her waist, I pull her to me. "Are you saying I've only been relaxed and happy with you in private?"

"Up to tonight? Yes," she teases, and I lean down to kiss her. Our lips only briefly touch before she pulls back. "I have your gift."

Opening her tan clutch, she pulls out a gold herringbone bracelet. It's wide and clearly designed for a man. I watch as she fastens it around my wrist, feeling slightly uneasy. I've never worn jewelry, and I don't want to hurt her feelings.

"I know it's old-school," she says, running her finger along the shiny surface before pushing it under my cuff and into my sleeve. "You don't have to wear it, but I want you to have it. It's eighteen karat gold."

She looks up, and the shyness in her eyes makes me want to hold her in my arms. "I'm not accustomed to jewelry," I say as gently as possible.

"I know. It's not fashionable anymore." Her chin drops.

"I'm not used to something around my wrist. I might damage it." Catching her chin, I lift her eyes to mine. "Still, I'll keep it on me during the race."

Her brow relaxes, and she smiles. "For luck."

Touching her cheek, I can't help a sense of wonder at this person. "You're my luck. I'll wear it for you."

Cal's voice cuts through our moment. "Had enough of all this nonsense? I know you hate it."

I look up at my brother, joining us with Zelda on his arm. "It's not so bad. I'm actually enjoying myself."

"I don't believe it." He slants an eye at me, and I shrug.

"Rowan," Zelda says, touching her friend's hand. "Do you mind if I steal her for just a bit?"

Stepping back, I nod. "Of course not."

Cal and I watch as they walk slowly to the other side the deck, stopping by the rail. For a moment, I observe how alike they move. I suppose it's because they're so close. Ava is several inches taller than Zee.

"It's her, isn't it?" A smile is in my brother's tone. "Ava is the reason you're enjoying yourself here."

"She's part of the reason." *A very big part*, I don't add. "I just spoke with Fayed. He's aware we got the green light on the deal with the Americans."

"How'd he take it?" Cal has been with me every step of the way in my efforts to diversify our economy. "Disappointed, but understanding. He's more interested in the race at present."

"It's a festival weekend—especially now that you've changed the conversation. We'll get back to business on Monday."

"I'll have to discuss it with the queen before I bring it to the council."

"Will you include Reggie in the conversation? She's met with him a few times since he's been back."

That flashes me. "About what?" I'm more than a little annoyed they've had meetings without my knowledge.

"From what I understand, she's trying to see if he has any ulterior motives for being here—other than bringing a certain wealthy American heiress to your attention."

"Zelda," I say with a nod, thinking how his matchmaking efforts are directly linked to his record for economic conservatism. "An oil heiress is more of his outdated way of thinking. Getting us further entrenched in waning technologies."

"They're not entirely outdated just yet."

"They're also not what I want for our future. Tourism, gambling, oil—all are dependent on the global economy and disposable income. I want us insulated against factors we can't control."

Cal holds up his hands. "I'm on your side."

"Reggie, however, is not." I'm less angry at my uncle, but I'm not ready to pull him into the inner circle just yet. Cal looks away to where the ladies have gone, and I can't resist a little prod. "At least his efforts weren't wasted. You seem to be enjoying your time with Miss Benedict."

He glances up, and I don't miss the change in his expression. "She's kind of perfect, but I don't know. It's a lot to consider."

"What is?"

"They're leaving soon. Going back to America."

Now I'm the one searching for them. "I didn't know that. When?"

"Zelda didn't say an exact date. It has something to do with her uncle's will."

"That doesn't impact Ava." I'm speaking as much to myself as to my brother. "She shouldn't have to leave."

I find Ava talking to Zelda across the deck, and the shadow I see passing over her face erodes my confidence.

"Maybe," Cal continues. "I get the feeling they stick together."

I've left my brother's side, and now I'm walking to where they stand. Zelda doesn't see me approach, and I catch the end of what she's saying before Ava cuts her off.

"I think he's satisfied for now, but I don't know what he might attempt—"

"Rowan!" Ava rushes forward, placing her hand on my forearm. "Zelda and I were just talking."

"Cal told me. You're leaving? Why didn't you say anything?"

Her green eyes go round. "I don't know." She looks rapidly to Zelda and back to me. "Everything is happening so quickly."

I cover her hand with mine, thinking of our day in Occitan, making love in the ocean. I remember eating strawberries and drinking champagne, discussing poetry and what I want my legacy to be. I want Ava at my side for all of it.

"It's my fault," Zelda says, drawing my attention away from the girl standing in front of me. "I wasn't sure if Ava wanted to stay... If I have to leave."

Ava releases my arm and returns to her friend. "Stay here alone? Without you?" I don't miss the worry in her voice.

"I was hoping..." Zelda looks up at me again. "I hoped you wouldn't be alone."

I reach for my lady, and the bracelet she gave me slips out of my sleeve, falling onto my hand.

Zelda's eyes fix on it, and her expression changes. "Did you give him that?"

Ava takes my hand, tucking the piece in my sleeve again. "Yes."

"In what way? As a trade? A farewell?"

My stomach twists, and I don't understand the meaning of these questions. I don't like what that meaning could be.

"It's for luck. It's for him," she says, looking up at me. "It's for all you've given me. I don't need anything in return."

Placing my hands on the sides of her face, I trace my thumbs along her cheekbones. She has no idea how much I want to give her. "I treasure it."

Zelda looks from me to her and back again before stepping away from us. "Have a good night. We can talk more tomorrow."

My eyes are consumed with the sight of the girl in front of me. I only just hear what Zelda is saying, and I pause.

"Zelda!" I call after her. She stops, and I tell her plainly, "You will stay through the race. You won't leave until after it's done."

Her mouth opens as if she'll argue with me, but

she seems to change her mind. "I'll do what I can," she says, but that's not good enough.

"No." My voice is sterner. "You will not leave until after the race on Sunday. If you have a problem, come and talk to me."

Her brow lines, and for a moment I hold Ava, watching her friend with an expression that won't take no for an answer.

At last she sighs. "I'll talk to you if something happens."

"Good."

She's not smiling, but she returns to where Cal is waiting, holding a champagne flute and watching. I don't know what he's thinking, but I'm not letting them go so easily.

CHAPTER 21: INSTINCT

Zelda

Cal hands me my champagne, and like the tiny bubbles rising in a straight line to the surface, Rowan's command is at the top of my mind.

On the one hand, it's reassuring that the future king is so adamant about us staying in the country. On the other, I can't promise him I won't leave. I'm more inclined to say Ava will stay — if he'll have her once the truth is out.

Cal's sexy tone pulls me out of my distraction. "Have I mentioned how beautiful you are tonight?"

Glancing up, I study his eyes. They change color, depending on what he wears, sometimes being all green, others more brown. Tonight they're warm, and that flippy fish I was sure had swum away for good when Seth appeared is back. He stirs these feelings I can't stop, even though I know they'll devastate me in the end.

"What do you see when you look at me?" I ask, thinking of what Seth said as we danced, who I really am.

"Well..." His large hand covers my lower back, pulling me close. "The first time I saw you, I noticed your top lip is a little fuller than your bottom."

"Oh!" Embarrassment heats my face. "It makes me look buck-toothed, doesn't it?" I pull the offending lip under my bottom teeth.

"No." He reaches up to touch my mouth, releasing it from my bite. "It makes you look like someone I want to do very naughty things with." His low voice is sultry at my ear, flooding my panties with heat.

"Cal—"

"Hang on, I'm not done." Taking my hand, he starts to walk, leading me down the stairs to the lower deck. "I like how the line in your chin is slightly off-center."

"It is?" *Oh my god!* I cover my chin.

That makes him laugh, and he takes my hand away. "I said I *like* it." He stops a moment and kisses my hand. "But most of all, I like when you speak."

Good grief, now he's going to say my voice is weird. I'm almost afraid to use it. "What happens when I speak?"

"Your blue eyes sparkle." Lifting my chin to look at him, I catch the gleam in his and my insides tighten. "It's like you have this amazing secret just for me."

Shaking my head, I do a little laugh. "Your imagination is very vivid."

"Don't crush my dream." He resumes walking, leading me across the smooth wooden deck. As we pass a server holding a tray of champagne flutes, he replaces our empties with two fulls.

"Why are you plying me with alcohol?" I tease.

"I like how champagne affects you."

He pulls me through a narrow door into an equally narrow passage. It's dim, with only a few recessed lights scattered around the corners. We reach another door, and he lifts the handle, stepping through it and going down another narrow hallway.

"Where are you taking me?" I hold his arm as I carefully maneuver down the passage, trying not to fall or spill my drink.

Finally, he reaches the last door. "I looked up the boat's layout. You've got to see this."

Leading us inside, he shuts the door behind us and locks it. I look around the room in wonder. We're in a plush bedroom with stark white carpeting. All the accents are shiny wood, and most of the space is filled with an enormous king bed. Two padded leather steps lead up to a Jacuzzi tub perched high and surrounded by narrow windows looking out at the night sky.

"It's beautiful!" I whisper. "Whose room is this?"

"Nobody's. They rented the yacht for the gala. No one is staying here…"

I don't miss the way his voice trails off. "I feel like there's a *but* coming."

"Did you see what we have here?" He puts his drink on a small shelf attached to the wall and walks to the enormous Jacuzzi.

"A Jacuzzi in the bedroom?" I do the same and join him at the steps.

Cal's eyebrows wriggle as he turns the tap. "Let's test this baby out."

Everything that happened tonight has me so tense and worried… A relaxing soak would be so nice.

"Again, you know exactly what I need," I say.

"I'll take care of you." He's back with me, pulling me close.

My insides unclench, and I rest my cheek against him. We're below the party in this private place. The door is locked, a Jacuzzi tub is filling, and this amazing man, this prince, is holding me so close. *Am I in a fairytale?*

"The gala will go all night," he says, running his hands down my hair. "We can sleep here if we want."

"How do you know?"

Warm teasing is in his voice. "I realize I don't tell you this enough, but I'm a prince. I tend to get certain privileges."

Closing my eyes, I only hold him. Ava is safe with the king; I'm here with this prince. It's almost funny I've never thought of him that way. Up to this point, he's always just been Cal.

"Sexy MacCallam Lockwood Tate," I say with a sigh.

He chuckles, "What was that?" His hand covers my lower back.

"I was thinking how I never think of you as a prince."

His cheek rests against the top of my head. "I'm going to take that as a compliment."

"I'm sorry—I don't mean it as a bad thing…"

"Don't apologize." Stepping back, he lifts my face, looking deep into my eyes. "I like that you see me as a man first. You're not looking for anything. You don't have an agenda."

My voice is quiet, serious. "I couldn't."

I never expected MacCallum Lockwood Tate. Even if I had, I would never have been prepared for him. He came straight out of left field and caught me totally off guard… and I've fallen for him so hard.

His expression changes, it turns focused and burning with intensity. Stepping back, he flicks his tie undone before moving to the cuffs of his white shirt. From there he starts on the front buttons.

"Take off that dress." It's a low order that starts my insides buzzing.

For a second, I'm transfixed, watching as he unfastens his clothes. Then I think of all the dirty things we can do in a hot tub.

"This is vaguely familiar," I tease.

"Dress. Off." It's a little louder, a little more stern, and all my teasing fades into lust.

I reach behind my neck to loosen the tie. My top falls to my waist, and our night in the Paris Hotel burns in my memory. I shiver watching him catch the bottom of his shirt and pull it over his head, leaving his thick hair a sexy mess.

"All the way," he commands. "I want to see that pussy."

"So bossy, MacCallum," I sigh.

He's in front of me in only black trousers, and the lines along his torso and stomach deepen in the dim light. Dark eyes hold me, waiting for me to obey.

This time I'm wearing panties, but when my dress hits the floor, it's possibly even hotter than if I weren't. I'm standing in heels and a matching nude-lace lingerie set I picked up as we passed through Agent Provocateur this morning. My hair is in soft waves around my shoulders, skimming my nipples like in his fantasy.

A hiss of air passes through his teeth, and he steps forward, running a finger along the black lines of the lace flowers. His touch is electric, heightening all the sensations humming under my skin.

"Let me see them," he says.

Reaching up, I slide my fingertips along the edge of the lace, pulling the bra cups down so my hardened nipples peek over them. Large hands immediately close over my breasts, cupping and squeezing them.

"You are so damn sexy."

It's my turn now. I trace my fingers along the lines of his chest, sliding my thumbs over his hardened nipples, loving that he's as turned on as I am. Dragging them lower, I watch as his skin tenses in the wake of my nails. I cup the erection straining in his pants, moving my hand up and down the rigid length. I love the way he moans as I tease him.

"What do you want?" I lift my mouth so my lips just graze his skin as they move, my fingers tracing his cock.

"All of you," he rasps. "In every way."

Stepping back, I unfasten my bra, so it falls away. I walk past him to the side of the Jacuzzi tub and reach up to shut off the water. The position arches my back, and I look over my shoulder at him, ass up.

He doesn't waste a moment removing the last of his clothes. In two steps, he's behind me, jerking my panties down my hips.

"Oh, god," I gasp, gripping the step for balance. My knee bends, and I brace myself on the padded leather as he holds my hip, running his cock along my slit, dipping it inside only a bit before sliding it forward to tease my clit.

"Cal... oh, yes," I moan, my fingers cutting into the leather.

In one quick thrust, he's inside. We both groan loudly as he stretches me, holding my hips a moment while we regain our bearings. He leans forward, over my back, to speak in my ear, and my body lights up like a torch.

"I'm going to fuck you so hard." He gives me a rough thrust, and I gasp. My hand flies forward to brace us against the side of the tub. "Then I'm going to do it again."

Another deep thrust, and my thighs tremble. He bites the top of my shoulder and a moan slips from my throat. He does it again, faster, going deeper.

"Cal..." I whisper, my eyes squeezed shut. The sensations rocketing through my stomach and core are overwhelming.

His grip on my waist is like iron. His thrusts become faster, relentless and punishing. He's hitting me so hard my feet rock forward onto my tiptoes. One hand slides around, and his long fingers taunt my clit.

"Come," he groans. "Come for me."

I'm clenching and gasping as he moves in a rhythm faster, provoking the orgasm spiking my veins. He's never been like this. The Playboy Prince is gone, and instead this conqueror has me, taking what he wants.

He kisses my back, and the scruff of his beard clenches my insides, causing him to groan. "I want you to know I've been here wherever you go."

"Oh, god... Yes!" I fumble my hand to cover his moving swiftly between my legs as my vision darkens, my brain scrambles.

I brace against the wall of the Jacuzzi as he blows my mind. Then all at once, he starts to jerk, groaning and pulsing. My insides break, and I come with a ragged cry. He continues rocking us as the sensations flutter and ripple through my legs, through the arches of my feet.

We're move together slower. I'm trembling, and he's pulsing above me, at my back, sliding his warm hands down the length of my back. I want to curl into his arms. I want him to hold me as I hold him. I want to wrap my arms around his neck and never leave. I want to bask in this afterglow, forgetting everything and pretending I can keep this beautiful man, this beautiful dream.

He slowly pulls out, and I feel the traces of cum on my thighs from an orgasm I can't wrap my mind around. Turning to on the padded leather step, he pulls me onto his lap.

My knees are bent, and my cheek is against his skin. We're breathing hard, still coming down, and he slides his hand gently down my hair. Turning my face, I kiss his neck. My heart feels shattered yet whole. He stormed in and took it, and I don't know if I'll ever get it back. He's right. No matter where I go, I'll remember this night. I'll remember how I gave him everything.

The hand that was stroking my hair moves around to my chin, and he lifts my face. Without a word, he kisses me so deeply. My mouth opens readily, and our tongues slide together. It's warm, tasting, bonding and urgent. Tears heat my closed eyes, and I reach up to hold him, to wrap my arms around his neck, as we communicate in a way words can't capture.

His lips chase mine, kissing me over and over, nipping my top lip and moving higher to my closed eyes. I'm sure he can taste the salty tears there, hiding behind my lids. He kisses my forehead and then holds me in a long embrace.

Moments slip by as we luxuriate in this closeness, as we let our hearts join with each other's. It's only a little while before he moves us slowly to stand.

"Here," he says, reaching for a soft white cloth and dipping it in the water. Squeezing the excess, he hands it to me then touches my cheek.

Our eyes hold for a moment, and it's so electric, so intense, I have to blink away for fear I'll say something I can't take back. He clears his throat, reaching again for the water as I use the cloth to clean myself.

"It isn't hot anymore," he says, and I hear the drain. "I'll have to refill it."

"I wish we could swim in the ocean." I think of the warm salt water swirling around our naked bodies.

Stepping down, he's in front of me again, placing his palm against my cheek. "We could go back to Occitan."

I slide my hand over the back of his, and our eyes meet in that incredible swirl of emotion. A loud, staccato banging from the door breaks it all. I squeal and jump back, dropping the cloth.

"Who's in there? Open this door!" An angry male voice shouts from the outside.

Panic hits me, and I step into my filmy panties, pulling them quickly over my hips. "I thought you said nobody was staying here!"

"I guess I was wrong," Cal says, grabbing his boxer briefs.

My bra is on in record time, and I'm reaching for my dress when the banging starts again, more violently.

The entire door vibrates from it, and Cal laughs as he steps into his trousers. "I wonder who it could be."

A noise like metal scraping against the knob is next. It's a sound I remember so well from the days when Ava and I used to sneak into boathouses to hide from the rain. *They're coming in!*

Instinct kicks in, and my dress is over my head in a flash. I scoop my shoes and clutch off the floor and dash up the leather steps, pushing the narrow window sideways and open. Cal's voice barely registers in my ears before I jump.

The water is like ice when I plunge into the sea. It's such a familiar memory, I don't even think as I kick hard, pumping my arms and swimming away from the luxury yacht as fast as I can. Another splash is behind me, and I swim harder. I don't know if they'll try to catch me, but I have to get away!

The second swimmer is stronger than I am, faster, and he's beside me in a few strokes, catching me and pulling me up. We've managed to swim around another yacht, and now we're hidden in the darkness.

"Wait for me," Cal chokes on a laugh, spitting out water and breathing loudly. I can't stop shaking, and he's laughing more, again spitting water as he holds my arm.

"You fucking jumped out the window!" he cries.

We're both dog paddling and the fear and adrenaline that flooded my mind are surging away, leaving my muscles spent and weak. *What the hell did I just do?*

"That guy," I gasp, spitting out salt water. "He scared me!"

"And you fucking jumped out the window?" Cal laughs again. "Jesus, Zee, I never know what the hell you'll do next!"

"I-I guess I panicked." My stomach cramps, and I'm exhausted all of a sudden.

He pulls me against his bare chest and wraps his arms around me. "You're shaking so hard," he says softly, running his hand up and down my back. "It's okay. Nothing's going to happen to you. Remember the part about how I'm a prince?"

I can't answer. I only hold him. My shoes are gone. I must've dropped them as I swam away. I still have my clutch, although I'm sure everything in it is ruined. Thank goodness for Lifeproof phone cases. I'm pretty confident Reggie won't be replacing any more of our things.

"I want to go... Back to the hotel." I almost said *home*. Where the hell would that be anymore? "Will you take me to my hotel?"

He leans back and smiles. "Sure, my little gypsy." Then he laughs again. "I swear, if I didn't know better, I'd think you were something out of *Oliver Twist*."

If only he knew. We paddle to one of the long concrete piers. A metal ladder leads out of the water, and we hold it, catching our breath before we climb.

"Sorry," I manage. "I'm not used to being caught breaking the law."

Once we're standing on the pier, I survey our appearance. My dress is soaked, and I'm barefoot. Cal is only in his soaked black tuxedo pants. He runs his hands back and forth through his hair, leaving it messy and cute, and his eyes are sparkling like his white smile.

Shaking my head, I open my clutch, turning it to the side so all the water can pour out. "I guess my credit card will still work." Lifting out my phone, I press the button and it lights up. "This case just paid for itself."

He's watching me, that amused expression firmly in place. "What are you doing?"

"Trying to figure out how we'll get back to my hotel." Looking up, I see we're on the far end of the marina. "We can probably walk."

"Hajib is with the car in the parking lot." He points to where we boarded the yacht just a few hours earlier."

We wait for a moment, watching the elegant guests leaving the boat in pairs, walking slowly to the waiting cars. A little break occurs every few minutes, but the photographers are still hanging around as are a few of the spectators.

"You're right," he says, glancing down at his pants. "We should probably skip the car. If those photographers catch us, it'll be all over the Internet."

Reaching up, I squeeze the water out of my hair. I try to do the same with my dress, but I'm pretty much stuck looking like a drowned rat. We start to walk, hanging close to the shadow of the tree line. Every few steps, I hit a sharp rock and do a little skip and yelp.

Ten paces more, and Cal stops and catches my shoulder. "Hop on."

He turns his bare back to me, and I hold up my hands.

"It's okay, I can manage. My feet are just... out of practice."

"Get on," he says impatiently. "I've been wanting to toss you on my back since the night you twisted your ankle."

Snorting a laugh, I take his shoulder and hop on, wiggling to a comfortable position as he slips his hands under my thighs. He's moving faster, heading away from the crowd at the pier.

"That night seems so long ago," I say, resting my chin on his neck, inhaling his warm man-scent mixed with the fresh, briney air. "It's strange to think I was supposed to be with Rowan."

"Supposed to be?" His voice isn't angry, more curious, and I decide to take a chance...

"Reggie wanted me to meet him."

"Right," Cal nods, surprising me. "He thought you might be a solution to Ro's problems."

That's news to me! "What are you talking about?"

He does a little exhale. "The economy has been bad—unemployment is up, oil prices are down, tourist spending is down. Reggie thought the money from your uncle's oil reserves could be a new source of revenue for the country."

"Oh," I say, quietly, my lips pressing into a frown.

That story doesn't get me off the hook, it only plays into the con Reggie was running—the con I knew about when I stepped out of that town car at the Royal Sports Club all those nights ago.

"I'm sorry," Cal's voice is quiet. "Marrying for political or economic advantage is a longstanding tradition in the monarchy."

Tilting my head to the side, I study his profile. He's frowning, but it only sharpens his square jaw, making him look even more attractive.

"You don't have to apologize. You killed any interest I had in your brother when you came to my bedroom that night."

He exhales a little laugh and glances over to me. "After the day we'd spent, I wasn't about to let Ro have you."

My heart fills with so much joy. Nothing I can

do will stop it, and I know it's only going to be so painful in the end. He slows walking. We're back at the Fairmont, and I slip off his back. It's quiet and the traffic is slow. We're standing in the moonlight on the beach facing each other. I know somewhere Ava is with Rowan.

"Would you like to come up?" My voice is quiet.

His handsome smile splits his cheeks. "Do you have to ask?"

Instinctively, I know I should be trying to detach. I should be putting distance between us, not pulling him closer. I should be guarding my heart and thinking of self-preservation.

I don't. I take his hand, leading us slowly to the back entrance. I find my door card and let us in, leading him to the elevator and ultimately my room so we can spend another night together. As long as he's here and we're in this same place, I just can't stay away.

Chapter 22: Trapped

Rowan

The engine roars as I blast through the straight. With a sharp downshift, I slow the pace so I can take the first curve. It's a nonstop pattern of trying to cover as much ground as possible in the straights, followed by dropping almost to a crawl in the hairpin turns. My speed fluctuates from nearly four hundred kilometers per hour to all the way down to sixty.

Still, I grew up running this track. It's the only race I've ever cared about. It's ridiculously hard and only included in the circuit because of how old and challenging it is, and it's right here in my own backyard. Winning has been a personal goal as long as I've been able to drive, and this year I'll do it.

Plunging into the tunnel, I'm blinded by the sudden darkness. Blinking fast, I hold the wheel steady, doing my best to avoid any swerving at this speed. Just as fast, I'm blasting into white-hot sunlight. More fast blinking, trying to see. Dirt on my visor annoys me, and I reach up to tear off the thin cover. I'll have three more tear-offs in the actual race.

"Keep it steady. You're doing great." Cal is in my ear, coaching me through the laps.

I ease off, preparing for the final hairpin, dropping to a crawl as my arms do a one-eighty turning the wheel. At last, I'm out. It's a straight shot to the finish line, and I shift then jam the accelerator to the floor to make up all the time I just lost.

"Keep going... Almost there..." The tension in my brother's voice grows as the black and white checks fly past me. "You did it!" he shouts. "It's the best qualifying time today!"

I'm breathing hard, my muscles loose as I coast into the pit area where Cal and my crew are waiting, cheering. Once I've stopped, I pull off the helmet, and Cal grabs my arm, giving it a rough shake.

"That's pole position, depending on Patel."

My jaw tightens as I bite back a *fuck*. I know the race will come down to the two of us, and I'm hoping to be pole sitter, the most favorable spot on the starting grid.

"It's okay," Cal says with a laugh, leaning closer to my ear. "I've been watching him practice. He's braking too much this year. Either it's a new car or he's distracted."

"The course is nothing but hazards. I'd forgotten how much we have to ride them."

We're walking back to the stands, waving and nodding thanks to the cheering spectators and fellow drivers watching from the sides of the track.

"Doesn't matter. Your speed is the best a driver could hope for. I don't see him overtaking you."

"I'm glad you're with me, brother." I slap his shoulder. "Get cleaned up. We've got meetings."

A brief stop at the desk to sign the official forms, and I'm heading out. The car will be locked in the *parc fermé*, the secured area where all competing cars are kept, until the race tomorrow.

In the town car on my way to the palace to shower, change, and start rolling out my proposal for the clean energy deal to the queen and members of parliament, I feel confident and optimistic. My mind drifts to Ava this morning, curled in the sheets asleep, her dark hair soft around her on the pillows.

I think about holding her on my lap last night in that same bed, watching her beautiful body tremble as she came apart in my arms. So far I've been gentle with her, easy. I look forward to introducing her to more interesting ways of making love. Once she feels more confident.

We left the gala last night shortly after I spoke to Zelda and returned to Occitan. After a brief swim in the cove *sans clothes*, we walked back to the house wrapped in thick white robes. Her hand was on my arm, and her body was tight against my side. Stopping on the terrace, I traced my thumbs down the sides of her face, watching how the moonlight shone in her eyes. I considered asking her to marry me then, but I decided to wait.

For starters, I don't have a ring. I need to put this race behind me, and I've got to present the new deal to parliament, sign all the contracts, and announce it publicly. With our economic troubles on the mend, everyone will be far more open to the idea of an outsider, an American, as their future queen.

My queen.

"If she'll have me," I exhale, speaking quietly to myself.

"She will, sir."

Glancing up, I catch Hajib's eyes in the rearview mirror. They're creased, and I can tell he's smiling. *Odd Job.*

"You think so?" I say louder, leaning back.

"With confidence, sir. I've seen the way the young lady looks at you. It's a love match."

It's the same thing Fayed said. *A love match...* I had always prepared myself to save love, should I find it, for a mistress. My wife would most likely be an arrangement based on political expediency and financial gain. Our marriage would be respectful and courteous, but *love*?

It seems I was wrong. I glance down at my hands as I turn the word over in my mind. The next time I see her, I'll have to tell her how I feel.

* * *

Zelda

Cal is gone when I open my eyes. A slip of paper is on the pillow where he slept, and I push up onto my elbows, reaching for it.

Have to be at the track for time trials with Ro. After that, meetings with the cabinet, dinner with the queen. I'll text or call as soon as possible. Miss you already. Last night was amazing. –MLT

My stomach warms, and that silly smile plasters across my face again. I drop my head with a little growl. "I've got to stop this!"

Folding the piece of paper in half, I tuck it into my phone case. Then I sit up and throw the blankets aside as I stomp across the room. The room service menu is on the desk. I flip through the pages and order... *it's after noon?* Lunch, I guess. I didn't mean to sleep so late, but in fairness, we didn't actually go to sleep until almost dawn.

Following that insanely mind-blowing fuck on the boat followed by the dive into the sea and the

294

walk back to the hotel, we crashed for a little while as *Cruel Intentions* played in the background.

Naturally, all the sexy in that movie led to more sexy for us, but it wasn't as insanely desperate or possessive. Still, the connection we'd made earlier lingered around us. We were closer, more bonded somehow.

I'm standing in the living room staring into space, trying to understand what happened between us when the door opens, and Ava walks in slowly. She's wearing a dark tee that must be Rowan's. It's five sizes too big, and her hair is a beachy-messy bedhead. She doesn't meet my eyes as she tosses her bag on the table. I'm pretty sure her expression mirrors the conflict I feel. *We weren't supposed to get emotionally involved.*

"Hey," I say, taking a step toward her. "I'm just ordering lunch. You want some?"

"Yeah," she nods, walking over to drop onto the sofa.

I sit on the arm and she scoots to the side, placing her dark head against my leg. I think about last night. "You gave him the bracelet."

Quiet answers me. Her chin lowers, and I slide my hand down her hair. After a few moments she speaks. "Remember when you said you only dreamed of safety and keeping us safe when you were a girl?"

"Yeah." I'm still sliding my hand down her head.

When she speaks again, her voice is quiet, almost ashamed. "I dreamed of being a princess. After we ran away and it was just the two of us and we were so scared? I dreamed of a handsome prince coming and saving us. I dreamed about it a lot."

My lips pull down in a frown. I don't know why her words make me want to cry. For a few moments, I look out the window remembering those early days. I remember how her little body would tremble when she was afraid. I remember how she would cling to me like I knew anything about keeping us safe. The only thing I had was stubbornness and luck.

Clearing my throat, I fight back my emotions. "That's okay. If it helped you not be afraid, you don't have to be embarrassed."

"I feel like..." She hesitates, a few moments pass. "I feel like these last few days my dream has come true. And I hate that it's all a lie."

My brow lines, and I think about my jobs, the cons I've run, the people I've cheated. As much as I've tried to keep her away from what I do, she's still a part of my world. She's never really out of danger as long as she's with me.

Threatening Ava is how Reggie trapped me here in the first place. When he said she could go to prison for five years, I panicked. I could go to prison for five years, but not Ava. For the first time, I'd seen how my actions can hurt her.

With a deep sigh, she pushes off the couch. "I'm going to shower."

I don't try to stop her. She disappears into her bedroom, and I place the order for our food. For a moment, I sit staring at the sapphire blue waters, thinking about that whole concept of freedom. I think about the beautiful moments I've shared with Cal. As much as I love those moments, as close as he is to my heart, I'm a liability to him as well. If his people knew who I really am, all the things I've done...

With a fortifying breath, I push off the sofa. It's time to confront Reggie. I have to get to the bottom of what's going on here. At the very least, I need to know what he expects from us now. After that, I'll deal with Seth.

I might have gotten a break from reality for a little while last night, but my problems are stacking up faster than waves coming in with the tide. It's time to sink or swim.

In my room, I pull on a pair of dark jeans and a black tank. My hair is a mess from jumping in the ocean followed by screwing Cal all night, but I smooth it into a side ponytail. I'm not trying to impress Reggie. He's seen me messy and unpolished.

Stepping into a pair of beige espadrilles, I give myself a reassuring look in the mirror, but it's no good. My face is lined with worry.

Lunch will be here when I get back, but I can't eat with this hanging over my head. I don't know what Reggie will do when I tell him I quit. He could call Rowan and destroy us. Or he could simply have us kicked out of the hotel.

That dark possibility has me dashing back to grab my clutch off the kitchen counter. My phone, the room key, and that black credit card are inside, and I put all three in my pockets just in case.

Reggie's room is only a few doors down from ours. As I walk, the space seems to expand like a telephoto lens. Cal is on my mind—what he'll say if Reggie exposes us, losing him. My insides shiver. I had thought I could figure out Reggie's plan and tell it to Cal. I had hoped it might redeem us in his eyes...

The thought *Ava doesn't know where I am* drifts through my mind. Too late. I'm at his door. I have to do this now.

Lifting my fist, I'm all set to knock when I notice the door isn't closed all the way. Placing my palm flat against the wood, I give it a gentle push, and the latch slips open. It falls away, revealing the vacant entrance. Two male voices are inside arguing, so I step quietly through the door, thankful my shoes make no sound.

"His deal with the Americans is finalized. He's meeting with parliament now, with the queen tonight... She *will* support him." Reggie's voice is tense and urgent, and I have no idea what he's talking about. "It's over, Wade. We're through"

"Calm yourself, Reginald," the male voice I assume is Wade's answers. "I'm meeting with Fayed this afternoon, and I intend to reassure him we will not be pulling out of his country. Their oil and gas production has just gotten off the ground, and with the countries unified, we'll invest deep in their operations."

"How do you intend to make that happen?" Reggie snaps back.

"Simple. The crown prince has given us the means to remove him as an obstacle."

"Is that so? Do explain."

My brain is moving fast. Cal said Wade Paxton was the Prime Minister of Totrington. He's the man Rowan suspected of plotting with Reggie and Hubert to kill their father.

"We've had a plan in place since before the king died for eliminating these... impediments." His voice is calm, sinister, and my chest tightens. "Rowan's decision to enter the Grand Prix made it easier than ever. I've already set the wheels in motion, if you will."

"What does that mean?" A tone I've never heard before is in Reggie's voice. It sounds like fear.

"I mean the removal of the crown prince has begun."

Ice filters through my veins. I sure as hell know that means.

Reggie's disgusted laugh makes me swallow hard. Every muscle in my body is tense. "Why even pretend we're working together, Wade? You've already planned everything without our council."

"Don't be a brooding old woman, Reginald. You had a plan. It was idiotic, so I launched a new one." He pauses to chortle. "Idiotic... Why would Rowan choose one female over all the others?"

"Money, political expediency. I'm familiar with my nephew's taste. I brought him a lady I knew would tempt him."

My nose wrinkles. His word choice makes me feel like a call girl.

"And still he chose another," Wade growls. "Such an obstinate young man. So arrogant and annoying."

"Back to the point," Reggie says. "Tell me about this plan."

"While your trick with the girl was idiotic, you showed great foresight in bringing along a spare."

"You mean Ava?" I hear movement as if he's pacing. "I don't see how she'll help us any more than Zelda did."

"She's already helped us immensely," Wade says. "He's in love with her, and he's doing this race to impress her."

"I think you're mistaken. He's never given up racing. He only stopped competing."

"Reginald." Wade's voice is condescending. "Are you being deliberately obtuse? Trust me. This is all about swinging around his big dick."

"You've always been so colorful." Reggie sniffs. "And what if it is?"

"What if he has an unfortunate *accident*?" Evil drips in his voice. "The poor, poor crown prince. It's too bad if he's taken out of the picture before he ever has the chance to finalize his deal."

My scalp prickles as I feel the blood drain from my face. *They're talking about killing Rowan at the race!*

The room is silent. I hold my breath waiting to hear what Reggie will say. *Do the right thing, Reginald...*

"You're planning to assassinate the crown prince." It isn't a question. It isn't even as shocked as it should be.

"Such an ugly word." Wade's slimy voice makes my skin crawl. "I'm merely observing it's a difficult track. It involves much braking and rapid acceleration. A hairpin turn is positioned at the top of a high cliff, and at one point, the drivers are plunged into almost total darkness."

"The tunnel," Reggie says quietly.

"Fatal crashes occur all the time in motorsport. It would be a shame if your future king's car failed. If he slammed into the wall and joined their ranks."

Closing my mouth, I swallow, trying to restart my breathing. I've got to get out of here. I've got to get back across the hall, to our room and tell Ava. She's got to warn Rowan... I start to move just as the men resume speaking.

"It won't work," Reggie says, and I stop to listen.

"Why the devil not?"

"MacCallam. He's the presumptive heir. If anything happens to Rowan, he becomes the crown prince, and he'll continue his brother's legacy."

"You disappoint me, Reginald," I hear him moving in the room. "You think my plan doesn't include MacCallam?"

I'm frozen in place. *Not Cal...*

Reggie hesitates a moment. "What have you planned?"

More movement. "As captain of the pit crew, Cal would know if the car had problems. He would be in charge of checking it out, top to bottom... Unless he had ambitions of his own. Unless he saw an opportunity to seize power."

Reggie makes a grunting sound. "Everyone knows how close the brothers are. No one will believe Cal would intentionally hurt Rowan."

My knuckles are white on the kitchen counter. I'm holding on, bracing myself against what they might say next.

"They don't have to believe it. They need only look at the evidence."

I push off the counter and start for the door, but just as I'm moving, my phone rings out my texting chime.

"Who's there?" Reggie shouts, and I hear them both heading my way fast.

My heart is flying, and I run around the corner, pushing off the wall as I skid to a stop at the door. Jerking the handle down, I'm pulling it toward me when it flies from my hand with a *SLAM!*

"What have we here?" Wade's voice is a sinister smile. He grabs my shoulder in an iron grip and slams my back against the wall, forcing an *Oof!* from my mouth. "What the fuck are you doing sneaking around our rooms?"

It takes me a moment to catch my breath. "I wasn't—" My text tone sounds again, and Wade's eyes drop to my waist.

"Take her phone," he says to Reggie.

"Zelda," Reggie says, taking my phone from my pocket. "You shouldn't have come here."

"Ah, Miss Wilder," Wade Paxton smiles, and I recognize the evil glint in his eyes. I've seen it before in our trashy foster "father," although I never called him that. "Do you know who I am?"

He has greasy black hair and a little mustache, and he's wearing a suit. On the pocket is an insignia. Lifting his lapel, he holds it closer for me to see.

"Wade Paxton," I say quickly.

"Correct. Prime Minister of Totrington." His painful grip moves to my upper arm, and he lifts me, half-dragging, half-pushing me into the living room of Reggie's suite. "You've been spying on classified state secrets. Do you know what we do with spies, Miss Wilder?"

"You don't have to kill me," I say fast. I might be out of my league with these guys, but I grew up talking my way out of trouble. "I won't tell anyone. I'll leave here and go back to Miami."

"You must think I'm a fool." He looks to my former associate. "Reggie, who is that text from?"

Reggie turns my phone over and touches the button. "Playboy prince." My heart plunges to my feet, and his blue eyes meet mine. "I'm going to assume that's MacCallam. It says, 'Are you wearing panties.'"

My eyes close, and any plans I had to convince them I wouldn't tell Cal are shot to hell now. If I were looking for something to pin on Reggie, I sure as hell found it. Too bad, it might cost me my life.

"She isn't leaving this room." Wade has my arm again, and he drags me to the wet bar, opening and shutting drawers quickly.

My mouth is dry, I'm shaking, but I've got to try. "I'm leaving him. I was coming here to tell Reggie. I'm going back to Miami. Cal doesn't know."

"Here." Wade pulls out a knife. "Do you have any rope, Reginald?"

"Stop this, Paxton," Reggie reclines on the sofa, a bored look on his face. "We're not killing her. Who will clean up the mess?"

Wade's sinister eyes are calculating. "What do you suggest?"

"Lock her in the bedroom until we've finished our business here then arrange for her disposal afterwards."

"Reggie," I whisper. "Just let me take Ava and go. I won't get in your way. You know I won't."

"I don't know anything now that you're romantically involved."

"I'm not romantically involved!" I cry, my voice cracking. "I'm a professional, Reggie. Remember the casino?"

"I thought you were a professional. Sadly I was mistaken." He rises from the couch, and walks toward the bedroom. Wade jerks my arm, pushing me after him.

"Very convenient, you providing your phone."

I watch as he begins texting. "What are you doing? Who are you texting?" Panic floods my veins.

"Message to Ava: Ran out to meet Cal. See you after the race. Zee." He glances toward Wade. "You said your plan is in motion. I presume it includes men stationed along the course?"

"On the pit crew, along the course," Wade says. "I've covered every possible outcome."

My eyes fly back and forth between them. I'm having difficulty breathing. "What will you do?"

Reggie steps directly in front of me, pushing my nose almost to his chest. "I might not trust you, but I know your Achilles heel. You'll cooperate—if only to protect your sister's life."

Jerking away from Wade, I swing my arm at Reggie's face. "You will *not* hurt Ava!"

He dodges easily, shoving me aside. "I *will* kill your beautiful sister if you do anything to interfere with our plans."

Stepping back, I take a breath. He's right about one thing—no matter what I have to do, I won't let him hurt Ava.

"You have a deal. I won't say a word."

I start for the door, and Wade Paxton actually laughs. "Where do you think you're going?"

Pausing, I look from him to Reggie. "I just gave you my word—"

"Whatever deal you make with Sir Winchester, it will begin *after* the race tomorrow. Not before."

My arm is back in his iron grip, and he drags me to the bedroom, shoving me inside. I slump against the wall as he walks around the room. He goes to the balcony door and then returns to where I'm doing my best to stay out of his way. He goes in the bathroom for a moment then returns with his hands on his hips.

"This won't work," he snaps. "Too many ways she can escape."

"She can't go through the lobby," Reggie argues. "The paparazzi are everywhere. She's a top story now that she's been seen with the prince numerous times."

The two men look at me again. Wade's eyes are glittering and cold, and I'm convinced he'd just as soon kill me. Reggie looks more impatient. My mind is racing.

"I can give you money. I'll give back all the money—"

"You stupid bitch, I bankrolled this entire venture." Wade's lip curls. "I *own* you."

Reggie walks through the suite again, looking around. "Every goddamn room has a window."

"Put her in the bathroom," Wade says. "I'll walk down to the corner and purchase rope, duct tape, and a bicycle chain to tie her hands and lock her in."

Reggie nods. "Get going. I'll guard her here."

The other man starts for the door, but then walks back to me. "Just in case you're thinking of trying to double-cross me."

With a loud *SMACK!* he whips his meaty palm across my face. Light explodes behind my eyes, and it takes me a moment to realize I'm on the floor, on my hands and knees. Pain radiates through my cheek, and my mouth is full of the thick, coppery taste of blood.

"You're determined to leave evidence behind," Reggie says, pushing a cloth handkerchief to me.

Wade bends down and grabs a handful of my hair right at the top of my head. He jerks my neck back, forcing me to look at him. I struggle not to cry out, but the pain makes it difficult.

"I'm not impressed by you, Zelda Wilder. I don't value your life over our plans for Monagasco. Do you understand?" He's so close, little drops of spit hit my face. "If it weren't for Reggie, you'd already be dead."

Blinking fast, I struggle to hold it together as I glare back at his hateful eyes.

"One sneaky trick. One attempt to escape, and I won't hesitate." He shoves my head away, and I sprawl onto the floor again.

His shoes squeak on the marble as he goes to the door. It closes with a slam, and he's gone, leaving only Reggie and me.

"Why are you here, Zelda? I told you to wait until I came for you."

"Let me go, Reggie." My heart aches and my swollen lip distorts my words. "It's not too late to change this."

"What's happening now goes way beyond what we discussed in Miami."

"How can you do this?" My voice cracks. "They're your nephews. Your family!" All I can think of is protecting Ava, saving Cal, saving Rowan.

His expression becomes closed. "In matters of state, family is sometimes a casualty."

"So you *did* help kill the king! Rowan was right!"

Clearing his throat, he walks to the wet bar, and I watch as he takes a handful of ice and puts it in a cloth napkin. "Philip was overweight. He had a short temper and high blood pressure. I can't be held responsible for his heart attack."

He hands me the makeshift ice pack, and I hold it to my throbbing cheek. "You stood by and let it happen. It's the same as helping."

He walks to the large glass doors overlooking the Mediterranean. "I like you Zelda. I'll do what I can to protect you, but if you cross Wade Paxton, I can't stop the consequences. He is not someone you want to play games with."

The door opens, and Wade returns. The only thing in his hand is a rope. "Sold out of duct tape," he growls as he passes, grabbing my forearm so hard, I stumble.

He drags me to the bathroom and shoves me inside. His hand goes to his pocket, and I watch as he pulls out a long knife. My throat closes.

"You see this?" His blue eyes slice into mine, and fear clenches my chest.

I don't answer and he charges me, pushing me all the way until my back slams against the wall. My head aches from hitting the plaster, and I struggle to fight back my tears. I can't appear weak. I have to be strong.

His face is right in mine, and I try to turn to avoid his sour onion breath. "Make any noise, scream..." His hand clamps around my wrist so hard, I'm afraid the bones will break.

Jerking my arm, he slams my palm flat on the granite countertop. I can't help a scream. My insides are shaking, and I struggle to get away.

"I'll start with the smallest one." The knife presses hard against the knuckle of my pinkie finger, breaking the skin as searing pain shoots through my hand.

"NO!" I shout, twisting and dropping to my knees. "DON'T!"

"SHUT UP!" He growls, kicking me in the stomach.

"Oh, god..." I'm gulping for air as pain cramps my midsection. Tears blur my vision. A roaring noise is in my ears, and I'm afraid I'll pass out. "Please... no."

"Wade!" Reggie's voice cuts through the din. "Think about what you're doing. This room is in my name. I will not be implicated in a blood bath!"

Wade pauses, looking down at me. The pressure of the knife grows stronger against my knuckle, and I cry louder. I can't stop shaking. My nose is hot. Snot is on my battered lip. His grip is a shackle around my wrist, and I'm on the floor, trying to pull away.

At once he releases me, and I fall to the hard marble. A startled cry slips from my lips. My knuckle is bloody, and I shove both hands under my arms, pushing with my heels until my back is against the wall. My knees are bent for protection.

Wade leans down, pointing the sharp knife at my nose. "I will cut them off, one by one. Then I will move to your toes. I'll take off your ears, followed by the tip of your nose. Your tongue..."

My stomach heaves, and I'm afraid I'll vomit.

"Good god, we get the point," Reggie says.

I press my eyes against the tops of my knees. I don't want to see his horrible face anymore. Everyone I know and love is in danger, and I've never been so afraid. I have no idea what I'm going to do. I only know I have to do something.

"She'll stay quiet," Reggie says in an eerily calm voice. "She won't jeopardize her sister."

"Yes," Wade's eyes flicker with sinister intent. "Your sister."

Rage and panic clash in my chest. "Don't hurt her." It's all I can manage to say.

They pause only a moment, staring down at me, before they leave. The double-doors of the bathroom slam, and I hear the rope being tied around the handles. Despair fills my chest as the tears start to fall. I've got to get out of here. I've got to get to Ava.

CHAPTER 23: SABOTAGE

Rowan

Race day dawns hot and bright. My spirits dim slightly as I look up at the cloudless sky.

"It would have been better if it were overcast," Cal says, reading my mind.

We're walking quickly to the track, and I'm going over the course, the system I've worked out for managing the curves, the braking, the slowing, and the flying into the straights full-throttle.

"The tunnel will be the hardest," I agree, thinking of the plunge into darkness followed by the immediate blinding white light.

"You're moving so fast at that point. Follow your instincts."

As we pass the other racers, we nod, shake hands with some. All are tense and jumpy. In my chest is a mixture of excitement and apprehension. Anything can happen on the track.

Fayed's team is the last group we encounter, and he steps forward grinning. "Good luck today, my friend!" He shakes my hand vigorously. "It was a lucky break getting pole position."

Our times around the track were identical, but officials gave him the coveted spot owing to his years on the circuit.

"Apparently there's an advantage to doing nothing but racing all the time," Cal says, crossing his arms.

"Don't be bitter, my friend Cal," Fayed slaps my brother's arm. "It will even out on the track."

My brow is lowered, but I give him a nod. "Have a good race."

A few more paces, and we're at my car. Cal is at my side reassuring me. "I've personally gone over everything. The car is in peak performance. It's all up to you now."

Reaching in my pocket, I close my hand around the gold bracelet Ava gave me. I haven't heard from her since Friday, and while we discussed this short separation, I long to hear her voice. She didn't return my call last night.

"Have you talked to Zelda today?" His expression changes only briefly, but it's enough to put me on edge. "What is it?"

"I don't know." He clears his throat. "We've been so slammed with meetings and race prep, I haven't been able to call her. She's not answering my texts."

My throat tightens. Here we are, a half-hour before the race begins, and I can't find Ava. Cal hasn't spoken to Zee. *If they left the country...*

I'll just fucking go after her.

"See what you can find out," I say, my voice rough as I pull on my helmet. It's time for our reconnaissance lap.

Cal's strong hand closes over my shoulder; his hazel eyes flash as he shouts over the noise of the engines. "Drive like you've been doing the last few weeks, and we'll worry about the rest later."

Nodding, I give him the thumbs up and pull onto the track. One by one, we'll make a slow lap around the course, stopping at our place on the grid. Fayed is in the lead, but I'm right behind him.

As we cover the course, my mind is on Ava. The weekend so far has been a success. The queen has agreed to support my deal, and every Member of Parliament I've spoken to has come onboard. Only two things are left—winning the race and Ava.

My focus sharpens as we reach the first hairpin, and my senses lock onto the car. The steering is sensitive to any movement, and in all my practices, I've felt immediate response. Taking the sharp corner, I notice a lag. It's the right front wheel.

Now I'm anxious to get back to the pit. Cal said he checked everything, but either a brace has come loose or an arm is failing.

We're coming down the final straight right into the tunnel, and all at once, I'm plunged into darkness. Blinking fast, I try to adjust my eyes. I hold the steering wheel steady, feeling the lag in that fucking right front, when just as fast, white light dazzles my eyes. *Hold steady.*

One final hairpin on the cliff above the ocean. I'm not pushing like I normally do for fear that tire will fly off into my windshield or one of my competitors'. *This isn't happening right now.* We slow into the grid, and I'm out of the cockpit in seconds waving for Cal.

Instantly, he's running across the track, the team right behind him. "What's wrong?"

"Right front." I'm breathing hard. "It's lagging, pulling to the center."

A crewmember I don't recognize dives under the chassis screwdriver in hand. I frown and look to my brother.

"Came over from Heinrick's team. Highly recommended." I nod, adjusting the tear offs on my visor.

"Stripped lug nut," the man says, climbing out and tossing up the silver piece as he runs for the pit. "Be right back."

We've got less than ten minutes. Fayed glances back to me, his brow lined. I give him the thumbs up as our newest crewmember finishes his work.

"Feel good?" Cal asks, massaging my shoulder. "You look good."

"Once I'm ahead of him, I'll be better."

The one-minute signal is shown, and Cal slaps my back before heading off the track. We start our formation lap, zigzagging back and forth, pumping the brakes. I'm heating up the tires, getting the engine hot, paying close attention to that right front.

"How's it feeling?" Cal's in my helmet now, and we'll communicate throughout the race.

"So far so good," I say, continuing to brake and rev the engine.

"Your temps are good."

We're back in the grid, and I pull into my space. We're all watching the lights, and the tension is razor sharp. Everything slows, I feel my breath going in... and out.

The lights disappear, and I hit the accelerator hard, shooting out as close on Fayed's tail as I can get.

"Great start!" Cal says in my helmet. "It's a two-man race!"

Seventy-eight laps to go, and it will be over. I've got ninety minutes to catch him, take the lead, then maintain my fastest time putting him far in my rearview mirror. After that, I can relax into the close.

* * *

Blinking my crusty eyes, I try to orient myself to the time. No one has come to check on me since I was locked in this room. No noises come from the other side of the door. I haven't gotten any food, and I drink water from the tap. At least I can use the bathroom. I push up to sit against the wall and wait, holding my fingers to my eyes, trying to think, trying not to cry.

Hours pass at a glacial pace. I wonder what's happening with Ava. Reggie texted her that I'm with Cal, which was sinister and genius. She won't worry about me, and she probably won't even call or text me back for fear of interrupting us. Fresh tears heat my eyes at the thought. I've got to get out of here. I've got to warn them.

For the second time, I pull myself off the floor and try the doors. The rope is so tight around the handles, they don't budge. I try to push them forward, and nothing happens. I try to pull them to me, and it's the same. Dropping my hands, I beat my head against them as the hot tears line my cheeks.

If I scream, Wade or Reggie might come. I don't know if that finger threat was a scare tactic or if he would really cut me. I don't want to find out.

Leaning against the doors, I feel utterly defeated and completely desperate. Staggering back to the wall, I slide down to a sitting position and wait, my hope almost gone.

My cheek is against the cold tile when I wake again. A high-pitched buzzing noise like an enormous swarm of bees fills the air. My forehead lines, and I try to get my bearings. I'm stiff all over as I move to sit up. *Did I sleep all night?* I reach for the light switch and turn it off. Sunlight shines through the cracks in the door, and I realize it must be Sunday.

The buzzing doesn't stop, and with a shuddering breath, I know what it is. The race has started.

"Oh, god!" I whisper, pacing the small room. I wrap my arms around my waist and try to calm my shaking insides.

The grand prix is less than two hours total. I have even less time to find a way out of here, to find a way to the track, to find Cal, and to get Rowan out of that car. Tears are in my eyes as I realize it's impossible.

"I'll never make it," I say in a broken whisper.

No! I have to try. I press my ear to the door and listen. Other than the noise of the cars, I hear nothing from the room. Grasping the door handles, I pull and push them with all my strength.

"Reggie?" I say it only a little louder than normal volume at first.

No response.

I pull the handles harder, forcing them to move as I call louder. "Reggie! I need your help! Reggie!"

It's a lie. I don't want Reggie to come. I hope he's gone. I hope he and Wade are both far from here, somewhere at the track where they can grow complacent, thinking their evil plan will succeed.

I stop and wait, listening. Several more minutes of silence pass, and I'm convinced I'm the only one in this room. Bolstered by this conviction, I grasp the door handles as hard as I can and throw my weight against them. They don't budge.

"Fuck!" I scream, jerking them to me as I throw all my weight in the opposite direction. *"Open you mother fuckers!"* I scream, running at them with all my might. It's like hitting a wall.

I'm on my knees again, trembling and crying, still holding the door. I'm too weak, and I can't get these damn doors open. I can't help them. My fingers slip off the silver handles, and I collapse on all fours, my forehead pressed against my hands on the tile.

It's quiet outside this little prison. The buzzing of the engines continues like the running down of a giant timer. My heart aches as I think of Rowan, as I think of Ava if Rowan is killed. She'll be devastated. They're going to blame Cal. A cramp hits my stomach, and I ball my fists. *I can't let this happen!*

Climbing up slowly, I'm ready to start pulling and pushing again when something hits the door with a loud *SMACK!* I jump back with a cry, eyes wide. *Are they here?* I scramble to the back wall.

"Reggie?" I call, my voice shaking. Fisting my hands, I shove them again under my arms. That Wade fucker will *not* cut off my fingers! My eyes fly around the room looking for anything I can use to defend myself. They cleaned everything out of here before locking me inside. I don't even have a cup.

My mind lights when I see the back of the toilet. Quietly, I lift the heavy ceramic cover from the tank and hold it like a bat over my shoulder. The doors continue to shake, moving back and forth, and I hear what sounds like sawing.

"Reggie?" I say again, a little more confidence in my tone. "Is that you?"

Moving carefully, I step to the side where I expect a head to appear. My only chance is to swing this slab of porcelain as hard as I can in the direction of his head.

A loud thud lets me know the ropes have broken. My heart seizes in my chest, and my arms quiver with fear. It's now or never. The doors fly open, and I scream as loud as I can while swinging the toilet lid with all my might.

"Zelda!" A voice shouts, catching the side of the lid and deflecting it away.

It flies from my hands and cracks into two large pieces on the floor tiles. I'm about to make a dive for one of them when my arm is jerked back roughly, and I turn to find myself face to face with...

"Seth!" I whisper-shriek.

"God dammit, Zelda!" He barks, pulling me out of the bathroom. "What the hell are you trying to do? Kill me?"

"Yes!" I say, shaking all over. "I thought you were Reggie. Or Wade!"

"Come on—we don't have time." He starts out of the bedroom, but I'm hesitant to follow him.

"Why are you here?"

He lunges back and grabs my arm, dragging me behind him as he runs into the living room of the empty suite and heads for the door.

"I called you three times yesterday!" He opens the door a crack and peeks out only a moment before flinging it wide and charging us both through it.

We're running for the elevator as he continues. "When you didn't answer, I decided to come here and investigate."

"W-why?" I'm trying to catch my breath.

"You owe me five thousand dollars," he barks, hitting the button for the lobby. "I'm not letting you skip town without paying."

"Oh my god." I collapse against the walls of the elevator, my insides flooding with am mixture of relief and panic. "But... how did you find me?"

He's digging in his backpack. "I was on my way to your room when I spotted that French guy from Miami. Put these on." He shoves a pair of Toms at me, and I slip my feet into them. "He was coming out of the room where I found you. Did that motherfucker beat you up?"

I turn and let out a hissing sound when I see myself in the mirrored wall. My cheek is bluish-purple, my lip is split, and my teeth and knuckles are covered in blood.

"It was his partner," I say, carefully touching my cheek. "Wade Paxton."

"We'll have to stop in the lobby bathroom—"

"NO!" I shout, my panic growing fiercer. "We've got to get to the track!"

"Are you crazy? It's a fucking mob out there. We'll never make it to the track. We've got to get to the airport."

"You don't understand, Seth! We've got to stop that race!"

"If the cops see you looking like this, they'll arrest us."

That makes me think... The police could help us faster than anyone. They could stop the race! But Wade threatened to kill Ava if I did anything.

"Where's Ava?"

"My guess is she's at the race—most likely in the royal box based on the company she's been keeping."

"Give me your phone!" We're at the lobby, and the elevator doors open. A crowd of people fills the space, and the buzzing noise of the engines is louder than ever. I can barely hear myself think.

"The course runs right in front of the hotel," he shouts. "It's the famous hairpin curve."

He takes my hand, leading me to the back entrance. We're facing the ocean, and the noises are like zippers going high to low as car after car goes from full speed to near stopping as they negotiate the 180-degree turn.

"Your phone!" I shout. "Give me your phone!"

"Those guys will kill you, Zee. We've got to get out of the country."

"Ava's in danger! GIVE ME YOUR PHONE!"

Finally, he shoves the device in my hand, and I dial her number. I'm pacing, trembling all over as it rings and rings. "Answer the phone, Ava!" I shout.

Pressing the end button, I immediately try again. Same result. "Dammit, Ava!" Then I realize.

Switching to text, I quickly type: *It's me, Zee! Answer the phone! I need you to hurry! Rowan's in danger! 911! 911!*

Immediately the phone rings in my hand. "Ava!" I cry.

"Zee!" Her voice is frantic. "Where are you? What's happening?"

"Stop talking and listen to me. Where are you?"

"I got your text, and since I was alone, I decided to walk around the streets. I ran into Felicity, and she has a pit pass. Only I didn't want to bother Rowan-"

"That's good! Can you get in touch with him?"

"I don't think so. He's in the race. I missed his call last night—"

"Ava, listen to me! You have to get to him. It's life or death!"

"What's happening, Zee?" Her voice is tight. "What's going on?"

Blinking hard, I scrub my forehead, thinking. *I need my damn phone!* "Is Felicity there? Ask her if she has Cal's number!"

Her phone moves away, and I hear her speaking to Felicity. "Five five four, eight two seven seven."

"I'll call you right back." Hitting end, my fingers shake as I enter the digits for Cal's phone. Again, it rings and rings, and I immediately end the call, knowing I've got to text him.

Again, I send the same 911 message I sent to Ava, but this time the phone doesn't ring back immediately. "Come on, Cal... Come on!" I'm pacing, shaking the phone. Seth is watching me, frowning and rubbing his chin.

"What's going on, Zee?" His voice calmer. "Let me help you."

I send the same text to Cal again, and as I hit send, I tell him. "Reggie — the French guy — brought us here to do a con on the crown prince. Only the con was on us. He used us to get him back in the country so he could do his own deal. They've sabotaged Rowan's car..." My voice cracks, and I feel the tears coming. "They're trying to kill him!"

As I'm saying the words, the phone vibrates in my hand. I do a little shriek as I press the green button. "Cal!" I cry, covering my face with my hand.

"Zee, where are you? I was worried — "

"Is Rowan okay? Can you get to him?"

"He's on the track..."

"You've got to stop the race, Cal! You've got to get Rowan out of that car!"

"What?" I hear the disbelief in his tone, and I almost lose it. "He's in the lead, Zee. He's going to win it!"

"He's going to die!" I'm screaming. "Reggie's working with Wade Paxton! They sabotaged Rowan's car! You've got to get him out of it!"

"Zelda... I checked the car myself. It's all good."

"You've got to believe me, Cal! They're going to blame you for it!"

Silence fills the line. The noise of the cars is louder than ever, and with every rip of an engine, my heart shudders.

"Please, Cal," I say, my voice breaking. "Just trust me!'

"Let me see what I can do."

The line goes dead, and I collapse to a sitting position on the back steps of the hotel. My face is in my hands, and I don't know how much more of this I can take. Glancing up, I see Seth returning from the water. I vaguely remember him walking away while I talked to Cal. Now he's back, carrying a damp tee.

"I might be able to get us to the track."

Blinking up, my eyes go round. "How?"

He hands me the wet shirt. "Clean your face. I'll call Lara Westingroot."

"The lady from the yacht?" I frown. "Why would she help us?"

"Not us, *me*." He gives me a wink. "How do you think I even got on that yacht?"

"I never thought about it." Seth has always had a knack for getting into any venue he wanted. Anyway, that night on the yacht had taken so many unexpected turns.

Seth chuckles. "Let's just say she barks like a baby seal when she comes."

My nose wrinkles. "Too much information." I hand his phone back, and he starts dialing, motioning for me to follow him.

Chapter 24: Running

Rowan

A bead of sweat rolls from my temple down the side of my face. My arms are exhausted, and that fucking right wheel is pulling again. I'm not as far ahead of Fayed as I need to be to make a pit stop. He'll retake the lead, and we've only four laps to go. Everything is focused on these final laps. One mistake could cost me the race.

"Ro, we have an issue," Cal is in my helmet. "It's possible your car has been sabotaged. I need you to bring it in."

"What? NO!" I can't come off the track at this point. "You checked it yourself!"

"I don't know how. It's possibly what's causing the cornering problem."

I feel a jerk to the right as I'm flying down the straight, and a quick look in my mirror shows Fayed right behind me. "I'm almost finished. I can make it."

Downshifting quickly, I hit the brakes as we take a tight corner. The wheel jerks in my hands and I hear a ping. *No*, I think straightening out of the turn and slamming the throttle down. We shoot into the straight, the tunnel looming just ahead. Plunge into blackness; blinding white on the other side. The stands pass so fast, they're a blur of color, and all I can think is I'm there. I'm hitting the top speeds. I've completed seventy-four laps, and I'm not quitting now. Victory is in my grasp.

Flying through the starting line, I don't hesitate. I pass the pit starting the seventy-fifth lap. Cal's in my ear again.

"Ro! I need you to bring it in NOW!"

Reaching up, my hand hovers over my headpiece. I don't turn it off, but I don't respond either. I'm coming up on the first of nineteen corners. Another downshift, another slam on the brakes, another groan from the front chassis. *Only three more laps.*

My speed drops from four hundred kilometers per hour all the way down to forty through the hairpin. One more curve, and I feel a slip in control. I feel the frame starting to give.

"Rowan?" The voice in my head now is not Cal's. My chest tightens when I hear her. I've been dreaming about her all night. "Ro, it's Ava. Please come in. Please."

"Where are you?" I say, easing off the accelerator as I take the next curve. Again the wheel vibrates hard.

"I'm in the pit. Felicity gave me her pass."

Shit. I'm on the straight, and the pedal is to the floor. My speed tops out at two ninety-three then plunge into darkness. The wheel shakes again. The car jerks to the right, and I'm dangerously close to the wall. Blinding white light hits me as I try to correct. My muscles flex as I fight with the steering column. I'm off the track, my speed goes all the way down.

Fuck! Shifting, I guide the car back onto the lanes. I'm one curve away from the pit, and I know I have to bring it in. I have to do it for Ava.

Fayed's coming out of the tunnel as I pull back onto the asphalt. He flies past, and my chest tightens. We have to move at lightening speed if I'm going to catch him again.

I'm around the curve and pulling into the pit, the crew surrounds me in a swarm. Tires off, they check the chassis. Cal's right with them, and I see the moment his face pales.

His head drops against his forearm, then he looks up at me. "The front arm is completely severed."

I'm out of the cockpit in seconds, running to see what he's seeing. He points to the damaged suspension. "Looks like it was bashed with a club. It's been a time bomb waiting to go off. You could've been killed."

"It's over." My shoulders fall, and I scrub my fingers over my brow. "*FUCK!*" I shout, slamming my helmet into the cockpit. Fists on my forehead, I blink out at the cars roaring past. *Only two laps to go...*

Cal walks around to where I'm standing, his brow lined. "This happened after qualifying. Who had access to the *parc fermé*?"

We both look to the crew. One person is missing. "Heinrick's guy?"

"Impossible. Heinrick wouldn't send someone to hurt you."

"Maybe he didn't know." I'm still looking toward the crew when I spot the one person able to bring me back, green eyes full of worry — *Ava*.

Leaving Cal beside the car, I cross the space. She's out of the gated area and running to me, her navy sleeveless dress moves in the breeze.

When we meet, I rest my forehead against hers, sliding my palms down her cheeks, to the sides of her neck. Her hand goes into the back of my damp hair; the other touches my cheek, and our eyes close as we breathe each other's air. My insides unclench.

"Thank you," she whispers. "I don't know what I would have done if you'd been hurt."

The fury in my chest eases. Lifting my chin, I kiss her forehead before looking into her beautiful eyes. I'm ready to ask her now, right this moment, but we only have this moment before the mob of reporters surrounds us.

"Your royal highness!" one yells. "Why did you pull out of the race when you were winning?"

Two more shout, "We've heard rumors of possible tampering with your vehicle!"

"Is it too soon to suggest a possible assassination attempt?"

I hear over the noise Fayed won the race, and my lips press into a frown. Touching Cal on the shoulder, I lean into his ear. "I'm passing this baton to you."

He nods, and my hand is on Ava's lower back. I hope to guide her through the confusion, through the restricted area beneath stands, and to my waiting limo. My plans for the beautiful woman at my side can continue at Occitan.

"Oh, wait! It's Zelda!" Ava takes off, out of my grasp into the crowd.

"Ava, stop!" I'm calling after her, but I know if I enter the fray, I'll be mobbed.

I call to her again, when I hear a sharp noise. It's popping like firecrackers, or the noise of a car backfiring.

Ava's face changes a moment. She looks confused... just before she drops like a stone.

"AVA!" My voice is a roar as I run to where she's fallen.

My brain registers it was a gunshot, and all of it—losing the race, the damaged car, the mob of bystanders, everything disappears in the face of losing Ava.

I'm throwing bodies aside as the crowd disperses around me. People are screaming and falling to the ground, or running from where my beautiful Ava lies on in a heap, her eyes closed.

* * *

Zelda

"NOOO!!!!" I scream as I see Ava's green eyes change from joy to horror. She falls so fast. She's on the ground like a rag doll, and people scatter in all directions away from her like oil fleeing a drop of water.

As I run to her, I notice another figure in a red jumpsuit also running in my direction. It's Rowan. We meet at my sister, and he has her in his arms before I can breathe.

"Follow me!" he shouts, heading toward the stands.

I'm right behind him, but I'm looking everywhere over my shoulder. I know who did this, and I'm afraid it's not over. They could be anywhere, aiming for us right this second.

"Run, Rowan! Run!" I shout. "Faster!"

We're through the metal door into the restricted area beneath the stands, and I push the doors closed behind us.

"Paramedics are here." He's at a red phone, dialing zero, but I see his fingers tremble. "The best emergency response crews in the country are on hand in case of an accident."

I'm at Ava's side, holding her hand. "Hang on, Ava-bug!" My voice breaks. My throat hurts and tears blur my eyes. She's ghastly pale, and blood soaks the navy dress she's wearing. "Don't die on me, Ava-bug! Please… Please, Ava-bug…"

My whole body is shaking. I'm searching all over for where they hit her when I'm shoved out of the way, and paramedics surround my sister.

Rowan is at my side, and I look up to see his jaw clenched. His eyes are wild, and I know it's taking all his power to stay back and let them work.

Plastic bags and tubes are drawn out and run to her body. I grip his arm as they move her onto a hard plastic stretcher.

"She's losing blood," a woman says, shoving a card at me. "We're taking her to Memorial East."

As fast as they appeared, they're rushing her out the door, into an ambulance and speeding away.

"NO!" I scream, running after them.

"Zelda! This way!" Rowan runs in the direction of a side door, and I'm right behind him.

Hajib has the car waiting, and we're in it, driving as quickly as possible after the ambulance.

* * *

It feels like hours pass before a female doctor with short brown hair comes out to tell us what's happening.

"*Majesté*," she does a little bow to Rowan. "Bonjour."

"Comment est-elle?" he says quickly.

"La dame est bien —"

"English, please!" I practically shriek, startling them both.

"Pardon!" The doctor says in a thick French accent. "I did not realize…"

"Will she be okay?" I plead.

The woman continues almost too quickly for me to follow through her accent. "She lost a lot of blood, so she's very weak. The bullet passed cleanly through her upper arm just missing her brachial artery. I stitched up the wound, and we're monitoring her vitals. She's very lucky it did not hit her heart."

My head goes light, and I'm sure I'll faint. Rowan catches me, helping me to a nearby chair. Bodyguards have cordoned off the area, so it's only the three of us in the waiting room. The doctor tells Rowan something I don't understand and disappears down the hall.

Overhead a television blasts in French. I read the subtitles explaining how the entire country is on high alert following two suspected assassination attempts on the crown prince at today's race.

Police have set up a tip line. The words tighten my chest.

Police are searching for anyone who knows anything about this attack. If you saw anything or know who might be behind this, call…

331

My mind is racing. I know who's behind this, and they know I know. How long before they track me down? I'm the only witness outside their group who can testify against them, who can expose them all.

"Cal is with the men examining the car," Rowan says, misinterpreting my dark expression. "Otherwise, he'd be here with you."

Cal... Another pain in my heart. *I won't see him again...*

"He's okay?" I ask.

"He just sent me a text. He couldn't reach your phone."

"My phone was... taken."

We don't speak for several moments as the television continues in French. A nurse approaches us and does a slight bow. Her voice is also accented.

"Do you know the young lady's next of kin?"

"Me," I stand quickly, going to her. "I'm her sister, Zelda Wilder."

I don't miss the way Rowan looks at me.

"Very good." The nurse hands me a clipboard. "I need you to fill out these forms as soon as you can."

I take the clipboard and turn to face the truth. Rowan is straight in his chair, his blue eyes fixed on me.

"I need to tell you something," I say, glancing down at the papers. "I don't have a lot of time. Do you think... do you think it's possible you can listen to what I have to say without asking questions? Even if it sounds ugly at first?"

"I won't promise anything." Rowan's voice is tense, anger just below the surface. I'm on the verge of tears.

"Ava is my sister," I say, clearing my throat. "We lied about her being my friend. I thought it would keep her safe. I didn't know the person who brought us here had his own agenda."

Rowan stands, and his hands are on his hips. "Is this about my uncle, the duke?"

I take a deep breath and walk past him to sit in the chair again. I'm not sure I can say this standing.

"I met Sir Reginald Winchester in Miami… at a casino. He hired me to come here and pretend to be an heiress, to seduce you. He said he wanted to humiliate you, to prove you weren't fit to be king."

I'm afraid to look up. I can't bear to see his face as I say this. "I brought Ava with me because I never leave her behind. Our parents are dead, and it's always been up to me to take care of us. We've been on our own since we were kids."

Rowan still doesn't speak. When I dare to glance up at him, his jaw is set, and a gleam of anger is in his eyes. My insides crumble.

"I'm telling you this because I'm so sorry, Rowan." I fight the tears. "As soon as I met you, I knew Reggie had lied to us. But it didn't matter. He wasn't interested in the original job anymore. He's been working with Wade Paxton. He used us as a distraction, a smoke screen to help him get back in the country. He was behind the sabotage of your car, and he had Ava shot… I'm next. I know too much about his plans. He's going to kill us both."

Rowan's hands lower, and I see them clench into fists. Ice-cold fury is in his voice. "Reggie did this."

He leaves me with that, and I watch as he crosses the room to one of the men standing guard. They speak in French, in low voices, and the man's eyes harden. He nods, speaking into his cuff before turning and striding quickly to the elevator. Rowan stays in the space where the man was a few moments longer, and I watch as his chin drops.

He takes a few deep breaths before returning to me. Anger is still in his eyes, and I swallow hard, summoning every bit of strength I have left to do this one last thing. I have to get this promise before I run.

Standing, I meet him halfway. "I only have one thing... one request."

"Zelda—"

"I know you hate me. I know you're going to throw me out, but if you would please, *please*, Rowan... Take care of Ava. Please believe me, she would never be here if it weren't for me."

"She lied to me."

"Only to protect me." My eyes heat, and I feel the pressure in my chest growing tighter. "You have to understand. Not being able to tell you the truth was breaking her heart. I've never seen her so happy... or so miserable."

His expression is closed, and I do the only thing I can think to do before a king. Dropping to my knees, I'm not ashamed to beg him. I look up at Rowan's eyes, and the anger has been replaced with confusion.

"You love her, don't you?" I'm taking a chance, but I have to do this for my sister.

He only pauses a moment, his blue eyes traveling around my face. Another beat, and he nods. "I do."

The slightest glimmer of hope encourages me on.

"She loves you." I take a shaky inhale. "I promised her I'd always take care of her, but now...

after all that's happened, I realize I'm putting her in danger. Only you can keep her safe now."

His lips press together a moment. He pauses again before answering me. "I intend to ask her to marry me."

My eyes slide closed as relief surges through my body. "You'll make her so happy."

"She's made me so happy."

Blinking fast, I rise to my feet. "I have to go. This is just the beginning. I know what they've done and who's involved. They're coming for me."

"No — you can't leave. We'll protect you —"

"Don't you understand? They've been planning this for years! They're way ahead of us. You saw how fast they got to Ava. They had a gunman at the track before I even got there."

"I won't let them hurt you." Rowan's voice is a low command. "We'll find them."

"The way you found the person who sabotaged your car?"

Anger burns in his eyes, and I know he's hearing me. I'm petrified with fear, but I have to get as far away from this place, from Ava, as I can. My insides tremble at the memory of what Wade Paxton promised to do to me. After all I've seen, I'm sure he wasn't bluffing now. I only hope I can stay ahead of them.

"Seth is waiting. He'll help me hide."

"Seth?"

Shaking my head, we don't have time. "I owe him money. Ava can explain it to you. Thank you, Rowan. Thank you so much. I'm so sorry for what I did, for helping them. One day I hope I can make it up — "

He takes a step forward. "But what about Cal?"

Those words rip through my stomach. As painful as everything I've endured in the last twenty-four hours, this question has the power to gut me.

"Please tell him I said goodbye." Tears thicken my throat. "He deserves someone better than me."

Turning away, I run to the elevator before he can stop me or see me break down. I'm in the small box, hiding in the corner by the control panel, pressing the *L* button over and over as the doors close.

In the mirrored walls I see my bruised cheek. It's nothing compared to my battered heart. Zelda Wilder is no princess. The closest I am is a dirty Cinderella, an orphan on the run, and that's not the kind of girl for a prince.

The door opens in the lobby, and standing there in dark jeans and a long-sleeved navy sweater is Seth. His amber brow arches, and our blue eyes meet.

"Ready?" he says.

"As ready as I'll ever be."

"Come on, then. Let's go."

I take his hand and follow him to the waiting cab. He pays the man and says one word: *airport*. Fishing in my pockets, I find the door card to our room at the Fairmont and the black American Express. It's a small relief.

"Thought you might need this," he says.

I look down, and he's holding the green ambassador's visa Reggie gave me.

"How did you get this?" I ask.

"I went back to your room and looked around."

My eyes narrow at the thought of him snooping in our stuff. "See anything interesting?"

"Not much."

Shaking my head, I return my gaze out the window to the passing traffic. Ava will be safe now and live happily ever after with her handsome prince. I won't let myself think about Cal. I've got to get as far away as possible, keep running, and hope the bad guys never catch me.

Chapter 25: Plans

Rowan

As soon as the elevator doors close, I speak to my chief security guard. "Keep me informed where she goes."

"Yes, your grace." He steps to the side to make the call, and I go to the room where Ava is recovering.

My promise to Zelda had been easy to make. Her words confirmed everything Ava already told me our very first night together at the Paris Hotel. The only thing she left out was Zelda is her sister — although, she'd actually told me that, too. I understand now she was trying to tell me everything that night, but she couldn't betray Zee.

Now it's time for me to become her security. I've been ready to assume that role since the night I swore to avenge her past. Her beautiful eyes blink open, and protective warmth surges in my chest. I sit at her bedside, taking her hand in mine and lifting her knuckles to my lips.

"How are you feeling, my beautiful lady?"

Her voice cracks when she answers. "What happened?"

I hesitate, not wanting to frighten her. "I don't have an easy way to say this... You were shot."

I see her pulse quicken on the monitor. Her fear stokes my anger at the men who did this.

"But... Who? Why?" she says.

"Your sister thinks it was to keep her silent, to warn her against telling what she knows."

Ava's eyes widen, and she starts to pull away. "You know about Zee?"

My grip tightens on her hand. "Zelda told me the truth, and I promised her I'd protect you. My entire secret service is searching for Reginald Winchester. When we find him, he'll wish he were dead."

"Reggie did this?" Her brow wrinkles. "But... I don't understand."

"I don't want you to worry," I say, gently, but she struggles to sit straighter.

"Rowan—is Zee okay? Where is she?"

"She left with a man named Seth. She said you could explain. Who is he?"

"Seth?" Ava exhales the word, and her chin drops. I watch as she rubs her forehead. "She went with Seth? Willingly?"

"She said she owes him money." Standing, I start to call my security team. "I can stop them if he's dangerous—"

"No," Ava shakes her head. "If she wanted to go with him, she must have a plan. I just... I can't believe she left me behind."

It's not what I want to hear. Returning to her bedside, I take her hand again. "Ava, I want to take care of you. Zee asked me to protect you, and I was glad to say yes."

Her pale cheeks blossom, but she's still quiet, thinking. I'm about to tell her everything I want for us when a noise in the lobby interrupts me.

"Where are they?" Cal bursts into the room and pauses at the end of the bed. "Ava—are you okay? I

340

came as soon as I could get away from those damn reporters."

"I'm a little weak…" she begins.

"You've lost a lot of blood," I say, explaining to her as well as to my brother what the doctor said. "The gunman was aiming for your chest. You were moving so fast, he missed by inches."

Her eyes slide closed, and my jaw tightens. I lift her fingers to my lips. "My men are searching for the gunman now. He will pay for this."

"Jesus," Cal hisses, walking around the room. "For what it's worth, Hampton De Clare called Mother," he says quietly.

"The King of Totrington?" I glance up at his face.

"They're searching for Wade Paxton. Supposedly, he's a 'person of interest.'"

"Is that so?" My voice is low, and I can't hide my disbelief. "Hampton has been silently funding Wade's efforts since before Father died. I wouldn't be surprised if he knew what that dog was doing."

"And now the dog is off the leash." Cal looks around. "Where's Zelda?"

My lips tighten. "She left."

"Left?" His eyes flash at me. "What the hell does that mean?"

"She said she was afraid to stay. She said the reason they shot Ava was to keep her from talking."

"And you let her go?" He's out the door, and I give Ava's hand a squeeze.

"I'll be right back." I'm two steps behind my brother. "I have a man watching her…"

I wait as he speaks to one of the guards. "I'm taking two of your men," he says, typing quickly on his phone. "Freddie and Logan. I'll have them meet me at the airport with my gear."

"You're going after her?"

"Fucking right I am. Where is she headed?"

"Miami," a soft voice behind us says.

I turn to see Ava is out of her bed, trying to follow us. She's holding the monitor with one hand and the back of her hospital gown with the other. One more step, and her face pales. Her legs give out, and I'm across the room in a flash, catching her in my arms.

"You shouldn't be out of bed," I soothe, carrying her to the room with Cal's help.

Once she's settled, my brother touches her arm gently. "Ava? Did you mean to say Texas?"

"No," she says, shaking her head. "Seth would go to Miami first."

I see the confusion on Cal's face, and I realize he's still in the dark. "I can explain—"

"Save it for the plane." He's already at the door.

"Cal!" Ava sits forward, reaching out to him. He pauses and returns to take her hand. I see her swallow back tears. "Don't let anything happen to her."

The muscle in his jaw moves, and his hazel eyes burn with determination. "I promise you. I won't come back without her."

I step to the door to watch him leave.

"Email me everything you know," he says before stepping into the elevator. "Fill me in on what I've missed."

"I will. Be careful, brother."

The doors close, and I return to Ava. Sitting beside her on the bed, she rests her dark head against my chest, and I wrap my arms around her, holding her body to mine.

Dropping my chin, I kiss the top of her head, speaking in a low voice. "When he returns with your sister, I will make you my queen."

Her body tenses, and she looks up at me. "What?"

I smile down at her. "Your ring is at Occitan. I had hoped to propose to you tonight by the ocean, but I'm afraid to wait any longer. I don't know what might happen next."

"But... Are you saying—?"

"Will you marry me, Ava Wilder?"

She blinks several times, and a little laugh erupts from her chest. "You want to marry me? ... *Me?*"

"If you would you consider being my wife, you would make me very happy."

"Consider it!" She grasps my arms in both hands. "Consider it? I've dreamed of it ever since I met you. I couldn't bear thinking of Zee with you. Thank goodness Cal—"

"Is that a yes?" I lower my head to kiss her cheek, which immediately moves in a rapid nod.

"Yes!" Despite her pallor, her face seems to glow. "Yes, yes, yes!"

My heart swells, and I cup her cheeks with my hands. Looking deep into her eyes, I say the words I've been thinking for so long. "I love you, Ava. I want to make you mine."

"I'm already yours," she whispers, eyes shining. "I've been yours since that first night."

Our mouths collide, and I push her lips apart so our tongues can slide together. She presses forward, and I hold her close, sliding my palms down her soft hair to her lower back. I want to pull her onto my lap and make love to her beautiful soul.

Breaking apart, I speak in her ear. "The doctor said you should recover quickly."

"It's already taking too long," she purrs, and I almost groan.

Another kiss, our lips chasing each other's in hungry motions until I lift my head. Her forehead rests against my neck, and her fingers lightly touch my collar as I hold her, loving how she feels in my arms.

As complete as I feel in this moment, worry tightens my stomach. If Zelda is right, the chain of events set in motion today is vast and deadly. I'm furious these political players tried to hurt my Ava. I will make them suffer for their crimes.

Cal is on his way to the airport. He's taking two of my best guards with him. As former military, the three of them have both the weapons and the training to find the men who are after Zee and bring her safely home.

Zelda Wilder might think she's on her own, but we'll find her. We'll find the people who did this, and I will personally oversee their punishment.

Then we'll have a week of celebration, culminating in a royal wedding.

This story isn't over…

EPILOGUE: HUNTING

MacCallum Lockwood Tate

The enormous jet touches down in the midst of a blinding Miami rainstorm. Powering off my laptop, I look out the window at the palm trees swaying in the wind as we taxi, and my mind drifts to the last time I saw Zee.

She was asleep in her bed at the Fairmont Hotel. Her blue eyes closed, a thick, pale blonde curl lay across her cheek, and her adorable mouth was relaxed. Still, I could hear her sassy voice, imagine the sparkle in her blue eyes as she taunted me. It made me laugh softly, and I'd wanted to wake her. I'd wanted to hear her voice and make love to her, but I had to get to the track.

Instead, I left her a note, telling her how amazing our night had been, starting with that fuck on the boat—*jesus*! I gave her my heart that time… Followed by that ice-cold, unexpected swim.

Watching the wind batter the palms, I shake my head. It all makes sense now—her panic, the reason she ran that night, her fear of being caught. I remember my shock at seeing her going out the window. Of course I went right after her. Just like I'm going after her now.

During the twelve-hour flight, I caught up on everything I've missed. Rowan emailed me explaining what Zelda said, what Ava told him—how Reggie found them in a casino in Miami, how he threatened them unless they helped with his plan to oust my brother, how they discovered it was all a ruse. Reggie used them to get back into the country so he could continue his plan to seize control of the government.

I confess, I'm surprised by how far our uncle is willing to go—to kill his own family—in order to ensure the success of his plans. My chest tightens when I realize how dangerous this situation is for Zelda. If these men won't back down from killing the crown prince, removing Zelda will be like swatting a fly.

She's the only person who can directly tie them to the crimes, and I intend to find her and take her back to Monagasco.

Rowan also let me know Wade Paxton has gone off the grid. Even though he's been stripped of his title, we have no reason to believe he's lost his power or his connections. If he's been planning this for years, Zelda's right—we've got a lot of catching up to do. And we have to watch our backs. It makes finding her even more urgent. At home I can keep her safe. I can keep her by my side.

We lost track of her once she and Seth landed in Miami, but Ava gave us two possible starting points—a woman named Helen Regis and a Ramada Hollywood Downtown. I have the address, and it's where we plan to start.

The plane finally stops moving, and a low tone sounds in the cabin. The lights flicker on, and we all stand, including Logan across the aisle from me, and Freddie a row in front of me.

We're using fake names, and we're dressed casually in jeans and button-down shirts. Our reason for this visit will be stated as "pleasure." We're simply European businessmen spending a week in South Beach. It's the best way to stay ahead of the game.

"I've made contact with our local guys," Freddie says, once we're through customs. "They'll meet us in the parking garage with weapons and vehicles."

"What's the latest on this weather?" I look out the window at the typhoon in which we've landed.

"Typical Miami rain?" Logan suggests.

"Let's hope it pushes through quickly."

We're in the garage, taking the elevator to the second to top level. Down twelve rows and over three, I see our men waiting beside a black SUV and a smaller black Mercedes sedan.

"That's not conspicuous at all," I say, shaking hands with Ronald Delahousse, our local contact. His light brown hair is longish and messy, and he's dressed the same way we are, except he has a thin nylon jacket on top.

He does a slight bow. "Your grace." He hands me a black leather wallet. "U.S. passport, Florida driver's license, and credit cards for one Bill Aucoin."

At the rear of the sedan, he opens the trunk and lifts the mat. Two rifles and a store of ammunition are housed in a secret compartment.

"Nice," I say.

"In the console area, you will find a drop-down compartment containing a thirty-five millimeter and a Diamondback DB-9."

"That would be a...?"

"Four-inch nine-millimeter handgun," he says. "Both are fully loaded."

"Sounds like we're all set."

He hands me the keys to the sedan, and I wave to Logan and Freddie. They'll shadow me to the hotel then wait from the SUV as I pretend to reserve a room. We'll maintain contact through our smart watches, which has the added benefit of letting them know my heart is still beating. I've worked with these guys before. They're two of the best from my regiment.

It takes a half-hour to reach the hotel in the rain. I pull into the parking lot, giving it a brief scan for anything unusual. All is grey and quiet in the downpour. I reach into the console and take out the tiny pistol. It's the size of my palm, and once I'm standing, I slide it into my jeans pocket before dashing into the lobby.

"Wahoo! You made it just in time for the hurricane party!" A tall, dark-haired male behind the desk is smiling and lively.

"Is a hurricane coming?" I glance behind me out the front doors. The black SUV is parallel parked on the street.

"Nah, it's just a thunderstorm, but any excuse for a party, right?" He does finger guns at me. "That's some accent. You from Louisiana?"

"Sure," I say, looking away to inspect the run-down lobby. *Not the greatest part of town.*

"Well, *laissez les bon temps rouler!*" He sings as he steps to the computer. I smile, playing along as I reach for my fake identification. "How long you staying with us, big guy?"

"One night." I hand over the license and credit card.

"Oh!" The guy squints at the card, and I my smile tightens. "How do you say that name? Aye-you-coin?"

"Close." My shoulders relax, and I smile. "Oh-kwan."

"I wasn't close!" he laughs. Then he whispers, staring at my card. "Oh-kwan... oh-kwan..."

Holding my hand out, I cock a brow. "May I have it back?"

"Oh, sure!" He passes it across. "Room 204. Elevator's around the corner. Enjoy your stay!"

"Thanks."

He's back to doing a little dance, playing on his phone, and I slip around the corner. The room I'm searching for is on the second floor, but it's on the other side of the hotel. I head straight down the empty hall, noting the faded carpets and peeling wallpaper.

"I'm *en route*," I say softly at my wrist, my eyes trained on the corner up ahead.

I haven't passed anyone in the hall, and I can only guess it's because of the unfashionable location or the poor weather—or both.

Around the corner, I stop as a blast of damp, warm air hits me. Keeping my back against the wall, I look down to see the exterior door is cracked, letting the rain and humid wind stream through the opening.

A quick glance to my right, and I see the room in question. My pulse ticks faster.

"I need backup," I say quietly in my watch. "Enter from the pool area. The back door is open."

A light thump from my watch tells me they're on the way. I fish out the small gun from my pocket and slowly creep down the shadowy hall. A flash of lightning makes me realize the power is out in the hotel, or at least in this wing.

Crossing quickly, I press my back against the opposite wall, on the same side as my destination. I have my gun against my chest, and I slide my hand out, testing the doorknob. It falls open easily.

"Shit," I say so quietly, it's not even a breath. I look to my right again. *Come on, guys.*

I'm standing at the last known whereabouts of Helen Regis, and I'm not about to enter until Logan and Freddie are in sight. No telling what I might walk into. Freddie is as tall as me, but a bit leaner, faster. Logan is both taller and beefier. They're the perfect combination in situations like this.

The soft noise of the exterior door opening makes me tense until my partners dash up, shaking water from their clothes. Nodding, I hold a finger to my lips before pointing to the door. Freddie takes the opposite wall, and Logan is right beside me.

Stretching out my leg, I kick it open, and Freddie points his gun straight ahead. Everything freezes.

I hold my breath, waiting, and...

Nothing.

Silence greets us from inside. A low rumble of thunder fills the quiet as we start to breathe again.

"Let's go," I whisper.

Freddie strides forward, stepping into the black room and reaching to flick the light switch. No dice. I'm right behind him as he pulls out a flashlight, and we quickly scan the seemingly vacant space. No luggage, no sign anyone's slept in the bed.

Pushing back the heavy curtains fills the room with grey daylight. "She must've checked out," Logan says behind me, moving around the magazines and a white plastic binder with his gun.

"Check the bathroom," I tell Freddie, and he nods.

He's only in the small, closet-sized space a moment. The noise of the shower curtain moving, and he calls to me. "Sir? I think I've found her."

Logan and I both rush to where he's waiting, and there, in the tub, lies a large, female body. She's wearing sweatpants and a shirt that reads, "I pooped today!"

A plastic bag is over her head, tied at the neck, and it's dotted with moisture. I'm just about to pull out our information to identify the body when the room phone blasts out a ring.

We all freeze, our eyes meet, and I take a second to decide what to do. "Identify her," I say, snatching a towel off the rack.

The harsh, metallic noise blasts another ring, and I slowly approach where it sits on the laminate table. One more ring, and I pick it up with the towel, holding the receiver near my ear without touching my skin.

I don't speak. Instead, I wait for the person calling to go first.

Silence. They're waiting as well.

I'm breathing fast, thinking as Freddie walks out of the bathroom. Clearing my throat, I pretend to cough.

"Helen?" the female voice I've been desperate to hear speaks.

"Zelda?" I say just as fast. "Zelda, it's Cal—where are you?"

Logan stumbles out of the bathroom, holding a towel over his mouth and nose. "It's her," he says.

"Zelda?" I say again fast. "Where are you, love?"

She doesn't hang up, which I take as a good sign, but she doesn't speak either. "Zelda, please. I'm trying to find you."

"Cal?" Her voice trembles. "What are you doing? Who's with you?"

"Two of my men. Tell me where you are. We're here to protect you."

A voice is with her. "Where is Helen?" I can tell she's repeating what it told her to say.

"I'm afraid she's had an accident—"

"Oh my god…" she gasps. "They're going to kill us all."

"Zelda, talk to me." My mind is racing. Helen and this hotel are the only leads we have. "I know you're afraid, but you're smarter than this. Let me help you."

She answers fast. "I can't drag you into this."

"I'm already in it."

"I'm not good for you."

"You're the best thing that's ever happened to me."

"You can't save me."

"Want to bet?" My tone is deadly serious. I will not let anything happen to this woman. "I love you, Zee."

She's silent a split second. "I have to hang up. They could be monitoring this line."

"Call my cell. You know the number—call me!" I'm shouting on the line as it goes dead. "*FUCK!*" I throw the receiver against the wall.

For a moment, we stand in the dark room. I'm breathing hard, frustration surging through my veins. A dead body is in the tub. The woman I love is out there, God knows where, in danger. I'm about to lose it, when my watch gives me a little thump.

Looking down, I see a text from an unknown number. *Must stay hidden. Seth has a friend who can hide us.*

"Yes!" I shout, motioning to the men. "Come on. We've got her."

Dashing out the back door, I'm speaking into my watch. "Send me your location. I'll come to you."

A quick touch, and the message is sent. I'm in the car, and the guys are dashing across the street to their vehicle. Seconds pass. They feel like hours. My jaw clenches. I'm staring at the small screen, waiting for her response. Waiting...

Finally, a thump. *Seth chartered a boat. Will text more when we're there.*

She's at the marina? Fuck! Which one?

"No," I speak fast into my watch. "Tell me where you're going now." A knot is in my throat as I hit send and wait.

More seconds tick by. The rain has slacked off, and little pellets of water make pinging sounds on the glass. The storm is passing over, moving further north, and away from the coastline. I drum my fingers on the steering wheel as the black SUV pulls into an empty parking space beside me. My forehead is tight as I watch the virtual second hand move around the clock on my wrist.

"Tell me, Zelda..." I growl, staring at the white hands on the black face. It's humid in the car, and a bead of sweat rolls down the center of my chest beneath my long-sleeved button-down. "Answer me."

Another second passes... another little eternity. My forehead tightens; I'm afraid she's not going to reply.

Then all at once a tap on my wrist; I almost shout when one word appears on the screen: *Tortola.*

I lower the window on the Mercedes. Freddie leans his dark head out toward me. "Get us on a flight to Tortola."

* * *

Don't miss the exciting chase, the return of Zelda,
the quest for justice, and a royal wedding in
A Player for a Princess!

* * *

Never miss a new release!

Sign up for my New Release newsletter, and get a **FREE Subscriber-only Story Bundle!**

Sign up here: **http://smarturl.it/TLMnews**

Your opinion counts!

If you enjoyed *The Prince & The Player*, please leave a short, sweet review wherever you purchased your copy.

Reviews help your favorite authors more than you know.

Thank you so much!

* * *

Get Exclusive Text Alerts and never miss a SALE or NEW RELEASE:

Text "TiaLouise" to 64600 Now!

(Max 6 messages per month; **HELP for help; STOP to cancel**; Text and Data rates may apply. Privacy policy available, allnightreads@gmail.com)

* * *

BOOKS BY TIA LOUISE

Signed Copies of all books can be found online at:
http://smarturl.it/SignedPBs

THE ONE TO HOLD SERIES

NOTE: All are stand-alone novels. Adult Contemporary/Erotic Romance: Due to strong language and sexual content, books are not intended for readers under the age of 18.

One to Hold

Derek Alexander is a retired Marine, ex-cop, and the top investigator in his field. Melissa Jones is a small-town girl trying to escape her troubled past.

When the two intersect in a bar in Arizona, their sexual chemistry is off the charts. But what is revealed during their "one week stand" only complicates matters.

Because she'll do everything in her power to get away from the past, but he'll do everything he can to hold her.

* * *

One to Protect

When Sloan Reynolds beats criminal charges, Melissa Jones stops believing her wealthy, connected ex-husband will ever pay for what he did to her.

Derek Alexander can't accept that—a tiny silver scar won't let him forget, and as a leader in the security business, he is determined to get the man who hurt his fiancée.

Then the body of a former call girl turns up dead. She's the breakthrough Derek's been waiting for, the link to Sloan's sordid past he needs. But as usual, legal paths to justice have been covered up or erased.

Derek's ready to do whatever it takes to protect his family when his partner Patrick Knight devises a plan that changes everything.

It's a plan that involves breaking rules and taking a walk on the dark side. It goes against everything on which Alexander-Knight, LLC, is based.

And it's a plan Derek's more than ready to follow.

* * *

One to Keep

There's a new guy in town...

"Patrick Knight, single, retired Guard-turned private investigator. I was a closer. A deal maker. I looked clients

in the eye and told them I'd get their shit done. And I did..."

Patrick doesn't do "nice."
At least, not anymore.
After his fiancée cheats, he follows up with a one-night stand and a disastrous office hook-up. His

358

business partner (Derek Alexander) sends him to the desert to get his head straight--and clean up the mess.

While there, Patrick meets Elaine, and blistering sparks fly, but she's not looking for any guy. Or a long-distance relationship.

Patrick's ready to do anything to keep her, but just when it seems he's changed her mind, the skeletons from his past life start coming back.

* * *

One to Love

Tattoos, bad boys, love...
Boxing, fame, fortune...
Loss.

It's the one thing Kenny and Slayde have in common. Until the night Fate throws them together and everything changes.

It's a story about fighting. It's about falling in love. And it's about losing everything only to find it again in the least likely place.

* * *

One to Leave

Stuart Knight is a wounded Marine turned Sexy Cowboy. Mariska Heron is the gypsy girl who stole his heart.

Some demons can't be shaken off.
Some wounds won't heal.

Until a pair of hazel eyes knocks you on your ass, and you realize it's time to stop running.

* * *

One to Save

"I lost myself in the darkness of trying to protect you..."

Some threats come at you as friendly fire.
Some threats take away everything.
Family won't let you go down without a fight.
The Secret isn't as secure as Derek's team originally thought it was, and a person on the inside of Alexander-Knight is set on exposing him, breaking him, and taking away all he holds dear.
Refusing to let anyone suffer for his crimes, Derek takes matters into his own hands. He's exposed, he's defenseless, but his friends are determined to save him.

* * *

One to Chase

Paris fashions,
Chicago nightlife,

Secrets and lies...
Welcome to the North Side.

Marcus Merritt doesn't chase women. He doesn't have to. But when the spirited and sexy blonde who left him wanting more shows up in his office looking for work, little things like the rules seem ready to be rewritten.

Amy Knight is smart, ambitious, and back home in Chicago to care for her mother. A courtesy meeting with one of the top lawyers in the city should be a boost to her career...

Until the polished green-eyed player turns out to be the same irresistible "random" she hooked up with at a friend's wedding in Wilmington. Bonus: He's the brother of her older brother's new wife. What the hell?!

Who's chasing whom? It all depends on the day. *Or the night.*

* * *

One to Take

Stuart Knight is a wounded Marine turned Sexy Cowboy. Mariska Heron is the gypsy girl who stole his heart. Now they're fighting for their Happily Ever After...

Life is never simple.
Even perfect couples face storms.
The question is whether our love is strong enough to survive.
I believe it is.

She told me to leave.
If I leave, I take her with me.
~Stuart Knight

* * *

PARANORMAL ROMANCES

One Immortal

Melissa is a vampire; Derek is a vampire hunter.

When beautiful, sad Melissa Jones flees to New Orleans with her telepathic best friend, she is looking for a cure—not an erotic encounter with a sexy former Marine.

Derek Alexander left the military intending to become a private investigator, but with two powerful shifters as partners and an immunity to vampire glamour, he instead rose to the top in paranormal justice.

At a bar on Bourbon Street, Derek and Melissa cross paths, and their sexual chemistry is off the charts. Acting on their feelings, they are pulled deeper into an affair, but Melissa is hiding, hoping to escape her cruel maker.

It doesn't take long before the shifters uncover her secret. Still, Derek is determined to confront the Old One and reclaim her mortality—even at the risk of losing his.

* * *

One Insatiable

(Loosely based on the Hades & Persephone myth.)

One wounded panther, one restless lynx: One insatiable hunger.

Mercy Quinlan is a whip-smart lynx and the youngest in her shifter clan. She's tough and independent and dreams of escaping her alpha sister's control and living life on her own terms.

When a lone black panther shows up in her hometown, Mercy is intrigued. He's just passing through, which makes him perfect... Along with his broad shoulders, defined muscles, and sexy fighter moves.

Koa "Stitch" Raiden is picking up what's left of his broken life. Exiled from his black panther clan, he's running from Princeton to Seattle when he's drawn to Woodland Creek.

He's aware Mercy is watching him. What he doesn't know is the sexy little vixen who sneaks through his window each night is both the trouble he doesn't need and the hope he can't live without.

* * *

THE DIRTY PLAYERS

Cinderella meets _Ocean's Eleven_ in this CONTEMPORARY ROMANCE DUET featuring secrets, lies, royal high jinks, scams and double-crosses; breathless, swooning lust, cocky princes, dominant alpha future-kings, and crafty courtiers, who are not always what they seem.

The Prince & The Player (#1)

Let the games begin...
Runaway Zelda Wilder will do whatever it takes to secure a better life for her and her sister Ava. Crown Prince Rowan Westringham Tate will do

whatever it takes to preserve his small country.

When Zee is blackmailed into helping a vengeful statesman take down Rowan, she never expects she'll be pulled into a web of lies and international intrigue--much less that she'll find herself falling for Cal, Rowan's "playboy" younger brother.

Ava's no help, as she finds quiet walks in the moonlight discussing poetry and leadership with the brooding future king irresistible. Even more irresistible is kissing his luscious lips.

They're in over their heads, and the more time passes, the more danger the sisters are in. Shots are fired, and it's soon clear even a prince might not be able to rescue these players.

* * *

A Player for A Princess (#2)

From the Mediterranean to the Caribbean, the game continues...

Zelda Wilder is on the run, this time from the ruthless assassins who've decided she knows too much to live.

"Playboy Prince" MacCallum Lockwood Tate isn't about to let the beautiful player who stole his heart get away — if only he could decide whether he wants to save her or strangle her for her dangerous choices.

After tracking her down to a casino in St. Croix, Cal follows Zee back to Tortola where he intends to keep her safe. One problem: Zelda's criminal liaisons are two steps ahead of her.

Lives are threatened, and all of the players' skills are tested in this plot to capture a killer and save a princess.

* * *

Dirty Dealers

My job is to protect.
I'm the best, the king's elite.
She's the only thing strong enough to make me look away...

Logan Hunt is a guard. He's constantly aware of his surroundings; he knows every angle. He'll take a bullet.

His new assignment is to protect the queen regent, keep his eyes on her at all times. He's more than up to the task...

Until a face from his past returns, and the one mission he's sworn to complete becomes his biggest liability.

* * *

Dirty Thief

Ava Wilder is beautiful, she lives in a pink castle, and she's a thief.

Crown Prince Rowan Westringham Tate craves speed, commands armies, and is devoted to Ava.

Their romance is straight out of an erotic Cinderella story, until the one man Ava is running from shows up to claim what she stole — or to claim her.

Now Ava may have to steal one more thing to protect Rowan: A life.

Acknowledgments

Starting a brand-new story after a very successful series is a bit daunting, and very scary. Thank God I'm surrounded by such supportive people cheering me on and anxiously awaiting this new adventure. I don't know how I'd do this otherwise.

Specifically, I must thank my husband "Mr. TL" for his encouragement, brainstorming support, and insightful critiques. You're my rock. Thanks to my beautiful daughters who are so patient and encouraging to me. I love you ladies!

As always, thanks so much to Ilona, Helene and Candy for their excellent feedback and eagle eyes. Huge thanks to my readers and to my "Babes" for your enthusiasm and for sharing my stories with your reading friends. (And special thanks for finding the PERFECT Prince Cal... Joseph Cannata = Wow!)

Thanks to Steven Novak for the incredible cover design that fits this story so perfectly. Thanks to Heather Roberts and L. Woods PR for helping me get the word out, and last but never least, thanks to my dear author friends for keeping me sane and organized while I'm in the writing cave.

I can't begin to put into words how much I appreciate the love and support of my readers, friends, and family. I love you guys! I hope you all love these new players as much as I do.

Stay sexy,
<3 *Tia*

Exclusive Sneak Peek

A Player for A Princess
(Dirty Players Duet #2)
© TLM Productions LLC, 2016

Zelda

My heart is beating too fast. Glancing down, I see my hands tremble, and I take a few measured breaths to try and make them stop.

I've never been this anxious on a job, but everything has changed in the last six weeks. Looking over my shoulder has become a nonstop addiction it seems.

For the first time, I'm alone with Seth, just the two of us. Unknown hit men took out our longtime partner Helen, and we don't even know how long ago it was. The radio report simply said her body was found in a bathtub in a cheap hotel in Miami. A plastic bag was over her head.

Clutching my black purse, again I look over my shoulder. Through the neon lights and arcade noises of the Divi casino in St. Croix, I see men in black blazers dotted among the gamblers. Men with curly earpieces in their ears, men with dark brows lowered over steely eyes, men sweeping the room for any signs of criminal activity.

I do another quick sweep, and I realize I'm looking for Ava. *Stop that, Zee.* My little sister is far away from this life, and it's because I chose to distance us. I decided her safety is more important than keeping our family together.

The last time I saw her, she was wounded and pale, unconscious in a hospital bed. It tore at my heart to leave her, but at least I know she's okay. Thanks to the Internet, I've been able to keep up with the "developing story" of the assassination attempt on the future king of Monagasco and the shooting of his fiancée, a.k.a., my sister. Rowan has taken Ava from the hospital to the palace, where she's recuperating under the watchful eyes of his royal guards.

With a steady exhale, I release the nerves, reminding myself it's for the best. She's with the man who loves her, who promised to take care of her. If a crown prince can't do that, I don't stand a chance.

Still… it isn't me.

I'm not watching out for her.

As the oldest, I've always had that job. I've taken care of us since our parents died, leaving us at the mercy of the foster system. I've protected her ever since that last asshole thought he'd try relieving his sexual frustrations on a little girl entrusted to his "care." It was me who'd bashed him over the head with the lamp, grabbed her hand, and run us out of there.

We'd hidden all night in the pouring rain in a concrete culvert, and I came up with a plan to keep us out of that life for good. Passing the baton to someone else—even a future king—hits me harder than I thought it would. My throat aches at her absence, my chest heavy. *Stay safe, Ava-bug.*

Tonight is the first time I've ever entered a place like this without her. Ava is the only person I can count on in any situation. Every security guard in this room reminds me of how we've always been a team. If anything goes wrong, I grab her hand and we run, just like always. We stay alive.

Only, I made the deal that changed everything. I shook hands with the devil.

I could argue I didn't have a choice. We were facing jail time, felony convictions in Florida for grand theft, and while I'd be willing to take my chances in jail, there's no way in hell I'm letting Ava go to prison. So yeah. Agreeing to work with Reginald Winchester might make me a "bad guy," but I'd do it again in heartbeat.

A heartbeat...

Squaring my shoulders, I slide a lock of jet-brown hair behind my ear and force confidence into my stride. I make my way through the glittering, noisy casino to my target—a shiny brass roulette wheel—and prepare to start the show.

The last time we worked this con in Miami, Helen had been waiting at the table when I got there. I can still hear her gravelly voice and see her "May Contain Alcohol" sweatshirt. Sadness followed closely by fear ricochets through my insides. Whoever killed her is looking for me.

We were on our way to Tortola to hide when Seth said we should stop in here and bank extra cash. As Americans, we don't need passports in St. Croix, and we can catch a cheap ferry and slip away in the night to our ultimate destination.

Keeping off the radar is the goal—as always. We'll pocket a few thousand and disappear unnoticed. At least that's the plan.

"No more bets!" The dealer passes his hand over the wheel just as I arrive, and I quickly assess the table rules. Minimum ten dollar bet. *Decent.*

Opening my clutch, I remove two hundreds and pass them to the dealer. He quickly exchanges them for twenty pale blue chips. I'll join the fray next spin.

Tonight the transmitter is hidden in my shoe as opposed to my cuff bracelet. I'm wearing a strappy black dress that stops mid-thigh, and my black heels show off my legs while hiding the device facilitating our winning streak.

I have to sit with my legs crossed and point my toe to activate it. One dainty point, one shiny silver ball drops right in the tray, predictable at ninety percent accuracy. So far the odds have been in our favor.

We'll play until Seth gives me the signal they're onto us. Then I'll calmly cash out, walk away, and meet him at the pier on Grapetree Point. From there we'll make the forty-mile cruise to Tortola.

An elegantly dressed woman shakes her head and gives me a bitter smile as I sit. "Don't stay longer than three spins," she grumbles.

I smile in response. "That's the rule, isn't it?"

"That's the rule." Her expression tells me she lost a lot tonight.

As a student of casinos, I know how steeply the odds in roulette are stacked in favor of the House—they're the worst of any game. The longer you sit, the greater your chances of losing, times a million. If I were giving advice to a rookie, I'd say stick to blackjack. At least there you can use strategy and possibly win a little. Walking away is something I learned early on. You can never be afraid to walk away—even when you're certain you're lucky. Luck is the biggest liar of all.

I place half my chips on the black rectangle and watch as the wheel begins to spin. The dealer snakes his hand to the side and releases the ball. It flies around the shining wood with a sharp rasp. I need to lose this round. The job doesn't start until Seth arrives, and I can't win for longer than a few spins or it'll look suspicious.

Another glance over my shoulder. He's still not here. Casting my eyes down, I watch the wheel spinning, *black-red, black-red, black-red, flashing brass.*

"Have you been here long?" A man in an elegant suit steps into the space beside me and fishes out his wallet as we wait for the ball to drop.

"I just sat down," I say without making eye contact. I'm not here to make friends.

He passes a crisp one hundred dollar bill to the dealer. "Then we have no way of knowing if it's a good table."

"Sorry," I shake my head. "I play red or black."

"Not much of a gambler?"

A glance, and I see he's tall and thick with dark brown hair and a cocky expression like he already knows the answer to his question.

"No," I say in a discouraging tone.

No, thank you. Even if I hadn't left my heart in Monagasco, I never let romance interfere with a job. Well, almost never.

"Logan Thomas." Mr. Persistent sticks a hand at me.

He waits, and I hesitate. *Two first names.*

"Regina Lampert," I lie only barely touching his fingers.

"Regina," he gives me a nod, but that twinkle of knowledge is in his eyes.

A knot forms in my throat. I don't like this. The ball drops on black seventeen, and a lady at the other end of the table emits a little cheer.

"You won," Logan's voice ripples toward me.

The dealer adds more chips to my pile, and I'm ready to hop up and intercept Seth. A swirl of warmth at my side tells me I'm too late.

* * *

Get A Player for A Princess *Today!*

Available in eBook, print, and audiobook on all eBook retailers, Amazon, iTunes, Createspace, Barnes & Noble, or Book Depository!

About the Author

The "Queen of Hot Romance," Tia Louise is the Award-Winning, International Bestselling author of the One to Hold series.

From "Readers' Choice" nominations, to *USA Today* "Happily Ever After" nods, to winning the 2015 "Favorite Erotica Author" and the 2014 "Lady Boner Award" (LOL!), nothing makes her happier than communicating with fans and weaving new tales into the Alexander-Knight world of stories.

A former journalist, Louise lives in the center of the USA with her lovely family and one grumpy cat.

Books by Tia Louise:
One to Hold (Derek & Melissa), 2013
One to Keep (Patrick & Elaine), 2014
One to Protect (Derek & Melissa), 2014
One to Love (Kenny & Slayde), 2014
One to Leave (Stuart & Mariska), 2014
One to Save (Derek & Melissa), 2015
One to Chase (Amy & Marcus), 2015
One to Take (Stuart & Mariska), 2016

The Prince & The Player, 2016
A Player for a Princess, 2016
Dirty Dealers, 2017
Dirty Thief, 2017

Paranormal Romances (all stand-alones):
One Immortal (Derek & Melissa, #SexyVampires), 2015
One Insatiable (Koa & Mercy, #SexyShifters), 2015

Connect with Tia:
Website: http://www.AuthorTiaLouise.com
Sign up for Tia's Book News: *http://smarturl.it/TLMnews*

Made in the USA
Lexington, KY
05 April 2017